THE

Vasundhara was born in New Delhi, India, and spent as little time there as possible, evidenced by her lack of understanding of what constitutes a good plate of pani puri. Or Gol Gappe as Delhiites like to call it. She spent her childhood moving between states and schools, leaving her with a lack of long-term friends but an overactive imagination. Thankfully she channelled this imagination into many stories from a young age. Of course she is a procrastinator so most of them are half finished but A for effort, as she likes to say.

Having started acting at the ripe old age of seventeen, she spent many years trying to make a mark for herself in the film industry by performing a variety of roles. Including being a part of some award-winning films. One fine day she decided to set her procrastination aside and actually finish a story. So she armed herself with one too many cups of filter kaapi and started writing this book. And BOOM, a couple of years and much procrastination later, she actually finished her first novel.

Now that the first milestone has been achieved she hopes to write many more books and secure her place in your shelves. Apart from acting and writing, Vasundhara spends her time painting, doomscrolling, baking cookies when she should be on a diet, and convincing her family to let her have a dog.

THE ACCUSED

VASUNDHARA

Published by Westland Books, a division of Nasadiya Technologies Private Limited, in 2025

No. 269/2B, First Floor, 'Irai Arul', Vimalraj Street, Nethaji Nagar, Alapakkam Main Road, Maduravoyal, Chennai 600095

Westland and the Westland logo are the trademarks of Nasadiya Technologies Private Limited, or its affiliates.

Copyright © Vasundhara C., 2025

Vasundhara C. asserts the moral right to be identified as the author of this work.

ISBN: 9789360454951

10 9 8 7 6 5 4 3 2 1

This is a work of fiction. Names, characters, organisations, places, events and incidents are either products of the author's imagination or used fictitiously.

All rights reserved

Typeset by Mukul

Printed at Thomson Press (India) Ltd

No part of this book may be reproduced, or stored in a retrieval system, or transmitted in any form or by any means, electronic, mechanical, photocopying, recording, or otherwise, without express written permission of the publisher.

*To Amma,
for being everything*

Prologue

THE TELEVISION PLAYED A SLOW-MOTION SHOT of a fielder sprinting to catch the ball. As he ran across the pitch, his hands cupped, the telecast cut to his wife sitting in the stands, her face taut in anticipation, her fists balled tightly. It cut back to the player who caught the ball and fell down, rolling to safety. A split second later, he stood up, holding the ball over his head, waving his arm in triumph.

Madhu slapped his knee and yelled, 'YES!'

In his excitement, he ended up spilling some of his drink. The floor would be sticky tomorrow. He knew she would hate to clean it up.

He hadn't noticed her yet. She had been careful to keep her movements quiet. She stood there, holding a knife that she'd brought from the kitchen.

He poured more rum into his glass and then reached for the water bottle lying on the floor next to him. He topped it off with water, his hands shaking slightly as he did it. He was too drunk to defend himself properly. The pills she had mixed into his biryani had started working. She could do this. She could. And just as he was about to place the bottle back down, she raised her arms over her head and brought the knife down into his back.

Her hands were trembling, and she wasn't as strong as she needed to be. The knife hit something, probably a bone, and didn't go in fully. He let out a gasp, followed by a gurgling sound, and turned to look at her. She squeaked in fear and pushed the knife down harder, biting her lip to keep from screaming.

'You bitch,' he slurred, reaching out to grab her. She took a few steps back. 'I knew it, I knew . . .' A bit of saliva dribbled down the corner of his mouth and he swallowed. He was going to throw up, she was sure of it.

'Bitch . . .' he said again, after a beat. This time it came out more like a moan, like the alcohol was no longer numbing his pain. As he tried standing, she desperately moved her hand behind her back, trying to get a hold of the balcony door. If the plan didn't work out, she could always jump from the balcony. Their flat wasn't high enough, but what other choice did she have? She had already provided for Priyanka.

He was stumbling towards her now, using the sofa for support.

She finally found the handle and unlatched the door to the balcony. She took a deep breath and stepped out. He lunged at her, but his shirt got caught on the pointed backrest of the sofa. This made him angrier and he swung back to try and free himself. But he turned too fast, too wildly, and ended up stumbling and falling on his back.

There was just a small, strangled sob. And then, silence. The sticky night air gently blew around her as she stood in the balcony, unsure if she was safe.

It was only when she heard the sound of laughter and the loud cricket commentary from the floor above that she took a deep breath and relaxed. She stepped back into the house and looked at his chest to check if he was breathing. He wasn't. His shirt's ends fluttered gently in the breeze that blew in from the balcony door, but other than that there was no movement.

He was gone.

The fall must have done the trick, driving the knife further into his back. She had to work quickly.

She stepped around him and surveyed the scene. It looked normal, except for the blood on the floor. She avoided touching him, in case he suddenly got up. She wouldn't put it past him; he had a knack for showing up when he wasn't wanted.

She went into the kitchen, put the remaining biryani back into the fridge and cleaned the counter. She grabbed a glass and poured some alcohol into it, making sure to wipe the glass clean with a small towel. Then she went to the bedroom and took out his spare phone from its hiding place, using the same towel.

Going back to the living room, she stood over him. He was definitely dead; his chest wasn't moving at all. There was no way he was still breathing. It seemed safe for her to unlock his phone, just as she had done on the night she first found out what he was up to.

That night, when she had seen the pictures and the messages, she'd dropped the phone and run to the bathroom to vomit. But today she had steeled herself for it. She had to make sure no one else saw them. She used the towel to hold his finger to unlock the phone and proceeded to delete the entire chat. Then she put the phone away back in its hiding place.

His actual phone, the one he took everywhere, was charging near the TV. Its twelve per cent battery would run out soon. She yanked the wire out and put it on the counter. She made sure she didn't leave her fingerprints anywhere.

She then went back to him and rolled him over. He was heavy, but she had done this many times before—dragging him from the sofa to the bed when he had passed out after another evening of drinking. Now, steadying herself with one hand on the floor, she tightened her hands around the knife's handle and yanked it out. The blood started gushing out. 'Shit,' she hissed, dropping the knife and turning him onto his back again in a hurry. Would the floor be covered in blood by morning?

She had no time to think about that right now. The towel had a few drops of blood on it. She would have to hide it. She went to the kitchen, washed the knife, removing all prints, and left it on the drying rack.

Then, she stood with her ear to the door.

She couldn't hear anything. The neighbours must have retired for the day. She looked through the peephole to make sure the elevator was inactive. Then she turned off the lights and opened the front door a crack. She went back inside, soaked the towel in alcohol and wiped the door handle, the outer padlock and the grille handles with it. She also wiped the bottle clean before putting it back in its place.

She stood back and surveyed the scene. It was exactly as she had planned it. She looked at him one more time. He was just as she had left him. Dead.

She was finally free.

She went into their bedroom and unlocked the attached bathroom's secondary door from the inside. Then, going out to the living room using the other bathroom door, she locked her bedroom from the outside and went back through the bathroom, locking the door behind her. She had to move the washing machine back in front of the door without making any noise. It was hard, but she managed it, moving it inch by inch into place. The neighbours living in the flat below might have heard something if they were awake, but she was almost certain they weren't.

Then, throwing the towels into the washing machine, she moved some clothes around and went back to their room.

The final step would be a hard one. She was okay with either outcome. Whether it worked or didn't, she was okay.

Grabbing the tumbler of milk she had kept in the room earlier, she added the crushed pills, the same ones she'd given him, and drank half a glass in one gulp.

It was four in the morning. Just a few more hours. Now all she had to do was wait.

1

LATER, WHEN JOSLIN READ THE HEADLINE IN the paper 'Local woman accused of murdering her husband', she would tell her friends that she always knew something was odd about that family.

She would gleefully gossip about the wife's alleged affair, the husband's notorious temper and the child's below average intelligence. But right now, Joslin was as surprised as anyone.

The residents of Green Tree Apartments had gathered outside house no. 8. They watched on as the policemen spoke to each other, pointing here, pointing there and finally pointing to the floor. At their feet lay the victim—Madhu. The man of the house. The most hated resident of their apartment society. And, for the foreseeable future, the biggest topic of conversation in their locality.

He lay in a perfectly peaceful position. Arms by his side, legs straightened out and his feet in a wide 'V'. His face was turned away from them, but the morning light that filtered in from the eastern window of the flat added a tinge of red to his silhouette.

As a constable called for an ambulance, speaking in hushed tones, more people joined the crowd. The watchman, the paper delivery boy, the maids, everyone was curious and they all asked the same questions: What happened? Why are the cops here? OH, GOD! Is he dead? This continued till the Inspector threatened to arrest them all for obstructing his investigation.

They turned to leave, but then surrounded the milkman, who was the one to discover the body. For once, someone other than Joslin had all the juicy information. Feeling left out, she followed the throng but not before looking around to see if she could spot the victim's wife.

The wife was nowhere to be seen.

2
Inspector Rakesh

WHEN INSPECTOR RAKESH HAD GOT THE CALL that morning from the constable on duty, he had jumped out of bed, quickly put on his uniform, barely managing to button it up, before rushing to his bike.

'Sir, there is a lady on the phone claiming someone killed her husband. She keeps repeating this over and over again. She specifically asked for you.'

'What are you saying?' he had mumbled incoherently.

Next to him lay his wife, snoring peacefully.

'Sir, there is a lady here who . . .'

'Don't repeat the same thing again,' he hissed. 'I heard you the first time. What is her name? What else can you tell me? Can't you handle this?'

The constable was new and, as was customary, he had been automatically handed the graveyard shift. He had begged them to let him have the daytime shift, claiming he was terrified of ghosts, but that had only sealed his fate.

'Sir, Mira, sir . . . Mira Madhu, sir . . . madam's name, sir.' He was blabbering in his panic, but Rakesh caught the name. By the time the constable had finished speaking, Rakesh had quickly put on his pants and was rushing to the door.

~

Rakesh watched as the body was carried away to the coroner's office. They first tried the elevator, but when they realised it wasn't wide enough, they manually carried the body down two flights of stairs, in full view of all the neighbours who were waiting outside their homes.

Atif, the head constable who'd recently joined them, had just finished his shift at the station and landed at the scene to help. The boy was very eager, a trait that Rakesh lacked—and hence despised. To get rid of Atif, he sent him off to control the crowd.

As soon as Atif was out of sight, Rakesh called his wife. 'Hello?' She sounded busy. She was probably in the kitchen.

'I had to run out.'

'I noticed.'

The crime scene photographer walked out and signalled that he was done. Rakesh nodded, waiting for the man to leave. 'Someone I know . . . called, there was a death in their house,' he said, unable to mention that it was a female someone. 'A murder.'

'Oh no!' she exclaimed. 'Sorry to hear.'

'Yes, so . . . It's our jurisdiction. I thought I'd help out; I mean, it's my job but . . . yeah. I'll come home as soon as some things are sorted.'

'Of course. Let me know if you need anything. And all the best,' she said, as she always did. He felt a little guilty, but what was he going to do? Tell her that the very first murder he was handling as an inspector was that of his first love's husband? No. He couldn't think of that now. He had to go downstairs to meet the secretary of the building.

Sunderesan had come upstairs from his ground-floor apartment while the police were taking Mrs Krishnan's statement. Apparently, the milkman had informed him of the morning's events. As the secretary, Sunderesan told them, it was his duty to ensure that all the residents were safe. It had taken longer than necessary to get rid of him, but Rakesh had sent him off with the assurance that he would come down and speak with him.

Half an hour later, Rakesh walked towards Sunderesan's home and took in the scene through the locked grille gate. Sunderesan was looking out of his living room window at the street. And Rakesh could hear the sounds of vessels being washed and a cooker whistling. He cleared his throat and rang the doorbell.

'Hi, sir. Inspector Rakesh . . .' he said, introducing himself, as he waited while the old man walked to the door, grabbed a set of keys from a fold in his veshti and started working the multiple padlocks on his door.

When the door was finally open, Sunderesan let him in and seated him. He shouted for two glasses of water. From the depths of the kitchen, behind a green patterned curtain which could have once been a sari, came an annoyed 'okay'. Sunderesan sat down opposite Rakesh and leaned forward. 'Tell me, sir, what happened in that flat? Is it really a murder?'

He had asked the same questions earlier too, and Rakesh had already answered them.

The cook set two tumblers on the table and went back into the kitchen, but Rakesh could see her feet peeping out from under the curtains where she stood eavesdropping. 'What happened to that fellow?' Sunderesan asked, 'Why did he die? Robbery? Are we safe?'

Rakesh opened his mouth to answer, but before he could say anything the old man started talking again.

'You know, sir, I had filed a request a long time back with the other building secretaries. We went to the municipal councillor and said we needed a police booth near our flats. The whole area only has one police station, and you are so far away. We can't just sit and wait for the residents to get murdered or robbed . . . That watchman fellow is also useless! Always on his stupid phone. What security is there? Where is Mira? Is she at her mother's house?'

As the smell of something burning wafted into the living room, Rakesh could hear the cook click her tongue and patter away back into the kitchen. Sunderesan, too, noticed the movement and turned his head in the direction of the kitchen.

Rakesh grabbed the gap in the monologue to speak. 'Sir, I will come back and answer all your questions, but first please just answer some of mine,' he said, taking out his pen and notepad. 'Did Mira and Madhu have financial problems?'

Sunderesan turned back to face him and thought about it for a second. 'Do you think that's what happened? Some moneylender's ruffian murdered them? Is she also dead? Yes, that is possible, no? They sold their bike recently. Madhu said he has sent it for repair when I asked him, but it has been almost two weeks and there is no sign of it yet. What kind of mechanic keeps a bike for two weeks? I'll tell you what kind—the made-up kind. Mira stopped wearing her real bangles too. I noticed that last month when she came to give the maintenance fee. See, we usually send the watchman to collect the maintenance cheque from everyone, but Mira said she didn't have any money with her at that time so she would give it in the evening after going to the ATM. She didn't give it for a few days—wait, I'll show you.' Sunderesan got up and walked to the overstuffed bookshelf in the corner of the living room. Taking a notebook from the drawer on the right, he came back to the sofa, sat down, moistening his finger on his tongue and began turning the pages.

'See,' Sunderesan pointed, 'here it is. She paid maintenance on the seventh instead of the first. And when she came to pay, she was wearing that shiny fake gold kind of bangle.' He shut the book in triumph and leaned back in his chair. 'They weren't like this when they moved into the building. Sometimes Madhu would cause issues, but Mira was always cooperative. She always paid the maintenance on time. But he started changing and picking fights with the other residents. We were actually speaking to the owner to try and get them evicted. I know they are his relatives, but enough is enough!'

'Relatives?' Rakesh's ears perked up.

'Yes, yes, I believe Madhu's uncle owns the house. Poor man, this uncle of his. Madhu also worked in his company. Imagine, having such a fellow as a tenant and an employee.'

'Do you know the name of the company?' Rakesh asked, writing as quickly as he could. Mira hadn't mentioned any financial issues, but why would she? It would have been embarrassing for anyone to mention it. Moreover, he hadn't had the chance to speak to her properly yet.

'No, I don't remember, but I can share his number. The owner has already been notified so he probably is expecting your call,' Sunderesan said as he picked up his phone and read off the number for Rakesh to take down.

'One more thing. Did you hear anything strange last night or early this morning?' Rakesh asked.

'No, last night I didn't see him come in when I went to sleep. You have to ask Mrs Krishnan. See, if there was a police booth nearby this wouldn't have happened . . .'

Before he could go off on another rant, Rakesh stood up and thanked Sunderesan, offering to do his best to get the police booth installed. As he turned to leave, he noticed Atif was waiting outside for him. 'Done?' he asked, impatiently.

'Yes, sir.'

'Fine, take an initial statement from the watchman and the neighbours upstairs. I'll come back and speak to them after making sure the victim's wife is okay. Then, just go home.'

Atif nodded and bolted upstairs, not bothering to use the elevator. Rakesh rolled his eyes and left, turning to thank Sunderesan again.

The cook's feet were back where they had been, sticking out from below the curtain.

3
Pooja

SHE WONDERED WHAT WOULD HAPPEN TO HER now.

She was sitting on the sofa and the anchor was screaming the news. The TV announcer's face blurred and pictures of her flashed across the screen—her at a party, at some event, posing with some fans at a shoot. Then his photo appeared next to hers. They changed her photo too. Now on the screen was a candid image of hers, one where she was pointing at something, her mouth open, ready to speak and her eyes half shut as if she had been captured in the midst of blinking.

The channel had done that on purpose, she realised. He looked charming and handsome and, depending on who you asked, she either looked frumpy or unhinged. From that moment, it all went downhill for her. The pictures that followed showed her 'flaunting' her cleavage, and there was one taken at a low angle that showed her legs crossed in an awkward pose.

The ticker read: 'SCANDAL OF THE YEAR! Affair behind her husband's back?' Their names flashed in red and white before the channel switched to *that* picture.

Sanjay, who had been pacing the length of the sofa, stopped to glare at her. She switched channels. But every channel was showing the same picture of her—her hair tousled, and she clutching his arm while looking behind furtively. Even though his face was unclear, he was easily recognisable. After all, he was one of the top actors of the country.

She changed channels again and paused at one that was showing her favourite show. On any other day she would have tuned in and called one of her friends to discuss the gossip the anchor was sharing. She'd always loved the smirk on the anchor's face when she shared salacious news. But not today. 'And in our biggest news of the day, you won't guess which big-shot producer's wife was caught red-handed with our favourite star. More after the break!' She laughed as the adverts cut in.

'Red-handed! Bloody red-handed?' Sanjay yelled from behind her. 'See what you have done!'

Pooja closed her eyes and quickly switched channels before the commercial break ended. Thankfully, this channel was airing news of a bomb blast that had happened somewhere. But at the bottom of the screen, a tiny thumbnail of her spun a few times before landing with gusto on the left of the screen next to a title that said, 'Mrs Reddy caught with Reddy's star actor. Affair? Or innocent meeting?'

Sanjay groaned and slapped his forehead.

Shyamal, their PR guy, looked up from his phone. 'Relax, sir, I have spoken to some friendly people in the media. I've told them it was just a meeting and that you were to join later . . .' The office phone rang, and Sanjay stared at it for a couple of seconds before turning to Shyamal. 'What am I paying you for? To stand in my house and be part of the decor?'

'Sorry, sir,' Shyamal replied, grabbing the phone. 'Yes?' he listened, before shaking his head. 'No, we already told you. Reddy sir was also supposed to be there, but he got delayed in traffic.

'No, why would they wait in the lobby? People come and disturb him, he's a big star . . .

'. . . Kunal sir, I've made it clear. They were discussing a project that is under wraps for now. You will know more when it launches. Okay?

'Of course she is involved in the project,' he continued as he started to walk out of the room. But he stopped at the doorway, listened for a bit more and hung up after saying they couldn't speak to her.

'Well?' she asked, looking at him expectantly. An oily smile appeared on Shyamal's face—the kind he had whenever he was avoiding something. Sanjay had had enough and snapped, 'Just fucking tell her. She wants to know what ripples her brilliant actions have caused!'

'Sir,' he stammered, shuffling his feet before turning to her and mumbling.

'It's okay, Shyamal-ji. Tell us what it is. It's better for me to know,' she said, hoping it wasn't as bad as she feared.

Shyamal nervously stared at his feet as he replied, 'Madam, they're asking if the two of you were lovers during that movie shoot.'

'SHIT! SHIT! SHIT!' Sanjay yelled, stomping his feet on the ground like a child. 'God only knows what stories they'll spin now. "Sanjay forced her to marry him, D always loved her but let her go because of friendship . . ."'

'You seem to be ready to give them headlines yourself,' she snapped and wrapped her arms tighter around her knees. She turned towards the television and changed channels to go back to the gossip show. The presenter (no longer her favourite!) was still speaking, her smirk giving way to an expression of pure glee. 'And they were caught entering a hotel room sneakily. Naturally, their PR team is denying all rumours,' the announcer said. 'But if you take a look at this picture,' the anchor continued, pointing to the image that popped up next to her head, 'Mrs Reddy is looking behind her. As if to make sure no one sees them going in.'

Behind her, Sanjay swore again and Shyamal dragged him out of the room and took him to the bar. She turned off the television and listened to the muffled abuses that could be heard from the locked room. She would normally have gone online to check out whatever news was being posted about them; she had an alert set up for all their names. But her husband had confiscated her phone, laptop and tablet. He'd even taken her Apple watch away, not that she used the damn thing anyway.

She was exhausted.

When she'd woken up that morning and grabbed her phone, she had found it switched off. It was strange as she remembered charging it the night before. Not thinking much of it, she had plugged the phone to charge it again. That's when Sanjay's phone had vibrated, followed by a frantic ringing of the doorbell below. As he woke up to answer the call, she heard the maid open the door downstairs. And then everything had changed.

Shyamal came bounding into the room followed by the maid. He was screaming at her to pack up and leave. Blabbering something about people coming and 'Shit, gone! Gone! Gone! Gone!'

Still in bed, paralysed by all the action happening around her, she saw Sanjay stopping midway through his phone call and turning slowly to glare at her, his face becoming red. She clutched her dead phone and stared at everyone.

'What the fuck did you do?' Sanjay had hissed. Shyamal looked like he was about to cry.

Before she knew what was happening, she had been bundled into a car and sneaked out of the house, just before the first reporter showed up. All they had on camera was Sanjay's car screeching out of the gates with Shyamal next to him. She lay hidden in the back seat, under a huge black coat, clueless about what was happening till they reached their beach house.

Frustrated that her only access to any information was the stupid television and Sanjay's phone, which was safely in his pocket, she turned the TV back on.

4
Inspector Rakesh

THE LAST TIME HE'D SEEN MIRA WAS A MONTH ago at the reunion. She'd spent most of her time talking to her friends from school, but when they left, he'd made sure to give her his new visiting card. He'd been promoted to Inspector and the cards had arrived just that morning. He passed them out to everyone, but wrote down his personal number on the one he gave her. It had been in her hands when he saw her that morning in the Krishnans' home.

Now, as she sat in front of him at the police station, Mira looked lost. She no longer had his visiting card with her. He wondered why she had called the station and not him. But this wasn't the time to dwell on that. He looked at Mira.

Her hair was pulled back, with a cheap gold barrette at the end of an almost blue-black braid. She'd always had thick hair, he remembered, as he looked at the plait resting on her shoulder. During their schooldays too, she would pull her hair to the front before she sat down so she wouldn't sit on her long hair. That husband of hers must have also liked it as much as the boys from their class, her plait swinging from side to side, moving in tune to her hips as she walked out of class. Now, it looked flimsy and weathered, like an old rope forgotten outdoors.

She looked so different from the Mira he remembered from school. He preferred picturing her in her school uniform instead of the sari she was wearing now. She sniffed, shaking him out of his thoughts. Clearing his throat, Rakesh got back to the questioning. 'Mira, please tell me clearly what happened.'

'I already said . . .' she trailed off, her lower lip trembling.

He felt like an asshole, but her incoherent ramblings earlier didn't make for much of a statement. When he'd reached the Krishnans' flat, Mira was waiting for him. Mr and Mrs Krishnan, whose statements he'd taken first, had been the ones to fill him in along with the milkman who'd discovered the body. Mira had been in no state to speak. She kept staring at the door to her house till Rakesh moved in front of her, blocking her view. When he'd finally managed to get her to say something, she'd collapsed into sobs, stammering a few words here and there. But other than the words 'How' and 'Madhu', Rakesh hadn't understood anything.

He asked again, more gently this time. 'Yes, I know. But I need to make an official statement here. If you need a moment . . .'

'I woke up this morning and found that he had locked me in,' she said, interrupting him with a slight shake of her head.

'Madhu?'

She took a deep breath and responded, 'Yes.'

'So, he locked you in.' Rakesh paused for a moment before asking, 'Did he do that normally?'

'Sometimes, but it was only when he didn't want to be disturbed.'

'Disturbed? Disturbed while doing what?'

'When he had friends over or when I told him to stop drinking.'

Rakesh raised his eyebrows but didn't probe further. He just made a note and continued. 'Do you know if someone was coming over?'

'No, but then he never told me anyway.'

'What about a motive? Any idea why someone would want to hurt Madhu?' He . . . I mean . . . we had . . .' she said but didn't continue.

'I get it,' he said, not wanting to make it more difficult for her. 'Did he have financial problems?'

She nodded and gave him a strained smile. 'Some of his debtors were harassing us.'

'Okay, what happened last night?'

'What else? Like what?' She was starting to panic and he rushed to reassure her.

'This is just procedure,' he said hastily. She looked so vulnerable sitting there, trying her best not to fall apart. 'I know you are scared. Don't worry, just tell me everything you remember. Okay?'

'Okay.' She raised her right hand and tucked an imaginary strand of hair behind her ear. Her gold earrings danced on impact. He remembered what Sunderesan had said and wondered if these were fake too. They were shiny and a little too gold.

'I was chopping vegetables for the next day. If I cut them the night before, it takes less time to cook in the morning. Last night, I was cutting cabbage at the dining table,' Mira said and she mimed the action.

'Madhu was angry as usual. He was screaming into his phone about losing some . . .' Glancing at the constable in the room, Mira paused, then leaned closer to Rakesh. He instinctively leaned in as well. '. . . losing some money,' she whispered. 'He was watching TV and having his dinner. Then he got another call and started shouting. When he shouts it's a bit hard to be around him, so I moved everything to the kitchen'

'And then?'

'I had some milk and then went to the bedroom to sleep. I woke up in the morning and went to the bathroom.'

'That's it?' Rakesh asked. Mira seemed to glare at him. For a second he wondered if he had imagined it, but then she blinked and it was gone. She shook her head and continued, 'When I came out of the bathroom, I realised Madhu wasn't in the bedroom. I called out to him and tried to open the bedroom door. But it was locked from the outside. I could hear someone screaming outside. My first thought was that Madhu had fallen; he once fell and broke his wrist after getting drunk, so I asked if he was all right and if he could please open the door. But then the milkman opened the door and Madhu was on the . . .' She gestured to the floor. 'I thought it was weird that he was sleeping there. I just . . . only when he moved . . .'

'Madhu moved?' Rakesh asked, his head snapping up so fast he cricked his neck. 'No, the milkman. Only when he moved out of the way did I see the . . .'

She stopped and ran her palms over her face. Tiny beads of sweat had formed on her upper lip and the sides of her forehead. Rakesh looked up at the fan that was spinning at full speed.

'Do you need something to drink? Water?' he asked.

'No . . . no, let me . . . I'll finish,' and took a deep breath. She looked older than how he had imagined her. Some wrinkles had formed at the corners of her eyes and on her forehead too. He suspected that Madhu was violent with her as he had been with everyone in school. But there were no signs of violence now—he couldn't see any bruises on Mira's face. Madhu could have broken her bones in the past—Rakesh would have to check on that—but today she looked unhurt. Like a normal, albeit a more beautiful than normal, housewife.

'Yes. So then . . . then Mrs Krishnan took me to her house and I called you. I waited there till you came.' She brought her hands back together on her lap and nodded. 'That's what happened.'

'No noise? Nothing?'

'I didn't hear anything.'

'You couldn't use the other bathroom door because the washing machine is leaning against it?' he said, looking at his notes.

'Yes. We never used the other door,' she said. 'Also, the washing machine is too heavy for me to move by myself.'

'Is there anything you can think of that was unusual? Anything at all, however insignificant? Maybe a phone call or a visitor?'

She thought about it, narrowing her eyes. 'He brought me my glass of milk,' she said.

'Is that unusual?' he asked.

'Well, he wasn't exactly that kind of husband.' she said, slowly choosing her words.

He decided against pressing further. 'You have somewhere to go, right?' he asked, shutting his notebook.

'Yes. My parents . . .' Suddenly her face crinkled. She slapped a hand over her mouth and shook her head violently.

'What happened?' he asked stupidly, even though it was obvious. She stood up, her handbag and phone falling off her lap onto the ground. She was starting to turn green. He was about to suggest she use the station washroom. But he realised in time that the smell would only make things worse. Moreover, it didn't seem like she could make it there; she was already gripping the end of the table and looking around wildly. He grabbed the dustbin by his desk and pushed it at her right on time. She pulled it towards her and vomited violently into it.

The others in the room got up from their seats and stared at Mira when they heard her hurling. Finally, one of them grabbed a water bottle and placed it on Rakesh's desk.

When she was done, she sat back exhausted. Despite her effort to contain the deluge, bits of vomit had spattered on her sari. 'Sorry,' she said, wiping her mouth with the end of her pallu. 'I'm really sorry.'

Her voice was hoarse and small now. He didn't know what to say, so he pushed the water bottle towards her and sat back.

When she'd drank a few mouthfuls, he asked if she needed to go to a hospital. 'Are you feeling sick? Dizzy? Sorry, I know it's a shock but . . .' he paused.

'It's fine,' she said, waving a hand at him. Her forehead was dotted with sweat, and she seemed to be having difficulty breathing.

'Maybe we should just go to your parents' house now? Once we get all the things we need, we may come back and speak to you,' he said, not wanting a repetition of the past few minutes.

'Okay,' she said, standing up and looking down at herself. 'Can I go home and get some clothes?'

'Yes. I . . .' he looked around for a constable, then changed his mind. 'Let me take you home.' He stood up quickly, reaching into his pocket for his car keys. 'Can you wait outside? I'll just finish something and meet you there.'

He walked to the washbasin in the corner of the corridor and splashed some water on his face. Unlike in the morning, the water flowing from the washbasin tap was warm now. From the window above the washbasin, he could see Mira waiting for him. She was sitting on the bench and staring in the distance, like a model in a Ravi Varma painting. The dancing earrings from earlier were frozen still.

5
Pooja

'MRS REDDY IN HIDING?'

That was the headline flashing on the news channel now. Before leaving the house, Sanjay had warned her not to watch TV, but she couldn't resist turning the damn thing on. It did occur to her that channels that didn't have the rights to her latest film were now playing it, and she wondered if Sanjay was trying to make money off her misery before remembering he'd sold the TV rights a long time ago.

It was some relief, she had to admit.

In their famous scene, D stood outside her balcony, watching her dance, sing into her hairbrush and entangle herself in pastel-coloured, translucent prop curtains so he could come in and set her free. She'd found the dialogue cute at the time: 'Would you like me to free you?'

The channel was now using it to twist the whole affair: 'Is D freeing Pooja from her unhappy marriage?' ran the ticker.

The camera zoomed into his twinkling and mischievous eyes. Then it focused on hers, shy and blushing, as she said, 'As if any girl in her right mind would smile at a stranger who walks into her bedroom from the balcony.' She watched as her character went on to do just that—letting D untangle her from the curtains while getting unnecessarily close.

He still wore the same perfume as he did then. She didn't know what it was, but she loved how well it went with the smell of cigarettes that constantly clung to him. Of course, they weren't together back then. It had started much later, after she got married.

One day, after she had found out that Sanjay was having yet another fling with yet another pretty young thing, she had called the last dialled number on his phone and started yelling as soon as someone answered the call. It turned out to be D's new number. She had been terribly embarrassed and told him her suspicions. D had comforted her, and had offered to meet her so she could let things off her chest. He was very comforting indeed, so much so that she hadn't even bothered to confront Sanjay about his next new girlfriend, or the one after that.

What followed were meetings once or twice a month. They didn't get much talking done. They made sure to clear their WhatsApp at the end of the day. Sometimes, Sanjay invited D along for their coffee dates, unaware that his wife and his friend were playing footsie under the table. Once, D accidentally began to caress Sanjay's foot. He immediately realised the mistake and apologised, complaining that his new shoes weren't comfortable.

D hadn't called her today.

Of course, there were no phones around her, but he could have reached her if he wanted to. The D on the TV screen was singing into her ear as she pushed him away playfully and ran up a snow-capped mountain in skimpy clothing. Maybe he had contacted her without knowing she didn't have her phone with her, and Sanjay was reading those messages now. Or maybe—she clenched her eyes shut—he hadn't tried at all.

She turned the TV off, lay back down on the sofa and wrapped her arms around her knees, rocking herself.

6
Inspector Rakesh

BY THE TIME THEY REACHED MIRA'S apartment, she'd stopped sweating and regained some of her colour. He waited while Mira fumbled with the keys. He picked them up after she dropped them, separated the silver key from the other two and, with a steady hand, slipped it into the keyhole.

As soon as he opened the door, he caught a glimpse of the bloodstain on the floor. He tried to step ahead of Mira so she didn't see it. But she stopped him.

'It's okay, Rakesh,' she said. 'I mean sir.'

'Are you sure?' he asked, stepping aside to let her enter. From one of the apartments behind them, he heard a creak. Someone was definitely leaning on the front door and peering at them through the peephole.

'Nosy neighbours,' he muttered, leaving the door wide open so no one would have one more thing to gossip about.

The forensics team had already taken away Madhu's body, but the bloodstain was still horrifying. Rakesh averted his eyes and walked towards the balcony. He wanted to see if an intruder could have climbed up and entered the house from the balcony.

The flimsy door swung open, banged against the metal railing and bounced back. Rakesh stepped out and looked around the narrow space. The second-floor balcony had no trees or buildings close enough to use as leverage. He shook the water pipes next to the balcony, but they were so old and thin that anyone using them to climb up would have fallen to their death.

'Maybe from the terrace?' he said out loud, looking up and catching the eye of someone who darted back so fast he wondered if he'd imagined it.

'You weren't fast enough,' he shouted. And a face slowly leaned over, looking sheepishly at him.

'May I help you?' he asked the woman.

'Nothing, sir. I just . . .' She blushed and had the civility to look embarrassed. 'Sorry. I was just checking what the noise was about.'

'Well, maybe your habit of checking things will help when I come to get your statement,' he said, keeping his voice pleasant. 'Maybe it will help you remember whatever noises you heard last night. Should I come up and get your statement?'

'No, no, please. Let me change and come downstairs,' the woman said, waving her hands furiously.

He nodded and went back in. He hadn't really managed to take a look at the house earlier; too much was going on then. Knowing he was in Mira's house, he hadn't been able to concentrate. But now, as he looked around, he noticed that everything was shabby. Yet, it was obvious that Mira had done a lot to keep it clean. His wife was a neat woman, but even she couldn't keep her house like this. The kitchen looked like cleaning advertisements had been shot here, only the walls weren't as brightly tiled and there was an oil stain on the ceiling over the stove. Mira, or someone, had tried to clean it, but the oil had instead spread and was streaked around the original stain.

He could hear Mira moving around her room. He thought he heard a muffled sob and decided to give her more time. Meanwhile, he explored the house on his own, checking the other bedroom's windows, the door and also looking under the sofas.

Of course, there would be a more thorough check later, but he thought he should get a move on it. After all, this was the first murder case he was in charge of.

He was interrupted by a timid-sounding voice from the living room. 'Sir?' He looked up from behind the TV stand and saw the neighbour. She had said she would dress up and come downstairs; apparently, dressing meant throwing on a gauzy dupatta over her nightie. He returned the papers he had found on the shelf behind the television and took out his phone to take notes.

'Your name?' he asked sternly.

'Joslin Philips.'

'Okay, Mrs Philips, did you hear anything last night?'

'No, sir.'

He rolled his eyes. 'Seriously?'

'Really, sir,' she said, her eyes all wide and innocent.

'Ma'am, you were performing circus acrobatics over the balcony railing in an attempt to hear what was happening in this house just a few minutes ago. Now either you have the instincts of a sleuth, or your ears are sharp enough to catch the sound of us entering the building. Which means . . .'

Her face fell. 'Sir, I really didn't hear anything.'

He ignored her statement and continued, 'Which means you would have heard Mr Madhukumar shouting at someone on the phone, you would have heard him yelling at Mira . . .'

'I didn't hear any of that.' Her mousy expression had changed. She now looked like a gossip columnist who'd found out something about her least favourite celebrity. 'There was no argument last night, none at all,' she said. 'Usually there is, but not yesterday. Everything was shhhh. I could only hear noise from the TV.'

'Around 9 p.m.?' he asked.

Joslin shook her head. 'I heard absolutely nothing but the TV last night.'

'What time did you last see Mira?' Rakesh stood up straighter, hoping he could intimidate her.

'I last saw her when she came over for tea yesterday evening.'

'So, you're friends, not just neighbours.'

'Better to get along with the people who live in the same apartment as you, right?' she said, neither confirming nor denying his assumption.

Also, it's easier to get more gossip, he thought.

'What happened after?' he asked.

'That's all. Then I saw her come home just now with you.'

'Not this morning?'

'No. I was busy sending my husband off to work. I didn't come down till the police arrived and all I saw was Madhu on the floor.' Her eyes glanced at the bloodstain on the floor before snapping back to Rakesh's face.

'And your husband didn't hear anything?' he asked.

'If he did, I wouldn't know. You have to ask him,' she said, shrugging.

He pulled out a business card from his pocket and handed it to her. 'I'll have to ask him when he calls me then,' he said. Joslin sheepishly took the card.

'Why were you eavesdropping in the first place?'

'I heard a rumour that you were asking for her, umm, alibi,' she said, searching for the correct word. She looked pleased with herself. Those damn crime shows and their fan following, he thought.

'We were not asking for her alibi,' he continued. 'We know that they were having money problems. And being the building snoop, I am sure you will know about that.'

'Snoop?'

'What else do you call it, Mrs Philips? Peeping into other people's houses, listening in on their conversations? That is snooping, right? Someone might file a complaint someday . . .'

'I don't snoop.' She spat the words out ferociously. 'And his money problems were common knowledge anyway. No one here needed to snoop to know about it. Moneylenders were banging at their door at all hours of the day. If the flat didn't belong to his relative, they would have been kicked out long ago. That's how much trouble they caused.'

Okay . . . now we're getting somewhere, he thought, allowing her to continue.

She took a deep breath and went on, a vicious gleam in her eyes. 'Not only that, she was selling off her jewellery. Bangles, earrings, the diamonds she wore for her wedding. She stopped wearing them a long time ago. She started wearing a plain gold ring. Who knows if that's even real! Madhu took all of it and still the moneylenders didn't stop coming.'

'Mira was working. I know she was a tuition teacher.'

'She stopped working when he came home drunk and vomited into a student's notebook,' Joslin said. Rakesh grimaced.

'Exactly! She actually copied whatever was in that notebook on a new one and gave it to the student before cancelling her classes. No one has come for tutoring here since.'

'When was that?'

'A few months ago,' she said, looking rather pleased with herself.

He typed that into his phone. Mira had lied at the reunion; she wasn't a teacher like she'd said she was. 'If you hear or recollect anything, call me immediately,' Rakesh said. He took down the descriptions of the last thugs who'd come to her door and sent Joslin on her way with a warning not to fall over the balcony railing.

She didn't look pleased with that.

When she left, he called Atif and asked him to check if the ring they had seen on Madhu's finger was fake. If it was, they could easily close the case, saying debtors were the problem. Maybe someone had come over to collect money last night and got into an argument with him. Goondas weren't really known for their anger management.

This way, he could close the case and impress Mira in one go. He slipped his phone back into his pocket and continued to check the papers he was going through earlier, this time finding a receipt from a local costume jewellery store. It was for a set of bangles. Sunderesan had been right. Rakesh took a picture of it and went back to the sheaf of receipts that Mira had carefully arranged in order of date of purchase.

A few minutes later, when he was done with that, Rakesh realised the house had gone quiet. He walked towards the bedroom door and called out. 'Mira?' There was no answer. Maybe she was in the bathroom. She had been waiting at the station for a while, maybe she needed to go to the loo. 'MIRA?' he called again and pressed his ear to the door.

Nothing.

He psyched himself up and turned the knob, hoping she hadn't locked the door. It wasn't that he was still scared of Madhu, the guy was dead afterall. He steeled himself up. This was Mira's bedroom that he was about to enter and he was scared she might freak out if he came bursting in.

As he entered, he found Mira lying unconscious on the floor next to the bed. 'FUCK!' he yelled. Someone outside the house heard him swear and asked if everything was all right.

'Call an ambulance,' he shouted. He heard the person—whoever it was—run away. Rakesh checked Mira's pulse.

It was weak. 'Oh God,' he cursed as he grabbed a bottle of water from the side table and splashed some on her face. He tried to recall the first-aid class he had taken as part of his training, but he couldn't think of anything at the moment. Mira's breathing was laboured, a rasping noise coming from her throat each time she inhaled.

'Did you call an ambulance?' he shouted to no one in particular. He ran out of the bedroom and towards the door. He was too tall, and kept bumping into everything. A man who he presumed lived in the house opposite Mira's said, 'I called. They are on the way.'

The woman from upstairs he had just met was standing behind him along with Mrs Krishnan who looked worried. 'What's happened?' she asked.

'I don't know, she just fainted . . . she just . . . she vomited earlier and fainted now . . .' He ran his hands over his sweaty face and shook his head. This was too much for him.

7
The Flat

AFTER MIRA WAS TAKEN TO THE HOSPITAL, A different policeman came and took away the evidence. The Krishnans watched from behind their locked grille door as the policeman walked around on the floor landing and barked instructions to everyone before stopping to ask them if he could get a cup of coffee.

Mrs Krishnan complied, hoping she could get some information out of him in return. But her efforts were wasted. She had even given him cashew cookies to loosen his tongue, but it didn't work. He just kept talking about how hot it was and how lucky housewives were to stay indoors all day while their husbands went out and worked. In the end, she was just relieved to get her dishes back and slammed the door in his face.

But upstairs, Joslin hadn't given up and was soon rewarded when the policeman got a phone call.

She figured it was someone from the police station because they were discussing the case. It didn't seem like anything was amiss till he said, 'I don't understand why sir is going gaga over her. Yes, they know each other but all this romance is too much!'

Joslin felt vindicated. For the first time, one of her suspicions had turned out to be right. She waited till the cop left, then rushed downstairs to Mrs Krishnan's house to tell her what she'd overheard.

By the end of the day, everyone in the building was convinced that Rakesh was having an affair with Mira, and that she had told him to kill her husband.

Rumours flew that Mira must have lured Rakesh with her homemade halwa and her beguiling smile and placed a knife in his hands after one of their passionate afternoons together. And Rakesh, hiding in the cupboard, had waited for an opportune moment to come out and slice poor Madhu open. Someone else was sure he had seen multiple stab wounds on Madhu's back, which were Rakesh's revenge for Madhu hitting his beloved Mira.

Another said that Mira must have done it because she knew that her inspector lover would get her off scot-free.

Mrs Krishnan was pressed for information till she feigned a headache and went back to the safety of her own flat.

8
Inspector Rakesh

'I'VE COLLECTED THE EVIDENCE,' KARTHIK SAID. Rakesh was sitting on a bench outside Mira's room at the hospital, waiting for someone to give him information regarding her condition. The sub-inspector had been away for his sister's wedding, but he had, thankfully, come back in time to help.

'So, what actually happened?' Karthik asked, sitting down next to him.

Rakesh filled him in, starting from everything that had happened that morning but omitting the fact that Mira had been his classmate. 'I used to know her family,' he said instead. 'So I really need this handled sensitively. If not for anything else . . .'

'I was wondering why she asked to speak to you directly,' Karthik said, and Rakesh looked up. Karthik seemed to have gone over everything with the others and looked like he was waiting for Rakesh's response.

'Like I said,' he replied carefully, 'I know her family from way back. I assume you know everything else or do I need to bring you up to speed.'

'No need. I've been filled in,' Karthik said and stood up. 'I think I'll go home, dump my luggage and come back.'

'You still haven't done that? I'm really sorry! Go ahead. And thank you for coming immediately,' Rakesh said and watched as Karthik walked away.

They'd been working together as sub-inspectors before Rakesh got promoted. It had been awkward at first because Karthik was one of the smartest people he knew. He should have got the promotion, not Rakesh. But familial connections mattered in every field and this one was no different. Rakesh's father-in-law had made sure that he had got the promotion. Things between Karthik and him were still okay. But Rakesh hoped this case would prove he was actually competent and deserved the promotion so Karthik could stop being resentful.

He got up and went to Mira's room. She lay on the bed, her eyes shut. She looked haggard. In her hospital gown, he could see her upper arms, and for the first time, he noticed a purple bruise. He couldn't have seen it earlier. She was wearing a long-sleeved blouse in the morning. Even when they had met at the reunion, her arms had been covered. Now he understood why she had dressed so conservatively.

Unfortunately, this gave her motive.

9
Pooja

IT WAS AN HOUR BEFORE SANJAY FINALLY dozed off. Shyamal left shortly after checking on her. She lay on the sofa till she heard the front door click shut and quietly went into the office to take Sanjay's phone.

The passcode, as she had guessed, was still his mother's birthday. She quickly went to the call logs and saw that he had dialled D's number ten minutes ago. They'd spoken for four minutes. She rushed to the kitchen and pressed dial. Before she could change her mind, the phone was ringing. 'Pick up . . . Please,' she whispered. He hadn't tried to speak to her since the news broke. It had only been a few hours, but it was still terrifying and she needed to speak with him just once. After four rings his low, gravelly voice filled her ears. 'Hello, Sanjay.'

'D? It's me,' she said.

The familiarity in his tone vanished immediately. It was replaced by the same high-pitched and cheerful voice he used while talking to fans. 'Yes! Hello! Are you holding up okay?'

'Yes, I just wanted to hear your . . . voi . . . opinion,' she faltered, instantly regretting her decision to call. What if someone found out? He didn't sound like he particularly was interested in speaking with her. The iciness in his voice spread to her stomach and for the tenth time since the morning, she felt nauseated. She gathered herself quickly.

'What are we going to do about these stupid stories?' she said, in her fake interview voice.

When he replied, she could feel his relief. 'Don't worry, Pooja, I've already spoken to Sanjay, and we will handle it. These people don't know what they're talking about. They spout garbage just to fill their news slots.' His voice was still polite. She took a deep breath before replying, 'That's wonderful to hear, D. Shyamal just left and I wanted to make sure things were okay at your end.' She was glad she sounded calm, controlled and just a bit unfriendly herself.

D was clearly done with the call, 'Of course, I'll speak to Sanjay again tomorrow. Have a good day.' She was about to disconnect when he said, 'Why haven't you answered your phone?'

'I . . . it's not with me. I can't contact anyone anytime soon.' She had expected him to feel bad for her, say something like, that's sad, I'll contact you somehow. Instead, he said, 'That's a good thing. It'll keep your mind at ease. Take care' and hung up.

She took a deep breath, inhaling the warm beachside air to take away the cold that had spread through her and wondered if she ought to check Sanjay's social networks for news. But his phone started ringing. She almost dropped it in her hurry to silence the call.

It was a journalist from a gossip rag that she hated. She held the phone away from her, tiptoeing back into the room to leave it next to Sanjay.

When she was back in the living room, she leaned back on the sofa and smiled. 'Why aren't you answering your phone.' she said, repeating D's words. He had tried to reach her after all. Even if he had sounded cold, it was probably because someone was listening. Once this was over, once the storm had passed, they'd be back together. The moments they had shared, the affection they had felt could not have been faked. She had watched all his movies; he wasn't that good an actor.

10
Inspector Rakesh

IT WAS EVENING BY THE TIME ATIF AND HE reached Madhu's childhood home. Rakesh had meant to come here immediately after taking Mira to the hospital. But between the hospital, asking around for the footage of CCTV camera (turns out, they were all dummies) and informing Mira's family, it had taken longer than he'd expected. He'd called ahead multiple times, but no one had answered. Instead of waiting for them to call him back, Atif and he had decided to just show up after finding the address on Madhu's old ID that they'd found in his wallet. Rakesh didn't want to tell anyone that he already knew where Madhu's childhood home was.

There was a time in school when he followed Madhu home after a fight had broken out between their two classes. His classmates had been planning revenge, but no one had the courage to make the move. Finally, one of them had jumped over Madhu's compound, stuck a nail in a bike's tyre and run out.

The next day, they had gone to take pleasure in seeing Madhu losing his temper—only to realise it was his father's bike they had damaged, not his. Rakesh was a grown man now, an inspector even, but he still hadn't gathered the courage to come to this house alone. He had brought Atif with him.

The outside of the house had hardly changed. The money plant was still twisting over the rusting grilles in the enclosed balcony, the garden was still overgrown with various flowering plants and there was still an unoccupied wooden swing in the middle of the entryway. Rakesh pushed the old iron gate and it moved easily, albeit with a loud clang that could have woken up the dead.

'Who is it?' someone from inside the house asked out loud.

Rakesh didn't answer. Instead, Atif walked up to the door and rang the bell, waiting for whoever it was to come outside. A plump old lady opened the door and peered out. 'Who is it?' she asked, despite noticing their uniforms.

'Madam, police.'

This was the first time Rakesh was meeting Madhu's mother. One would think that with all the skirmishes Madhu got into at school and the number of times his parents were called to the principal's office, most students would have met her. But no, Madhu's mother never showed up. Rakesh had only seen Madhu's father a few times—on the way to the principal's office, hitting his son.

'What do you want?' she asked, raising one eyebrow and bringing Rakesh back from his memories. Atif turned to Rakesh who finally decided to take the lead.

'Madam, we are here about your son.'

'Which one?' She still sounded stern. He didn't know Madhu had brothers. 'Madhu.'

'That useless bastard. What did he do now?'

'Madam, if you can open the gate.'

She glared at both of them before grudgingly taking out a gigantic set of keys from a hook and ambling towards them. When they were seated inside, she snapped at them again, 'What did that fellow do now?'

'Madam . . . we are sorry to inform you that yesterday, Mr Madhukumar was found dead in his apartment.'

Her reaction was not one he had expected. She didn't seem sad. Shocked, yes, but the tears weren't forthcoming. She just sat there, like Mira had, mouth open, staring at both their faces. Atif cleared his throat, uncomfortable with the silence, and asked if she needed a glass of water. She didn't answer so he stood up, went closer and asked if she'd like them to call someone.

'Ma'am? We called earlier but . . .' Atif started.

'Suji!!!' She shouted next to his ear, making Atif jump back. Someone replied from inside. 'Yes, ma.'

'Madhu is dead.'

'What?' A patter of feet and a woman appeared from the bedroom.

'What do you mean by what? Madhu, your brother-in-law. He is dead. Call your husband and ask him to come home sooner.'

'What happened?' Suji turned to them now. She was still wearing her ID card from work and holding a child's toy in her hands. She was a smart-looking woman, not at all like how Rakesh had pictured Madhu's family.

'He was stabbed to death.'

'And Mira?'

'She is fine . . . she found the . . . she found Madhu,' Atif continued. 'She fainted from the shock, we think. She is in the hospital now.'

'Poor thing,' the mother said, shaking her head. 'Which hospital? Is she going to be okay?'

'The doctor seems to think so,' Rakesh nodded. 'We were wondering . . .' He was interrupted by two kids coming out of one of the inner rooms, one of them running to Madhu's mother and shouting, 'Paati! She isn't sharing her colour pencils with me.'

Pretty with almond-shaped eyes, just like her mother, Rakesh thought, looking at the kid. Mira had never uploaded any family pictures on Facebook, but he could tell from the girl's delicate face and her long hair that she was Mira's daughter. 'Take them inside. I don't want them to hear anything,' the mother-in-law hissed at Suji, who ushered both of them inside. 'What about Priyanka?' Mira's mother-in-law asked.

Rakesh understood. She didn't seem like the kind of grandmother who could take care of her grandchildren on her own. He'd have to convince her. 'Well, that can be decided later. But right now, I think she should remain with her grandparents. After all, only family can protect her till her mother is fine.'

'Yes, I suppose that is best. So, when do you think Mira will be fine? I can't deal with things on my own, you know. My husband is dead . . . my older son is very busy . . . Suji is a team leader, so she has no time.'

'I will let you know as soon as I know, madam,' Rakesh reassured her and finally got to the question he'd come to ask. 'Madam, we wondered if Madhu had any debts. Mira said he owed . . .'

She cut him off. 'He owed a lot of money to a lot of people. Him and his big plans and business ideas. Hmpf! He owes me a lot of money too. Thankfully, I realised his worth soon.' She spat out the last words. 'Thank God I have two sons. Imagine my plight if I'd only had one! Who would take care of me?'

'Do you know who all he owed money to?'

'It would be easier to say whom he didn't owe money to. I hope the moneylender doesn't come here thinking we will pay him back. I am not paying anyone anything.'

Atif and Rakesh looked at each other. 'Madam, you do understand what I'm saying right? Your son . . . Madhu . . . is dead.'

'I do.' She looked irritated. 'Do you think I'm stupid? I understand what you're saying. He is dead. He was dead to me when he stole my ring and sold it to buy his first bike.'

Rakesh was shocked.

'Oh,' the woman said, looking at his expression. 'You've been thinking an upstanding citizen has been murdered. No, Mr Inspector, sir. My son was not a good man. He was my biggest mistake. In fact, we all believed he would kill himself and his family because of all the loans. Instead, a loan shark killed him. A bit stupid really, isn't it? Who will pay the loan now? Mira? That poor girl couldn't even stand up for herself.

'So . . . thank you for informing me,' the old woman said, standing up.

'Yes, madam,' Rakesh hurriedly said. 'When was the last time you saw him?'

'Priyanka's first birthday,' she said and walked to the door, clearly expecting them to leave.

11
Pooja

THE ANCHOR'S PRETTY LITTLE MOUTH MOVED rapidly. Her eyebrows wiggled and false eyelashes fluttered, a lash precariously hanging on by the remnants of dried glue. The make-up artist would surely be pulled up after the live telecast ended.

Even as she was engrossed in the TV show, Pooja knew that Sanjay was making some plans without her. He had already left their beach house before she'd woken up. A few hours later, he had shown up with some ideas that he claimed would solve the 'mess she had landed them in because she had no mind to speak of or self-control'.

Pooja had ignored him and continued watching TV while he sat with Shyamal. But her ears were pricked in the direction of the men who were whispering like ghosts in a low-budget horror film. She blinked. Once.

And then again.

Pooja shut her eyes tightly, trying to drown out what was happening around her. She could feel the room buzzing with suppressed emotion. A shiver ran down her spine and she shook herself. Shyamal showed Sanjay something on his phone and Sanjay whooped loudly, slapping his thigh, his mouth curling into a grin.

She turned back to the TV. The ticker told her why Sanjay was suddenly so happy. 'Project announcement to be made later this week. But for now, we, as fans of Pooja, are so excited she's making a comeback in a new avatar.'

Fans of Pooja, it seems. What a bunch of liars! She barked out a rough laugh before it hit her. New avatar? Her? What avatar? Sanjay hadn't told her anything. But he was a businessman and money mattered more to him than anything else. Even more than his wife. There was no way he would spend so much trying to bring her back as an actor. Would he? She pursed her lips, wondering if her husband really suffered from a hero complex.

'What do you say, Pooja?' Sanjay said, interrupting her thoughts.

She looked at the empty space between him and Shyamal, shaking her head slowly, trying to gain control of the situation. 'About what?'

'You saw the news. Wanna be a director?'

'A what?' She had, for a second, thought Sanjay still found her good-looking enough to be an actor. Apparently not. She turned away. 'I have to think about it.'

'Think? Are you fucking kidding me?' he asked. 'I have given you a golden goose. Not only are you, an unqualified idiot, going to become a director, you will be working with one of the biggest stars in the country. Never mind that he is your fucking boyfriend; we will handle that when it comes.'

'I . . . I will think about it, Sanjay. I don't even have a script,' she said and got up to leave the room. He stood up too, wiped his sweaty face with his palm and took a deep breath. 'You're always reading, right? You read so many books all the time—reading in the bathtub, reading on holiday. Fuck, you even read during sex. I don't care if you steal a story from another language and turn it into a script! Or find something from one of those podcasts you're always listening to—those disgusting crime ones. Or if that is too much work for you, my princess, just let me buy a script off some broke idiot.'

'Just . . .'

'No just. No buts. This is what you're doing. We will announce the details next week and have a press meet,' he snapped, turning to sit back on the sofa.

'I don't want to do some crap just because you snapped your fingers and told me to,' she yelled, the TV remote flying from her hand as she shook her fist at him.

'Oh! Madam has principles now, is it?' he said, his voice dripping with sarcasm. 'You happily slept with someone else and now you're pretending to have principles?!' Sanjay was yelling now.

Through the corner of her eye, she saw Shyamal making a hurried exit into the kitchen. 'Would you prefer to just keep doing that then? Fuck him in the daytime when I'm at work and then pretend to be a good wife when I'm around? You will ruin my reputation, woman,' Sanjay spat.

'You're taking care of that quite well yourself. Which of your many women have you spent these last few days with?' she yelled back.

'What?'

'I know you were out with one of your women last night. You came in late.'

'You're kidding, right?' Sanjay looked exhausted. 'I've been spending the whole day brainstorming with Shyamal . . .' He looked around, '. . . trying to figure out what to do about your blunder.'

'Oh, shut up, Sanjay. My blunder? You've gone to that hotel with your whores so many times and the ONE TIME I do it they catch me? You don't think that's a coincidence?' This hadn't occurred to her until she just said it. Someone, probably one of his minions, must have followed her and D and informed Sanjay. This was just his way of punishing her for daring to have a life of her own!

'I don't know what the hell you're talking about now.' He kicked his chair to the side where it rattled on the floor before crashing down. 'Conspiracy theories, is it? God, I always call you crazy, but I just realised it's true!'

'Fuck you,' she said as she began to tear up. She sat back down, turning away from him so he wouldn't see her crying.

'You had one job, Pooja—to stand by my side and look pretty. You can't even do that properly. You know what? Just fucking suffer. I've given you an easy way out. Do it or just go out and tell everyone you're screwing my star behind my back. But don't expect D to back you up. He's doing his next film with me, and he will not give up on that hefty advance for someone as worthless as you—a one-time actor who has nothing to her name. Don't you forget that I am the only thing you have ever achieved.' Sanjay snarled as he said those last few words and walked away, leaving her alone in the living room.

Outside, he started his car and honked impatiently till Shyamal came out of the kitchen, bid her goodnight with a sheepish smile and left with her husband.

12
Inspector Rakesh

THAT NIGHT HE ENTERED HIS HOUSE TO THE sound of two people arguing on TV and the smell of his wife's chicken curry. Bindhu, his wife, was sitting on the sofa, peeling the skin off some dried jackfruit seeds. She looked up when he walked in.

'Hey,' he said, taking off his shirt on the way to the bedroom. He needed a shower to get the day off him.

'Rough day?' Bindhu asked.

'Yeah. I'm exhausted. I'll just take a shower and come back,' he said, shutting the bathroom door. He couldn't quite look her in the eye yet. Somehow, it felt like he had been out cheating even though he had done nothing.

As he hung the towel on a hook behind the bathroom door, he caught a glimpse of himself in the mirror. He hadn't really contemplated his reflection before. He'd been married for a while and both of them had settled into a nice roundedness of the body that comes with marriage and having kids. Or, in his case, being a cop.

He patted his tummy and turned away, wondering what Mira must think of him. She was as petite and pretty as she had been back in school, while he was starting to look like a well-seasoned cop. He sucked his stomach in and turned back to the mirror. It gave him a constipated, deflated look. Rakesh exhaled, his stomach jiggling back into place in relief.

When he came out, his wife had already set his plate for him. 'Chicken curry and rice,' she announced. He gratefully started eating. This was worth the belly.

'What happened to that person you know?' Bindhu asked, pulling out a chair and settling down next to him.

'He's dead,' he said, swallowing and taking a sip of water, still not looking at her.

'Sorry to hear that. Any leads?'

The TV behind them reflected on his tall steel tumbler of water. Someone in a pink sari, similar to the one Mira had been wearing, moved across the convex surface, distorted by the shape of it. It suddenly occurred to him that she must have changed before going to Mrs Krishnan's house. Did she always sleep in a pretty sari, or did she grab the chance to change in the morning?

He hadn't asked her.

'Were you close to him?' his wife interrupted his thoughts.

When he still didn't answer, she reached over and patted his hand. 'I wasn't close to him. He was a rowdy in school. Always bullying kids and stuff.'

He could feel her observing him. He tried to keep a neutral expression but failed.

'I'm guessing he treated his wife badly too?' she said.

'She has bruises on her.'

'Poor thing. Whom do you suspect?' she asked.

'Moneylenders. But she has . . .' he said, his mouth full. He swallowed and continued. 'Anyway. He owed a lot of people money. He probably had a fight with someone before he died, about why he hadn't paid them back.'

'Gambler?'

'I guess.'

'And she was working?'

'Was, after-school classes. Quit because of him.'

'That's just sad,' she said, clicking her tongue.

'They even had a kid,' he added. 'She is at her grandmother's house.'

'Poor girl!' Bindhu said, crossing her arms. She was wearing a faded nightie with the in-skirt peeking out from the bottom. Neither matched. He tried to picture Mira in a similar outfit, but it didn't work. All he could see her in was her pink sari. Or their school uniform, which would probably still fit her.

'The neighbours said he was an alcoholic and came home drunk all the time. Anyway, I hope she is able to recover soon and give another statement.'

'Recover?'

'Yeah, she vomited when we were questioning her. Then she fainted at her house. I think it was the shock.' Bindhu raised her eyebrows but didn't interrupt. 'Her statement was a bit confusing . . . I need to get a clearer picture.'

'What was it? Are you allowed to say? You've never handled a murder by yourself, so if you don't want to . . .'

'No . . . she said nothing interesting. The husband came home late, had a fight with someone on the phone, she gave him food. Before she went to bed, he gave her a glass of milk. When she woke up, she found she was locked in.'

'Gave her a glass of milk?' she asked with a sharp intake of breath.

'Yes, why?'

'Honey, think about it,' she said, raising her eyebrows.

'I don't under—'

'If you were in debt, a drunk, a wife beater, just had a fight with someone on the phone, would you suddenly become a loving husband who brings a warm glass of milk to his wife before she goes to bed? Not to mention the vomiting and fainting. Women aren't as fragile as you think.'

'You mean he . . .'

'Murder–suicide? Yeah,' she said, shaking her head. She had been watching too many TV serials, he thought. But there had been a few similar cases in the past when Parameshwaran sir was his boss. Maybe there was something here that he could explore. His brilliant wife clicked her tongue and went to the kitchen to put away the leftovers.

He washed his hands and grabbed his phone to call the hospital where Mira was. 'I'm Inspector Rakesh,' he said to the lady who answered.

'How can I help you?' she replied.

'I need to speak to the doctor handling Mira Madhukumar; I admitted her today. She's a witness in a case. It's urgent,' he said, speaking faster than normal, almost stumbling over his words.

'Sir, we cannot . . .'

'Idiot woman, this is urgent, regarding a murder investigation. Can you put the doctor on the phone or not? Just give me a simple answer. Or at least get me a nurse.'

He heard a sharp intake of breath; she was clearly taken aback by his words. But he didn't hear her calling out to anyone. A clipped voice answered after a few seconds. 'Can I help you?'

'Yes, can you please check Mira for poisoning? We suspect . . .'

'Sir, Mira Madhukumar, right?'

'Yes.'

'And who are you to her?'

'I am the inspector . . . can you just do it?!' Rakesh could feel his voice getting louder. Bindhu had returned to the room and was watching him panic. She gestured at him, showing him that he had to take a deep breath in. He did that and continued.

'Madam, she is a witness in my case, and she is a family friend. Can you . . .'

'We have already pumped her stomach, sir,' the voice on the other end said. 'I cannot give you more information since I can't confirm your relationship with her or identity . . .'

'Why didn't someone inform me?'

'We have informed her family. Are you her family!' It wasn't a question.

He cut her off. 'But she's fine, right?'

The nurse had already hung up. Bindhu shook her head at him and went back into the kitchen.

Once she was gone, Rakesh checked his phone. Mira was still a part of the WhatsApp group of classmates. He clicked on her face and zoomed into her display picture. It was an old one. It looked like she had taken a picture of a photograph. Light was reflecting off the surface and the person next to her had been cropped out. But he spotted a part of an arm, a man's arm. It was probably Madhu.

Rakesh clicked on 'Send message' and texted Mira: 'Are you okay? I heard that the hospital performed some procedure.'

13
Pooja

IT WAS MORNING AND POOJA WAS IN FRONT OF the TV again. Sanjay had taken out the batteries of the remote control because of how much she'd been crying. But did he think she couldn't find where the spare batteries were kept in her own home? Or that she didn't know how to operate a TV without its remote control?

She had grabbed the batteries from the AC's remote control in Sanjay's office as soon as he'd left. Now she was sitting on the couch, clutching a cushion for support, and flipping channels. The TV anchor was talking about some secret source who apparently was close to her.

'We have some information from one of Pooja Reddy's closest friends!' she exclaimed to the camera. 'And she has some seriously juicy revelations.'

'Pooja told her friend that she has been planning to leave her producer husband for his main actor. Unfortunately, it seems D didn't think that was part of the bargain. Instead of breaking up her marriage, Pooja just continued her relationship with D in the hope that he would, one day, change his mind.'

'Ugh!' she cursed, changing the channel and moving to the one she hated. If this is what a news channel was showing its viewers, she could only imagine what a gossipy entertainment channel was telecasting. The anchor who had once been Pooja's favourite appeared on screen with a glint in her eye. 'Fuck!' Pooja said as she saw a picture of herself pop across the screen. It was from a particularly risqué photoshoot she had done for a magazine spread before her only movie had released.

The anchor said, 'I don't know if you all remember this photoshoot Pooja did with superstar D back in the day. But we do. And we wondered if something was going on between the two then.'

'Nothing was going on then,' Pooja screamed at the screen.

'We spoke to one of the photographer's assistants and he was quite happy to tell us that both D and his leading lady were extremely comfortable on set.'

'Who the fuck is this idiot!'

'In fact, they were sure that D was finally going to put an end to his bachelor lifestyle and get serious about Pooja. So it was quite a surprise when Pooja settled for the balding producer Reddy.'

Her co-host appeared on screen, and she turned to him. 'So, what you think about this whole affair?'

'Honestly, I've always been a fan of Pooja's,' he said. 'Even though she only acted in one film, I still think the chemistry between her and D was amazing.'

Pooja smiled.

'But . . .' he said, raising a finger and looking into the camera, 'But . . . I will say this. This is probably the first time in the history of our show that we have discovered a woman cheating on her husband. For all you people out there who say men are dogs, well, women seem to be following the same path.'

'Who knows what our country is coming to,' the female anchor said.

'Well, I guess you could say it's going to the dogs,' the co-anchor said and both of them laughed.

Pooja had had enough. This wasn't helping her in any way. She turned off the television just in time to hear a scraping sound outside. Peering through the gap in the curtains, she saw a head bobbing up and down from behind the fence. After a few seconds, a man's head poked up over the fence and looked around her backyard.

'What the fuck?' she said, watching as the man tried to jump over. There used to be barbed wire over the fence, but Sanjay had it removed because it 'spoiled the look' for an international client meeting. Thankfully, they had left some random nails in here and there and she gave a satisfied smirk as the man's hand snagged on something and he pulled it off the fence in pain.

He squinted at the house again and shook his head. Pooja instinctively took a step back before remembering that the windowpanes were tinted. However, they weren't blackout, so she pushed herself down on the sofa, almost lying on her stomach, and watched him. He put his denim jacket on the jagged bits of the fence and leapt over it in one swift motion.

'Lakshmi Ma!' Pooja hissed from her position. She recognised the man now. He worked at a gossip blog everyone hated. The sneaky fellow had found out where she was. The cook, who had been brought over to keep her company, was in the kitchen, chopping vegetables too loudly to hear her. Pooja slid off the sofa as smoothly as she could while keeping an eye on the approaching man. He was halfway across the lawn now, walking in a very sneaky way. The idiot seemed to think he needed to be quiet on a wet lawn.

She managed to land on the floor without injuring herself and scrambled on all fours to the kitchen.

'Madam?' Lakshmi Ma looked bewildered as she spotted Pooja crawling into the kitchen.

'Lakshmi Ma, there is someone on the lawn. He jumped over the fence,' she whispered. 'And he is outside the TV room now.'

Lakshmi narrowed her eyes and grabbed the ladle she was mixing the sambar with. 'One minute, Ma, you wait here,' she said and stomped out. Pooja sat on the floor, hugging her knees and listening.

The lock clicked open, and Lakshmi's shrill voice filled the house. 'WHO ARE YOU?' she yelled. The rumble of her voice was followed by a loud whacking sound.

The man stammered something that she couldn't hear. 'DON'T LIE,' she warned, her voice intimidating. 'POOJA MADAM IS IN AMREEKA. WHAT MEETING? LIAR!'

Sanjay was not going to like that twist in the story, thought Pooja. She heard the intruder ask something. 'HOW DOES IT MATTER TO YOU WHEN SHE LEFT? HUH?' Laksmi Ma sounded livid.

He tried to talk over her, but Lakshmi Ma wasn't having any of it. Pooja listened in glee as she belted out a few abuses before calling loudly for the watchman. 'USELESS FELLOW, WHERE ARE YOU?' she shouted, her voice getting hoarse.

'I'll leave, madam,' the man pleaded.

'GOOD. GO. OR I'LL CALL POLICE!' she snapped and slammed the door shut. The glass pane clattered in its frame and Pooja heard Lakshmi lock it. She tentatively stuck her head out from behind the kitchen wall. Lakshmi was still standing by the door, hands on her hips, watching to make sure that the man left.

After she saw him jump back over the fence, she returned to the kitchen beaming. 'All done. Now, how many dosas do you want?'

14
Inspector Rakesh

HE HEADED BACK TO MIRA'S APARTMENT building the next morning, this time accompanied by Karthik. They went early so they could catch residents before they left for work. They had asked for everyone to gather in the common area at 7:30 a.m. A few residents protested about packing lunches, getting stuck in traffic and missing a meeting, but when the policemen wouldn't budge, the residents gave in.

'Thank you for coming,' Rakesh started. 'As you are aware there was a murder in this building.' Some people nodded, others flinched. 'We are doing our best to find out what happened. But we need your help too. As neighbours, you might have seen or heard something that may not seem out of the ordinary but can help this investigation move in the right direction.'

No one said a thing. Their faces were turned to him, expectant and waiting. He glanced at Karthik who shrugged. He continued. 'So if you can, one by one, please tell us anything about Mira and Madhukumar and their life that we should know. Or about any suspicious characters you may have seen. Please do not feel shy.' They continued staring at him and he shook his head. 'I'm finished talking,' he added. The whispering began immediately. He felt like a schoolteacher who couldn't control his class.

Rakesh let the people talk amongst themselves and went to join Karthik at the dining table that had been set up to serve tea and biscuits. 'These people sure know how to live life even when such a horrible thing has happened,' Karthik said, pointing at the feast that was laid out. Rakesh discreetly slid his hand across the table and grabbed a cream biscuit.

'Probably keeps them sane,' he said, munching.

'Look at them talk. It's like watching some TV serial,' Karthik muttered.

One of them, a woman, raised her hand.

'Yes?' Karthik asked before Rakesh could swallow his mouthful. 'Is Mira still alive?' she asked.

'Well, yes,' Mrs Krishnan answered, annoyed at the question. 'I spoke to her just this morning!' Sunderesan clicked his tongue and the woman looked embarrassed. 'Sorry, just wanted to ask.'

Rakesh chewed faster as Karthik took control. 'She is fine. Yes, she is in the hospital, but she is fine.'

'Are we in danger?' someone asked.

'No, nothing . . .' he started, but the residents broke out in whispers again.

'Are we all supposed to be living in fear?' 'Inspector, it is your responsibility to provide security for this building till the murder is solved.' 'I am an old person living alone . . .' Rakesh waited for the complaints to subside before raising both his hands and saying, 'No danger, nothing. Now, did anyone see anything?'

'I saw someone I didn't recognise going into their house once or twice,' a man said. The one who had first panicked.

'Someone?'

'Yes. Once when Madhu was there and once when he wasn't. He stayed for less than an hour the second time. The door was shut both times.'

'Who're you again?' 'Sharma, flat no. 4.'

'Couldn't it have been a plumber or an electrician?' someone asked. 'It was her brother,' Mrs Krishnan interjected.

'As if! It was obviously someone else,' Sharma said, looking smug.

'How do you know?' Rakesh snapped. He didn't like what was being suggested.

'She always kept her door open when any worker came over,' Mrs Krishnan snapped. 'And when guests came over, she always told me about them. So, it must have been the brother.'

'Yes. It must have been her brother. Moreover, you said that he came over when her husband was present,' Rakesh said. He had started pacing and repeating the sentence over and over again.

Rakesh only realised what he was doing when he looked up and everyone was staring at him. He stopped immediately, embarrassed, and turned to Karthik. 'What else?'

Karthik took over, asking questions about this mystery visitor while Rakesh cooled off.

No way was Mira having an affair. And if she was, who was this mystery lover and why hadn't he visited her in the hospital?

'He had come around lunchtime,' the man said. 'I come home for lunch; we shared the elevator on the way up.'

'What time did he leave?' Karthik asked.

'Maybe at 2:30 p.m.? I saw him from my balcony.'

'Anyone could have left. How do you know from your floor that it was the same visitor?' Rakesh asked.

'Same checked shirt, sir,' the man said, his voice sure.

'Thank you,' Karthik said and Rakesh felt his heart fall to his stomach.

'It could have been anyone,' he told himself. A cousin, her brother. Of course, it was her brother. Her brother had come home when Madhu wasn't there. Probably to spend time with his sister, probably to try and save her from her bad marriage and drunk husband. It had to be her brother.

'Does anyone have anything to say about the husband?'

'He was a nuisance,' Sunderesan started, and one by one everyone joined him in complaining about Madhu. Broken flowerpots, a damaged car mirror, alcohol bottles falling from his balcony in the middle of the night. The list went on and on.

Rakesh let Karthik take notes while he gestured to Mrs Krishnan.

'Did Mira talk to you about her husband? If he was being affectionate? Or angry?' he asked when she joined him at the snack table. She furrowed her brows and thought for a second.

'I don't think she ever spoke about him. She spoke about Priyanka a lot. Nothing about him except to say he was busy or working late.'

'Was he ever concerned about her health? Did he cook for her when she was sick or something?'

Mrs Krishnan snorted. 'If she was sick, I gave her food. Not a thing from that useless fellow!'

Rakesh nodded and made a note before thanking her. Mrs Krishnan went back to join the others.

15
Pooja

SHE WAITED FOR SANJAY TO COME HOME. BUT when he didn't come until midnight, she drifted off to sleep on the sofa in the living room. Before Lakshmi Ma left, she asked if Pooja wanted to use her phone to call Sanjay. As she handed her phone back after the call was rejected, Pooja pretended not to notice the look of pity on Lakshmi Ma's face.

The next morning, she found Sanjay sitting by the window, the curtains drawn open, reading the gossip section of the newspaper.

'Hey,' she said, sitting up and pushing off the blanket she didn't remember using. 'Hey,' he replied, folding one corner of the paper to look at her. 'Good morning.'

'Morning,' she said, rubbing her eyes. 'Does it say anything?'

'Well, apparently you are in New York, shopping your troubles away,' he said, chuckling. 'Lakshmi told me what happened yesterday. I have to say, it was pretty genius of her.'

'Why didn't you answer my calls?' Pooja asked. She immediately regretted asking him. Maybe she was imagining it, but Sanjay looked smug at the thought of her unable to do anything or go anywhere without him.

'Sorry. I was in a meeting and just thought it wasn't important. I mean, if it was that urgent, you would have called Shyamal, right?'

'Who remembers his number?' she replied, getting off the sofa and folding the blanket. She had memorised her husband's number but never their PR guy's number. She placed the soft sheet on the sofa arm and sat down again.

'Doesn't that mean my phone should be with me?' she asked, hoping he'd agree.

'Yes. It does. But I think we can pull off something a little more elaborate,' he replied instead, dropping the newspaper on the floor.

'Like?'

'Like you coming back from the USA?'

'I'm not in the USA,' she said, her mind still foggy with sleep.

'Let's look at flight timings,' he continued, like she hadn't spoken. 'We can get you dressed up and photographed exiting the airport.' He spread his arms wide as if presenting some magic trick. 'It's simple. I've already asked a personal shopper to find you a good designer outfit. She knows your size so . . . she should be at my office sometime today. I'll bring it over and take you to the airport.'

'And what if someone spots me going to the airport?'

He grinned, 'I have a wig.'

'A wig. Like that would work.'

'No make-up, a wig, you can get ready there. It's a genius idea. I should make Lakshmi Ma our PR head.'

Pooja didn't want to admit it, but it seemed like it would actually work. 'So . . .' she asked, 'when are we doing this?'

'This week. I'm thinking the day after.' He pulled out his phone. 'There is a flight coming in early in the morning. That's the best option. We can get you to the airport when it's dark and you'll come out looking nice and fresh.'

'Okay,' she replied, 'It would work. It would totally work. Yes!'

'I should really make Lakshmi my PR head,' Sanjay said again, laughing.

Pooja smiled, glancing at the kitchen where the coffee machine was making its usual whistling sound. 'I'll remember to thank her.'

'Me too,' he said, picking up the paper. 'The picture is nice,' he said, before hiding behind the newspaper again.

By the time Pooja showered, Sanjay was having breakfast on the lawn. The curtains were still half-drawn so no one could see her coming down the stairs. Lakshmi greeted her at the foot of the stairs with a mug of coffee, 'Sir said not to come out. So no one sees you.'

She nodded and took the coffee mug from Lakshmi. This was the first time in weeks that Sanjay had spoken to her nicely. Even before the scandal broke, conversation between them was stilted and stiff. Only necessary information was exchanged even as their 'love' was put on display on Instagram, Facebook and TV interviews.

She walked to the window and looked out. Sanjay was on the phone, laughing and whispering. His voice normally carried over in the open space, but she couldn't hear anything right now. He glanced up and spotted her. She shook her head and went back into the room. She expected him to hang up and come over to her, maybe tell her that they'd have breakfast indoors instead. But a few seconds passed, and she could hear him laughing again.

Pooja wiped off the lip gloss she'd put on and went upstairs to drink her coffee alone.

16
Inspector Rakesh

AFTER THE MEETING AT MIRA'S APARTMENT building ended, Sunderesan handed over the contact details of Mira's landlord to Karthik while Rakesh headed off to speak to the two watchmen.

Sunderesan followed Rakesh and started lecturing the watchmen for not using the logbook for visitors' entry despite his insistence in the past. The two men looked like they wished they could be anywhere else. Rakesh decided to rescue them. Moreover, he doubted he would get an honest word out of them while the old man was around.

'For investigative purposes, sir, I have to talk to each of them separately,' Rakesh insisted a third time after Sunderesan told him to question them in his living room. He finally agreed, albeit reluctantly.

Rakesh and one of the men headed to the motor room. The watchman offered Rakesh a plastic chair while he sat down on a little boulder that seemed to be otherwise used as a footstool.

'Tell me,' Rakesh began after making himself comfortable. 'What time did you show up for duty that night?'

'Usual time, sir, 8:30 p.m.'

'What about the other watchman? Rakesh jotted down the time in his little notebook and waited.

'He leaves at 7:00 p.m., sir.'

'His shift ends at 7 p.m., but you come at 8:30? Why is that?'

'Sir, I told the building authorities that I can only come at that time. And they were fine with it. I have to pick up and drop my wife home after her work . . .'

Rakesh nodded and made another note. 'Then?'

'Sir, I came at 8.30, had dinner at 10.00, and then went to sleep,' he said sheepishly. 'I'm a light sleeper, sir. I sleep right by the gate so I always wake up when anyone comes or goes.'

'But you didn't wake up when Madhu came.'

'Sir . . .' He dragged out the word like it was a note in a song, 'No, sir. I went to the bathroom once or twice that evening, so I didn't . . . I have diabetes so I have to pee often.'

'Where is the toilet?' Rakesh asked, looking around. It didn't look like there was one in the building for staff use.

'On the terrace,' he pointed upwards.

Rakesh was surprised. 'You have to go all the way from the ground floor to the top for that?'

The man shrugged. Once they had covered the events of that night, Rakesh asked him about Madhu's behaviour in particular. He wasn't sure why he was so hell bent on making him seem like a villain. Rakesh, though, didn't have to try too hard. If the words that came out of the watchman's mouth were anything to go by, Madhu was a regular old drunk who either came home late to beat up his wife or stayed out for days.

'He didn't come home sometimes? Are you sure?'

'Yes, sir, he wasn't a quiet guy. His motorbike makes a lot of noise. He did too. Once I found him sleeping outside the building gate. His bike had fallen down, and he must have passed out right there,' the watchman said. Rakesh urged him to continue. 'A couple of times, a friend dropped him home drunk in the middle of the day.'

'Who?'

'Don't know, sir. Never asked his name.'

'Was Mira madam awake when her husband came home drunk?'

'I don't know, sir. I heard some noise once or twice. Mira madam is very quiet. I never heard them fight. I heard him shout, but she never made any noise.' Rakesh pursed his lips. The neighbours had said the same. But they too had seen Mira with bruises. He could just picture her cowering and shielding her child as her drunk husband rained punches down on her. It was enough to make him flinch.

'Sir, I thought she would escape,' the watchman said after a minute. 'But she came back.'

'What?' Rakesh asked blankly.

'She had asked me for the number of a pawnshop.'

'Why?'

'Sir, I pawned my wife's jewellery to get my son into college. She must have remembered.'

'What do you mean about her coming back?' Rakesh asked.

'She went away for a few days.'

'And then?'

The watchman shook his head. 'Madhu sir was very angry. He came down in the morning and asked me if I knew where she went, when she left, which autorickshaw she took . . .'

'Did you tell him?' Rakesh asked.

'I wasn't going to help him find her. No way!' he said vehemently. 'I told him I didn't see anything because I had to leave early that morning.'

'She took an autorickshaw from there?' he asked, pointing at the autorickshaw stand down the street. The watchman nodded. 'And did you give her the number?'

'Number?'

'Of the pawnshop,' he said.

'Oh. Yes, sir.' The watchman pulled out his phone without being asked. 'Mahavir Pawnshop, sir. Shop no. 72 down that road.' He pointed to a lane that led to a small marketplace. Rakesh took down the number.

'Oh, I heard a man came once or twice to visit Mira, checked shirt. Any idea?'

'Who?'

'Someone said it might be her brother?' Rakesh prompted, feeling hopeful.

'Her brother? Yes, yes, he did. Maran sir. It seems he lives out of station. He came to visit Mira ma'am a couple of times.'

So it had been her brother. Rakesh felt relieved. By the time Rakesh finished interviewing everyone, it was lunchtime and his stomach was growling. But he was too excited to stop to eat. He wanted to follow on the autorickshaw driver's lead and see if he could find anything there. He could then stop for lunch before proceeding to the pawnshop. Rakesh knew what he would find at the pawnshop—all the jewellery that Sunderesan and the others thought Madhu had sold. But it was Mira who had actually sold the jewellery. But why hadn't she escaped if she had the money to?

17
Pooja

IT WAS NOON AND SANJAY WAS PACING THE living room again. 'Well?' he said, turning to Shyamal.

'He'll be here any second, sir,' Shyamal said, glancing at his phone.

They had rented a car for that night, just to drive Pooja to the airport, so she could go there in an unknown vehicle and come back out to their car. Pooja had told them it would look weird if she exited through the departure gates, but Sanjay had assured her that the photographer they'd hired would ensure that it wouldn't be obvious where she was. As she waited for the car to arrive, Pooja held her new Gucci bag, sunglasses and Burberry coat in one hand and checked her reflection in full-length mirror on the living room wall.

She went through her checklist of things she usually carried on a flight. She had everything, including an eye mask that she would strategically leave dangling from her bag.

Shyamal's phone pinged and everyone turned to look at him. 'He's here,' Shyamal said.

Pooja's bags were quickly placed in the back seat and she got in. 'Remember, check in and continue till the security check is done,' Sanjay said.

'Okay.'

'You have to look like you've just gotten off a long-haul flight. Those zip ties and stickers need to be there on your luggage.'

'Yes, got it,' she replied, her heart pounding.

They had to pull this off well. If they failed, it would make the whole situation much worse. Sanjay's anxiety had rubbed off on Pooja. He was sure that by the time she reached their home, one or both of them would have had a heart attack.

The airport was quite empty when they reached. She checked her wig to make sure it was secure and got out of the car. Sanjay had given her a phone with a new SIM card, without internet, with just her ticket loaded in. 'I don't want you to accidentally post an image which will give you away,' he had said curtly. She didn't bother arguing; his face was already red with the stress of planning this.

Sanjay stayed in the car as the driver loaded the suitcases on to a trolley. As Pooja wheeled it into the airport, she suddenly realised that she was all alone. Her fate was in her hands.

The wig didn't really change her face, so she had to be extra careful about her movements. Sanjay had forbidden her from going to the spa, fearing she might get recognised. He had also asked her not to wear make-up.

Thankfully, she managed to get past the security checks undetected. She settled down in the airport lounge, wearing her reading glasses, while she waited for the alarm she'd set to go off. Her coat, handbag and other things were tucked in a small bag by her side.

18
Inspector Rakesh

AT THE AUTORICKSHAW STAND, HE SHOOK A sleeping driver awake. He removed the checked towel off his face and woke up with a jerk. 'Savari, sir?' he said, asking if Rakesh needed a ride. Rakesh shook his head and pointed to his badge instead.

'Inspector Rakesh. I need to ask you a few questions about a lady.' He showed him Mira's picture on his phone. Another curious autorickshaw driver heard Rakesh's question and walked up to them.

'That's Mira madam,' the driver said. 'Poor lady, her problems don't seem to end.'

Rakesh looked the second driver up and down. He was tall and built like a fighter. He probably spent a lot of time at the gym, hoping to impress a girl he drove regularly— or maybe to impress Mira, thought Rakesh. No, he was too young for Mira. But he had come across Facebook groups where young boys shared their obsession with older women. Young boys these days were very weird, he thought. 'What's your name?' Rakesh asked.

'Muthu, sir.'

'I'm Palani,' the first autorickshaw driver said, climbing out of the back seat.

'So, you both know Mira madam?' he asked, wondering how well they knew the residents of the building. Maybe he should have questioned these guys first.

'Yes. Madam took one ride every week to drop off her child at her grandmother's place. Then we stopped at the market on the way back.'

'She didn't take the bus then?'

'Not when her child was there,' Palani said. Muthu kept looking at the building behind Rakesh.

'When did you last see her?'

'Maybe a week or ten days ago?' Palani replied. 'I dropped her at Koyembedu bus stop.' Rakesh saw Muthu glaring at Palani.

'Is there a problem?' Rakesh asked, shutting his notebook.

'No, sir.'

'You seem to be glaring at Palani.'

'Sir, nothing at all. I was just wondering why you wanted to know where Mira madam went. I thought the suspect was one of the moneylenders who madam's husband borrowed from.'

Rakesh noted how the driver didn't mention Madhu by name. He was just Mira madam's husband. 'Poor Mira madam with her shitty husband' seemed to be the general consensus in this area.

'I am just making sure the timeline is clear when I file my reports,' Rakesh said, wondering why he was even bothering to answer the question. 'I want to ask you about Madhu sir too.'

'Who?'

'Mira madam's husband.'

'I thought his name was Kumar?' Palani turned to Muthu.

'Madhukumar,' Rakesh said.

'No, sir, Muthukumar, sir.'

'No, Madhukumar.'

'Sir, I am Muthukumar, sir.'

'Oh. I meant Mira madam's husband was Madhukumar. You said Kumar. I said Madhu,' Rakesh replied, trying to get the conversation back on track. The two of them nodded, still looking confused.

'We know nothing about him, sir,' one of them said. 'Unless you want to know how drunk he came back each night and how many times he fell off his bike while trying to park.'

'He didn't take public transport or a taxi when he was drunk?'

'Once we took Mira ma'am to his favourite Tasmac wine shop when he was drunk. They called her to come get him. It was a big problem.'

'Why?' Rakesh asked, alert again.

'Sir, he got drunk and beat up someone for being loud. That man and his friends hit Mira madam's husband and the people accompanying him. Big problem, sir!'

'That was the only time?'

'That was the only time we went, sir.'

'Do you remember when?'

The two men looked at each other. 'Maybe two months ago?' one of them said.

'Can't be. Maybe a month ago,' the other one replied.

'Forget it,' said an irritated Rakesh. 'Do you remember which one?'

'That I do, sir,' Muthu said, leaning forward and giving him directions and street names that he was all too familiar with. This one was near his house.

Rakesh asked a few more questions and left. The drivers had offered nothing worthy except the bit about having dropped Mira at the Koyembedu bus stop.

Mira had left with Priyanka and a bag. She hadn't mentioned the troubles she was facing with Madhu to him. Was it because she thought it was irrelevant, or was she hiding something?

As Rakesh walked towards Mira's building, he saw Karthik exiting. He was glad Karthik hadn't been around to hear this conversation. He hoped Karthik wouldn't ask to see his notes.

'I'm done. By the way, we need to check out that male visitor. It might have been an affair partner she colluded with to . . .'

'It was her brother,' Rakesh interrupted. 'I just asked the watchman.'

Karthik nodded, thoughtful.

'Lunch?' Rakesh asked.

'There's no time for lunch. The post-mortem reports have arrived,' Karthik said, waving his phone. Rakesh pulled out his own and there was a message from Dr Salman asking them to come by.

'Better eat later,' Karthik said. 'We don't want a repeat of last time.' Rakesh blushed as he recalled vomiting over the hospital sink as the senior doctor looked on in distaste. Karthik started the bike with a chuckle.

19
Pooja

AIRPORT LOUNGES IN MUMBAI ARE USUALLY teeming with people, but today it was deserted. Pooja passed time by observing an Asian couple sitting in one corner. They looked like business associates, but she was sure there was more going on. She watched them chat, with drinks in hand and eyes lingering on each other, and wondered what D would say when he heard of this plan.

He would definitely think it was ridiculous and unnecessary. 'This shit will just blow over,' he'd say. She couldn't believe he hadn't called her even once. There must be people around him too, watching his every move. That's what she wanted to believe, as nothing else made sense.

An Indian man walked into the lounge and Pooja bent her head lower. He took a moment to survey the lounge and sat two chairs down. 'Fuck,' she hissed. She tucked her bag closer and put her left hand on the table to shield her face from him. With her free hand, she pulled out a book and opened it.

'Hi,' the man said, his weight shifting towards her. 'Where are you off to?'

She didn't reply. Why hadn't she carried her headphones? If she had, the man wouldn't have tried talking to her.

'Um . . .' he said, switching to Hindi and repeating the same question. Pooja shook her head, bending forward so her hair covered her face, and mumbled something in Tamil. He stammered and tried again. She clicked her tongue and he muttered something about ugly stuck-up women before sliding away.

After a while, she turned a page just as another traveller walked in. A woman this time, young and pretty, dressed in a tank top and skinny jeans. The man grabbed his drink and went over to the girl who seemed to have given him a similar response. Cursing, he came back to his seat, grabbed his bag and left.

An hour passed and Pooja ordered a sandwich to go with her drink. 'Would you like something else?' the bartender asked when he brought it to her. She shook her head, still trying to hide her face, keeping her nose deep in the book, pretending to read.

When the phone finally pinged, she had just about finished turning the pages of four chapters and was starting to get a knot in her neck.

'Outside, madam,' the message read. It was Shyamal. It was 5.00 a.m. and her 'flight' would have landed fifteen minutes ago. She went to the restroom to fix her make-up and hair. Then she took out her new handbag, coat and sunglasses. Her hair was flat and greasy from being under a wig, but she couldn't do anything about that. She ruffled it as much as she could. She still looked tired. Photoshop would have to take care of that.

Taking a deep breath, she walked out.

20
Inspector Rakesh

THE DRIVE TO THE HOSPITAL WASN'T LONG, but based on the growing tightness of Rakesh's belt he could do without food for a few hours.

On the way, Karthik updated him about his conversation with the flat's owner. 'Fucker says he's in mourning. Then told me to speak later.'

'What took you so long then?' Rakesh asked.

'Oh God, there's this woman . . .'

'Joslin?' Rakesh immediately intervened.

'YES!' Karthik swore. 'She was peeping over the railing and listening to me talk to the guy. I kept having to move around so she wouldn't hear me.'

Rakesh nodded, telling him about his encounter with Joslin. 'She'll be a fount of information,' Karthik said. Something about the way he said it set Rakesh on edge. He didn't press further because they had already reached the hospital.

Inside, the doctor, a young woman in her late twenties, stood tapping her feet with a notepad in hand. She heard them coming and, turning around with a swish of her coat, opened the doors and went into the room at the end of the corridor. 'Pretty,' Rakesh commented and Karthik agreed with a grin.

'Ma'am, is Dr Salman here?' Rakesh asked, as they followed her.

She rolled her eyes and cleared her throat. 'As you can see, it is a homicide,' she said, pointing to a stitched-up Madhu lying in front of her. Rakesh shivered.

'Anything specific we need to know?' Rakesh asked, tearing his eyes away from the dead man.

'Well, he abused alcohol. His liver was in bad shape.' She continued, 'There was a bit of cabbage in his stab wound,' she said in a matter-of-fact manner, picking up a clear plastic container and showing it to them. Karthik looked impressed.

'Umm . . .' Rakesh started, but Karthik interrupted.

'Time of death?' Karthik asked.

'Based on liver temperature and lividity pattern, I would say he died between 11 p.m. and 2 a.m.,' she said. 'His toxicology screen came back negative for most things except rat poison. Since he was drunk as a skunk, I don't think he could have,' she waved one arm around in a Karate chop motion, '. . . defended himself.'

She looked at their surprised faces and continued, 'I mean, if it makes a difference to your case.'

Karthik asked, 'Did you say rat poison?' Rakesh realised he had forgotten to tell Karthik about what he'd learnt the previous night.

'Yes,' the doctor said, shaking her pad at them. 'Not much. Just a bit, not really enough to kill a grown man. Someone went through a bit of trial and error to kill this man.'

'What the . . .'

'Yeah, I mean with the internet and all, you'd think people would be better at this,' she said and the two of them exchanged a glance. The doctor seemed too happy.

'Um . . . any other injuries?' Karthik asked.

'Nothing new enough that can be related to this incident. There are a few old injuries, cuts here and there. I think he may have had a bike accident recently, he definitely wasn't wearing his helmet. He got some stitches in the past. But apart from that, I don't see anything that could suggest there was a fight.'

'Thank you, Dr . . .' Rakesh's eyes went to her lab coat where her badge should have been. 'Dr Salma,' she said, her voice a little louder than before. 'As I said on the phone.'

Rakesh's face went hot, and he looked away. He should have paid more attention. 'Everything you need to know is in here,' she continued, pointing to the file she had compiled.

'Thank you, Doc,' Karthik said, looking at Rakesh with a twinkle in his eye.

'Fuck, I thought Dr Salma was Dr Salman. She's . . .' Rakesh hissed once they were a safe distance away and Karthik laughed, slapping him on the back.

'Well, the last one was a grumpy old man, so this is at least an upgrade,' Karthik replied, still laughing.

'Anyway, the important thing is the rat poison,' Rakesh said, trying to focus. 'Yeah?'

'Yeah?'

'We need to speak with Mira.'

'Maybe she tried to get rid of him,' Karthik chuckled.

'They pumped her stomach at the hospital last night,' Rakesh said, avoiding Karthik's eyes. 'He probably tried to kill her.'

21
Pooja

SHE PEERED OUT OF THE EXIT GATES, wondering if someone would catch her now. What if someone who had seen her inside the airport spotted her outside? Pooja looked around carefully, keeping half her face hidden behind her hair till she saw a familiar face.

Shyamal was waiting with someone she'd never met before. She tried her best to be casual while walking towards him. 'Hi,' she said, once she was close enough. Shyamal nodded and told her to walk to the area that had plants in the background.

'This is so weird,' she said, wheeling her suitcase stylishly behind her. She smiled and waved at the camera as she walked past. They had to do this discreetly, so it would not look deliberate. They did it a few more times, using one professional camera and two phones. Thankfully, the airport was relatively deserted. There were only a few passengers sleepily ambling out and greeting their waiting family, or making their way to taxi or bus stands. No one seemed interested in what they were doing.

Then, before she knew it, they were done.

Shyamal told the photographer to follow them out to where one of their nicer cars was parked. There they snapped some more pictures—of Sanjay helping her with her luggage, hugging her and then of her getting into the car.

'So, that's done then,' Sanjay said, as they drove back to their house in the city.

'What happens now?' Pooja asked.

'Wait and watch, my darling wife,' he smirked. 'Wait and watch.'

22
Inspector Rakesh

HE STOPPED FOR LUNCH ON THE WAY TO THE Tasmac bar the autorickshaw drivers had mentioned. It was late afternoon, and the bar was starting to get crowded. 'Fuckers can't go one day without a drink, can they?' he muttered under his breath and walked up to the counter where the manager was ignoring the crowd and checking his account book.

'Are you in charge?' Rakesh asked, tapping the table.

'Sorry, closed right now. We open a little later,' the man replied, not looking up.

Rakesh tapped the table harder and cleared his throat. The guy looked up annoyed. His mouth was open, as if he was about to say something rude but had stopped, having noticed Rakesh's uniform.

'Sir, tell me. How can I help?' His demeanour changed completely.

Rakesh pointed at the cameras he'd seen on his way in. 'I'm guessing those work?' There was a soft blinking red light under one of them, so it was clearly recording.

'Yes, sir, what happened?' the man asked warily.

'There was a fight maybe a month or so back. Do you remember?' Rakesh asked, wishing he had an accurate date to give.

'Sir, this is a wine shop with a bar attached. There are fights almost every day,' he replied.

'What's your name?' Rakesh asked.

'Jayaseelan, sir.'

'Okay, Jayaseelan, listen. A man called Madhu had a fight a month or so ago at your bar. He is now dead, murdered. If you can check your records and tell me if you know the guy or who hit him or what the fight was about, it would be great,' Rakesh said, glancing at a boy's head that was peeping out from the back room.

'Madhu? That's a common name . . .' Jayaseelan mumbled, grabbing another notebook from under the one that was open.

'Dei Gopal, come here,' he suddenly shouted, making Rakesh jump.

The boy came over, head bowed, looking at Rakesh through the corner of his eye. He wasn't from here, that was obvious. His fair skin and light eyes gave him away. Maybe he was from the northern states.

'Was there a fight in our bar? Some guy called Madhu? Sir wants to know,' Jayaseelan said, shutting the notebook and opening another one.

'Sir, which Madhu, sir?' the boy asked in fluent but accented Tamil.

Rakesh showed them a picture.

'Sir, that fellow never pays his bills on time,' Gopal said, recalling his experience with Madhu at the bar. The manager nodded in agreement, before adding, 'Yes. If you can get me the date, I can try to find the footage. We only keep sixty days' worth in the main office, so if it was before that I can't help you.'

Rakesh left, wondering if Gopal would remember more than Jayaseelan. He'd have to ask once he had the exact date.

23
Pooja

'POOJAAA!' SANJAY YELLED AS HE RAN UP THE stairs.

She woke with a start, thinking something bad had happened again. Someone had confirmed her affair with D. Or the media had figured out her trip abroad was fake. No, someone had spotted her hiding at the airport. Fuck!

'YES!' she yelled back, trying to untangle her left leg from the sheets as he burst into the room.

'Turn the TV on,' he said, panting and clutching his bad knee.

She grabbed the remote from the side table and turned it on. He took the remote from her, changing to another channel.

'. . . And this morning Mrs Pooja Reddy arrived in Mumbai after a short holiday in Los Angeles. Sources say she went there on business while others say it was a well-deserved holiday after the hard work she'd been putting in here in India.'

'What work?' she asked but Sanjay shushed her. The newsreader continued. '. . . A fan posted a picture of her at the airport.' The pictures they'd taken that morning appeared on the screen with a completely different background. There was a crowd of people behind her now! It was a very good Photoshop job, she smiled.

The newsreader continued, 'We hope Mrs Reddy will now break her silence and speak to the press. Apart from one playful tweet to D, where she tagged her husband Sanjay Reddy, there has been no response from her at all. D had nothing to say when confronted with the news but, hopefully, Mrs Reddy does.'

'Did you ask them to say Mrs Reddy over and over again?' Pooja asked. 'And what playful tweet did I send D?'

'Oh yeah,' he replied, pulling out her phone from his pocket. 'You can have this now. Don't tweet anything, don't post anything.' He tossed the phone onto the bed. 'D shared the link of some article with you, which said why D and you would make a nice couple. And we had someone tweet from your account, tagging me and saying that maybe a comeback movie was due.'

She searched his face, but Sanjay had already pulled out his phone and was scrolling through some feed.

'Okay,' she replied, trying to unlock her phone.

'No battery,' he said and walked out. Pooja placed the phone into the drawer on her side table and lay back down, watching the anchor talk about a famous couple who had scolded someone for littering. The internet was angry again. This time at someone else.

24
Inspector Rakesh

HE REACHED THE HOSPITAL WHERE MIRA WAS admitted and wondered if it was rude to meet someone empty handed around lunchtime. It was close to 3 p.m. though and she was probably done with lunch anyway. When he reached, he saw a constable sitting outside Mira's room. It was Sujeeth, one of Karthik's men.

He squared his shoulders and marched up to Sujeeth. 'What are you doing here?' he asked. The man had been playing a game on his phone and almost dropped it when interrupted.

'Sir. Karthik sir asked me to be here,' he said, standing up straight and pocketing his phone. 'Why?'

'Sir, he said madam might be unsafe. So, we need to keep her safe,' he recited. 'When? I didn't . . . never mind. When?'

'Just now, sir. I came after lunch.' Rakesh narrowed his eyes and nodded. 'Fine,' he said. The man was worse than a school dunce memorising lines from a textbook. But he had no business snapping at the constable because he was angry with Karthik. Moreover, he had questions to ask.

He opened the door to Mira's room and looked at her dozing figure from the doorway before letting himself in quietly. A sound came from the bathroom behind her, and he stepped out quietly, glaring at the constable.

'Is someone else here with her?'

'Yes, sir,' Sujeeth said, as if he just remembered. 'Her mother is here.'

'Didn't occur to tell me first?' he snapped, shutting the door and knocking loudly, before opening it again.

'Can I come in?' he asked, smiling as the older woman came out of the bathroom.

Yes, yes. Come in Pa.'

Mira opened her eyes and hurriedly pushed herself up by the arm that wasn't attached to the IV. 'Ma, this is Inspector Rakesh. I mentioned earlier, didn't I, that he was my classmate in school?'

Mira's voice was still tired, he noticed. The doctor had said she was still running a fever, probably due to the stress, and was quite malnourished. Her collar bones stuck out at a sharp angle.

The older lady, a small woman with an exhausted face, smiled at him. One of her upper teeth was missing. 'Hi, Ma. I'm Mira's classmate. Don't worry. She was just a bit overwhelmed by everything. She's fine otherwise. We will definitely find out who did this,' he told her.

She looked relieved. 'I can't imagine that someone was sneaking around the house when she was asleep. Oh God. I'm just so glad they did nothing to her.'

'They probably didn't know I was there, Ma,' Mira said.

Mira's mother turned to him, 'Did she tell you, Pa? Did she? How many times people came to her door to shout at her, to harass her? And that fellow would leave her all alone in the house and vanish! No consideration for her safety at all!'

'Amma, you should really get some rest,' he said, trying to calm her down.

Mira jumped in, 'Yes, Ma. Go home. Appa needs you, right? Go back home to him.'

Her mother sipped a mouthful of water and nodded at both of them. Droplets rolled off her chin and onto her polyester sari. She shook it off and put the bottle back into a cloth bag she must have brought with her. 'I'll send your brother,' she told Mira, slinging the bag over her shoulder and turning back to Rakesh to thank him.

The door had barely shut when Mira spoke, 'Any news?'

'Yes,' Rakesh said, bringing his attention back to her. 'In the autopsy . . . I mean in the lab tests . . .'

'There is no need to tip-toe around me,' she interrupted, 'I know autopsies exist. But why was it done? I thought it was . . . obvious.'

'It is standard procedure,' he said, sitting and running his hands over his knees. 'Anyway, I wanted to tell you that we found some poison in his system. He . . . I suspect that he was in a lot of debt . . . and . . .' Rakesh couldn't finish.

Mira's eyes widened. 'Is that why they . . .', she began, her expressions a mix of realisation and fear. She paused, her hand unconsciously moving to her stomach. '. . . I mean, is that why I vomited again. I thought it was the shock, but now . . .'

'Yeah . . . that's why. I guess it's a good thing you left your daughter at your in-laws' place . . .'

'What?' she said, then nodded. 'Right. Although it was Madhu's suggestion.'

They sat there in awkward silence for a moment before Rakesh remembered what he'd wanted to ask her. 'Listen, Mira . . .' he started, but she interuppted him. 'One second . . .'

'Go ahead,' they said at the same time, and he chuckled. 'Sorry,' he said. 'You go ahead.'

'I just need to go to the . . .' She pointed awkwardly behind her to the bathroom door, and he stood up.

'Should I call the nurse?' he asked and she nodded. He marched out of the room to look for one.

As the nurse was helping Mira, Rakesh looked around the room. For a government hospital, it wasn't as bad as many others he had been to for work. In fact, except for the faded stains on the wall and the cheap pastel colour, it looked rather clean.

He was about to wait outside when Mira's phone vibrated and a message from an unknown number popped up on the screen.

He hadn't meant to read it. In fact, if it hadn't buzzed, he wouldn't even have looked at it.

'We reached safely. Please don't worry. We had decided to cut off all contact, right? Let's start now. It is only best for . . .' The rest of the message was hidden, and he didn't think he would be able to read it. What did it mean? Who was this person? So many questions flooded his mind.

When the nurse exited the bathroom, Rakesh smiled at her and introduced himself.

'Oh, you're the one who yelled at me over the phone yesterday?' she asked, raising an eyebrow at him. He felt his smile vanish. Thankfully, Mira called the nurse back in and he busied himself on his phone till Mira came out.

'Sorry, you were saying?' Mira asked once the nurse left the room, closing the door behind her.

'Ah, yes,' Rakesh said. 'A while back Madhu had a fight with someone at a Tasmac?'

'Oh yeah, yeah he did,' she replied, scrunching up her face. 'I had to go and pick him up.'

'Do you remember the date?' She thought about it for a few moments, then grabbed her phone. Rakesh was looking intently at her face and he saw that her expression changed when she unlocked the phone—but only for a second. Then it went back to her normal aggrieved look. Rakesh was sure he would have missed the slight change in Mira's expression had he not read the message earlier.

'It was a month and a half ago,' she said, 'On the 18th. Why? Is it relevant?'

'Well, murder or suicide aside, there clearly was someone else in your house. I needed the date to check the CCTV footage.'

When he left, his mind was buzzing. Luckily, he had managed to memorise the first few digits of the phone number from which Mira had received the message. The country code was of America. Who was it and why did they want to cut contact? Rakesh would give anything right now to get his hands on Mira's phone.

25
Pooja

SHE SAT ON THE EDGE OF HER BED, FRESHLY showered and still in her robe. Her phone was charging on the side table. She was sure that Sanjay must have read at least some of the chats between her and D. She had been smart enough to delete most of them, but who knows if she'd missed some—a flirty message about his intoxicating smell or how he felt inside her. She racked her brain trying to remember if she had sent any texts to D the night before it all blew up in her face.

She couldn't recall.

Of course, even if Sanjay had read any, he would have deleted the messages. To make sure she didn't know he had read them.

'How does it even matter!' she cried, stomping on the bedroom carpet like a frustrated child. He had slept with every woman who'd said yes. He would parade them around on his arm and call them his new 'discovery' in case anyone ever asked. She too had once been his 'discovery'. And it had taken him no time to replace her with a newer model.

Pooja turned her phone on as soon as there was enough charge.

Wire still plugged into the socket, she held it in her hand, feeling it vibrate and ping with each notification. She couldn't bring herself to read the messages; instead, she leaned back in her chair, taking the deep breaths her yoga instructor had taught her and tried to calm down.

Each time her phone pinged, as message after message came in, her heart pounded harder than it had on her first day of shooting. The deep breaths weren't having the desired effect.

'I need a drink,' she said, reaching for a glass. But her hands shook so violently that she put the glass back on the table.

Finally, when the shaking subsided, she picked up her phone and unlocked it.

'Come on now,' she muttered, scrolling through her messages to find the ones where she'd sent D their plans.

Phew! She'd deleted them.

It looked like she'd learnt a lot about hiding messages from Sanjay.

Now, with that out of the way, she opened the most vicious app first.

Her Twitter feed was full of notifications, which was surprising since she had turned the notifications off for anyone she wasn't following. But she did follow all the accounts of magazines and they had tagged her in each article. She went through them all.

Pooja Reddy caught in a romantic rendezvous with Bollywood heartthrob D. Mrs Reddy embroiled in controversy with her husband handling the crisis. D denies having an affair with Pooja Reddy, Pooja Reddy missing.

They had made it sound as if she had been murdered.

Pooja Reddy missing from her house, security guard denies knowledge of whereabouts. Mrs Reddy caught red-handed.

Then there were tweets from people she didn't follow. Some childish ones about her and D sitting on a tree and K.I.S.S.I.N.G., and several nasty ones. There were even tweets where people were threatening to harm her or kill her for daring to bewitch two men. She scrolled through them all—more than five thousand of them.

'You fucking bitch, so desperate for men that you'll spread your legs for anyone.'

'What a cunt. Heroine hai na, 100% randi hogi.'

'What else do you expect from someone who used to be an actress and probably slept her way to her marriage with Sanjay sir?'

But there was someone who had defended her as well. 'Leave @poojareddyoff alone for God's sake. She was seen with a man, big deal. Losers.' She checked the girl's profile and saw that she was from Chennai. She bookmarked the tweet and continued torturing herself before moving to Facebook.

Her personal Facebook account had quite a few messages. Dhakshi, one of her closest friends, had messaged her asking if she was okay. Her concern was evident in the tone of the message, 'Poo where the hell are you? I can't reach any of your numbers and Sanjay said you will be temporarily unavailable. What the hell is happening? Are you okay? Don't bother about what people are saying and just call me, okay? Please?'

Dhakshi again, 'Sweetie, please call me, I'm getting worried. I tried coming to your house but there was such a large crowd that I couldn't even get through. Are you there or are you at your place? She was referring to Pooja's house in Chennai that she still had. She hadn't gone there since she started seeing D. 'Pooja, please yaar, reply karo. Where have you vanished? Wherever you are, just tell me if you are safe.'

She typed out a quick reply: 'Hey Dhakshi, sorry I didn't have my phone. Turned everything off. Will connect asap, thanks so much for checking up on me. xx'

The other messages were from friends and family. Her cousins were wondering if she was getting divorced, her aunt had told her not to worry and to stay strong regardless of whether she was getting a divorce, and her uncle wanted to know if he could get free tickets to a movie he wanted to watch in Kerala. She thanked and reassured her aunt that she wasn't getting a divorce, replied to some messages and deleted the others—all while ignoring the requests tab that was flashing an obscene number of messages. Her parents didn't have Facebook accounts, neither did D.

She went to her official Facebook page. Her last post had been a picture of the flowers in her garden. The chrysanthemums had bloomed, and she was proud to have worked on them herself. 'Proud momma with her babies' was the caption. It was the morning before the news had broken out. She had returned home after meeting D and had taken the picture during the golden hour like her friends had told her to. She thought she looked lovely, the sunlight bringing out the brown in her eyes. She remembered setting down her chai and book and running out to the garden to take the picture. She had posted it on Facebook and also sent it to D.

There were over eight hundred comments on the picture the last time she had checked. Now there were more than twenty-five thousand! Things like, 'Proud mummy? Is she trying to say something?', 'yeh randi hai (she is a whore)', 'Indian cinema's number one randi', 'Pretending to be a sati savithri with her cooking and gardening when really she is the poisonous villain', 'Sanjay films are having losses, so he is now pimping his wife out.' The last one got quite a few likes and laughing emojis in response.

Her phone started vibrating in her hand, startling her. Dhakshi had seen her Facebook message. She let it ring through and went back to the comments. 'Always knew she was the cheating type, even in the film she broke off her engagement to be with D na. Should have known then that she would do it in real life too.'

There was a reply under the comment: 'If you're right then it's meant to be. Can we stop judging her?' Taken aback, Pooja clicked on the girl's profile. Unfortunately, the girl's account was locked and the display picture was that of a dog. Pooja went back to her Facebook page when her phone rang. Cheered up by the sole positive comment, she answered.

'Pooja?' Dhakshi started, almost yelling into the phone. 'Are you okay? I just saw your message on Facebook. Where are you?'

'I'm fine, don't worry. I'm back in Mumbai, I was in the US for a bit, work stuff.'

'Are you at home?'

'No,' she said in a hurry, worried that Dhakshi might come over. She lived just a couple of streets away.

'At a hotel then. Do you want me to come over?' she asked. Pooja could hear dogs in the background; she must be at Fluffy's dog obedience class.

'No, I am going back home in a bit. Can I call you back? I just turned on my phone and I have a lot of notifications to go through.' Even as she said this, Pooja hoped she wasn't being rude to the only person who seemed to care enough to contact her.

'Pooja, are you sure you're okay? Like, do you want to talk?' The barking sounds in the background continued. Pooja closed her eyes tightly, fighting off a gradually increasing headache and replied, 'Yes. Sorry, I just need to see what people are saying . . .'

'Don't do that please. Trust me, it isn't going to do you any good. How is Sanjay? When I spoke to him, he seemed rather brusque.'

'Sorry about that, he has been finding it hard to cope with the publicity and these silly rumours . . .' she lied again, trying hard to stop her voice from breaking. '. . . they're taking a toll on him.'

'Yeah . . . I can imagine,' Dhakshi said. It didn't sound like she believed Pooja. There was an awkward silence before Dhakshi started again, 'Listen, I have to go now, sweetie, but if you need anything, anything at all, please don't hesitate to call. Okay?'

'Sure, yeah. I will,' Pooja said and quickly hung up in relief. With trembling hands, she dove back into the hell that was social media.

26
Inspector Rakesh

AS HE LEFT THE HOSPITAL, RAKESH COULDN'T stop thinking about the message on Mira's phone. The tone of familiarity implied that the person knew her.

It took Rakesh half an hour to reach the Tasmac bar, the school traffic slowing him down.

'I'm back! Where's sir?' he asked a cleaner, looking around for the manager he'd spoken to earlier. The man clicked his tongue and went to find Jayaseelan. The tables were neatly arranged, ready for customers. Rakesh didn't remember Tasmacs being this organised even a few years ago. The fairy lights on the wall were a nice touch.

Jayaseelan popped in and stood grumpily. 'The 18th,' Rakesh said. 'I need CCTV footage from the 18th.'

'This 18th should still be with us. We . . .'

'No, I mean the 18th of last month,' Rakesh interrupted. Jayaseelan looked annoyed.

'Sir, for that I have to check the hard drive. We can't have footage of every single day. Do you know how much data it consumes for one evening? We can't . . .'

'Okay, okay,' Rakesh said, raising his hands. 'When do you think you can get it for me?'

The man took out his phone and called someone. After a minute of conferring, he turned back to Rakesh and said, 'Four to five days.'

Rakesh nodded. 'Can't you at least remember who he fought with? I'm sure you were there.'

'Sir, how do I remember everyone who came here? He probably fought with someone for bumping into him or being too loud.'

Rakesh fished out his phone and navigated to his gallery. 'This woman came to get him,' he said, zooming into Mira's face.

'This one?' he laughed. 'I remember her. She came the next day to pay his bill.'

Rakesh was confused. What did that have to do with the fight? Jayaseelan was still chuckling. 'Poor woman. She's lucky I was present. If my boss had been here, he would have suggested another way for her to pay her husband's dues.'

Rakesh flinched.

'Yes, yes,' Jayaseelan continued, eager to tell this story. 'He racked up a bill of Rs 15,000 in just two weeks. If I recall correctly, we refused to serve him unless he paid his tab. That's when he started hitting Gopal Raj,' Jayaseelan said, pointing to the cleaner who was listening to the conversation with interest.

Gopal Raj looked like he could take down two men at once and Rakesh wondered how a scrawny Madhu would have handled him.

'Gopal hit him. He started bleeding and shouting, saying we are trying to kill him,' Jayaseelan continued. 'It became a big issue, sir. He broke some unopened bottles. Thankfully, it was cheap beer, and no one was hurt. He stopped when his phone started ringing. He answered and started shouting at the person who had called.'

'How did the wife come here then?'

'Oh, we took his phone and spoke to her. Told her to come get her husband or we'll take him to the police station. She agreed to come. When that man heard the word "police", he shut up.' Jayaseelan chuckled as he showed a photo in his phone to Rakesh. It was a photo of the very room where they were standing now—the room as it looked after the fight Madhu had at the bar. In the low light, Rakesh could see a few broken bottles and dark patches of liquid on the floor.

Jayaseelan scrolled through his phone to show Rakesh a couple more pictures before continuing. 'When the wife arrived, she and the autorickshaw driver took him away. She didn't have the money to clear her husband's bill, but told us that she would come back in a couple of days. I did want the money right then, but couldn't risk the husband getting angry and breaking more things. So I told her to pay for the broken bottles.'

'When did she pay you?'

'She came the next day, right about this time in fact, after lunch. She paid in cash and left, telling us that she was sorry, again.'

'Do you know whom he hangs out with here? Their names?'

'Sorry, sir. I don't interfere in all this.'

Rakesh had a feeling he was lying. But he stayed silent. He had to figure out how Mira got the money. Giving Jayaseelan his number and reminding him to call when the CCTV footage was ready, Rakesh went home for some much needed rest.

27
Pooja

IT WAS 10 P.M. WHEN SHE SPOTTED THE notification. She would have seen it earlier, but she had been busy deleting all the nasty comments on her Facebook page. After deleting the last of the 'whore', 'randi' and 'bitch' comments and blocking those accounts, Pooja turned off her laptop and climbed into bed. Exhausted but unable to stay still, she picked up her phone and saw the message from Dhakshi that had her on full alert again.

It was a link to a story whose headline said: 'D parties with mystery girl, his new girlfriend?' The website, a typical gossip site, featured a thumbnail of D at a local club, dancing with a girl in a tiny dress. Pooja's hands hovered over the screen before she clicked on the picture and was immediately assaulted by a page full of thumbnail images. As she went through them all—twice—she realised that the girl's face wasn't visible in a single one of them. She was either covering her face with her hand, laughing or she was shielded by D who had one arm around her with a palm in front of her face.

'PR mechanism at work,' she said to no one. Pooja stared at the hazy image of the girl. She was probably some model who had been hired for this job, someone unknown, so no one would recognise her. It probably wasn't even a real party, just something set up at a club and the pictures 'leaked'. She tossed her phone on the bed with a sigh and started applying her night cream.

She hadn't aged, not much. She looked pretty close to that twenty-six-year-old woman who had made her film debut and stolen the hearts of D and Sanjay. 'At least Sanjay's,' she mumbled, applying a thick layer of lip balm over her chapped lips. D hadn't paid her any heed. It was Sanjay who had pursued her, attending to her every need and listening to every word she said. She, on the other hand, was interested in D and found Sanjay's attention a little tedious.

When D didn't reciprocate her affection, she had hitched her wagon to Sanjay—he was, after all, her only option. But she had made a mistake in marrying Sanjay. People who say it's better to marry someone who loves you instead of someone you love never take into account the fact that the love can vanish as soon as the next shiny young thing comes into the picture.

Pooja lay down. Sanjay would stay out tonight, going by how he had looked at his phone before leaving home. She switched off the lights and put on a podcast she had been listening to. The latest episode had dropped; the host was talking about a man who had killed his wife for objecting to the presence of his other wives.

'Wow, asshole!' she mumbled, and fell asleep to the sound of murder.

28
Inspector Rakesh

THE NEXT MORNING, HE STOOD OUTSIDE THE pawnshop, waiting for the crowd inside to disperse. A young woman was begging the owner to be a little less stingy. Rakesh looked her up and down before putting down another five hundred rupees. Behind her another woman waited, holding a small child. There were two more behind her. Rakesh looked at his watch and sipped on his bottle of icy cold water, letting the condensation drip onto his dark blue jeans.

Ten minutes later, the last guy left, and Rakesh slipped into the store and shut the door. The shopkeeper stood up, 'Yes, how can I help you?'

'Rakesh, Inspector.' It occurred to Rakesh that he might have to show his ID, so he set his bottle down on the counter and took out his badge from his shirt pocket.

'I am not responsible for any theft,' the shopkeeper immediately blurted out and Rakesh rolled his eyes.

'I am aware of all that . . .'

'You can't hold me responsible. I have CCTV cameras installed here, so you can check who brought what,' he continued, pointing around the small room. Sure enough, there were CCTV cameras everywhere.

'I am not here for anything like that, for God's sake. Calm down,' Rakesh snapped. 'Are you Mahavir?'

'My father is, I am Anil,' he said, his face still sweating.

'Okay, this woman came to your pawnshop a while back. Just look at this picture and tell me if you recognise her.'

'Any theft . . .' he started again.

'FOR FUCK'S SAKE!' Rakesh yelled. The man looked shocked.

'This,' he said, showing him a picture of Mira he took while filling her file. 'Her name is Mira Madhukumar. She might have pawned something here.'

'Pretty,' the guy muttered, exposing his stained teeth. Up close he smelled like cheap tobacco and Axe body spray. Rakesh tried not to breathe while the man leaned towards him and examined the picture. He zoomed in and out even though it was a pretty clear image and Rakesh wondered if he should suggest that the man put on the glasses that were hanging off his neck from a string. But the man clicked his tongue and returned his phone.

'I don't know, sir,' said Anil, dragging out the words slowly. Rakesh pushed the phone closer to his face, 'Look closer.'

'Sir, so many people come every day. How can you expect me to remember all their faces?' her said, scratching the overhang of his stomach.

'She would have come from nearby. Third street? Green Tree Apartments. I am sure you take down details?'

'Yes, but . . .' Rakesh hated himself for missing Karthik at this moment. He would have made this sloth of a man divulge details even before showing him the picture.

Rakesh straightened up, adopting the stern demeanour he had learnt at the police academy. 'Alright, here's what we are going to do. I need you to come down to the police station with me. We'll need to take a formal statement, and maybe seeing her in person will jog your memory. I'll wait outside while you shut your shop.' He turned around to leave, hoping the man would relent. 'Oh, by the way,' Rakesh added glancing back at Anil like he had seen cops in movies do, 'her husband was murdered in the most horrific way. I'm sure you've heard of cases like this. You said she was pretty, right?' He paused. 'You liked her . . . who knows. Maybe you killed her husband. I'll wait for you to get ready. It'll help business to see a policeman standing outside, I'm sure.'

The man turned white as Rakesh walked out and leaned against his bike. A minute later, Anil opened the door and gestured to Rakesh who shrugged. The man looked at him with pleading eyes, so Rakesh relented and went back into the shop.

The drawers were pulled open and there were a few notebooks on the table. Anil pointed to an entry and pushed the notebook towards Rakesh along with a bill.

'Diamond earrings?' he gasped. Then he noticed the date. It was the 19th of last month. 'American diamonds, sir. Not real ones. But the gold is real.'

'She just pawned it?'

'Yes.'

'Why didn't she sell it to a jewellery store?'

'Not many stores offer value. You really have to ask her.' Shaking his head, he added, 'I wouldn't know. I just take the stuff.'

'She sold it to you?' Rakesh asked, pulling out his phone to take a photograph of the bill.

'No, collateral. It wasn't a sale. See, it says right there,' he pointed at the writing on the wall that said that. Rakesh snapped a photo of that as well.

'Did she say why?' he asked, knowing that Anil wouldn't remember because it was so long ago.

'I didn't ask. I never ask.'

Rakesh nodded again and asked if he had a picture of the jewellery. Anil shook his head but pointed at the safe.

When he had all the information he wanted and a picture of the earrings from Anil's safe, Rakesh left for the police station.

So, she had pawned her earrings to pay the drunkard's bill, Rakesh thought. Sunderesan had said that she paid the maintenance bill by pawning her bangles. If he could find other bills and receipts from other shops, he could check. Mira hadn't pawned anything other than the earrings at Anil's shop. Then there was that weird message on her phone. 'Fuck,' Rakesh muttered.

He needed to go to Mira's apartment and have another look around. There had to be a receipt they'd missed.

29
Pooja

'WHAT HAPPENS NOW?' SHE ASKED SANJAY, dusting the toast crumbs off her pyjamas. They were eating breakfast indoors because a few photographers were still hanging outside their home. People had mostly moved on, but there were a few who were still interested in what was happing to her and D, and Pooja wanted to know their next steps.

But Sanjay wasn't worried. 'Now, I get some more coffee,' he replied, waving to Lakshmi who nodded and went to the kitchen.

'No, I mean . . .' Pooja shook her head in frustration. Sanjay was starting to become thick in the head, especially after a heavy night of partying. Age was catching up with him and if he didn't stop soon, he would become the butt of people's jokes. 'We pulled off a rather extravagant stunt. What do we do next?' she explained what she meant.

'We are having lunch with D today. We can decide how to move forward,' he said nonchalantly.

She snorted, 'I'm not doing that.'

'It's all arranged.'

'You'll have to drag me out for that,' she said, glancing at the gate. The photographers would have a field day.

'Or you could just meet some people for a casual outing and slowly integrate yourself back among our friends—as if nothing happened. Why not join that kitty party group of yours? I'll meet D myself.'

'It's not a kitty party; it's a group of women who come together to support social causes,' she snapped.

'Right . . . social causes. Like having tea at the Taj and dinner at the Oberoi. Social causes indeed,' he mocked, rolling his eyes.

'I can't decide where they choose to meet,' she replied. She hated that group more than Sanjay, but being part of it gave her entry into his damn social circle.

Lakshmi Ma came back with coffee and waited while Sanjay tasted it. Their new coffee machine had been delivered when Pooja was at the beach house and Sanjay had taken great pains to teach Lakshmi how to use it.

'Perfect, Ma,' he said, closing his eyes in exaggerated enjoyment.

'Good? Good.' Then, turning to Pooja, she said, 'You?'

'No, thanks. Also, don't make lunch for us today. We have a meeting to attend. At my favourite café, it seems.'

'Good. Go out and have fun,' Lakshmi Ma said, beaming, and went back to the kitchen.

'She seems happy to get the afternoon off as if we were working her to the bone,' Sanjay commented after Lakshmi had gone inside. 'By the way . . . did you check Twitter last night?' Sanjay said. 'D was . . .'

'D was spotted squeezing his new squeeze? Yes, I did,' Pooja replied, keeping her face as straight as possible. She wasn't going to give him the satisfaction.

30
Inspector Rakesh

'WHY CAN'T WE JUST CHECK THEIR COMPUTER?' Atif asked while outlining his plan vaguely over lunch. Rakesh hadn't given him all the details. He had only told him that Mira had pawned her jewellery to pay people and said that if they narrowed down the ones that hadn't been paid, they could find the murder suspect.

'What time did the IT guys say they'll be free?' he asked. The murder of a drunkard who was known to start problems wasn't really high on the priority list. They were supposed to arrive before lunch with details on Madhu's computer, but hadn't shown up yet.

Rakesh and Atif washed down their meal with buttermilk and went back to the police station where they found Karthik speaking with a young man.

'Just in time. We have our call records and our tech guy Raghav!' Karthik said too pleasantly and stood up. Atif slunk away next to him as he walked up to the duo. 'He is new to you, but I know this chap', he added, patting the tech guy on his back. 'He's a very smart fellow. He's come to go through the victim's phone and computer.'

Rakesh didn't like how friendly Karthik was being, but he was pleased to note that the young boy seemed more uncomfortable than enthusiastic.

'Thanks for coming,' Rakesh said 'The system is in one of the rooms. Why don't you go with Atif?'

Atif who had just taken a seat at his desk jumped up like he had a spring underneath him. Rakesh turned to follow them, leaving Karthik behind with the call records.

'Fucking hell! Windows XP?' Raghav said.

Rakesh chuckled at the tech guy's reaction and placed the file from the lab on his desk. 'Who still has Windows XP?!' he continued, yelling at the beat-up computer they had taken from Madhu's house as it slowly whirred to life. 'Jesus, this is going to take ages,' Raghav mumbled. 'I bet it's not been maintained, nothing ever deleted, filled with viruses and it looks . . . like garbage.'

'That's good, right? We can access everything on it then,' Rakesh said. 'How long will it take to go through everything?'

'This could take hours!'

'Oh!' Rakesh hadn't thought of that. 'For now, just tell me about the search history, emails, and anything else that looks suspicious. I can make do with that for now. I don't think the victim was tech-savvy.'

Raghav set to work, and Rakesh flipped through the file, phone in hand so he could Google things he didn't understand. A few minutes later Raghav called him.

'Nothing interesting. I have a lot of cooking-related searches. How to bake a cake without oven. Little girl birthday cake. Healthy snacks for children after school,' he chuckled. 'You were right about them not being tech-savvy. There are basic questions here like: can my friends find out if I see their profile, how to delete a Facebook friend. I mean, a monkey could figure that out! Then . . .' he continued, but Rakesh interrupted him.

'Just go as far back as two months. That should be sufficient,' he said, remembering the date of the reunion.

'Okay. There are a few searches for people . . .' He paused. 'Sir, your name is here as well.'

'My name?' Rakesh asked.

'Yeah, see,' Raghav said, turning the monitor towards him and moving out of the way.

He was right. There it was: Inspector S. Rakesh, Satyam Matriculation School. He felt special for a moment before realising that his name was one amongst others. Every person who'd attended the school reunion had been Googled with Sudha and him appearing a few times more than the others.

She had searched for him . . . one, two . . . seven times, he counted. That was six more than the other guys who had turned up at the reunion. But why? 'It shows searches for all of us,' he said instead, pointing out at the other names.

'Us?'

'Yeah, same school,' he replied, stepping back. 'Could you compile everything in a file for me?'

'Sure, boss,' Raghav said, his eyes already focused on the screen.

Rakesh was determined to unravel the mystery of the message on Mira's phone. He checked his notes where he'd scrawled the visible portion of the message. 'We reached safely. Please don't worry. We had decided to cut off all contact, right? Let's start now. It is only best for . . .' The timestamp on the message nagged at him. Mira had sent the message just two days before Madhu's death. What had she been planning?

As he left the room, Rakesh realised that the search on the names of those who attended the reunion were done the day after the reunion and then again a week before Madhu died. And then there was that message. He had to figure out a way to get his hands on Mira's phone.

31
Pooja

SHE WAS MEETING D PUBLICLY FOR THE FIRST time since the media onslaught. A brunch at a café favoured by celebrities. It was public enough for them to be spotted.

Sanjay had chosen the location and the reporters who would be 'alerted' about the meeting. 'Shyamal casually mentioned the meeting while having drinks with some of his buddies who in turn will inform their friends at the gossip mags,' Sanjay had said this morning over breakfast. She had rolled her eyes, Sanjay was behaving as if they were Brangelina.

Her worries were cast aside as paranoia. 'Of course we are a big deal. Moreover, D is a famous person, so shut up and look pretty,' Sanjay had spat out

Pooja looked at herself in the mirror now. She looked fresh-faced and radiant, not like a woman whose life was ruined by an affair that wasn't worth it but more like a happy wife having brunch with her husband and their friend.

She walked over to the bed where Sanjay had laid out an outfit for her. He had gone through her entire wardrobe to pick one outfit that would say everything their non-existent press statement should have: 'Look at my beautiful wife. She wouldn't cheat on me. She is perfect and dutiful.'

As she slipped on the soft, white cotton kurta, she said to herself, 'Look at her innocent face! Could she do any wrong?' Her voice sounded condescending even to herself, so she stopped and took a deep breath.

Sanjay had chosen well; she did look innocent, the white making her glow and look younger, almost like a virgin. He had chosen a pair of white bottoms, but Pooja slipped into a bright pink pair of palazzos instead, just to make sure it looked like they weren't trying too hard.

Sanjay would be livid. She smiled at that thought and went downstairs.

Through the entire ride, Sanjay kept glaring at the pink of her pants, but he didn't say anything. He didn't want to spoil his mood, she thought. Or maybe he was tired of arguing. Either way, they were on the way to meet D and her heart was starting to pound.

D hadn't reached yet. The table they had reserved was away from the entrance but close enough to the tall outer fence so that people could peer over to get a glimpse of them, maybe stick their camera over the fence and get a few shots. Sanjay sat down facing the fence, and she was left to pick one of the remaining three chairs.

They sat awkwardly, shifting from one position to the other, and struggled to make conversation. Sanjay ordered for both of them, a coffee for himself and a lemon tea for her. Her usual hot chocolate and cookies wouldn't make her feel better, so why risk the calories, she thought, and let the waiter go.

Their drinks arrived and Sanjay got busy replying to each message with a smile on his face, conscious of the camera shutter sounds she was sure she heard between the pauses of the loud music playing at the café.

Sanjay's phone pinged again and his smile fell for a second before it was back. 'The fucker is going to be late,' he said through gritted teeth.

She thought he looked like a Cheshire cat just then, but nodded quietly. 'He's probably stuck in traffic,' she replied.

'Defending your lover in front of your husband doesn't make for a very good photo op, Pooja,' he said, the grin not matching the tone of his voice. She looked at him calmly and took a sip of her tea. She was about to say something nasty but remembered why she was here. This, in Sanjay's opinion, seemed to be a better photo op—a husband and wife staring at their phone screens while they waited for the wife's boyfriend to arrive.

And arrive he did, in a tight black tee that stretched across his muscled torso. He was wearing his reflective sunglasses and his hair, as usual, fell over his eyes. Pooja took a deep breath and stood up to say hi, but D turned to Sanjay first. The camera shutters started going off, with photographers trying to elbow each other to get the best shot. They pretended to ignore it all. D bent down, gave Sanjay a one-armed hug, turned to her, hugged her the same way and sat down. It was over before she knew it. Their first physical contact after the scandal and all she got was a fast-fading feeling of warmth where his hand had gripped her back. She sat down before she could make a fool of herself and slid the menu towards D. But he was already talking to Sanjay and didn't notice her gesture.

He called for the waiter who was lurking behind a pillar and ordered an iced lemon tea. Sanjay visibly flinched at that and glared at her, as if she had made D order what she was having. D, having noticed nothing, asked them what they wanted to eat. The awkwardness hadn't dissipated by the time the food came, so they smiled and laughed uncomfortably, made poor jokes. D led the conversation easily. And even though he was talking to her like he usually did, it felt like he was putting up an act.

'Are you guys doing okay though?' he asked after the waiter brought another bottle of water.

'Yes, we are,' Sanjay answered quickly and nodded to her. 'Pooja is handling it very well. The pressure isn't getting to her at all. Me, on the other hand, since I go out to work every day, I have to handle the reporters and cameras,' he continued, shaking his head sadly. 'It's okay though. How are things for you?'

'Nothing I can't handle,' D replied, glancing at both of them. He reached out for the hot sauce and his hand, cool despite the hot day, brushed against Pooja's. She snatched it away, but realising her mistake, she quickly reached into her handbag, pretending to look for something. Both Sanjay and D stared at her for a second before resuming the conversation. The shuffling outside had stopped; the reporters had probably expected a fighting match and were bored. Pooja snorted while playing with her salad, as Sanjay and D were engrossed in a conversation.

They stayed for an hour longer. As long as they could tolerate. Each one saying something to keep the flow of conversation going. Sanjay and D discussed the movie for which she was supposed to be writing the screenplay. D suggested a ghostwriter in case she was too stressed to write, speaking as if she wasn't there at all. Sanjay interrupted the conversation by showing off a new game he had downloaded and was spending nights playing. It was an action-packed game that gave you points to upgrade your monster warriors. 'My new wife,' he joked distastefully. Pooja started tuning out and before she knew it, D was hugging her goodbye, pressing her into his body before letting her go and walking away. Sanjay gave her a glare, grabbed his keys from the table and snatched her hand from her side, squeezing it tightly, as they walked towards their car.

32
Inspector Rakesh

'I KNOW YOU'RE BUSY, BUT YOU CAN VERY WELL let me know if you aren't coming home for lunch,' the message on his phone read.

He had forgotten to tell Bindhu. He would get an earful when he got home. But right now, he had other things on his mind. Raghav had asked for Madhu's phone after going through the computer. Rakesh checked the last few numbers, both incoming and outgoing, before handing it over. Then he called the first number on his list.

'Are you ready to pay me back, asshole?' barked a rough voice on the other end and Rakesh stiffened. This person definitely sounded like a murderer. He cleared his throat. 'Hello. This was the last dialled number from the phone of Madhukumar. Who is this? I am Inspector . . .'

The rude man hung up.

Rakesh and Karthik looked at each other. 'Sounds like a ruffian,' Rakesh said.

'Don't call from that phone, idiot. Use the station's phone!' Karthik said, his voice rising a couple of notches.

Rakesh looked around to see everyone in the room staring at him. There was pin drop silence and everyone was watching the exchange. Karthik's face changed as he realised his mistake. Rakesh slapped his forehead forcefully. 'I thought it was my phone. Same colour . . .' he said, laughing awkwardly.

Everyone went back to their work, a couple of them smirking at Karthik who had turned his back to the others.

Feeling stupid, Rakesh dialled the same number from the landline and waited. The phone rang till it got disconnected and Rakesh pressed redial again. 'Yes,' a polite voice asked. He couldn't make out if it was the same person. Rakesh repeated what he had said earlier, adding that Madhu had passed away. He avoided the word 'murdered'. 'We are just calling the last dialled number to check who it is.'

Karthik gestured that he would call another number and went to his own desk.

'Um . . . Ram?'

'Okay. Ram. Who are you to Madhukumar? Friend? Relative? Lover?' Rakesh asked blandly.

'Sir, I am a . . . I offer services in . . .'

'In? You aren't in trouble if you aren't doing anything illegal.' Rakesh didn't know why he said that. Ram was calm and didn't sound worried at all.

'Sir, I am not doing anything illegal. But Madhu . . . is sort of a client.'

'Okay. What kind of client?'

'He bets on events, and I help . . . place the bet. Nothing illegal. Just sports and horse racing and the like.'

'Okay. And how much money did Madhu owe you?'

'Sir, small amount . . .' the man hesitated.

'If it was such a small amount, why did you shout at me earlier? You asked if Madhu was finally ready to pay you.'

'See, sir, he doesn't owe me. I work for Areef bhai. So technically, Madhu owes him money.'

Rakesh stiffened. Ram had mentioned the name of one of the biggest 'businessmen' in the area. That name drop meant Rakesh could not pursue this, or they would pursue him. The higher-ups wouldn't allow it. Ram sensed the pause and continued, 'Anyway, the amount was so small that it doesn't really mean much.'

'Okay. Thank you,' said Rakesh and hung up. He could have sworn he heard a chuckle on the other end of the line. Karthik was still on a call, so Rakesh ticked off the first number on his list and handed the phone over to Raghav.

33
Pooja

SANJAY DROPPED HER AT THE DOOR AND LEFT to attend 'an important meeting . . . it's a work thing'. She watched him drive away from behind the living room curtains and changed into more comfortable clothes. By the time she was done, she could hear notifications ping one after another from the alerts she had set up. Pictures flooded her feed from the brunch earlier. She wouldn't have known if the photos were of D hugging her hello or him hugging her goodbye if it weren't for the plates on the table. One story said, 'Pooja looked radiant as she met up with the man she has been linked with along with her husband.' They'd missed a comma.

Another headline went: 'Pooja with D, Sanjay looks on.'

'Crap,' she said as she clicked the link. One picture captured an unfortunate moment of Sanjay watching D hug her goodbye. He had glanced up from his phone, and the photographer had captured him looking suspicious. Pooja sighed again and closed the link. She had been told to expect negative comments, but she felt like she had been through a storm for nothing if people were continuing to write about it.

'All not well in Reddy household' was another headline, with a picture of Sanjay and her scrolling through their phones and looking bored. The next picture had both of them grinning while speaking with D. 'Future director Pooja Reddy discussing movie with D and husband Sanjay Reddy' read another. It had a picture of the three of them laughing. She clicked share and posted it on Twitter, tagging both Sanjay and D.

'Pooja wears an Anusha Rao kurta to meet her bae.' What's a bae? she wondered as she retweeted it and continued scrolling through the others which mentioned pretty much nothing but the affair. She didn't think to check what bae meant.

She sat on the sofa looking out into their garden when she suddenly realised that all she could hear was silence. The crowd outside had dispersed. They'd had their morsel and were satisfied for now. She could deal with the tweets and Facebook comments, but what bothered her most about today was how D had not paid any attention to her. The last time they had been together, she had come back to this same empty house and sat on the sofa, just like she were doing now. She couldn't stop smiling that day. What a difference a few days can make. She shook her head, forced herself off the couch and went into Sanjay's stock of whisky to pour herself a glass.

34
Inspector Rakesh

AN HOUR LATER, RAGHAV CALLED RAKESH AND Karthik over. 'I have recovered some files from the phone and it's mostly weird,' he said, pointing at the screen.

'What's weird?' Rakesh asked, putting his phone back into his pocket.

'A lot of pictures of women, obviously. Seems like he's a part of those creepy WhatsApp groups. Or was at one point, because there's no evidence of it on his current WhatsApp account. I have recovered deleted SMSes, you can see them here.' Raghav opened another window and showed them.

'U dkls bstrd, u shd kil urslf.'

'What the fuck does that even mean?' Rakesh asked, trying to jog his memories of text lingo.

'You dickless bastard, you should kill yourself,' Raghav and Atif said at the same time.

'Well, that's . . . pleasant,' Rakesh said, jotting the number down in his notebook and checking to see if there were any calls to Madhu from the same number. There were—it was the number he had called earlier.

'Other messages from the same number as well, sir,' Raghav said, pointing out a few highlighted messages.

'12%' was one. 'Pymnt due' was another. Madhu had received almost twenty calls from this number in the last few months. 'That's a lot,' he said and highlighted them.

Most other messages were generic. Messages from Mira, from various friends and a few spam ones. Rakesh ignored all of them and continued searching for messages from loan sharks and other unknown numbers.

'Look at these,' Karthik said.

'What about them?' Rakesh asked. Karthik was pointing out the messages from Mira to Madhu. 'They're also weird,' he replied.

Rakesh read them and shrugged. 'They seem like any other couple,' he said to Karthik. 'Except maybe they spoke a lot less.'

'Spoke a lot less? I don't think they spoke at all! Look at these messages. She asks him, "When are you coming home." But Madhu doesn't respond at all. It's like he hates her.'

'It was a love marriage,' Rakesh responded.

'Yeah, but that was years ago,' Karthik insisted. 'These messages aren't normal.'

'Sir . . .' Raghav interrupted. 'There is evidence of another phone.'

Rakesh's ears perked up. 'Another phone?'

'Yes. In a few chats, he says he will send it from his other number or that he has sent it from another number.'

'We didn't find another phone,' Karthik said, leaning forward.

'Time to look for it then,' said Raghav.

'Did he have a mistress?' asked Atif, and everyone nodded. He'd said what they all were thinking.

'Let's go and find out,' Rakesh said once Raghav had left. He had meant Atif, but Karthik also nodded and stood up. Looked like they were all going to search a tiny apartment.

35
Pooja

WHEN SANJAY CAME HOME THAT EVENING, HE found her asleep on the sofa. An empty glass, sticky with alcohol, was on the floor next to her. He picked up the glass and dropped it in the sink. He had met D that evening again, before coming home, but Pooja didn't know that. They had finalised a story, something they had picked up from the pile of scripts received by post every day, one where the writer was desperate enough to sell his story to be filmed in her name. The writer saw this an entry point into the industry that could otherwise be very difficult to break into.

Sanjay wanted to give Pooja the good news. He was ready to forgive her but then she had shared the stupid tweet that called D her bae. He knew that she didn't do it on purpose, she probably didn't even know what bae meant, despite being younger than him by several years. But he was frustrated by her stupidity. For all the books she read, she wasn't always the brightest in the room. He pulled his phone out of his pocket and dialled Pooja's number. He heard it vibrating somewhere in the room before the shrill ringtone started and Pooja jumped awake, looking around warily.

He disconnected the call.

'Hi,' she said, noticing him, 'What time is it?'

'Do you even use your brains, or does it just occupy space in your head? Huh?'

'What?'

'Did you think even for a second before sharing the tweet that calls D your boyfriend?'

'I didn't share any such tweet, Sanjay. What're you saying?' She picked up her phone and, still half asleep, tried to open her Twitter app. He walked up to her and yanked it out of her hands.

'I didn't do anything,' he said in a high-pitched mocking tone, fiddling with her phone before turning it to face her.

'There, Bae D and husband Sanjay. Do you even know what bae is? I am not a stupid actress, I am well read and intelligent. That's what you keep telling me. I see no evidence of it. Or are you pretending to not know so you can embarrass me again?'

Pooja tried to reach for the phone, but he kept it out of reach and scrolled, reading some of the replies, '"Whoa, did she just confess?", "Omg, I cannot believe she's so out of it that she retweeted this. Poor Sanjay, he should just divorce her now", "D and she make a better couple anyway, why didn't they get married in the first place?", "How embarrassing for her ya. How come she hasn't deleted it yet?" Shall I continue? People are already celebrating our divorce and your reunion with "the hunky" D.'

Pooja was wide awake now and managed to yank her phone out of Sanjay's hands. 'I'll delete it,' she said and did it, quickly tweeting that she didn't know what a bae was. 'Sorry, folks, I guess I'm not cool enough to keep up with all the new lingo. Deleted the tweet, apologies for the confusion. Now please leave @sanjayreddy alone.'

She pressed send and his phone pinged. He checked it, grunted and went to his office without saying another word. Pooja sank back onto the sofa, her weariness bone-deep. As she half-heartedly cleared the remnants of the meal she had had earlier, she caught her reflection in the window. The carefully curated image of a Bollywood wife stared back at her. She turned away, feeling uncomfortable.

Just then, her phone pinged. It was a WhatsApp message from Sanjay. 'BTW we've found a story, the writer has decided to give it to you. Script will be here tomorrow morning.'

She closed the chat and went upstairs, shutting the bedroom door behind her.

36
Inspector Rakesh

AS THEY MADE THEIR WAY THROUGH THE four rooms of the house, Rakesh was starting to get an idea of what life was like for Mira and Madhu. She cooked, cleaned, taught the neighbourhood kids, raised their child while he drank and gambled. Filed and stored in one corner of the living room were receipts and account books for various businesses that had failed. The failures were Madhu's, the organisation clearly Mira's.

'I'll take the bedroom,' Karthik said just as Rakesh turned towards it. They shared an awkward moment before Rakesh turned towards the kitchen. It was a kitchen typical to an apartment like this. Small, congested, but with a large window on one side where multiple metal wires held cut-up plastic containers filled with soil. He peered outside to look at the makeshift planters. He could only recognise the money plant and a small tender sprig of coriander.

Just as Rakesh sat down to check the shelves under the countertop, his phone rang.

'What time are you coming home?' Bindhu asked, speaking over the din of the TV in the background.

'Don't know, but not early for sure,' he replied, opening the shelf closest to him. It had an assortment of empty containers and blender jars. 'We are at the victim's apartment trying to find a second phone we think he had.'

'If it were a woman, I'd tell you to check the rice. I've no clue how men work,' she said, chuckling. In the background, someone on TV screamed loudly.

'The what?'

'The rice. Anyway, tell me soon when you'll be home. We might have guests,' Bindhu said before hanging up.

It occurred to him that Mira could also be hiding things. The mysterious message came to mind. He decided to take Bindhu's suggestion. He moved from shelf to shelf, opening lids of all the containers he found, till he found the one that stored rice.

He yanked the lid open with some effort, took off his glove, wiped his hand on his pants and stuck it in. As he swirled his fingers through the grains, he touched something. He paused, closing his hand around it. As he pulled it out, rogue grains of rice scattered all over the kitchen floor.

It was a plastic bag containing a cell phone and a set of gold bangles! The phone was a cheap Chinese make, the kind you buy from shady stores on the black market. 'Fuck me!' he whispered. His wife was right. Mira was hiding things. He threw the bangles back into the rice and checked the phone. It was turned off. Either it was out of charge, or it had been turned off on purpose. He put it back inside the plastic bag.

'Found something?' Atif asked, coming out of Priyanka's room. He found Rakesh holding the rice container in one hand and the bag in another. Atif raised an eyebrow and said nothing. From inside the bedroom Karthik asked if someone had a knife.

'Yeah, I do,' Atif replied, looking at Rakesh again before going in. Rakesh pushed the container to the back of the shelf, tucked the phone—which he presumed was Mira's—into his pocket and quickly cleaned the grains of rice off the floor.

Then, he went to the living room and sat on the sofa, moving a stack of papers on the coffee table with the edge of his pen. In a drawer attached to the table were some boxes. He opened a shoe box to find it full of receipts. The family pack ice cream box contained the family's miscellaneous bills. Mira had stored everything and was maintaining accounts meticulously.

There was also a bunch of stapled faded fuel slips where she had written the amount over the faded font. He smiled sadly as he made a note of it in his little book.

'They were having serious problems,' Karthik said out loud from the bedroom.

'That's an understatement,' Rakesh replied, flipping through a notebook the pages of which were filled with the dates and amounts of Priyanka's school fees. He even found two late payment notices from a few weeks ago. No wonder Mira had decided to send the girl off on an early holiday, she didn't really have a choice. He sighed and wrote that down as well.

'See this,' Karthik said as he walked towards Rakesh, holding a small box in his hands. He rattled it and it sounded like a Maligai shop's change box. Rakesh pushed himself off the floor with his hands, shook out his legs and wobbled over to where Karthik was opening the box.

Inside, amidst the small coins, Karthik lifted up a false bottom using the edge of a kitchen knife. 'Whoa,' Rakesh said, looking at five hundred and two thousand rupee notes. 'Did you count it?'

'No. I saw it and came out,' Karthik said.

Rakesh took the notes out and checked them. There was about eight thousand rupees in there. 'That isn't much,' he said.

'It isn't a small amount either.'

'Certainly not worth killing for.'

'True,' said Karthik, 'But looks like she was used to hiding things. The box is old, as is the metal plate. We don't really need to take it into evidence. I mean, she didn't kill him with a metal box.'

'She didn't kill him,' Rakesh hissed.

'Hmmm,' Karthik replied, taking the box and money from Rakesh and sliding everything into place. If Madhu had borrowed money and had left a paper trail, there was certainly no proof of it in the house. But thankfully it wasn't just Mira's word they were going by. His family, the neighbours, even the watchman had said that moneylenders' goondas came visiting every few days, demanding that month's payment.

Madhu did bet on horses though. Rakesh had the slips to prove it. He also tried his luck at lottery tickets. They had found a whole sheaf of them in Madhu's cupboard.

Just then Karthik bent down and started feeling around under the sofa. 'What're you doing?' Rakesh asked.

'One guy I know taped his phone to the bottom of the sofa. AHA!' he cried, jumping up and triumphantly holding up a phone.

'Smart,' Rakesh said, feeling queasy as he saw Karthik waving it around. So both Madhu and Mira had secret phones. Well, at least Karthik hadn't managed to find Mira's. That was his secret for now. 'Let's take it back to the station and see what's on it,' said Rakesh.

Karthik shook his head and turned the phone on. 'It's not locked,' he said, raising his eyebrows. Rakesh joined him as Karthik scrolled to find a messaging app.

'The app has a password lock! What the hell!' Karthik said as he unsuccessfully tried to log in.

'Doesn't ISIS also use such encrypted apps?'

'Yes, but so do a lot of other people. Journalists, students, whistle-blowers.'

'But the tech guy can unlock it.'

'You think so?'

'We'll figure something out,' said Rakesh. 'Let's leave, unless you think there's more to look for. I'm going to take a leak.' He went to the bathroom attached to Mira's bedroom and felt out of place. When he went to wash his hands after flushing, Rakesh noticed something he hadn't seen the first day he was here. The washing machine, the one that was supposedly blocking the second entrance from the living room, had been moved. The clear lines cutting through the dust on the floor looked new. Who had moved it? Mira? But why would she? She'd always been a straight arrow. Not to mention that when he had questioned her, she had said she couldn't leave her bedroom since the washing machine was blocking the way. That it had been too heavy for her to move.

He couldn't imagine Mira—his first love, Mira—killing anyone. He couldn't even imagine her lying! No way. It had to be someone from his team who'd moved it while searching for evidence.

'Are you done?' Karthik called, banging on the door. Rakesh rushed out before Karthik could come in and take a look at the floor.

As they were leaving the house, Karthik said, 'Listen, about earlier . . .'

Rakesh knew where this was going and interrupted him. 'Yes, about that. We are friends. But you cannot yell at me. It's probably hard to accept that I got promoted. But so what? You'll be promoted next time. Till then I'm your superior and you cannot yell at me,' Rakesh said quickly.

Karthik stiffened. Rakesh regretted his words immediately. It felt like Karthik had been about to apologise, but he had fucked up. 'Of course, sir,' Karthik said, forcing a smile and walking ahead of him.

37
Pooja

SHE UNDERSTOOD SANJAY'S ANGER. ESPECIALLY after she noticed that a few people online had cropped Sanjay out of the picture and were 'shipping' D and her. She'd had to Google what shipping meant, but when she found out, she laughed. God, people are so flaky. D was his nickname after his most famous character, Dhiraj. Now fans were calling them Dhooja and Pooraj. She laughed again and went through a thread of conversation on D's fan page where people were discussing how cute their babies would be.

Pooja was lying in bed and scrolling through Twitter when Sanjay knocked on the door. She quickly slipped her phone under her pillow, unsure what made her do so, and sat up in bed. Sanjay stepped into the bedroom, bringing in the familiar smell of whisky with him. She pulled her sheets around herself and sat up straighter. 'Yes, Sanjay?'

'So, that almost went well. It would seem . . .' he slurred.

'Sorry?'

'Yeah, right! Like you haven't spent all day going through Twitter, Facebook and Instagram,' he said sarcastically. You tagged me and D in the picture!'

'Yes, Sanjay, because you asked me to.'

'You wouldn't have tagged me otherwise?'

'I wouldn't have tagged D otherwise,' she corrected and waited for him to leave like he normally did after yelling at her. But Sanjay just stood there, staring at the curtains. A couple of minutes went by before he asked her in a sad voice, 'Do you like him then?'

'Sanjay. . . . ' she started, not sure what to say. What right did he have to act like she had broken his heart when he probably had multiple girlfriends right now?

'I know he is handsome.'

'And you are a philanderer,' she snapped back. His puppy face was making her angry.

'I am a man, men have needs,' he said, the sadness giving way to anger.

'Men have needs?' she yelled, 'And what do women have?'

Sanjay didn't answer. Instead, he continued rambling. 'Did you wear pink because it's his favourite colour?'

'What?'

'PINK!' he yelled, walking to her and shoving his phone screen in her face. 'Did you wear the bloody pink pants despite me instructing you to wear white because it is his favourite colour?'

She looked at the phone after his hand stopped shaking. An article was open, an old interview of D's, where it said, 'D likes his girlfriend to wear pink.' Fuck, she thought, and gently pushed the phone away. Sanjay's eyes were red, not from crying, she was sure.

'No! I didn't even know that he liked pink,' she said, waiting for a response. There was none.

'Sanjay, why don't you go to bed? It's been a long day and you look tired.' He shook his head and put his phone in his pants pocket. He tried to wrap his arms around her but she pushed him away. 'Sanjay, listen.'

'You bought pink lingerie recently. It was for him, right?'

'Sanjay . . .'

'Has to be, I've never seen it.'

'You've not been around.' she replied, not liking where the conversation was going.

'I'm around now.'

'This is neither the time nor the place.'

'This is not the place? This is MY bedroom, in MY house,' he yelled at her, spit flying out of his mouth. 'If this is not the time or the place, where would you prefer we do it? In D's house?'

'Sanjay, calm down. You're acting crazy.' She was now out of bed and backing up into the wall. 'Why don't we talk in the morning when you're feeling better?'

'I'm crazy? She thinks I'm crazy!' he screamed. 'I am a man asking his wife to show him some love, and I am acting crazy? This is why I started having affairs.'

'That's bullshit. You were having an affair even when we were supposedly happy so don't give me this crap about men having needs and me not showing you love. You were the one who made this happen.'

'Oh, I was the one? Tell me, did you marry me because D wouldn't marry you?'

Pooja felt her back touch the wall and now there was nowhere else to go. Sanjay was standing in front of her with his hands on the wall by her side. 'Answer me, woman. Am I the idiot who thinks he got the girl? I thought I won the competition, that I had the pretty young thing. But no, you're not really a prize, are you?'

'Sanjay,' she started, but couldn't continue. Her tongue had got thick, and her words were mumbled. She put her hands on his chest and tried to push him away, but her strength seemed to have left her.

'Don't you dare push me away, you are mine,' he snarled in her face. The smell of the whisky was making Pooja's stomach churn, even though it was one of her favourites.

'I'm tired, Sanjay. Please,' she finally managed to say before trying to turn away and move his arm. He removed it from the wall but grabbed her face.

'Yeah, well, I am not.'

Pooja struggled to free herself from his grip, but he had already pressed his mouth to hers. She gagged and put both her hands on his face to push him away. His grip on her cheeks tightened, she could feel his fingers pressing into her teeth. His other hand clumsily groped at her waistband and yanked her pants and panties down. His mouth moved off her as he looked down to undo his pants.

'You're hurting me,' she said one last time, but she could barely hear herself. Instead, she bit the inside of her cheek and tried not to swallow the blood.

'Stop making faces,' he snapped. 'At least try to look at me the way you look at him.'

Pooja stopped fighting. But Sanjay had more to say. 'This is your fault. You think he will save you from your horrible husband? He isn't the marrying kind, you know. Even if he likes you, he isn't going to marry you. There will never be a Mrs D, especially not you.' He whispered the last bit in her ear.

She felt her head bang into the wall and tried not to look at them in the mirror on the opposite wall. Outside, their neighbours were returning home, probably from their weekend dinner at a restaurant. Their car honked impatiently in the distance followed by the creak of the gate as the watchman opened it.

38
Inspector Rakesh

THAT EVENING, AFTER KARTHIK DEPOSITED Madhu's phone with Raghav, he excused himself and left early without looking at Rakesh who was in the room.

But Rakesh was too busy wondering about Mira's spare phone to notice.

Once Karthik left, Rakesh called Atif. The boy took a while to answer. Having just left the police station, he was probably riding his bike. 'Listen, I know I said you could go home . . .' Rakesh started as soon as Atif answered.

'Aiyo, sir, please don't put me on night shift again,' Atif whined.

'I'm not doing that. I just need you to meet me somewhere. Unless you're busy,' Rakesh added, guilt-tripping the guy.

He didn't know Atif that well yet, but he seemed to be the only one not in love with Karthik. Rakesh asked Atif to meet him at Koyembedu bus stand. It was a smaller bus stand but still crowded. There was certainly no way to figure out who was coming and going at any time of the day. But maybe, as the autorickshaw drivers had told him a couple of days ago, someone had spotted Mira there.

As he waited for Atif to arrive, Rakesh parked his bike and his thoughts went back to Mira. Nothing made sense to him anymore. If Madhu had really wanted to kill himself and her, maybe she knew about it and so had run away? Then again, he thought, Bindhu too had left with their son several times to go to her parents' place after they had a nasty fight. Maybe Mira left to warn Madhu to change his ways.

But why did she have a spare phone?

He decided to try his luck and pressed the power button. Surprisingly, it turned on, making an obnoxiously loud noise and flashing brightly.

Rakesh went through the call history, messages and pictures, but there was nothing. Everything seemed to have been deleted. Disappointed, he turned the phone off. Just as he had put it back in the plastic bag and tucked it into his bike pouch, his phone rang.

'I'm here, sir.' Atif had reached the bus stand. Rakesh got off his bike and walked around to look for him.

Together, they went to the ticket counter and asked for information on all the buses leaving a week or ten days before Madhu's murder. The man behind the counter was grudgingly helpful. As they walked away with a list, Rakesh sniffed the air. 'Are you wearing perfume, Atif?' he asked, realising that the man was well dressed.

'Yes, sir,' he said, sheepishly running his hand through his hair. 'I just dropped Jamina home. We went to have coffee.'

'That's why you're late.'

'Sorry, sir. She wanted to stop and do some grocery shopping. I convinced her we would do it later and left her at home and came rushing.'

Rakesh shook his head. 'You don't realise how much grocery shopping you'll have to do when you get married. Why are you doing it already?'

Atif grinned, not saying anything more. Rakesh wondered if he had ever been that infatuated with Bindhu. He couldn't remember.

'Okay, so here's Mira's picture. I'll start here, you question the ones there,' said Rakesh, standing in front of a bus company's booth. 'Remember, don't tell Karthik.' Atif nodded.

It was tedious and boring work, but Rakesh was hopeful. They slowly made their way through the location, names and numbers of conductors and drivers. Most of them were away on a trip but thankfully the stand had their contact information.

Rakesh had reached the middle of the row when he heard Atif call out his name. He turned to see Atif jogging towards him with a guy in tow.

'Sir,' Atif said, 'this is Nagavelu, sir, he said he saw the . . . person.'

'Ah yes,' Rakesh nodded, guiding them all to a less crowded spot. 'You saw her?' he asked Nagavelu when they had some privacy.

'Yes, sir, the woman? Sir showed me a picture of her.'

'How do you know you saw her? I mean, how are you sure?' This man probably saw hundreds, if not thousands of people, every day.

'Sir, she wanted biscuits, sir.'

'Biscuits?'

'Nagavelu runs a shop there,' Atif said, pointing at one end of the bus stand. 'He said he saw Mira that day. She was in a hurry because her child was crying and she bought some biscuits and snacks to calm her down.'

'Oh, what time did she buy?'

'Sir, one packet of cream biscuit, some Eclairs chocolates and one bottle of Fanta.'

'No, not what did she buy, what time did she buy.'

'That I don't remember, sir,' he said, scratching his head. 'It was just getting dark. Maybe around 6 p.m.?'

'Okay. Did you see which bus she got into?'

'No, sir, sorry, sir. I had other customers.' Rakesh thanked the guy and they sent him away with a crisp note in his hand and a promise not to tell anyone else the same thing.

'How did you find him?' Rakesh asked, impressed with Atif's work.

'Well, that's what my family does before any trip. We buy snacks if there are kids. I just thought, if she hadn't taken snacks with her, she might have bought some. That neighbour said that Mira madam rarely gave her daughter any sugary food, which means she didn't have snacks at home.'

Rakesh stopped in his tracks, staring at Atif admiringly. Was everyone a better cop than him? This hadn't even occurred to him, and he had a son!

'What, sir?' Atif asked, looking worried.

'Nothing. You did well, good job, Atif. Let's try and follow this lead. It'll be easier now, won't it? Beautiful woman travelling alone with a crying child. People will remember.' Atif raised an eyebrow at the word 'beautiful' but didn't say anything.

As they crossed the roadside vegetable hawkers, Atif stopped, looking at the okras.

'What is it?' Rakesh asked.

'Sir, I thought, since Jamina wanted to buy groceries, I . . .' He pointed at the vegetables in front of them.

'Go ahead,' Rakesh said with a chuckle.

As he left, he glanced back at Atif who was enthusiastically pulling a cloth bag out of his pocket and holding it out to the seller. It made Rakesh feel old and jaded.

39
Pooja

POOJA COULDN'T REMEMBER WHEN SHE HAD fallen asleep last night. The room was bright now. It must be late, she thought, closing her eyes and groaning.

Last night, after Sanjay left her half-naked on the floor, Pooja managed to drag herself to the door and lock it. It had been a restless night, filled with nightmares of D and Sanjay pushing her out of a window and telling her that everything was her fault. Sanjay was maniacally laughing while D was hugging the mystery woman whose face was still half covered.

Pooja got off the bed and looked out the window. She couldn't see the entire driveway, but Sanjay usually parked his car in front of hers where she could spot it.

It wasn't there right now.

She grabbed her phone and checked her social media accounts. There were hundreds of notifications from Twitter, as usual. Pooja wished she could just delete her fucking account. Even when she limited replies, people could still tag her. Determined to not dwell on people's comments, she searched 'my husband had sex with me without my permission' in the browser. She couldn't bring herself to use the dreaded word yet. There is no way that SHE was going to use THAT word.

As she read through the posts, she got increasingly incensed. Someone on a platform called Reddit had asked the same question. The comments fell into two groups: polar opposites, one saying that women had no right to say no after marriage, and the other saying women weren't pieces of meat to be used and discarded. 'I'm a man and honestly that's a horrible thing for him to do. You should leave him' was followed by 'Look at the white knight here, do you think she's going to fall for you if you say this?' which had 143 downvotes. At least she had some faceless allies.

She should leave Sanjay, she thought. But how could she, especially after what they had just gone through?

Downstairs, Lakshmi Ma was busy in the kitchen. The sounds of vessels clinking and a cooker whistling reached her ears, lending a sort of normality that didn't reflect her state of mind.

40
Inspector Rakesh

RAKESH WOKE UP EARLY THE NEXT MORNING and went to the kitchen. He found Bindhu making his favourite masala omelette with extra cheese. His son, Anthony, was already at the table, tearing into his own plate and busy on his phone. Rakesh ruffled his hair and sneaked up behind his wife, putting his arms around her. His son was too busy on his phone to notice anyway.

'Don't! He's right here,' Bindhu protested, pushing his arms away.

'He won't realise if a tsunami hit the house, he's playing that racing game,' Rakesh whispered, embracing her again. After seeing how Atif spoke about his fiancée, Rakesh wondered if he had ever spoken about or to Bindhu in that soft voice. His was an arranged marriage, one his family had finalised. He had got used to living with Bindhu, but getting used to someone wasn't the same as love.

'What's with the sudden affection? You're never like this,' she said, flipping the omelette with a clean twist of her wrist. She really was good at this. His stomach growled at the smell of eggs and cheese. 'Or is it because I'm making your favourite meal?' she asked.

'I was wondering,' he said, ignoring her teasing, 'have I ever taken you grocery shopping?'

'Eh?' she said, turning around to look at him.

'Just asked . . .'

'Is this your idea of romance, or do you want me to make something you're craving?' she said.

He clicked his tongue. 'Nothing like that, I was just wondering.'

'Anyway, let's discuss this at night, your son is sitting right there.'

'He's playing his game.'

'My game is done . . . I died' came his son's squeaky voice from behind them and Bindhu pushed Rakesh off her immediately. The kid looked at his parents and asked his father, 'What did you do?' leaving Bindhu holding her stomach in laughter.

Rakesh shooed his son away and got to eating. He had planned to go to Mira's house today and look for more clues. He was halfway through his omelette when his phone rang. It was Karthik. Rakesh felt bad about snapping at him the previous evening, so he answered Karthik's call immediately.

A politician's son had crashed his SUV into a smaller car, setting it rolling down the side of the highway before it burst into flames. The car had been carrying a family of five, including a grandparent and two little kids, returning to Chennai from a wedding in Bangalore. There were no survivors.

At the police station, Karthik was yelling when Rakesh walked in. 'That boy never has Shani in his horoscope, bastard.'

'Is this the bastard that I have woken up for?' Rakesh asked, setting his cap down on the table.

Karthik turned around and said, 'The very same.'

'What happened? He lives nearby, right?' Rakesh asked a furious Karthik, gesturing to the TV. Karthik increased the volume. A balding man, a local minister associated with the culprit's father, was saying 'No comment. No comment. Let there be an investigation first', before being stuffed into his car by his bodyguards.

Karthik finally answered Rakesh's question. 'Yes, two streets down from here.'

The newsreader came back on screen. 'The charred remains of the family are still being examined, but it is safe to say that it was indeed a case of irresponsible driving. As you can see from the CCTV footage, the car was speeding before it lost control on one of the speed breakers, crashing into the vehicle on the other side of the road. One of the passengers in politician Sunder's son's car was also injured but is alive and in the ICU for now.

'Our team has recovered pictures from the social media accounts of the driver's friends, and it seems they were drinking before hitting the road. And let's not forget that Sunder's son is underage. He is just seventeen years old and is already driving. The opposition has demanded that parents should be held liable if their children are found driving under the legal age. What do you think?

'We will now be taking callers. Call the number on the screen to let us know your thoughts or post on social media with the hashtag #UnderageDrivingLaws.'

Karthik handed the remote to Rakesh who listened to the first conversation before turning off the TV. 'We have to go there,' Rakesh said. 'We have been told to stand outside the minister's house to make sure there is no trouble. He will land in two hours.'

Karthik scowled. 'I expected as much. As if we have no other work. We had a domestic disturbance in that house again.'

'Which one?'

'That lady doctor.'

Rakesh remembered her. The woman who married the guy she'd loved in school and ended up with an abusive husband. It reminded him of Mira. 'Did he try to hit her again?' Rakesh asked

'Yes, and this time he accused her of trying to poison him and started banging on the door. Idiot He kept shouting that she had locked him in, but the idiot had locked himself inside and was too bloody drunk to realise it. Atif waited there for an hour before she came. Had to get her permission to break open the door.' Karthik slapped his forehead.

'Anything else?' Rakesh asked.

'Tests on the knife came back,' Karthik said, taking out another file from the pile on his desk.

'The DNA matched with Madhu's, obviously, and there were no fingerprints on the handle of the knife. Isn't it strange that Mira's fingerprints are nowhere on it, considering it is her knife?'

Rakesh had an answer for that. 'The killer would have wiped the knife, removing all fingerprints on it. Including hers.' Karthik didn't seem too happy with his reply. But Rakesh continued, 'We dusted the rest of the apartment for prints, didn't we? Results on that?'

'Apart from the ones on the approved list? Nothing.'

'Nowhere?'

'Well, there were a few prints in the living room, but so many parents came to pick up their children from Mira's tuition class.' Karthik looked a little deflated.

'Anyway, let's get ready. Who knows when the minister will want us there?' Rakesh said, resigned to spending a boring day guarding a politician's home.

41
Pooja

POOJA SPENT THE ENTIRE MORNING IN THE room and came downstairs only after Laksmi Ma had set the table for lunch and left. She would be back at dinner time, but till then Pooja had the house to herself.

Pooja had chosen every single thing in this house; her touch was everywhere. Yet, today, it felt like it belonged to someone else. She went to the living room and turned on the TV to check the news. Surely, they would have moved on from her. As she flipped through channels, she noticed a spiral bound notebook on the side table.

It had a Post-it which read, 'This is the script, read it. We will announce once I'm back.'

She tossed the notebook back onto the table and turned it face down. She hated this entire situation. If Sanjay had been caught cheating, he wouldn't have gone through so much trouble to make himself look innocent. He'd have laughed it off and moved on without caring what the media said. Why was her mistake such a big deal?

The TV news was droning on in the background. But the mention of Sanjay's name caught her attention. She turned around and increased the volume to see that Sanjay had left town. They showed a selfie that D had posted. It was of Sanjay, D and a few others that she knew on a boat.

'As you can tell,' the news anchor said, 'all's well in Bollywood with our favourite group of boys back together again. The last few days were much ado about nothing, don't you think? We can't wait to hear about D and Sanjay's next project together.'

'They're MEN! Not boys. MEN!' Pooja yelled at the TV. 'And YOU are the one who made the ado about nothing, you fucking bitch!'

The anchor had gone off the screen and an advertisement was playing. Pooja threw the remote at the wall and went back upstairs. She had to find out about her fucking husband going on a trip from the fucking news!

Upstairs, Pooja grabbed her phone off its charging point and went to D's Instagram page. The newest post was a carousel of images. She knew all the men in the pictures. She also knew their wives; they were a part of her 'kitty party group', as Sanjay liked to call them.

She looked around the room and saw that the top shelf in the wardrobe was empty. When had Sanjay taken out his suitcase? Was the trip planned a long time ago? She had locked the door behind him last night and the door was locked when she woke up.

She looked at the caption: 'Boys weekend with my favourite bros!!! #SummerSplash #Dsworld #BoysAreBackTogether'

If things were normal, she would have left a funny comment. So she pretended it was and typed out a comment: 'When the cat's away, the mice shall play. Time for the ladies to have their own fun!'

Then, grabbing the footstool from the corner of the room, she retrieved her own suitcase from the top shelf. It was time for her to take a trip of her own. Sanjay didn't deserve her consideration or forgiveness anyway.

42
Inspector Rakesh

THE CALL CAME AS SOON AS THE MINISTER landed in the city. Rakesh gathered Karthik and a couple of others before heading to the minister's house.

Over a hundred people had gathered outside. Every major paper and their regional language counterparts were peering down the road to see if the minister's official car was making an appearance. As soon as Rakesh and his colleagues arrived in their police vehicle, they could hear a collective groan.

'We are happy to see you too,' Karthik yelled, as the gate opened and they were let in. A couple of journalists tried to get into the house, but the security guards were experienced enough to slam the gate quickly.

The minister's son was already there, somehow free of any injury. His mother was sitting hunched over the dining table, her head in her palms. Rakesh removed his shoes at the door, unnecessarily wiped his socks on the doormat and took off his cap. 'The police is here,' a helper said. The lady snapped her head up, nodding wearily. 'When will my husband arrive? He isn't answering any calls yet.'

'It will probably take another forty minutes, madam, given the traffic,' Rakesh replied.

'What about the people outside? Any chance we can clear them out? This is the first time something like this has happened. They should give us a free pass this time.

It's a first-time offence. Kamala, give them water,' she said, without stopping for breath.

'Madam, if we ask them to leave, they will make a bigger fuss,' Karthik said. 'It is better if we let them stand there and get tired. When did they arrive?'

'Early in the morning. Right after Priyansh came back from the hospital.' She pointed to the boy in the living room, who was taking pictures of the media outside his home. 'STOP IT, PRIYANSH!' she yelled, striding over to him and snatching his phone. The boy rolled his eyes at her and sat back down on the sofa, sulking. Muttering under her breath, she made her way back to the dining room. Rakesh doubted she truly felt bad about the deaths.

'How old were the children?' she asked, setting the phone next to hers—matching iPhones, or so he thought, he could never tell them apart. 'One was five years old, madam.'

'And both girls?'

'Yes,' he replied, not sure how that made a difference.

'Poor things,' she said, adjusting her hands nervously. 'And the old man? What was his age?'

'They didn't mention, madam, he was probably in his seventies.'

'Of course, they will focus on the children, show their picture everywhere. Such a nightmare . . .' She put her face back in her hands and groaned. 'You can go, let my husband come first,' she said, getting up and calling Priyansh to her. He dragged his feet angrily but followed her up the stairs anyway. Rakesh drained the tumbler of water that was rapidly losing its coolness before heading back out to face the crowd.

There was just enough room for a fourth car in the compound; their police car was clearly too small for the parking space. The crashed car must be parked here. There were two imported cars: an Audi that belonged to the minister's wife and a small Honda that was probably used by the help for grocery shopping. Karthik stood admiring the cars, especially the Audi. He ran his fingers around each circle of the logo before joining Rakesh at the gate.

Just before the minister turned the corner, Rakesh's phone rang, telling him to be ready. He nodded to the others. The car came calmly down the road, much slower than the speed limit of forty. The security opened the gates, and the constables pushed the excited crowd back while Karthik and Rakesh walked in with the car, hiding the minister from view as he got out.

The man charged into the house, veshti flapping, as his assistants and lackeys followed behind at a respectable distance. Rakesh had forgotten to salute after noticing how angry he was. Karthik seemed to share his state of mind. They saw him climb up the stairs, and soon they could hear voices from above.

'Stop whining!' the minister screamed over his wife's voice. 'You can't control this boy for the one week I'm not here?'

Everyone looked at each other.

'No, not possible. Didn't you see the news? The idiot posted a picture of himself behind the wheel, else we could have said it was the driver.'

Now everyone turned to the driver who looked terrified. The guy next to him holding a purse patted him on the back and whispered, 'You've escaped. Don't worry.' The driver nodded, still looking dazed.

'Do we still need to be here?' Karthik asked and Rakesh shushed him, pulling out a phone from his pocket and showing him a message.

'Stay there till the minister leaves for his party meeting. Then accompany the boy to the airport.'

'Are we personal bodyguards now?' Karthik grumbled. The maid walked around them, pulling the curtains tighter and making sure the windows were shut. The boy was yelling now. 'I'm not going anywhere. I have plans here, Pa, Monica's birthday is coming up.'

There was a moment of silence before a loud slap rang through the house. Rakesh could feel the sting and didn't want to imagine the plight of the person who had actually been slapped. They could hear the minister's wife shouting now. 'Don't touch him, it's because you spoiled . . .'

'Pa, I'll go after her birthday . . .'

'SHUT UP! BOTH OF YOU!' the minister bellowed. 'I don't care if your little girlfriend has a fucking birthday. Pack your stuff. Don't waste my time anymore. I have to go to a meeting. By the time this issue is forgotten, you would have changed girlfriends three times!'

The boy whined a bit more, but they could hear his feet stomping across the floor above them. Karthik rolled his eyes again; Rakesh messaged an update to his superiors, saying the minister was safe and indoors. Of course, they would know that by now, the channels were streaming live, but he wanted to do his bit and avoid a scolding.

43
Pooja

A FEW HOURS AFTER LOOKING AT SANJAY'S holiday pictures, Pooja found herself at the airport, wearing oversized glasses and a ratty old tee that would hopefully ensure she wasn't recognised. She hadn't told anyone about this spontaneous trip, not even her close friends and definitely not Sanjay or Shyamal. She had packed up her bags and called an Uber to the airport after booking the earliest flight she could catch to Chennai.

She could have gone anywhere, but she was worried she would find herself stranded somewhere abroad with her credit cards cancelled and no way home. Sanjay was capable of anything now. She flashed her ID to the excited young woman behind the counter and made her way past security before she could change her mind.

The journey was mostly uneventful except for a few teenage girls pointing at her and giggling into each other's ears. She ignored them and looked out the window.

Pooja reached her house at 4 p.m., Chennai's heat already melting her carefully applied concealer. It seemed hotter than Mumbai even though it was, according to her weather app, both the same temperature and humidity. She had asked the housekeeper to wait till she reached home, so she wouldn't have to search for her keys.

She sent the housekeeper off with a generous tip and grocery list and went into the room to curl up in her old bed. Leaving town without informing anyone wasn't a big deal, now that she thought about it. No one would believe she had run away; she had already announced that she was taking off on a holiday with her comment on D's Instagram post. She rolled over on the bright sheets that smelled of fabric softener and shut her eyes before falling into a disturbed sleep.

She thought she wouldn't wake up before next morning, but half an hour later, her head thudding from the incessant honking on the street outside, she was wide awake. She pulled herself off the bed and splashed her face with cold water. The housekeeper had come and gone while she was asleep. The groceries had been laid out neatly on the kitchen counter, eggs and milk in the fridge and everything else where it belonged. She opened the freezer to check if she had got the low-fat low-sugar chocolate chip ice cream she wanted but found regular chocolate ice cream instead. 'It will have to do,' she croaked.

Outside, the honking got worse, this time with a few angry voices thrown in, and Pooja started shutting all the windows of the house. After a quick shower, she settled on the sofa with the tub of ice cream and called Dakshi.

She must have fallen asleep right after the call with Dakski. When she woke up it was evening and she found that the ice cream had melted and her phone had a bunch of missed calls and messages from Sanjay and Shyamal.

'Where the fuck are you?'

'Madam, please return calls, madam.'

'Pooja, answer the fucking phone.'

'You think I don't know where you've gone?'

And after half an hour, 'D says you didn't even call him. Where are you, Pooja?'

She chuckled and turned off notifications for both of them. There was a message from D as well, 'Hey, Pooja, where've you vanished? D' But it was from a different number. Who knew if it was really him or some creep fishing for a scoop using D's Twitter avatar as his display picture.

She set her phone aside, promising to ignore it and the men in her life for the rest of the day.

44
Inspector Rakesh

BY THE TIME THE MINISTER CAME BACK downstairs, it was well past lunchtime and they were all relaxing on the couch, trying to digest the biriyani they'd been served. 'I hope you guys ate?' he asked, freshly showered, changed and smelling strongly of perfume. 'Yes, sir,' Rakesh and Karthik replied in unison, standing up. 'Good, good.' He gestured for them to sit back down and sunk into one of the leather armchairs.

'What's happening outside? The noise seems to have reduced.'

'Half of them have left, but the local channels are still here,' one of the security guys replied.

'Bastards! They won't leave anything alone until it resembles a bloody carcass.' Then, turning to the cops, he said, 'Boys, I will need you here till my stupid son reaches the airport, even better if you can accompany him and make sure no one bothers him along the way. We will get his luggage into the car without anyone seeing it and . . . Mani . . .' The short man with the purse hurried over. 'We must divert the media's attention,' the minister continued. 'Find out what else is happening in the city and let me know immediately. No accidents, of course. The media will club the two events together. There has to be something else—drugs, rape, fraud, anything.' He got up and turned towards the stairs before giving one last instruction. 'Mani, wait, nothing about children dying either.'

Mani nodded, pulled out his phone from his breast pocket and started furiously scrolling through his contacts. Priyansh's luggage was quickly loaded into the Honda as it was closest to the door, and the boy was dragged downstairs with his mother chasing after him with a jacket in her hand. Priyansh had changed into a sleeveless shirt that showed off a large wound covered with gauze and tape. Rakesh couldn't help feeling satisfied that Priyansh had also got hurt.

The boy, it seems, wanted to show off his wounds. After some protest, he reluctantly wore the jacket and sat down on the sofa, waiting for further instructions. 'He is a juvenile,' the mother said sheepishly. 'We need to be somewhere safe until the charges are pressed. There is after all no proof that he was driving.' Rakesh glanced at the driver from the corner of his eye. 'So it is better to keep him safe where that lot can't get to him,' the minister's wife continued.

No one replied, but she continued talking to the room, explaining that they weren't doing anything against the law since charges hadn't been pressed yet. The boy was mumbling into the phone that was back in his possession and the minister whispered something to Mani.

'Okay,' the minister finally said out loud. 'Mani will handle everything. Let us first get Priyansh out.' Rakesh stood up. He and Mani would accompany the minister and his wife as they answered the mediapersons' questions. While they were distracting the group the boy would sneak into the car. As soon as they were done, a car would exit the compound. The wife would get inside the car and leave with Priyansh hiding inside.

It mostly went according to plan.

The minister's wife had combed and retied her hair and he had sprayed on some more perfume, and now both of them stood together and spoke about how sorry they were. 'All we can say right now is that we are very sorry for the loss of the family, and that the public and media should let law take its course.'

Rakesh took a quick look at the car, and he could see the boy's head sticking out from between the two seats, staring at the crowd, looking a bit surprised.

'Till then I request you all to leave us and their family alone,' they finished.

As they turned to go back inside the gates, someone from the crowd shouted, 'Leave what family alone? Your son killed all of them. Who is left to trouble?' The minister's façade dropped but his security guards managed to move him back into the house. His wife got into the waiting Honda, took her handbag from the maid and the car rolled out of the gates, hurtling down the road as fast as it could legally go. No one spotted the boy.

As soon as they were inside, Rakesh asked the maid where the bathroom was and went in. His phone had been vibrating the entire time they were outside. He pulled it out and checked. It was Bindhu. He texted her a quick reply.

Once he was done, he called Atif to ask how Mira was. He had requested Atif to go to the hospital earlier since she was going to be discharged soon.

'She is fine, sir. She ate, watched the news and took her medicines properly. She is sleeping now.'

'Did she ask for me?' His voice was more eager than he anticipated. There was a pause at the other end. Rakesh immediately regretted it and was about to retract his question when Atif replied, 'Yes, when you came on TV next to the politician.'

'Oh, what did she say?'

'Nothing, just asked if that was you.'

'Okay, yes, okay. Thank you,' he said and hung up. He looked at his reflection in the tiny mirror, checked if his zipper was up and went out just in time to overhear Karthik say, 'Don't worry, sir, I can get it done. People will forget soon.'

Karthik didn't say anything more when he spotted Rakesh exiting the bathroom. But Rakesh didn't notice.

'We will leave in half an hour,' the minister said to everyone in the room and went back upstairs, phone in hand, after patting Karthik on the back.

45
Pooja

WHEN SHE WOKE UP THE NEXT MORNING Pooja dug out her old things from one of the cupboards—clothes, sheets, towels and even expired skincare products. She spread the old musty sheets on the clothesline and hit them to shake out the dust. She spotted a hole that wasn't there the last time. The sheets were getting old, it was probably best to get new ones.

But she wouldn't throw away these sheets; they were a reminder of her childhood. Although she remembered her mother's words about never wearing or using anything torn or broken because it could ruin your life. 'Too late for that now,' she sighed and headed back inside. Once the smell of mothballs dissipated, she would use them for some time.

Her parents, just like most other middle-class families, filled their home with traditional Indian designs, making it a mismatched menagerie of block printed animals in vegetable dye and appliqué work. She had lost a patchwork wall-hanging of a red tiger to moths. She had been more careful ever since, ordering a yearly clean-up and always calling up to check on the condition of the cottons and the silks.

These sheets, a mix of the old Indian patterns of kalamkari and various other block prints, brought her so much comfort, as did the quilted cushion covers with mirror work that they happily flaunted as wealth. She didn't dare show them to Sanjay who thought thread counts and pale white sheets, maybe a grey in winter, was the way to go. His mother's international travels had clearly influenced his choices.

Pooja locked the balcony door behind her, carefully bolting both top and bottom latches, and called Shyamal. He hadn't, she reasoned with herself, done anything wrong. Why punish him for the mistakes her husband had made? Moreover, she didn't want to be responsible for giving the old man a heart attack.

46
Inspector Rakesh

SOMEONE HAD INFORMED THE PRESS THAT the boy was making a getaway. It took a lot of effort to hide him at the airport. They had requested another group of policemen to take him inside, so Rakesh's team would act as decoy security guards. As soon as the media realised what was happening, they rushed to find the other group, but it was too late by then. The plainclothes officers had managed to escort the boy in on time.

After half a day of action with the minister's family, Karthik's thoughts were back on Mira. During the entire drive back to the police station, he could not talk about anything else, not even about the stunt they'd just pulled. He was more convinced that Mira was the culprit because of the lack of fingerprints. 'See that seventeen-year-old boy? He looked so innocent, but we know what he did. The ones who look decent and righteous turn out to be frauds,' he said, slapping the dashboard.

'Doesn't matter,' Rakesh said. 'The politician gets all our attention now. I've already got four calls.'

He wasn't lying. The commissioner had told their station to stop everything else and focus on this matter. He wasn't sure if he was relieved. Regardless, he was free for the rest of the day and had enough time to give Mira's phone to his sleuth friend.

When he arrived at his friend's mobile shop, after giving Karthik a lame excuse, there were a few other customers. Once the last customer left, Shankar told Rakesh to come to the back of the store while he checked Mira's phone. He plugged the phone to his computer and worked while Rakesh read an article about the minister's son escaping the city. 'Done,' Shankar said half an hour later.

'That was fast!' Rakesh exclaimed, turning to Shankar's screen.

'Yeah, it's an old model. I was able to recover most of the files. Some were corrupt, I don't know why.' He moved so Rakesh could get a better look.

'No problem, let's see what you found.'

'First,' Shankar started, 'there were no pictures, no videos and no saved contacts.'

Rakesh was perplexed. A phone with absolutely no information on it could only mean two things: either Mira had something to hide or . . . she was hiding from someone.

'That's unusual,' Shankar continued. 'But there are a lot of messages and call logs.'

'Calls and messages? To whom?'

'The number doesn't appear in my database, sorry. You will have to go via the usual methods.'

Rakesh knew it wasn't possible. Not unless the same number appeared in Madhu's phone or their no-longer-functioning landline. He couldn't very well present her secret phone to the police IT department without knowing what she was up to first. What was he going to say? That his first love might be suspicious and he had found the phone and was hiding it? Not possible. 'And the messages?' he asked, trying to focus on the positives.

'The messages are a bit odd,' Shankar replied with a bit of hesitation. 'An affair?'

'Not even remotely. It seems like she was discussing travel and a job,' he said. 'Whose is this, by the way? Your wife? Are you guys having problems?'

'No, it's . . .' Rakesh did not want to lie to one of his closest friends. He had already removed the SIM from Mira's phone, so he couldn't check whom it was registered to. He decided to go with a version of the truth, 'It's a schoolmate's wife. I am just trying to figure out the reason for the secret second cell phone.'

'Yet when I wanted to stalk the girl I liked, you refused to let me,' Shankar laughed.

'Just continue.' Rakesh snapped.

'Fine, fine. Like I was saying, she discusses a trip. Mostly it's just time and place, nothing else. There was one where there is mention of an interview and a sister. Does this person have a sister?' Rakesh shook his head as he read the messages. The trip was the one the autorickshaw drivers had told her about, from Koyembedu bus stand. But Rakesh was still to find out why and where Mira had gone.

'Well, anyway, the last message was sent a few days ago. It just says, "Thank you for everything. Take care." After that, all the messages were deleted.'

'Anything about a guy?' Rakesh asked, squinting at the computer screen.

'It doesn't look like she was having an affair. But . . .' Shankar paused. 'I found one message. Have a look.' He pointed to the message in question.

'Sorry, he is drunk and home. Not safe. Can you collect it tomorrow?'

'Collect what? Does she say?' Rakesh asked, reaching over to check the previous messages. 'It doesn't say. But . . . not safe. Is your friend a violent man?'

'He is an angry man,' Rakesh replied, absentmindedly. His mind was racing with thoughts. It seemed like Mira was getting ready to leave Madhu. She was looking for a job, maybe at a hospital. But she couldn't be a nurse, that required special training. Or maybe her friend was a nurse. What else could 'sister' mean?

If the neighbours were to be believed, Madhu was angrier and more violent when he was drunk. Maybe Mira was trying to get herself and her daughter to safety.

47
Somewhere . . .

WHILE RAKESH AND POOJA WERE TRYING TO decide what to do next, something sinister was happening. Something that Sanjay Reddy and the politician were doing without even communicating with each other. Something that was about to make their lives a lot more difficult.

Somewhere in a small town in a corner of Andhra Pradesh, a young college boy lay on a mattress in a room he shared with four others. They had the weekend to themselves and were waiting for a call to make some quick money. When the phone rang, the boy and his friends sat up in their beds like meerkats, looking at each other to figure out whose phone it was.

One of them pointed at the other's phone and he quickly answered. 'Hello?'

The voice at the other end rattled off instructions slowly, details that should have ideally been written down but the boy wasn't worried. He had done this many times before. He had a superpower; it was his excellent memory.

Once the caller finished speaking, the boy muted the call and discussed the rates with the other four. This was a harder job, something that needed more time and effort. They would charge a little higher than usual. When the commercials were agreed upon, they hung up and waited for the notification to come through.

After they received a message notifying them that the payment had been credited, the boys pulled out their laptops and multiple phones, each one opening a different account on a different social media network. Usually, they spoke in favour of one politician or the other. Or posted about movies, celebrities and cricket. Their posts about cricket were usually of their own accord and for free. But this time they had to make news about a nobody go viral. The advance amount they received was large, but if they pulled it off, their final payment would be even larger.

One of them typed out the tweet and showed it to the boy who was clearly their leader, for approval. 'Is dis what da world has come to? Murder is a solution to everything? #JusticeForMadhu'

'Perfect, ra,' the leader replied, and the boy clicked to post it online.

The other three followed suit and soon, unknown to Mira and Rakesh, the Twitterverse was buzzing with news about an innocent man who was murdered by a wily housewife just so she could run away with her policeman lover.

There were many different versions of the story. But the most common one was about how an inspector and a housewife fell in love in school and finally found a way to elope after collecting life insurance money from each of their murdered spouses.

It is said that if you say something long enough it becomes the truth. And lying in a hospital bed, half asleep from her medicines and the IV, Mira didn't know that the truth about her was changing in the public's eye. Rakesh, unfortunately, was about to watch the whole thing unfold.

48
Inspector Rakesh

WHEN HE GOT HOME FROM SHANKAR'S SHOP, Rakesh ate a lovingly prepared meal, called his wife's masseuse for a foot massage and even got to watch sports instead of the soap his wife liked. Bindhu was at her parents' house preparing for a cousin's wedding.

He was relaxing now and browsing through his favourite Facebook groups. As he was about to like a cricket meme about M.S. Dhoni before and after marriage, a notification popped up, followed by a message.

Sunil has invited you to join Crime Watch Page. He checked it out. It was a closed group with about one lakh members. Probably invited me because I'm a policeman, Rakesh thought to himself. He noticed that a few of his cop friends were also a part of the group. He checked the message next.

'Bro, there's a crime that happened in your area, I think you are probably in charge of it. Check this out.' There was also link to a post in the group.

Rakesh quickly joined the group and checked the post.

'I recently found out from some of my friends that a murder took place in a building on my street. A man was murdered, and his body found in the morning. Police have not arrested the prime suspect, his wife. He was stabbed in the back with a knife that she uses for kitchen work. Women always get away with anything in today's society, thanks to Westernisation of our culture and feminism. Anyway, it seems the woman is missing. I heard her name is Meera. We must get her to pay for her crime. I will start a petition to pressure the police to arrest her. I will post the link to the petition here to ensure the police do their job.'

Rakesh blinked a few times, sure that he was seeing things. 'What the fuck!' he said, reading it slowly again.

A message notification popped up, again from Sunil, this time asking if he was handling the case.

'Yes, but I can't share details and the information in the post is incorrect,' he typed and closed the chat to focus on the post again.

How the hell did this person know it was a knife wound? How did they find out Mira's name? Sure, the spelling was wrong but there was no way any random person would know about her. The only people who knew were on his team. The building's residents knew about the murder but not about the knife. The forensics department knew about the knife but didn't know Mira's backstory.

It had to be someone from his team! 'Fuck!' he hissed.

49
The Newspaper Office

JAMES WAS AT HIS DESK, GOING THROUGH THE article he had just finished writing, when he got a call. He glanced at the name flashing on the screen and groaned loudly. Rukmini, who sat nearby writing her own article, looked up and raised an eyebrow. James saved the file and got up to answer the call.

'Good morning, sir,' he said as soon as he was in the stairway, smiling widely so it reflected in his voice.

'Good morning, Pa,' the person replied. 'I saw the article you wrote on our boy.'

'Sir, I had to . . .' James sputtered. 'I had no choice. The editor put a lot of pressure on me to finish it. But, if you read it, you'll notice the article is about the hazardous roads in the area instead of the accident.'

'Yes . . . I saw that. Sad that our own journalist is writing about us,' he paused. James could hear the clink of metal against teeth as if he was sipping something from a steel glass.

'Sorry, sir. Is there anything else I can do for you today?' James asked, uncomfortable with the long silence.

'Yes. Actually, you can,' the man said. 'You are so busy dragging sir's name through the mud you didn't even stop to notice the murder that happened right in your area.'

'Sir?' he asked, not sure what to say. A single murder was not going to take attention away a politician's underage son driving and killing people in a drunken state.

'Yes. Apparently, the wife will go scot-free even though all the evidence points towards her,' he said in a slow and measured tone. 'I heard from someone that the chief inspector is in love with her. She's really pretty, it seems.'

'Oh, really?' James's ears had pricked up.

'Yes. And they were also friends in school. He even admitted to one of the constables that she was his first love.'

'First love? This is definitely news.'

'I'm glad you think so. The wife seems to have fainted after the police questioned her. She's now in hospital. Of course, the rest is up to you. When can I expect the article? Tomorrow morning would be good,' he said.

'Sir, the editor has to agree first. It'll take time to investigate properly . . .'

'I'll send you everything I have. My source is on the inside. So, everything is legit and backed up with reports and facts. Tomorrow morning, okay? First page,' he said and hung up.

James's Telegram app pinged immediately, and he saw a bunch of files arrive in a zip folder. There was one recording too. James put his headphones on and played it as he walked back to his desk.

He found Rukmini sitting in his chair. She had one hand in his second drawer, the one where he kept his snacks, and was smiling sheepishly. 'One of these days you're going to get diabetes,' James told her, shooing her away with his hands.

'Says the man who has a desk full of chocolates,' she retorted, still smiling at him.

'You have chocolate in your teeth,' he replied, and she immediately closed her mouth, moving her tongue over her teeth to remove the residue.

He locked the drawer while pointedly staring at Rukmini. 'Not fair,' she mumbled, making a face at him. Then, she pulled a chair from one of the other desks and sat beside him.

'What was that call about? You seemed pretty annoyed,' Rukmini said, still trying to find the non-existent piece of chocolate in her teeth.

'That politician,' he said, putting his phone in his pocket. 'The one whose son . . .'

'Crashed and didn't burn?' she asked. 'Rather, crashed and burned his father's career?'

'His career will never burn,' James said under his breath and opened his search browser. 'He gave me a tip of another story. It isn't really a big deal even though I told him it was.'

'What's the story?' she asked.

'Some woman killed her husband, or rather he says the evidence says she did. She is hospitalised after the police questioned her. And . . . yes, the police inspector who is handling the case is her first love.'

'Holy shit,' said Rukmini. 'This kind of story is becoming really common these days, isn't it?'

'Yeah. Two stories like this in just the last week,' James said.

'The only difference is the cop love triangle,' she pointed out, putting her hand in her pocket and taking out one of his chocolate bars. He watched as she nonchalantly unwrapped it.

'You owe me a year's worth of chocolates,' he told Rukmini.

She ignored him and continued chewing. 'Whayougondoo?' she asked, her mouth full. 'I'm going to write it,' James sighed. 'What else can I fucking do? I owe the bastard.'

'Fine. Then stop whining and start writing.' She stood up. 'Let me know if you need any help. And when you're done, I'll show you how I can open a desk draw with a hairpin,' Rukmini said while walking away with an exaggerated hair flip. He chuckled watching her.

Once James had checked the facts, called the concerned police station, checked with hospitals and managed to get the name of the guy who died from his contact at the mortuary, he wrote everything down.

He didn't think the editor would agree to carry the story. He already had an article, a pretty big one, in tomorrow's paper. This one wouldn't make a difference. James got up, running his hands down the front of his shirt nervously, and went to the editor's office to pitch the idea. Might as well ask him, he thought. When the editor says no, James could blame him and be free.

50
Pooja

POOJA WOKE UP FEELING LIKE SHE HAD BEEN hit over the head. She'd forgotten how hot Chennai could be and the power cut at 5 a.m. hadn't helped. The fan was now spinning again with a slow creak. She forced herself to get out of bed, turned on the AC and climbed back in.

A few hours of rest and a breakfast delivery would get rid of her headache, she was sure. She ordered a coffee, a masala dosa and an indulgent plate of vadai, and started going through her notifications while she waited for the food to arrive.

The news alert for her and Sanjay's names had come up with quite a few things.

'Pooja Reddy spotted at the airport in Chennai' was one of the first ones. She cursed. She wasn't really known in this city, but the stupid scandal had unfortunately remedied that. She clicked on the next article. 'Pooja Reddy in Chennai on personal business. Spotted sporting a very casual airport style.'

That was code for 'she looked like trash'.

'Sanjay Reddy and D in talks for new project, spotted partying at pub opening.' That was new. Pooja clicked on the link and checked the images. Surprisingly neither man had arm candy with him. It seemed like a boys' night out.

Pooja went through the rest of the notifications but there was nothing to worry about. Of course, some shady sites were still posting about the affair but that would die down soon. She checked Twitter next. She'd spent the previous day and night sleeping, so there was a lot she had missed.

She replied to the important notifications and checked the trending topics to see if her name had been knocked off. And it had! There was now a whole new slew of topics being commented on by angry trolls. A woman had accused her start-up boss of harassing her and a few of her colleagues had also corroborated her story. A brand had made a less-than-ideal advertisement and was facing the wrath of the internet. A local celebrity's new movie had released and a politician's son had caused a car crash while driving drunk.

Pooja briefly skimmed the trending hashtags and checked out the top tweets related to them. She knew the start-up founder; if she remembered correctly, D had invested in his company. She hoped people wouldn't find out and come after her and D again. The politician belonged to a party a lot of people in the film industry supported. Just as she was about to click on the #BoycottOGMasalas hashtag, her phone rang.

'Hi Shyamal-ji,' she said, cheerfully.

'Madam, why, madam? Why!' he whined.

Their conversation last night had gone as predicted. He begged her to come back, reminding her of Sanjay's escalating blood pressure, and apologised on behalf of Sanjay for taking a trip without informing her.

'Why? I don't have any work there. Sanjay said I was jobless, remember?' Pooja said, opening the door for the delivery guy who had knocked.

'Madam, you have to do that movie na.'

'You guys chose a script without asking me, decided to announce that I had written it without checking with me, basically planned everything without involving me. What work do I have left there? I wrote it and left. Let someone else direct it, I don't care,' she said.

'But what are you going to do in Chennai, madam? So boring, right? Nothing to do. Your friends are all here, your club is here.'

'I don't know, Shyamal-ji. I'm sure I'll find something to do here. Maybe I'll like it here so much I won't even come back!' Pooja said and hung up. She placed her phone on silent mode, tore into the silver foil packet and took a deep breath.

51
Green Tree Apartments

JOSLIN HAD CALLED MRS KRISHNAN EARLIER IN the day and told her that she had done something stupid, terribly stupid.

After some cajoling, she finally blurted out what she had done. And it had shocked Mrs Krishnan so much that she immediately called her friends to come home as soon as possible.

They began to arrive one by one, and sat down on the sofa, next to Joslin, having lukewarm snacks with ginger tea. The news channel was playing the last bits of an advertisement before going back to the telecast. The anchor cut to a reporter in a red shirt standing in front of their building, waiting for someone to come out.

Then, she appeared.

'Madam, madam, are you a resident here?' the guy cornered a tired-looking Joslin who was bringing her son back from school. 'Who are you?' she snapped, looking at the camera suspiciously. The camera moved a bit till it had both of them in the frame, smartly hiding the boy's face. 'We are from a local news channel, madam, Channel 2 News. We hear that there was a murder in this apartment complex, and that you were friends with the family.'

'What?' she snapped loudly. 'I was not friends with the family. That fellow, *chhe*! I was never friends with him.' Joslin had started walking away but the reporter was not done.

'We hear his wife was spared, that she is somewhere safe in police custody. Is that correct?' The reporter gestured for the cameraman to follow him and caught up with Joslin.

'Yes . . . I don't know. But why are you asking questions? Murders happen all the time, no?'

'Yes, madam, but the wife never kills the husband.' Everyone around her gasped. Joslin hadn't said anything about that. Mrs Krishnan and her friends saw Joslin stop and turn with her mouth open. And the camera zoomed into her face. Joslin cringed as she took in her dishevelled appearance on TV. Her kajal was smudged and her skin so sweaty she looked like she had just run a marathon.

Everyone started asking her questions, but she shushed them and pointed at the TV screen. The man continued with his questions.

'Madam, we hear from a source close to the police that she hasn't been arrested.'

'That means she's not the criminal,' Joslin snapped.

'Do you know who the criminal is?'

'How would I know?' She sounded so stupid that Joslin wanted to slap the woman on the screen who looked like her. 'Only the police would know that!'

'But our sources say that she is very close to . . .'

'. . . the inspector,' Joslin interrupted without thinking. 'So, it's true then? I don't think Mira did it. But how will the case get solved when the inspector is too busy being in love with her?' With that, Joslin turned and shut the gate, her hair bouncing as she marched to the elevator.

'There you have it, folks,' the reporter turned towards the camera and said. 'One of the accused's friends and neighbours doesn't think the case will be solved because she has no faith in the police. Is this goonda raj under the current government where the upholders of the law feel like they can break it for personal reasons . . .'

Mrs Krishnan muted the TV and turned towards Joslin. 'What have you done?! Aiyo, that policeman will come for you now!'

'I don't know!' Joslin wailed. Someone had unmuted the TV again and it was blaring the headline: 'WOMAN MURDERS HUSBAND WITH HELP OF LOCAL POLICEMAN.'

The residents of Green Tree Apartments would have never expected their dingy building to ever appear on TV. And now it was on the news! They didn't know how they were going to handle this, but as they sat there in Mrs Krishnan's living room, eating pakodas and drinking tea, they all thought the same thing—they should have sold the flat to the developer who'd come knocking last year.

52
Inspector Rakesh

RAKESH REPORTED THE POST TO THE FACEBOOK admin and forgot it as a one-off thing. He needed to find out who had leaked the news but that could wait. Raghav had texted saying he was almost finished with the recovery of all the deleted files on Madhu's phone.

As soon as Rakesh entered the police station, Atif cornered him.

'What is it?' he asked.

'Sir . . . a news channel has interviewed the residents of Madhu's building.'

'Who?'

'Sir, that local channel, People's News. They found that woman you don't like, that Joslin woman.'

'Okay. And?'

'The interview, it's . . . well, that woman said, she said that she . . . thinks . . . that you . . . helped.' He squeaked out the last few words in a rush and looked down at his hands. Rakesh was dumbstruck.

'Show me,' Rakesh said and Atif, shaking his head, pulled his phone out of his pocket and clicked on the YouTube link.

53
Pooja

SHE WOKE UP TO A MESSAGE FROM SANJAY. 'I've done everything I can to get you off the news. I even ruined that start-up fellow's life for you. Why can't you, for once in your life, just listen to me?'

Pooja was walking towards the kitchen with the phone in her hands and froze. What was Sanjay talking about? She didn't want to ask him directly, so she called Shyamal again.

'What start-up fellow is he talking about?' she asked as soon as he said hello.

'Madam, a woman filed a complaint against a start-up founder for harassing her. Sanjay sir heard about it from D sir. He made it trend so that you would disappear from trending,' Shyamal said.

'It's the top trending topic today!' she yelled.

'I didn't think it would become this popular either. We've used these guys in the past to get movie news to trend. But this harassment story became so much more popular than that, and so much faster too!' Shyamal replied.

'You told them to make chatter about me go away?' she asked, wondering who these guys were who now had confirmation that she had indeed had an affair.

'No, we told them to make whatever they can popular. We also gave them some topics.'

'What other topics?' she asked, gritting her teeth.

'Nothing important, madam.'

'Shyamal!'

'Sanjay sir did it because he didn't want you to get hurt.'

'Bullshit!' she snapped. 'Sanjay sir did it because he didn't want his precious reputation tarnished.'

'Madam, see the top three tending topics today.' She put Shyamal on speaker and checked Twitter.

Along with her and D's hashtag, a politician's son who was trending yesterday had completely vanished. Instead, the top three trends were the start-up founder, a murder that had happened in Chennai and a behind-the-scenes video of an upcoming actor's martial arts training that had gone wrong.

'What the fuck! Couldn't Sanjay have done this on day one, Shyamal-ji?' she asked.

'Madam . . . it didn't . . . well, it only happened now. Sir has been trying for a while, that ad boycott didn't work and . . .' he continued. She slapped her forehead, surprised at how little she knew about what Sanjay was up to.

54
Inspector Rakesh

'WHAT THE FUCK!' RAKESH SAID, CHECKING THE channel logo. This was an actual news channel, not some random group on Facebook or WhatsApp.

While Rakesh was watching the video for the third time, Karthik burst into the police station and stood there gasping for air. It looked like he had run up the stairs.

'Sir. . . . ' he panted. Rakesh paused the video and looked up. Karthik was coming back from the minister's house so maybe the brat had run someone else over. 'What is it?' Rakesh asked as his phone started vibrating.

'Sir, you should watch the news,' he said, switching on the TV.

Another news channel was airing a replay of the clip he'd just watched. The news anchor was saying, 'Yesterday we found out that the accused Mira has still not been arrested for her husband's murder. Today, we will confront the man who has been shielding her—Inspector Rakesh.'

'What?' he stammered, confused.

'I don't know, sir.'

'What is happening? When did Mira become the accused?' Rakesh asked, goosebumps prickling up on his neck. He had managed to take down that one Facebook post. And the admin had taken down another one soon after. But this felt different.

'Change the channel,' Rakesh told Karthik, hoping others weren't carrying this piece of 'news'. He switched to a national channel now and the same information was being telecast there as well.

'Meninists have threatened Mira online, and some are even saying they will take justice into their hands. We will now go to our on-ground reporter who is outside the police station where the accused is being held.'

The camera panned to a shot of men shouting slogans. 'Swift justice is the need of the hour in cases like this,' one of the men said into the reporter's mic. The people behind him, mostly men, were holding up placards and screaming slogans like 'Feminism is cancer' and 'Feminism is against equality'.

'She's not being held . . . what the . . .' Rakesh said, walking to the door. There was no way he hadn't heard two dozen people on camera claiming they were in front of his police station. But the only people he saw were the usual idli seller and her drunkard husband.

'WE WANT JUSTICE! WE WANT JUSTICE!' the men chanted on camera.

'There's no one outside! What is this drama!' Rakesh said.

'Did they get the location wrong?' Karthik wondered aloud.

'They have got everything wrong,' Rakesh snapped in response, not quite catching the look on Karthik's face.

'People are angry, Sharmila,' the reporter said to the anchor, 'And they want justice. We will try to get an interview with Inspector Rakesh as soon as possible. But for now, he is nowhere to be seen.'

'But . . . I AM RIGHT HERE!' Rakesh shrieked. 'Stop LYING!' Rakesh was dumbfounded. He couldn't understand what was happening.

'Sir, calm down,' Karthik said. 'We need to handle the situation. Let us think practically. We just need to talk to someone higher up. Look at how angry people are . . .' The TV screen was now showing close-ups of angry men screaming at the camera.

'I have to call Mira. Actually, I should go there,' Rakesh said, getting up to leave.

'No, what if they follow you there?' Karthik said. 'So far they don't know where she is. Just call her.'

Rakesh nodded, taking his phone out of his pocket and frantically scrolling through the call list. Karthik's phone rang and he answered it while walking outside. Rakesh watched him go, running his hands over his hair nervously. The channel continued showing various shots of the 'protesters' screaming slogans into the camera. The men didn't look as angry as they sounded, but the way they were screaming was enough to send a chill down anyone's spine.

'NO! What rubbish!' Karthik suddenly shouted into the phone. Everyone in the station turned to him. 'No, she did not castrate her husband,' he said, laughing. 'She's not mad, you know.'

Rakesh felt the blood drain from his face.

55
Breaking News

THE MINISTER HAD PULLED EVERY STRING HE could to ensure his son was no longer in the news for 'evading arrest'. Overnight, Madhu's murder and the fact that no one had been arrested yet had started trickling into the national news channels.

On one channel, two prominent feminist influencers were arguing that the case must be treated like any other.

'Domestic abuse can be traumatising,' said a psychologist. 'It can make the victim take extreme steps to ensure her and her child's safety. God only knows what happens behind closed doors. The laws of this country do not handle domestic abuse well. If you go to file a complaint with the police, they dissuade you, calling it a family matter.'

'NO, NO, MADAM . . . a balding man interrupted, his moustache twitching. 'All you feminists are all the same. Why must you always blame the man? He is a poor fellow who married a mad woman . . .'

'MR KESHAV . . .' the psychologist said sternly. 'Mr Keshav, let me speak. I haven't finished. Please let me speak.'

'Affairs are common now. Women can also be villains. She was, after all, a housewife . . .'

'Therein lies the problem. SEE!' the psychologist yelled, her voice cracking as she tried to speak over him. 'A mere housewife, you say. Men inherently have no respect for women. They pressure women to remain in traditional gender roles and then shame those very roles!'

The argument continued for a while. By midnight, #MurderessMira, a Twitter hashtag started by a few trolls, was trending with over five thousand tweets. The next morning, even Facebook had taken it up, with retired uncles and aunties arguing in various groups about what the world was coming to.

56
Pooja

POOJA STOPPED TO GRAB A NEWSPAPER ON the way back from her morning walk. Back at home, as she settled down on the sofa, the first news item she saw was about Mira.

Murder Mystery in Malar Colony

Mira, a housewife, whose husband, a local import–export businessman, was murdered earlier last week, has become a suspect. The police haven't been able to acquire any other information, but it has been confirmed that her husband's body has been sent for post-mortem and . . . (Cont. on page 4)

Pooja turned to page 4 and continued reading, '. . . it has been officially called a homicide. Police are currently investigating the case but Mira seems to be receiving special treatment. DSP Siddharth Balan has informed us that the body will be returned to the husband's family once all police procedures are completed. Mira and Madhukumar have a three-year-old daughter who is currently staying with her grandparents. She hasn't gone back to school since the news went public. Mira is also rumoured to have been having an affair with her classmate and first love, Inspector Rakesh. When we called the police department, they didn't respond to our queries. Crimes like this have increased . . .' It went on.

Pooja leaned back on the sofa and scanned the other news stories. The start-up founder had issued a statement, saying he was drunk when he had texted his woman colleague and that he was sorry for his actions. But it had only infuriated the author of the article, Rukmini Menon, who had called it a non-apology.

Pooja checked Twitter to see if this was gathering steam there.

It was among the top trending topics along with the release of a film's first poster and a hashtag telling a politician to go back. She clicked on #JusticeForMadhu and went through the top tweets.

'Honest businessmen take such cheap women as their wives, and this is how they get rewarded. But nice girls like us can't find a husband. Fml,' a tweet said. Pooja rolled her eyes when she saw the girl's profile picture. The top reply had a link to an article which read, 'Madhukumar, a businessman, was known to have many failed ventures

and had a debt and gambling problem. Residents of his apartment complex said that he often fell asleep drunk on the staircase, which required his wife to drag him home.'
Pooja bookmarked the tweet. She was all too familiar with drunken husbands.

Pooja checked her phone to see if Sanjay had called or texted. He hadn't. He was, as usual, giving her the silent treatment. She would happily return the favour.

After reading a few more articles about the case, she was sure that the poor woman was falsely accused. She had been victimised twice, first by her husband and now by the media and public. Pooja felt a sort of kinship with Mira who looked so frail and lost in the images posted by the media. She felt she had to do something. But what?

Suddenly, she got an idea. Grabbing her phone, she called Shyamal back.

'Madam, you finally returned my call.'

'Sorry, Shyamal-ji, I was out getting some breakfast and my phone was at home. How are you?'

'How will I be, madam? I'm sure I have another ulcer. Madam . . .'

'One second,' she interrupted. 'I have a deal to make with you.'

'Deal?'

'Yes. I am going to start a podcast. Obviously, I will need resources. So, how about you help me, and I will tweet and post whatever you guys want? I'm not interested in seeing Sanjay's face, but I can tweet . . . for you.'

'That's fine, madam, but what is a podcast?'

'Oh,' she paused, wondering how to explain it. 'It's like a radio show, but on the internet.'

'Oh. Like Spotify and Saavn?' he asked.

'Yes, exactly.'

'What podcast, madam? About the film industry?'

'Now that's my secret. Don't worry, I won't say anything bad about anyone we know. It has nothing to do with any of your or Sanjay's secrets.'

'Okay. Do you need anything, madam?'

'An audio editor and an assistant. I'll find the second person myself.'

'Okay,' Shyamal replied and she hung up.

Shyamal was used to such demands by now. He would comply because it would bring her back. Or so he thought.

Then, she went to the tweet she had bookmarked earlier and checked the girl's profile again. It was the same girl who had tweeted in support of her a few days ago. She is perfect, Pooja thought, and clicked the direct message button.

57
Crime Watch Facebook Group

WE HAVE A POSSIBLE BLACK WIDOW IN CHENNAI. Mira is capable of beguiling even the most faithful of men. Inspector Rakesh is one of them. Married and recently blessed with a boy, Inspector Rakesh seems to be pushing for her release. It has recently come to our attention that Inspector Rakesh was Mira's classmate at school. He was an average student and we can understand that he was in awe of top ranker Mira, not just because of her academic performance but also because of her beauty. Maybe he is recalling those days of his youth and doesn't want his first love to become a noted murderess! We just hope he doesn't fall for her charms and end up becoming the second victim.

4283 likes/reactions, 809 comments

58
Inspector Rakesh

'NO, MA, PLEASE LISTEN TO ME. NOTHING OF this sort is happening,' he said, exasperated. His usually kind and understanding wife had turned vicious last night after her cousin Lily had forwarded the Facebook post about Mira being his first love.

After spending a restless night on the sofa, Rakesh woke up to his in-laws ringing the doorbell. And since then, there had been no stopping his mother-in-law from saying how all policemen were frauds. His father-in-law, a former policeman himself, was defending their profession.

Bindhu, meanwhile, was bustling around the kitchen, cleaning after their son's breakfast and preparing her own.

She hadn't yet cooked anything for him, and he was ignoring his hunger pangs to explain to her that he really had no feelings for Mira. 'Aren't you getting late for work?' she said with an expressionless face, clearly not listening to anything he had to say.

His in-laws hadn't stopped talking. 'Listen, Pammu,' his father-in-law said, 'let us give him a chance to explain. Mapplai, tell us what this is? What is all this rubbish we keep hearing on TV? Bindhu told us nothing happening, but when Lily sent that post last night, I was shocked. I have done so much for you; how could you do this to my daughter?'

'I didn't do anything, Pa,' Rakesh replied. 'Believe me, please. Bindhu, listen, I didn't do anything,' Rakesh stammered, trying to get up from the sofa, but his father-in-law's hand on his shoulder was a bit too firm. So he gave up and turned back to his father-in-law. The white hair in this father-in-law's bushy eyebrows was sticking out threateningly, and Rakesh hesitated for a moment.

'I don't know what is happening,' Rakesh said. He was innocent, but the ex-policeman's gaze made him feel like a criminal. His father-in-law tightened his grip further on Rakesh's shoulder and with his other hand manoeuvred a chair behind him and sat down.

'Listen, I cannot help you if you are involved with anyone. Not cannot, I will not. In fact, I will make sure that you suffer for it. If you have betrayed my daughter, tell me now and make it easier for yourself.'

'No, no, I didn't do any such thing. I don't know where these stories came from.'

'All of us have fun every now and then, Rakesh,' his father-in-law whispered. 'But none of us leave our wives and we certainly don't murder our mistress's husband over it either.'

'No, Pa, I didn't do it. They keep saying I am in love with her because I don't believe she killed him. That's all.'

'She looks innocent,' his father-in-law said, rather than asked; Rakesh nodded.

'Does she look beautiful?' The man's eyes bored into his. He heard the sound of anklets and knew Bindhu was standing behind the kitchen wall to listen in. 'She is my classmate,' he whispered, hoping Bindhu couldn't hear.

'You know her?'

'Yes, Pa, and I felt sorry for her.'

'How did she know to call you?' Bindhu asked from the kitchen door, her head peeping out. The woman had ears like a wolf.

'Reunion,' he replied immediately.

His father-in-law let go and Rakesh quickly followed Bindhu into the kitchen. She was starting making dosais. He tried to help, but she shooed him away. 'I haven't had breakfast yet, I'll just have coffee and leave . . . okay?' He tried to ignore her furrowed brows and started opening cabinets, smelling the brown powders till he opened the correct one. He added a spoon to his tumbler and poured lukewarm milk over it. He could feel Bindhu staring at him, and he smiled at her as he mixed the coffee powder with milk.

Only, it didn't mix. She snorted, put the last dosai on her plate and walked out to join her parents in the dining room.

Rakesh gave the coffee another vigorous stir, but dark brown granules floated to the top and stuck to the side of the stainless steel tumbler. He could feel Bindhu watching him struggle. Grumbling that he should have heated the milk properly, he gulped the liquid in one go and briskly walked out, choking out a goodbye to everyone. He spent the next ten minutes manoeuvring traffic while coughing and digging out bits of coffee from his mouth.

59
Pooja

THE GIRL'S NAME WAS SHALINI. SHE WAS between jobs and looking to shift careers.

Pooja had Googled for a nice café nearby and sent a DM to Shalini, asking her to meet. Shalini was waiting when Pooja reached. She had expected to see a young, stylish girl, but was taken aback by the person who stood up and smiled at her.

Shalini looked like she didn't mess around. Loose khadi kurta, ruddy-looking face and mismatched accessories. She looked like she didn't give a damn, and Pooja liked that. She smiled and walked up to Shalini. 'How old are you, Shalini?' she asked before she thought better of it. She liked to think she wasn't one to judge people by their appearances, but she couldn't help wondering how much thought Shalini would put into the case she was working on, if this was the amount of thought she had put into an important meeting.

'Twenty-four, madam,' Shalini answered without hesitation.

Years of watching women hover around her husband had trained Pooja to spot the starstruck ones. But they were usually older than twenty-four and looked about ten years younger than this one. 'You mentioned that you left your previous job at an IT firm a while back?'

'Yes, I needed a mental health break, not enough spoons,' she said. Pooja nodded as if she understood.

'Now I just do creative things. Corporate jobs are all right, but I thought I'd do something to feed my soul.' Pooja tried to see if Shalini was joking, but the expression was genuine.

'And that would be?' Shalini asked, picking up the menu when the waiter arrived. 'An iced tea, please,' she said, turning to Shalini who asked for a cold coffee.

'I've worked with children before. There's a slum near my house, I taught them English. They wanted me to teach them maths, but I am so bad at it that even the good students will fail if I teach them.'

Pooja laughed. 'I didn't mention what the podcast was about, right? It doesn't really have much to do with kids . . .'

'Yes, you did. Crimes against women, starting with Mira, right? I actually did some research . . .' Shalini pulled out a folded printout from her pocket. It was warm and damp, and Pooja gingerly held the corners of the paper and unfolded it.

'It seems like the police have questioned the neighbours and they say he was a drunkard. Mira would sometimes send the daughter to her or his mother's house and on those days there would be loud fights. They aren't sure if he hit her, but I think he must have. Someone interviewed her friends who said he used to hit her even when they were dating . . .'

Pooja was impressed. The girl had done more research than she had. That too in just a few hours. The waiter came by with their order.

'I'm not really sure what the job would entail, but I want you to write the script for the podcast and assist me in research. You might have to conduct a few interviews, but for the most part I'll be doing the recording. The work may increase or reduce depending on the circumstances,' Pooja said, pausing to take a sip. The smell of melting cheese wafted over from the next table. She ignored it, remembering that she had ordered new clothes because she wasn't fitting into her old ones.

Shalini was waiting for her to continue.

'So go home, take your time and send me a text with your salary expectations and we can get started.'

60

Green Tree Apartments

MRS KRISHNAN AND JOSLIN WERE SITTING IN the Krishnans' living room, eating ragi butter murruku and scrolling through their women's Facebook group when Joslin spotted the picture shared by one user.

'Hey! Isn't that you?' Joslin said.

'What?'

'Go back.'

'Okay.'

'No, not to the home page. Tsk, go back to the group and scroll down. I just saw a picture someone shared,' Joslin snapped, grabbing the mouse and scrolling up.

'Of me?' Mrs Krishnan said, shocked.

'Of us, I think. Just move.' Joslin pushed Mrs Krishnan's chair away and started scrolling quickly till she got to the post. 'See, I told you. It's from the birthday party. It's all of us.'

Mrs Krishnan peered over Joslin's shoulder. It was a picture of them from the birthday party. Their faces had been blurred on TV, but not here.

'Delete it!' Mrs Krishnan shrieked, grabbing Joslin by the arm and shaking her. 'I can't delete it, it's not my post!' Joslin said, yanking her hand away.

'Do something, my face is right there!'

'So is mine!' Joslin snapped, pushing her hair out of her eyes. 'Wait, let me report the post.'

The computer pinged and a red notification dot appeared on the top right corner.

'Shit!' Joslin said, clicking on it.

'What?'

'Someone has tagged you in the comments.'

'Make them stop!' Mrs Krishnan shrieked.

'I can't make them stop. Get a hold of yourself.'

'What did they say?' Mrs Krishnan grabbed the mouse from Joslin's hand and started clicking it furiously.

'Hey, Malathi Krishnan, isn't this you?'

'Who is this bitch?' Mrs Krishnan snarled, all decency forgotten. 'How do I delete this comment? Joslin? How do I . . .'

'Let me see if I can report it. Wait.'

'Report this Ravi Patel too. The bastard is posting pictures that don't belong to him. Why is he in a women's group? Men are not allowed here!' Mrs Krishnan wailed, slapping the mouse on the table wildly.

'Calm down. I will report the picture, all right?'

'I have to call my husband,' said Mrs Krishnan, tears filling her eyes as she looked around for her phone.

61
Inspector Rakesh

THIS MORNING, THE CROWD SEEMED TO HAVE found the right police station.

Atif had called and warned him, but he hadn't expected the situation to be so bad. Rakesh parked his bike opposite the station and tried to walk in casually, but his uniform gave him away.

As soon as one person in the crowd spotted him, everyone ran towards him. 'Is it true that you have the suspect in custody?' 'Is it really the wife?' 'Do you have any other suspects?' The questions kept coming, one after the other.

'We are currently looking at all angles,' Rakesh replied, overwhelmed by the number of people around him.

'Sir, is it true that the main suspect is injured?'

'I can't say anything right now,' he said feebly.

'Sir, is she the main suspect then? Are you confirming that?'

'She is a victim of a horrible crime!' he protested, but his words fell on deaf ears.

'So, when are you going to question her?' someone else asked.

'She is in a critical condition,' he said into one of the multiple microphones in front of him. 'And she is not a suspect.'

'Who is the suspect then?' 'What happened to her, sir?' 'Could you give us the name of the suspect?' 'Whom do you suspect, sir?'

Rakesh had had enough. 'Shall I give you the suspect's name and address too? So you can air this on television and he will run away. Then you'll blame us for not doing our job efficiently.'

'Sir . . .'

'Move please,' Rakesh snapped, trying to push past people. He wished he had somewhere else to be today, but all the reports he had to go through were at the station. 'I have to get on with my work. If you could all just wait till the investigation is actually over . . . I would appreciate it,' he yelled, his voice cracking from the strain.

A younger journalist, a boy barely out of college, jabbed a microphone in his face just as Rakesh removed his water bottle from his bag. The bottle hit the boy hard on the eyebrow even though he swerved to avoid it. 'For fuck's sake!' Rakesh swore and the boy backed off, startled and apologetic. The cameras trained on his face seemed closer now and the boy rubbed his eyebrow while Rakesh glared at everyone.

'You are interfering with the investigation,' he said, trying to keep his voice even. 'Once we have a suspect in custody we will let you know. Please let us do our work.'

Rakesh turned and went into the building.

Inside the police station, he found Karthik on the phone, talking urgently to someone. Rakesh ran the news flash through his mind and wondered about Mira's reaction to his statement. He felt ill at the thought of it. As soon as Karthik hung up, Rakesh grabbed him. 'Did anyone ask anything?'

'About?'

'Anyone? The commissioner?'

'About the news? I don't think it is important enough, sir. The investigation is proceeding normally.'

'Okay,' he said. It was probably time to focus on the actual investigation. 'What is the update on that front? Did we find anything on Madhu's second phone? Any signs of an affair?'

'Nothing yet, I just spoke to Raghav.'

'Okay,' Rakesh said, feeling dejected. It hadn't happened yet, but it was a matter of time before he got the dreaded call. He could survive a suspension, but he was sure that his wife would leave him if this nonsense went any further.

Just when Rakesh thought it couldn't get any worse, his phone rang.

62
Pooja

THE NEXT DAY SHE WAS IN THE NEWS AGAIN. 'Pooja Reddy is in Chennai to start the first season of her new podcast' was the headline on an entertainment website. No doubt Shyamal's doing, but this time she was glad for it. Pooja went through the article where Sanjay was quoted saying, 'My wife is a hands-on person. I had suggested that she let others do the research while she can take care of the recording, but she's refused. If she doesn't put in the work she feels useless. So I am glad she's doing this. She needs a break, anyway, don't you think?'

Sanjay had sent her the link himself. She read the article and replied to Shyamal, who had sent her the same message. Her phone pinged with Twitter notifications, but she didn't bother opening the app. She typed out a 'Thank you' to Shyamal and turned off her phone so she could focus on Shalini who she had invited home.

'Nice place, ma'am,' Shalini said, fidgeting. Her arms had half-moon stains under them and there was sweat under her eyes and on her chin. Pooja got up to turned up the air conditioning and offered Shalini some cold cranberry juice.

'No, ma'am, thank you. Just water. I have everything here,' she replied, pointing at her phone and some papers in front of her. 'Most of the articles are pretty vicious.'

Shalini had called last night and accepted the job. Pooja could manage to pay her what she wanted for the one month she planned to be in Chennai if she kept her shopping to a minimum. She glanced at the papers Shalini had printed out.

'I know,' Pooja replied. 'They tend to be that way when a woman is involved.'

'What are we going to do now?'

'Well, Shalini, the plan is to get the truth out. It's not fair what they've done to Mira only because a stupid policeman is infatuated with her. So we will have to hire her a good lawyer, get her a psychiatrist if she needs one and maybe talk to a few people who know her personally. As long as we don't talk about the evidence itself, we won't get into trouble legally.'

Pooja had watched a lot of crime dramas and even though none of them was Indian, she was sure the rules were the same.

Shalini agreed, sipping her water and looking around at the house. It didn't bother Pooja if Shalini found it lacking. She had, after all, mentioned that it was her childhood home and their makeshift office.

'The recording might not be the best,' Shalini said, pointing to the window.

'Oh, I have another room for that,' Pooja replied. 'My old room. It has only one window and faces the building behind us. It's quiet in there. We just need some heavy curtains and a carpet. I'll get those.'

'Okay. What do you want me to start with first, ma'am?'

'I think we should start with a small summation of the case for our listeners. If the media is covering this case, then I guess we should think of ourselves as the media as well. I will record that. Then we can start speaking with people who know Mira well.'

Shalini nodded and began making an action plan.

Pooja was feeling reckless. As reckless as she had felt the day she'd seen the call for movie auditions in Mumbai and boarded a train from Chennai without informing anyone. That had worked out reasonably well. She hoped this would too.

63
Inspector Rakesh

HE WAS ON HIS WAY TO MEET THE commissioner and had already practised what he was going to say a few times.

Rakesh was worried about leaving the situation, but Karthik had assured him that he would be fine. He would speak to any journalist in case they called. 'Yes, Madhu was killed. Yes, Mira's fingerprints were in the house, but it was her house too! Yes, Madhu didn't fight back; there are no signs of a struggle. He never saw it coming, the stab wound was on his back. And no, he wasn't backstabbed.'

Rakesh took a deep breath. He checked the files he was carrying with him one last time. He wanted the commissioner to know that he had done some work. Because if the commissioner believed the news channels, Rakesh was sure he would get suspended, if not worse.

Rakesh was ushered in immediately on his arrival, without having the chance to catch his breath, and found the commissioner pacing in his office.

'Inspector Rakesh, sir,' the man who showed him in announced, sticking his head in through the door. 'Ya, ya' came the gruff voice he remembered.

'Sir,' Rakesh said, snapping his feet in place and saluting. The commissioner rolled his eyes.

'Tell me, Inspector Rakesh, how are you? I'm hearing a lot of things about you.'

'Sir, that is . . . I, sir, I, sorry, I am handling the case,' he stammered, looking at the magnificent moustache that looked a little too much like his father-in-law's. The commissioner nodded his head. 'Tell you what, Rakesh. Why don't you give me your autograph?'

'Sir?' Rakesh said, confused.

'Your autograph, Rakesh, you seem to be getting more famous than me these days.'

'Sir, nothing like that, sir.'

'Then what is it like?'

'Sir, I don't know who is spreading these rumours.'

'How is your girlfriend?'

'Sir, she's not my girlfriend.'

'You've married her then? I thought you already had a wife. Getting a second wife is illegal, you know that, right?'

Rakesh felt his face turn red and he looked down, thinking it was better if he kept his mouth shut. 'Inspector Rakesh kills girlfriend's husband and tries to run away.' The commissioner read off his computer. 'Mira, a murder suspect, knew the officer from their school days. They are probably waiting for the right opportunity to elope.'

Rakesh looked away and the commissioner snapped, 'What rubbish am I reading? Can't you keep your personal matters to yourself?'

'Sir, there isn't anything perso—'

'You're lucky none of the good newspapers have mentioned your love story. If they do, you can kiss your job goodbye. People are already saying that your sub-inspector does all the work while you're romancing your murderess.' The commissioner cleared his throat and continued, 'Answer my questions. Do you know her?'

'Yes, sir.'

'Girlfriend?'

'No, sir. She is not my girlfriend, sir. Just a classmate, sir.'

'She's your classmate now?'

'No, sir, she was in school, sir. She was my classmate then, sir.'

'So, you were only friends all these years? Can a man and a woman really be friends for that long without anything happening? Come on, tell me the truth.'

'Nothing happened, sir. The first time I met her after school was on the day of the murder, sir.'

'First love?'

Rakesh didn't reply.

The commissioner continued unperturbed. 'Is she?'

'No, sir,' Rakesh said, his voice shaking.

'Why are you trembling? Act like a police officer!'

'Yes, sir,' Rakesh whined in response.

'Why are you taking so long to arrest her?'

'She isn't a suspect, sir. We think it is a murder–suicide gone wrong. They found rat poison in the milk he gave her the previous night. And in her system when she was hospitalised. The husband had a lot of debt, and rowdies kept threatening them.'

'And no one saw these men except the wife, right?'

'Sir, the watchman, the neighbours and even the autorickshaw drivers outside heard the commotion they caused,' Rakesh confidently replied.

'Oh,' the commissioner was taken aback. He leaned forward, resting his chin on his palms, and scratched his moustache. Then he took the file Rakesh was carrying and started to read. Rakesh glanced at the computer screen.

The website open on the screen was called *Murder Masala*. Rakesh cringed.

'So, there is no proper evidence against anyone.'

'There were so many moneylenders . . . he borrowed from one to give to the other. There's one more angle but we are still looking into that,' Rakesh answered.

'I am only being kind because your father-in-law and I are friends,' the commissioner said, closing the file. 'If you do not handle this case properly, you will be suspended; you may even lose your job. Do you understand?' he snapped. 'One drunk fellow dies and suddenly the whole country is up in arms. Tell me,' he paused, shaking his head. '. . . Is it true?'

'What, sir?' Rakesh asked, unable to understand the eye movements the commissioner was making.

'Tsk. Was he really castrated?' he whispered, as if saying it out loud would make it all too real.

'No, no, no, no, sir! No,' Rakesh countered hurriedly. 'That is not true at all. Nothing that's on the news is true.'

'Oh, thank God,' the commissioner relaxed. Anyway, aren't you supposed to meet your family in the evening?'

'Yes, sir,' Rakesh nodded, flustered.

'Finish this and then go. Don't make my life difficult. Go.'

'Yes, sir.' Rakesh said, grabbing the files and exiting the room as fast as he could. Once outside, he felt a sudden need to pee. But he ran to his vehicle instead, not wanting to remain at the head office a minute longer.

64
Inspector Rakesh

AS HE WAS DRIVING BACK, RAKESH DECIDED TO call the numbers on Mira's secret phone. He hadn't had a chance to do it earlier amidst all the confusion created by the news channels.

With one eye on the road, he pulled out the call sheets and ran his finger down the list of calls and messages. Mira had called one particular number twelve times in the week leading up to Madhu's death. Without thinking, Rakesh grabbed his phone, dialled the number and waited.

A male voice answered. Strong yet not too manly. The gruff hello reminded him of his school maths teacher. Ignoring the sinking feeling in his stomach, he spoke. 'Hello, this is Inspector Rakesh, this number has turned up in one of our investigations. Who is this?'

'Ah,' the voice said. He sounded self-assured and Rakesh didn't like that. He was expecting the person to show some panic, maybe a bit of worry. Surely Mira's secret boyfriend, if that's who he was, would have known that her husband was murdered. Hell, he might have murdered him himself! The person continued, 'Could you hold on for a second, Inspector? I'm in the middle of a meeting, let me leave the room so I can speak with you.'

There were some muffled sounds followed by the noise of a chair scraping against the floor. Some footsteps and a door slam later, he was back on the phone. 'Yes, Inspector, how can I help you?'

'Can you tell me who I'm speaking with?'

'All right,' he said, sounding amused. 'I am Anand, a lawyer. Now can you tell me what this case is about?'

'Lawyer?' Rakesh sputtered. 'You're Mira's boyfriend?' Something wasn't adding up, but other man sounded amused as he gave a short laugh.

'My boy, I am definitely not anyone's boyfriend. And I am too old to be considered a boy! Now if you can give me some more information, I can help you.'

'Oh . . .'

Rakesh thought about it for a moment; the man could be lying for all he knew. 'Could we meet somewhere? I can come to your office, if that works. It's an urgent matter.'

'Of course,' the man replied. 'Sometime after lunch tomorrow?'

'Today would be better,' Rakesh said, hoping he sounded firm. He didn't want to go back to the station and face the crowd that was now accusing him of assaulting a journalist with his water bottle.

'Okay. I have meetings lined up for the next hour. Maybe we can meet after that? I will SMS you the address.'

Rakesh thanked him and hung up. He definitely was an older man. Who else used SMS these days?

65
Pooja

'HELLO, EVERYONE. WELCOME TO *THE ACCUSED*. I'm your host Pooja Reddy and I'd like to welcome you to the first episode of season one, Mira.' Pooja paused the recording to take a sip of water and checked her script again.

Shalini had taken charge after she signed her contract. She took Pooja along to purchase some things they needed to create a makeshift recording room: a microphone, some thick curtains. The carpet Pooja had sent her parents a couple of years ago and some Thermocol on the windows had help soundproof the room. It wasn't a very thorough job—she could still hear the odd koel screaming in the background—but she could record those parts again if needed; at least the room was echo-free.

'This isn't an investigative podcast. We are not here to challenge the official investigation. What we offer instead is a voice to those who are being judged by strangers—the public and channels that claim to telecast news. We are here to show you the other side of the coin, to speak for the voiceless, and to let you know that behind every sensational story are things no one knows about.'

Pooja paused and replayed it. She had to admit that she had gone a pretty good job. Years of watching Sanjay go through press releases and practise speeches had paid off. She grimaced at the thought of him and put him out of her mind.

She flipped to the next page and recorded it. When she was done, she named each file and uploaded it for Shalini to access. The girl was extremely efficient. She had already contacted Mira's family and her school headmistress for interviews.

Surprisingly, both had agreed.

66
Inspector Rakesh

THE LAWYER'S OFFICE LOOKED QUITE SHABBY, but it was definitely a place of work. The shelves were stuffed, from floor to ceiling, with legal books. The receptionist, a flat-faced, young thing, had asked Rakesh to wait in the sitting room.

She brought him a glass of cold water and resumed her typing.

Moments later, one of the doors opened and a man stomped out. He looked furious and the young man behind him kept saying, 'What else can we possibly do!'

As soon as the angry man left, the lawyer turned back and asked him, 'Inspector Rakesh?'

'Yes,' he replied.

'Sir is waiting for you, please come with me.' Rakesh abandoned the half-full glass on top of a magazine and followed him into the room.

This room was shabby too, covered from floor to ceiling with files. They went through another door to the main office where an older man, the one who actually looked like a lawyer, was waiting.

'Hi, sir,' Rakesh said, immediately deferential. He couldn't help it; the man's vibe warranted it.

'Hello, Inspector, please have a seat,' he replied, looking at the other man who backed out and shut the door.

'What can I help you with?'

Rakesh pulled out his phone to show him a picture of Mira. 'Do you know this woman?' he asked.

The lawyer looked at the picture and narrowed his eyes. 'I do, yes,' he said after a few seconds.

'How do you know her, if I may ask?'

'She's a client. But that's all I can tell you. Sorry, Inspector,' the lawyer said, returning his phone and crossing his hands in front of him.

'Your board says you're a corporate lawyer.'

The lawyer laughed. 'I know, yes. But I also practise family law, or I used to, and I was advising Mira on something related to that.'

Rakesh realised what he was trying not to say. 'She was trying to get a divorce?'

'I can't tell you that,' the lawyer said, shaking his head.

'But her husband is dead.' Rakesh was sure that confidentiality was no longer an issue.

'Is he?' The lawyer looked surprised. 'So that's why she stopped calling me.'

'You didn't know?'

'I didn't know,' he said. 'But it makes no difference. She is still a client, and confidentiality applies.'

Rakesh smiled. 'Come on, sir, this is India. No one is strict about that here. As someone who works in law enforcement, I can't tell you how many lawyers I've met who don't follow a single law. Even we don't follow most of them!' He hoped what he was saying would help. He had seen an ex-boss do it and it had worked every time.

'Inspector,' the lawyer said, his face grave, 'I cannot tell you how seriously I take my job. I am a third-generation lawyer and my job is like my God. I don't take my clients or their problems for granted.'

'Sorry . . .' Rakesh backtracked. 'I just meant, I am a friend of Mira's, from school.' He dropped his voice a notch. 'Some people believe she is a suspect, that she was having an affair and that the two of them conspired to murder Madhu. It doesn't make sense to me. She was found locked in a room, and the milkman discovered the body because the main door was left open.'

'What . . . you said he died! It was a murder?' Rakesh had finally got the lawyer's attention.

'Yes. I know Mira; she was very loyal to Madhu even in school. I just cannot imagine her having an affair. I found this phone, her secret phone, and I panicked. Can you imagine what would happen to her if I didn't clear her name? Her life will become a nightmare. Please just tell me anything that will be helpful.'

The lawyer leaned back in his chair, his eyebrows knotted. Finally, after looking like he had thought it over, he leaned forward again. 'Well, I cannot tell you much, to be honest,' he said, 'but there was no reason for her to kill him as she could have easily got a divorce on grounds of domestic abuse and torture. She thought of me like her father. More than for legal advice, she would call me to share what was happening with her. I believe . . .' he pursed his lips, '. . . yes . . . last week she called me saying she and Madhu were penniless and that she had to sell her chain to pay rent and buy groceries. I told her she didn't have to pay me anything, I was just helping her. What can I say, Inspector? She could have easily left him if she wanted to. She was even looking for a job. Why would she kill him! She wouldn't have had the courage to do it anyway.'

Rakesh nodded, a wave of relief washing over him.

67
Pooja

SHALINI HAD EDITED THE FIRST EPISODE OF the podcast. 'It's a little short,' she told Pooja after they heard it a couple of times. 'But short with a punch, which is better than long and boring.'

'I agree,' Pooja replied. 'Now for the rest of the formalities. I don't think we need to publicise this. My husband doesn't want me to anyway.'

Pooja had received an angry voice message from Sanjay that morning. 'If you are covering this murder, don't expect me to help you publicise it or pay for it. I am not going to be involved in something so ridiculous. Why couldn't you just interview people from the film industry? At least you'd have had a hit podcast on your hands. How do you think it will look if Sanjay Reddy's wife is involved in a podcast about a woman who was caught after murdering her husband with her lover? Right after we have solved your stupid mess? Do you want people to think you're getting tips from her?'

It went on and on for five minutes. In the end, Pooja had replied with just one word: 'Cool.'

Her response had infuriated him even more and he started calling her incessantly. When he wouldn't stop, she had turned off her phone. 'Shall we play the next episode's edits?' Shalini asked, her finger poised over the trackpad. Pooja nodded and she pressed play.

Shalini's voice filled the room. 'I'm at Mira's parents' home.' There was a pause before Shalini spoke again, 'You can speak now, Aunty.'

An old woman's voice filled the room. 'What to say, Ma. This is very difficult.'

'Tell us about Mira as a young girl. Do you think she did this? If yes, why?'

'You are going to spread rumours about my daughter, no? Like the others?'

'No, Aunty, I promise. I like Mira, I'm just trying to lend support.'

'You are her friend?'

'Yes, Aunty,' Shalini said. Pooja paused the recording and raised her eyebrows. 'Well, I'm as much a friend as she can have right now,' Shalini protested and Pooja shook her head. 'Can we keep the lies to a minimum?'

'My Mira was a sweetheart, you know. She would never do something like this. It was him; it was his fault. She was the best daughter in the world. My son doesn't take care of me. But Mira does,' she said shrilly. 'He is of no use to me. I know him, he runs after women and when he gets married, he will leave me for his wife. His wife will make him do whatever she wants, and he will leave me to fend for myself. I won't even get a card for Diwali; I won't get phone calls. If something happens to Mira, I might as well throw away my phone. No one calls us anyway.'

Pooja paused the audio. Mira's mother sounded senile. She took a deep breath and wrote down, 'Father sick, mother blabbering, bad childhood?' on her notepad before pressing play. 'So, you don't think she did it despite what the news channels are saying?'

'Why aren't you understanding, Ma? She didn't tell me how things were in her house, but I knew from the way she limped and the way her face was suddenly swollen!' Her voice broke. 'She may have not told me, but I knew.'

'Was he beating her?' Shalini interrupted, and Pooja shut her eyes in frustration. She had told Shalini specifically not to interrupt people when they were talking! She heard someone click their tongue, presumably the mother. 'That's what I'm saying! She was terrified of him and didn't tell anyone. One day she couldn't walk! She came to pick up Pri and she couldn't even walk properly. She was limping badly. I should have known when she came here unannounced to drop Pri off that Madhu was drunk and angry again.'

There was a long pause, and Pooja realised she was clenching her teeth. 'Sorry, Aunty,' Shalini said in a soft voice.

'Turn that off. I don't want—' the woman said, before a scuffling sound cut off the audio.

'That's when she said her husband used to beat her as well but never as badly as Madhu hit Mira,' Shalini said. 'Just a bit of disciplining.' Pooja rolled her eyes. 'I asked why neither of them divorced their husbands. And she told me to get out because I was trying to badmouth her daughter just like the people on TV. I did my best to reassure her that I was on her side, and that I have to ask these questions, but she wouldn't listen to me.'

'So, what's next?' Pooja asked.

'Well, next we talk to the headmistress. I'm meeting her this evening.'

68
Inspector Rakesh

RAKESH WAS EATING HIS LUNCH AT A PARK when Atif messaged him to say it was safe to come back to the police station; the reporters had left for the day. He immediately packed up and left. All morning, he had been avoiding calls like the plague. Any call from an unknown number was diligently ignored.

Only messages got through. Unfortunately, the messages were getting worse. 'Macha, this is you, right?' It was accompanied by a video of the water bottle accident. Here, it looked like he had deliberately hit the man. He didn't reply.

The next one was a forward to the school WhatsApp group. They had seen the news now and most had left. He had been avoiding Mira since the news broadcast, he couldn't bear to see her. She hadn't messaged him either. It was better this way. Who knew who would see the messages and create another sensational story. Trial by public opinion was bad enough without the extra fuel.

Atif was waiting for him at the police station with a file in his hand. Karthik was nowhere to be seen.

'Where is . . .' Rakesh started, but Atif shook his head. 'Meeting.' He pointed towards the ceiling. Karthik was meeting with some higher-ups. Rakesh hadn't been informed of this meeting nor had he been called to it. Today was turning out to be a really fucked-up day.

Atif handed him the file. 'A list of everyone Madhu spoke to over the past three months using his secret phone.'

'Has Karthik seen this?' he asked, opening the file and flipping through it.

'Not yet, we just got it. He'll be back after lunch, I believe. So will Raghav who is eager to show us other things he's found on the phone.' Rakesh went through the list and took pictures of the numbers.

69
Breaking News

A NEWS CHANNEL HAD FOUND THE PICTURES taken at the reunion. No one had any idea how, but the photos that had so far been shared only on the Facebook group were now on the news. All faces except those of Rakesh and Mira were blurred. The man who had posted the pictures checked his settings again and again till he realised that anyone on his friend list could have shared them.

The channels had highlighted Rakesh and Mira's faces with two red circles. Unfortunately for Rakesh, in one of the photos he was looking at Mira.'

People online were comparing it to a famous scene in a movie where the lead actress looks at the lead actor right as the picture was being clicked. The video of the movie scene along with their picture was now doing the rounds on social media and WhatsApp groups, and soon reached Bindhu, the police commissioner and Joslin.

As the pictures were flashing, the anchor on a news channel said, 'That was a romance, this is a thriller. Love may conquer all, but this time the law will conquer love.

70
Inspector Rakesh

RAKESH'S PHONE HAD BEEN VIBRATING FOR A while in his pocket. But he had more important matters to deal with right now. He was with Raghav who had finally managed to get into Madhu's secret messaging app.

He stared at the screen in front of him in shock. Next to him, Karthik visibly squirmed. 'Okay, turn it off,' Rakesh finally said. 'I don't think I want to understand what's going on.'

'I've seen worse,' Raghav said. 'I can blur the girl's face and give you the printouts.'

'Why do we need printouts?'

'To give to the press?' Raghav said, raising an eyebrow.

'Why the fuck would we give it to the press?' Karthik snapped. 'This is a child, dude.' He wrung his hands in frustration.

'What does the message say again?' Rakesh asked.

'Nice. Excellent quality,' he read it out.

'Quality?' Atif snarled. 'What kind of language is this?'

The rest of the conversation between Madhu and the unknown number was on similar lines. The line that horrified everyone was, 'Kids this age don't remember anything.'

'I can't believe this . . .' Karthik said.

'Karthik, we'll address this tomorrow,' Rakesh said. 'Let's look at the other things Raghav has found.'

Karthik excused himself and walked out towards the tea shop.

Atif glanced up at where Rakesh was looking and nodded. Rakesh and Atif turned back to the screen.

The person Madhu had been communicating with and the chat screenshots Madhu had taken all had the same number.

'The number is registered to some import–export company,' Atif said.

'Does the company actually exist or . . . ?'

'I couldn't find anything about it online, but it was registered a few years ago.'

'Didn't one news channel claim that Madhu had started an import–export company?'

'I'll find out more.'

Rakesh went through the images again, quickly skipping the ones of the little girl in her birthday dress, smiling and posing for the camera. While the images were shocking on their own, what was even more concerning was that the girl in the photo didn't look like the girl he'd seen in Madhu's mother's house.

'If Mira knew this . . .' Rakesh trailed off. If she had found out that Madhu, her worthless piece of shit of a husband, was part of a child-trafficking ring doing something like this to pay off a debt and possibly helping traffic other young children and women . . .

'. . . she might have decided to kill him,' Atif concluded.

Rakesh had always protested whenever Karthik had said this, but now that Atif was saying the same thing, it seemed like an actual possibility. The evidence was right in front of him. Either Mira had found out and killed her husband, or there was a whole new list of suspects that he was yet to discover.

From the window, Rakesh could see the bright blue phone case pressed to Karthik's ear as he paced up and down while waiting for his tea.

He looked at Atif who nodded and left.

71
Pooja

A GOOGLE ALERT TOLD HER THAT SANJAY HAD been a guest on a popular talk show along with D. The PR drive to move on from the scandal was in full swing. Unfortunately for them, she was not there.

She hadn't planned on watching the show, but she was free that evening because none of the other people they had contacted for the podcast had responded. She wanted at least three episodes' worth of content before she released the first one, so instead of worrying and repeatedly calling the people who didn't respond, Pooja tuned in to see Sanjay and D's show.

They discussed the usual things, D's career, Sanjay's last film, Pooja's new project, while deftly avoiding any talk of the scandal. Pooja wondered what strings Sanjay had pulled to make this happen. Then, finally, they came to the topic of Pooja's visit to Chennai.

'It is a sad situation in our country today. Women are abused by their husbands who drink more than they can handle. Poo believes, I mean Pooja . . .' Sanjay stopped to laugh, 'Pooja believes that something must have gone wrong for that woman to act in such a manner, and I agree.'

'Right you are, Sanjay. But why this case and why now? Why not have someone else take it up? Aren't you two worried about what it might do to her image and to your marriage? And the movie? Forgive my nosiness,' the anchor asked.

'Pooja thinks Mira was going through a particularly harsh time. Having experienced some nastiness from online trolls herself following this unfortunate incident, she wanted to help a woman who couldn't help herself.' Pooja smiled. Sanjay had taken the bait but turned it around. He had mentioned the scandal himself without saying the word 'scandal'. She wouldn't have been able to do such a good job.

'She does deserve to go to jail though; after all, she murdered her husband,' the anchor continued.

'Rita, we should let the police investigate before we jump to conclusions,' Sanjay said, giving the anchor a snarky smile. 'Have you ever heard of trolls abusing a husband who kills his wife? No! Men get away with anything and women always face the brunt of it. If he had killed her, yes, he would have been arrested, but it wouldn't have happened with all this drama. It would have been a small story in the back pages of a newspaper. Now, because it's a woman, she is being ripped to shreds! We must all apologise to the women in our lives.' Sanjay looked into the camera. Was he apologising to her? Maybe he was, especially since she wasn't responding to his messages.

'How right you are, Sanjay! Women do suffer. I myself have face so many trolls,' the anchor said. 'With that we go to our first break. When we come back, we will meet everyone's favourite superstar, D, on *Meet the Celebrity* sponsored by Quality biscuits. *Bas quantity nahi, quality bhi.*'

D was next, which meant the film's actress would be with him. They wouldn't talk about Pooja anymore. She wanted to turn off the TV. The last time she had seen D was when he had shared an advert for a protein supplement company. 'This protein shake promises extra manly power.' He had said and winked at the camera. D was making money off the scandal while she was languishing in hiding.

It was fucking unfair.

They were back on TV and the camera showed D sitting next to Sona Sharma, the next big thing, according to the media. 'I'm so happy to be here,' she preened at the anchor.

'Sona, you always have such a radiant smile for everyone. How do you stay so happy?'

'When I have such amazing people to work with, how can I not be happy, Rita!' Sona giggled, and both Sanjay and D laughed with her.

'Sona is way too kind to us idiot men,' D said. Their words trailed off and Pooja turned her attention to the packet of potato chips that she had somehow finished in a short time. Tossing the empty packet on the floor, she texted Shalini to ask if she'd made any progress tracking down Mira's childhood friends.

A change in the anchor's tone of voice grabbed Pooja's attention again. 'You're launching it?' she asked D.

She saw a look of surprise pass through Sanjay's face before he rearranged. 'Yes,' D said, 'I will be launching the first episode of Pooja's podcast as soon as it is ready. I've played the hero in so many films, but I've done so little to be a hero in real life. I would like to start before it's too late. Unfortunately, the release didn't go as planned because of the drama that unfolded.'

The anchor nodded enthusiastically as D went on. 'She told me so many young men look up to me that I should be an example for them. Pooja asked if I was willing to launch something in support of women. We met privately for it a few times and now it is ready to be launched.'

D had handled their situation better than Sanjay. She laughed out loud. Sanjay had not wanted to spend a penny on her show. Now he had no choice.

72
Inspector Rakesh

RAKESH WENT BACK TO AN EMPTY HOUSE THAT evening. He had received a text from Bindhu telling him that she was going to her parents' home. The message came right after Lily, Bindhu's awful cousin, had sent the reunion picture to him. Even though Lily had deleted the message in a few seconds, he had seen it. She must have sent it to Bindhu as well.

He checked the fridge to see if Bindhu had left any food for him. It was mostly empty with just a few spoons of leftovers. The okra fry that he hated seemed to be mocking him. Normally when Bindhu spent the night at her parents' house, he would order takeout. But he didn't want the delivery guy recognising him. Two men had recognised him when he'd removed his helmet to wipe his sweaty face at a traffic signal.

He took out a packet of the noodles that had been bought exclusively for his son. After putting the noodles to boil, following the instructions on the back of the packet, he checked all the WhatsApp groups he had muted and noticed that he had been removed from a couple of them. His weekend cricket and extended family groups had acted swiftly. At least he would no longer be subjected to their constant forwarded messages and chatter.

When Rakesh clicked on his college group, he found out that he had been tagged in messages quite a few times. The first tag, an image, said, 'Da @rakesh, isn't this you?'

It was the picture from the reunion.

Taking the bowl of noodles to the living room, he sat on the floor and turned on the news. Every major news channel was covering the case and his part in it. One or two national ones had even sent reporters to Chennai to update viewers on what was happening. Why was an ordinary murder case such a big deal?

Rakesh was lost in his thoughts and was brought back to reality when his phone rang. It was Atif. 'Hello?'

'Sir, the hospital has asked us to take Mira to a different place.'

'Why?'

'Someone leaked her location. Reporters have gathered outside and the noise is disturbing the other patients.'

'But didn't she need to stay for a few days to recover? It's only been four days, isn't it?' Rakesh realised he had lost track of time. So much had happened to him of late that he'd forgotten when the murder had come to light. The enormity of the events didn't match the crime.

'Sir, they want us to take her away right now. But I said that we would take her tomorrow.'

'Fine,' Rakesh said. 'By the way, did you speak to the idli lady?'

'Not yet, sir. I'll catch her in the morning. There were people around all the time,' Atif replied.

'Got it. Let me know when you go,' he said and hung up.

Just then, the news channel changed its coverage. A bearded man was standing outside Mira's hospital, speaking enthusiastically to the camera. 'We have found out that Mira is currently receiving treatment in the hospital behind me. Police have been stationed outside to prevent her from running away.'

'More like to prevent you from going inside,' Rakesh muttered.

'We do not know if Mira was injured or if she was admitted for reasons of safety. But it is clear that she is being guarded. We asked the doctor who is treating her about her condition, but he refused to share any details.'

Rakesh checked the time. It was 10.00 p.m. This news channel had claimed that it was the first one to have this information. That means not many viewers would have watched it at this time. He should reach the hospital early tomorrow morning.

73
Pooja

'WHY CAN'T YOU RECORD YOUR STUPID PODCAST from here?' Sanjay snapped into the phone. He had called her right after the live broadcast of the talk show. This time she had answered his call. Sanjay told her to come back home since D was launching her podcast.

'I don't think so,' Pooja said. 'Just because you plan things without consulting me doesn't mean I have to go along with it.'

'What the fuck is wrong with you . . .' he started again. She listened to his rant for a while, keeping the phone away from her ear.

'I was interviewed the other day. Did you even listen to that?' he asked. 'They kept asking about you—as if you had left me. I didn't know what to say.'

Pooja hadn't been aware of any other interview. 'You seem to have managed just fine,' she replied, quickly checking Sanjay's Twitter feed to see if he had posted a link to it. There was nothing on his timeline. If they had asked questions about her, he wouldn't have shared it. So that's why he had agreed to be a part of the chat show. It was damage control.

'I had to, right? I had to manage.'

'Since you know how to manage without me, I'm sure you can continue to do so for a while longer,' Pooja snapped. 'We are recording another episode in a bit, and we do not have the time to come back.'

'Oh, fuck you!' he said angrily. 'Stop acting as if your podcast matters. You don't do the grunt work anyway. You're probably sitting you ass at home or in some salon getting your nails done while . . .'

'Yes, Sanjay. You're right. I'm a lazy cow and my podcast doesn't matter, my feelings don't matter, my opinion doesn't matter, and I don't matter.' She was furious now. 'If nothing I do matters, then I guess my existence doesn't matter either. Why don't you just stop calling and file for a fucking divorce?'

There was silence at the other end. Maybe she'd hit a nerve. But then she heard Shyamal's voice in the background.

'Hello,' Sanjay said, after he was done talking with Shyamal. 'I have to go. Let me know if you're okay with an online launch. We can at least figure that shit out. Bye.'

He hung up.

He hadn't even heard what she'd said.

She threw her phone across the room where it bounced off the spongy soundproof walls and hit the bed. 'FUCK!' she yelled.

74
Inspector Rakesh

'WE ARE OUTSIDE THE HOSPITAL RIGHT NOW and Mira is about to be discharged. We have been informed that she will come out any minute now. As you can see, police presence has increased tremendously since last night. This means we will soon be able to see the infamous murderer with her lover, the inspector.'

Rakesh was watching the live broadcast on his phone as Atif and he drove to the hospital in an unmarked car.

'Just ignore it, sir,' Atif told him.

'I am ignoring it. Just want to know the size of the crowd,' he said, turning it off. 'Has the other car reached?'

'Yes.'

Rakesh nodded. They had placed the police vehicle that Rakesh would take to the police station in the basement. The press would follow him, allowing Atif in the hatchback to take Mira to her mother's house. He would see Mira only for a minute or so while escorting her to the car.

He hoped she would understand.

He hadn't seen Mira since that day at the hospital when he'd found a strange message on her phone. Atif had been the one keeping tabs on her at the hospital. He didn't know how she would react when she saw him. He hoped she didn't think that the man she trusted had abandoned her to strangers, or that he had made her life more difficult.

As they got closer to the hospital, Rakesh ducked in the back seat. The crowd moved aside after peering into the window at Atif who was in plainclothes. Atif parked the car in the basement next to the elevator.

Atif had received a text from the constable stationed outside Mira's room that she was ready. When they reached her room, Mira was sitting on the edge of the bed with her small bag in her hand. She didn't look up when they entered.

'Ready, ma'am?' Atif asked and she smiled at him and nodded.

Rakesh could feel the tension in the air. The nurses who had been previously friendly with Mira seemed hostile to her presence. The head nurse who had kindly told him about Mira's injuries last time had glared at him when he got off the elevator. It hadn't occurred to him that she was going through worse than he was.

Mira covered her face with her sari as soon as she entered the lift.

'Don't,' Rakesh said. She stiffened. 'That will draw attention to us. Just be casual.'

'Yes, ma'am,' Atif added. 'Sir is right. I've done this before, and the media always spots us if we hide faces.'

She nodded and let the pallu fall back down over her shoulders.

The elevator ride was short and silent. Rakesh, Atif and the constable had formed a ring around Mira, in case someone had found their way to the basement.

Once there, they quickly guided Mira to the back seat. The noise outside was deafening. Mira flinched as soon as the door was opened. Rakesh went to the car they had come in, opening the back door for Mira to get in. Once she was comfortable, he asked her to lie down on the seat and covered her with a black cloth. Just before shutting the door, he whispered, 'I'm really sorry about everything that's happening.' Mira didn't respond. He shut the door and went to the decoy vehicle. A policewoman was waiting inside, already covered in a big black cloth. He nodded to her and started the car, pulling his cap low on his face and adjusting his sunglasses.

He took a deep breath and drove out. As soon as the cameramen spotted his car, they ran towards it. He ploughed past everyone, honking furiously. Thankfully, no one jumped in front of his car or seemed to get injured.

He drove as fast as he could, manoeuvring between cars and accelerating to avoid red lights till he made it to the station. Halfway through the drive, a few of the bikes chasing him had realised that Mira was not in his car. The cover had slipped just a little and revealed the policewoman's face. She put her cap on and smiled smugly at the reporters chasing them.

They yelled the update to each other and soon left Rakesh and the car alone. A couple of vehicles were still following him but that didn't matter. Now that the situation was under control, he thought about Mira's mute reaction to his apology. Why hadn't she acknowledged his presence at all this morning? Rakesh slowed down till he was driving within the legal limit and headed to the police station.

75
Pooja

POOJA WAS IN THE STUDIO GOING THROUGH the script of the next episode when Shalini asked her to come to the living room urgently.

The news channel was showing footage of a car chase involving Inspector Rakesh as he drove recklessly out of the hospital. 'Damn,' Shalini said as they watched the media chasing him. This channel's cameraperson was lagging behind the other cars and Pooja was shocked to see just how many vehicles were trying to catch with the police car.

'We need to speak to him as well,' Pooja told Shalini. 'If we can actually get him.'

The reporter was screaming into her microphone. 'As you can see, Inspector Rakesh is speeding away from our cameras. But there is no place to hide on the open road. As our vehicles try to catch up with him . . .'

The reporter suddenly seemed to realise that the person under the black cloth in the back seat wasn't Mira; it was a young policewoman. And the channel's car slowed down immediately.

This ridiculous car chase reminded Pooja of the time Sanjay and Shyamal had hidden her in the back seat of their car and driven to the beach house.

On the screen, the anchor continued narrating what was unfolding in front of them. '. . . As you can tell, folks, this was a distraction. The police department created a diversion to get the accused to safety while taking us on a wild goose chase. But don't worry, we will get to the bottom of this and secure an interview with the woman in the eye of the storm soon.'

Shalini switched channels but the news being telecast was the same there too. This channel's reporter, though, was in front of Mira's mother's house, where Shalini had gone just a few days ago. 'Jesus Christ!' she said as they saw Mira's mother dart away from the window and pull the curtains shut.

'The poor thing,' Shalini sighed.

'How was the house? Was it secure? Do you think someone can get in?' Pooja asked, thinking of how high walls and CCTV cameras had given her a sense of security when she was being hounded.

'Of course they can get in easily. It's a normal house. They don't even have a security guard like apartment buildings do,' Shalini said, switching channels again.

It was the same scene playing everywhere.

As she was thinking about Mira, Pooja's phone pinged. It was a message from Shyamal: 'Madam, D sir is trying to contact you. You blocked his new number? Here it is. Please unblock.'

76
Inspector Rakesh

RAKESH PARKED THE CAR, AND HE AND THE policewoman hurried inside. 'Well done,' he told her. 'First time?'

'Yes, sir, it was really exciting,' she said.

As usual, the news channels were talking about only one story. 'Awesome driving, sir. Like movie stunt!' one constable said, grinning at Rakesh as he entered.

'Have they found where she went?' Rakesh asked, squinting at the small print on the TV.

'Not yet, but I don't think Atif will be able to take Mira to her parents' home. The media has gheraoed the house.'

'And her flat too,' said another, eyes still glued to the television.

Rakesh called Atif again, who still wasn't answering. 'He's probably driving around not sure what to do,' Rakesh muttered as he hung up. As soon as he did, his phone rang. It wasn't Atif like he'd hoped. It was the commissioner.

'Sir, hello, sir,' Rakesh said, standing at attention without even realising it.

'Come to the office when you've dropped off that woman,' the commissioner ordered and disconnected the call before Rakesh could respond.

I'm fucked, Rakesh thought. He then turned his attention back to the news. One channel's car had stationed itself outside their station. The boy who served them tea every day walked past the camera and grinned at it before stylishly walking towards the station.

'No one asked for tea,' one of the constables said. The boy stopped at the entrance, pushed his hair back, imitating a famous actor's signature style, and walked in.

As everyone laughed, Rakesh grabbed his keys and ran out to his car again. He might as well get the meeting with the commissioner over with.

Twenty minutes later, he was at the police headquarters. And he couldn't believe what he'd just heard. 'Sorry, sir?' Rakesh said, sure he had misheard his boss.

'Take some time off, maybe two or three weeks to, you know, relax a bit,' the commissioner repeated.

'But, sir, I did everything properly.'

'I know, Inspector. This is for your own good. It's not like I'm suspending you, Pa. Don't worry. Just go on a vacation. Spend some time with your wife and kid. Doesn't he have holidays soon?'

'Yes, sir.'

'Then take him on a vacation,' the commissioner repeated, a tad too enthusiastically.

'But, sir . . .'

'See, Rakesh,' he said, taking his phone and unlocking it. 'Look at this.'

Rakesh stepped forward to see what the commissioner was showing him and felt his face turn red.

'The love is real. Look at this picture taken at the recent reunion of Inspector Rakesh's class.' There were two red circles around his and Mira's faces; he was staring stupidly at her and she was staring at the camera with no expression on her face.

'Sorry, sir. I promise there's nothing happening between Mira and me.'

'Are you a child? What is all this talk of promise? Before this gets worse and I'm held accountable, take some time off. Go on holiday, do something.'

'Okay, sir.' Rakesh said, finally realising that this was an unofficial suspension. As he drove back to the police station, he wondered if the situation was really as bad as the commissioner implied it was. Honestly, he wouldn't mind the break. He could take his son to a theme park, maybe take Bindhu to Yelagiri hills; she had been pestering him about it ever since their neighbours had posted their holiday pictures on Facebook.

It occurred to him that if he was spotted him on holiday, pictures of his vacation would go viral and the media would claim that he was taking a much needed break after helping his girlfriend murder her husband. Also, what would happen to Mira if he left? And what about those images on Madhu's phone? Should he have mentioned that to the commissioner? It was too late now.

Parking the jeep, he pulled out his phone and called Bindhu. Once again there was no answer. Karthik was back in office and talking on the phone again, whispering away with a smirk on his face.

Rakesh ignored everyone and went to his desk to pack a few essentials that he would need at home.

77
Pooja

POOJA CHANGED HER EARRINGS AND CHECKED her reflection in the bathroom mirror once again. This Facebook Live session would be one more attempt to put rumours about her and D to rest.

She was applying lip gloss when her phone pinged. D had tagged her in a post.

'Don't forget to see me and @pooja_reddyoff live on Facebook in 15 minutes!!!! Love you guys!' She liked it, shared it and went back to her reflection. Just yesterday, she had refused once again to go back to Mumbai. So Sanjay had instructed her to do this online session with D.

Shalini stuck her head into the room, 'I have your notes here. Hope they're all right. But I don't understand why we're not doing this at your place.'

'You've seen my house, Shalini,' Pooja replied, taking the notebook from Shalini. 'It would take ages to make it pretty for social media. But this would totally work for social media.' She glanced at the generically decorated hotel room.

'Well, I'll be in the other room if you need me,' Shalini said and stepped out.

Pooja grabbed her phone and checked some tweets. Sure enough, there were nameless and faceless accounts who had nothing better to do.

'Maybe it will be a Facebook Live of them fucking.' 'We already saw you kiss in your movie. Going to show us more?' 'Pooja Reddy and Hero D, is he going to give her the D. rofl'

She blocked them all and vowed once again to not to let them get to her. How hard was it to leave people alone! Instead of responding to the rude messages, she posted '10 minutes to go!!!' and put her phone down.

Her Wi-Fi connection was strong, the lighting good, and her teeth lipstick-free. Pooja counted down the time and clicked live at 3.00 p.m. sharp.

'Hello, everyone!' she said into the camera as messages rolled down the side.

'Bitch is wearing clothes. Disappointed.' 'Chitting hore.'

'Ma'am, so proud of you for coming online and facing these assholes.' The rare positive message gave her strength.

'Thank you all for being here,' she continued cheerfully, pinching her nails into her palms to remind herself to keep smiling. D joined her and the screen split. She recognised the awards behind him. He was at their house, sitting in Sanjay's office.

'Hi, Pooja!' he rasped. 'Hi, D! So glad you could do this!'

'Me too! I can't wait for people to hear what you have going on!'

'I'm just here to see some banging!' 'Get to it!' 'Okay, this is too PG 13 for my taste. I'm logging off.'

Both of them ignored the messages and Pooja continued. 'I am sure you've all been wondering what we've been up to.'

'And we'd like to announce that not only is Pooja penning the script for my next film, a story based on violence against women,' D added, repeating the news from their press release, 'but she is also launching a podcast for women!' He then started clapping, making her ears ring with the sound.

She laughed, 'Yes. I am so happy to announce that *The Accused*, a podcast that focuses on crimes and women, will be available to listen very soon.'

'Boring!' '*Ye podcast kya hotha hai.*'

D grabbed the cue. 'For those of you who don't know,' he said, switching to Hindi, 'a podcast is like a radio show. This one focuses on women who have been victims of a crime or have been accused of committing one.'

'*RJ banne wali hai kya.*'

'As you all know, I'm a huge fan of podcasts. After listening to so many and sharing my recommendations with all of you, I thought, why not start my own and see if we can replicate what other podcasts have done—helping women who have been falsely accused and identify those who have got away with committing crimes . . .'

'We are starting with a case you are all well aware of,' D added. 'Mira, a victim of domestic abuse, is being falsely accused of murdering her husband. The police inspector who tried to protect her after seeing the medical reports that showed the extent of her abuse has been called her accomplice!'

'Not just by the media, but by members of the public and on social media too!' Pooja added, wondering how the fuck D knew more about the case than she did.

'Exactly,' he said, nodding at the camera. 'The aim of this podcast is show the other side of the story to the public.'

'You can ask us any questions about the podcast, and we will answer them.'

The comments poured in. Almost all of them were about D's new movie which was up for release soon. Even though both D and Pooja kept insisting that they were only taking questions about the podcast, she knew it wouldn't happen. Few people cared about such things.

When they ended the session, they told the viewers that they were going to release the first episode of the podcast now and that they should stick around to listen to it. Pooja logged off before D did, waving enthusiastically at the camera and thanking him for taking the time to be there for her and her newest venture.

The truth, however, was that D wasn't doing much except launching it. His new movie was one of the 'sponsors' of her podcast. Pooja had to keep up appearances, so she had recorded the advertisement for it. 'Now to our sponsor, D's new film, *The Girl Is Mine*. Releasing in theatres near you in just two weeks.'

As much as it pained her to work with him, it was necessary to smooth things over. It would also kick-start the process of getting over him and coming to terms with the fact that, just like Sanjay had said, D cared more about his freedom and his pay cheque to actually see her as more than a fun time.

78
Inspector Rakesh

IF RAKESH WAS FINALLY BEING HONEST WITH himself, his pride had taken a beating and he was still smarting from it. A few days at home with nothing to do but think about the case had given him some clarity. He really believed that he was a better cop than he had proved to be. Sure, he hadn't been good to begin with, but he had thought that his love for thrillers and detective books would kick in at some point and he'd have a remarkable insight that would solve Madhu's murder in a matter of hours.

Atif had told him last night that he'd finally found out what Karthik was speaking on the phone. And why he would suddenly run off to the tea shop outside the police station whenever he got a call. 'The shop owner said that Karthik told the person on the phone that he can no longer do this now that a child was involved. That he had done all he could for the minister but now he had to back out.'

What was going on? Rakesh ran through the events of the last few days in his mind.

Mira had been taken to the hospital and Karthik had collected the evidence from her house—the knife, the computer, Madhu's phone and now they had Madhu's second secret phone. All the news channels said that they were getting information on the case from an inside source. He remembered how Karthik's demeanour had changed when he was with the minister. They had started talking post lunch while Rakesh was on the phone checking on Mira. He remembered walking out of the restroom after checking on Mira's condition and Karthik whispering to the minister.

'Fuck,' he said.

Had he really done it? Was Karthik the one who had been cooking up stories and sharing them with the press? But why had the minister helped?

As the realisation dawned on him, Rakesh slapped his forehead.

Bindhu walked into the living room after hearing him swear. 'What happened?' she asked. He had been grateful that she had come back from her parents' house after hearing about his suspension. 'Nothing, Ma, is he asleep?' he asked, looking at their son's bedroom.

'Hmm,' she replied and went back into the room. Rakesh wanted to share the conclusion he'd come to with someone. But Bindhu wasn't that person. She anyway didn't believe him when he said he didn't love Mira. Why would she believe him now? She would think he was a fool for not knowing what his team was up to. No, it was better to keep his thoughts to himself.

79
Pooja

THE LAUNCH WAS A SUCCESS. SORT OF.

Pooja checked the stats of the first episode. They'd managed to get an impressive number of listeners. But, she realised, it was mostly due to the efforts Shalini had put in. She had edited most of the first episode and got it ready in time for the launch. All she had done was listen to the final cut. Sanjay was right. She had done nothing here, Shalini was the one doing all the hard work. They had sent the episode to D, and he'd recorded an introduction to it, which Shalini had managed to patch in at the last minute. They had released it right after the live ended and the numbers were already increasing.

Pooja looked over at Shalini who was removing the wires from the equipment they had used for the Live. She looked exhausted but she hadn't complained. 'Why don't you stay here today? The hotel room is all paid for anyway. You can relax, order room service, enjoy the rest of the day,' Pooja said

'No, I have to edit the episode with the principal,' she replied. 'I also thought I would stop by Mira's flat today and see if . . .'

'Should I come with you?' Pooja asked.

Shalini turned to look at her. Pooja tried to act nonchalant. 'I mean, the launch is done so there's nothing for me to do but record the episode.'

Sanjay's statement about her sitting around all day while others did her work was playing over and over again in her mind. It was getting to her. Shalini nodded. 'It might help with the people in the flat. I've seen some of their social media pages, they're movie maniacs. Particularly fans of D,' Shalini said, without looking at Pooja.

Pooja smiled to herself. So, she was of some use.

80
Inspector Rakesh

'MY PARENTS WILL PICK US UP IN THE EVENING,' Bindhu said as soon as the show she was watching got over.

'Us?' he asked, distractedly, reading the message that had come in. Someone had forwarded a link to a Facebook Live session that had taken place between his favourite actor, D, and an actress who he was supposedly having an affair with. His friend informed him that they had spoken about Mira's case while announcing the launch of some podcast they were making.

Bindu was still talking in the background, he realised. 'Yes, you don't have to go to work so you may as well come to the engagement,' she said.

'Okay,' he murmured, not really listening to her. He checked the electronics drawer where he kept his headphones and clicked play. He was worried that D, whose fan club he had once been a member of, had also joined the others in abusing him.

Inspector Rakesh has borne the brunt of a public trial. He has been called an accomplice even before the real accused has been found, the first episode said. *In a world where news goes viral before it is verified, where mass lynchings based on rumours have been normalised, we must take the time to check before we share.*

Rakesh was pleasantly surprised. Maybe he did have a friend after all.

We don't know what really happened. Nor should we, considering this is an ongoing investigation. But since the damage has been done, we at *The Accused* have decided to offer the other party a platform as well. Don't get us wrong, we aren't condoning murder, whatever the reason. We are offering the public a chance to see both sides of the story before deciding which one they want to support.

The rest of the episode continued in the same vein. They spoke about Mira—some negative and some positive.

They didn't mention him again, but they didn't have to. It was enough to fill him with renewed energy about this case. He was going to get to the bottom of it.

Rakesh finished listening to the episode and quickly sent the link to Atif. His finger hovered over the share button in the school WhatsApp group, which had been surprisingly silent since the news broke. Instinct told him to keep it to himself. A few more members had left the group. The only people who remained were his friends, a few people who were rarely active anyway and Mira. She was the only woman left now.

81
Pooja

AFTER THEY GOT TO HER HOUSE, SHE AND Shalini went through the comments on the Facebook Live session. D's vocal support had brought in many listeners in a short time. But, as expected, quite a few of the comments were negative.

'Look at this one,' Shalini said, rolling her eyes. She had started a Twitter account for the podcast so Pooja's personal account wouldn't be tagged.

'Saying what this time?' Pooja asked, rubbing her temples.

'Oh the usual, you're planning on murdering Sanjay and that's why you're interviewing Mira—to ask for tips.' Shalini shook her head.

'Yes, because that makes so much sense. Wouldn't it make more sense to ask someone who is a little more low-profile at the moment?' Pooja groaned. The coffee she'd had before leaving the hotel wasn't helping, nor were the comments. Shalini started typing a reply but stopped. 'Let them seethe,' she said, reading the next tweet. 'Oh, this is nice.'

'What's nice?' Pooja asked, perking up. She could use some good news.

'Someone really enjoyed the episode . . .'

'Enjoyed the unbiased narration of Pooja-ji's podcast. It is a pleasure to hear someone give you the facts of the case without trying to pull you in one direction or the other. A good listen despite the rather grim topic. Keep it up, ma'am.'

'Not bad! Not bad at all! Who is that?' Pooja got up from her chair and leaned over Shalini's shoulder.

'It seems to be . . .' Shalini replied, clicking on the account, 'a stockbroker? Well, that's boring.'

'Nevertheless, it's nice to read that. Very sweet of him or her,' Pooja said, pulling out her phone as a notification pinged. Sanjay was going live on Instagram.

What was he up to now?

'Hi, everyone,' Sanjay said, looking freshly groomed. 'My darling wife, Pooja, released the first episode of her podcast today. It has already garnered so many downloads! I want to thank all of you for making it a success. She has worked very hard on this podcast and is resting right now,' he said, turning back to look at the door behind him as if she was inside sleeping. He had clearly not realised that she had joined the live feed along with hundreds of others. 'I thought I'd take this chance to answer any questions you might have about this podcast. But before that, let me tell you why you should listen to it, if you haven't already.'

Bored, Pooja exited the live feed and went back to Shalini and the Twitter comments. Suddenly, she thought of an idea. 'Listen, Shalini,' she said, 'why don't we try and get that inspector on the show? He probably wants a chance to tell his side of the story.'

'I don't know if he'll be allowed to,' Shalini replied, looking up from the message she was typing.

'But no harm in trying, right?'

Shalini nodded and called a journalist friend to find Inspector Rakesh's number.

82
Inspector Rakesh

'SIR, GULAB JAMUN,' THE WAITER SAID, interrupting Rakesh's thoughts. He nodded and the man placed a small bowl with two marble-sized sweets next to his plate.

Rakesh had no interest in attending Bindhu's cousin's engagement party. Earlier in the evening, he had changed into a shirt to meet Atif when his wife walked into the bedroom, scolding him for picking such a casual shirt for a formal event. 'I have already set your clothes aside for you. I don't know if the suit will fit you anymore, but the rest should be fine,' she had said, marching to the cupboard and yanking a grey garment bag out.

Handing it to him, she had continued, 'Do something about your hair as well. No need to hide the fact that you're balding, it's more obvious when you do that. Appa and Amma will be here soon to pick us up. Lily said the party starts on time so get ready quickly.'

Only then did he notice Bindhu's outfit. She was draped in a soft silk sari that she had showed him about a month ago. Her hair was coiled in a bun at the back, held in place by a glittery pin. 'You look nice,' he said, and she smiled.

'Do I have to go?' he asked, hoping she would take his side. 'I mean, after the news . . .'

'. . . You'd rather have me go there by myself to face the rumours?' she asked, raising her eyebrows and glaring at him.

Rakesh resigned himself to his fate and shook his head. She nodded, jabbed a finger at the clothes and left the room.

He took out the suit from the garment bag. Bindhu must have laundered it recently. It smelled fresh and clean. The last time he'd worn it, he had been two years younger and definitely thinner. He tried it on and it fit! Surprised, he checked to see if any seams had given way and realised that Bindhu had them let out. 'No wonder,' he said, checking his reflection in the mirror.

'Everything okay?' Bindhu asked now. 'Why aren't you eating the gulab jamun. They're your favourite.'

'Yes, they are,' he said, smiling at her and popping one into his mouth. She turned her attention to Antony who was eyeing the extra bowl of ice cream the child next to him had been given.

Rakesh was about to tell Antony to get himself some more ice cream when he felt a gentle slap on his back. 'Relax, Pa,' his father-in-law said. 'Just enjoy your holiday.'

'Not a holiday,' he mumbled.

His father-in-law nodded before asking, 'How long have you been suspended for?' Rakesh swallowed. 'Not suspended, Pa, I'm taking time off, that's all.'

'Yes, yes, that's what I meant. How many days are you taking off work?'

'Not sure,' Rakesh said, unable to meet his eyes. His father-in-law knew the truth; after all, his friend, the commissioner, was the one to suspend him. But it was easier to stick with the lie, especially in front of Bindhu.

'Take this time to reflect on your actions, really think about them and realise where you've gone wrong.'

'Okay,' said Rakesh, uninterested in continuing this conversation.

'What are your priorities? You have to know them. You need to have better instincts as a policeman if you want promotions. You can't be throwing away your family and your job for some pretty thing you used to know back in the day,' the older man said, his voice lower now.

Rakesh was getting annoyed. The people in his life trusted the news more than they trusted him. 'Have to pee,' he said, putting his spoon down and wriggling out of his father-in-law's grip. People stared at him the entire way and he locked himself in the washroom stall. Even the ones who didn't know him seemed to have realised who he was. 'Fucking WhatsApp forwards,' he cursed.

As Rakesh was mentally preparing himself to get back out and face people again, his phone buzzed.

It was a number that had been withheld, and he frowned before answering it. 'Hello?' said a pleasant female voice. 'Am I speaking to Inspector Rakesh?'

'Yes?' he said, ready to hang up if it was a reporter.

'I'm Pooja, calling on behalf of *The Accused* podcast,' the woman said.

'What?'

'A podcast. An audio show?'

Rakesh knew what it was. He had just listened to an episode earlier that day. He hadn't expected them to contact him so soon though.

'How can I help you, ma'am?' he asked, putting on his most professional and intimidating voice.

'Can we meet sometime tomorrow?'

'I am not sure . . .'

'Please. I promise I won't ask you any horrible or disrespectful questions. If it helps, I don't really believe any of the rumours.'

Rakesh stood silently by the sink as an attendant walked in with a mop in his hand. He could meet this woman. But would he be allowed to? Would their interaction be considered a press release? The department might not approve if it was.

He was about to ask her if he could contact his boss first when he spotted Bindhu walking towards the restroom, clearly looking for him.

'I will message you,' he said urgently and disconnected the call.

83
Pooja

'WELL?' SHALINI ASKED.

'That was abrupt,' Pooja replied, looking at her phone screen. 'He said he'd message me and hung up.'

'Maybe his boss is around.'

'He got suspended, remember? The news said so.'

'Maybe he will message,' Shalini said, as Pooja turned to listen to the interview she had recorded.

'What about her husband? Could you tell me about him?'

Madhu and Mira's school principal was struggling to say a single polite thing about him. Surprisingly, she remembered Rakesh as well. 'Madhu picked on everyone in school, even that poor Inspector Rakesh. Typical male chauvinist. Rowdy. Roadside rogue.'

Pooja paused the file and asked Shalini to message the inspector. The man must be terrified of the media and she wanted to inform him that theirs was a safe space.

'Do you think he will reply?' Shalini asked.

'No, but let's try and continue with the next episode anyway,' Pooja said, going through the list of people still to be interviewed. She'd made the list after the reunion picture had come out.

'I have a question,' Shalini said. 'What if we don't find the real killer ourselves? I know this isn't a Nancy Drew novel, so I am mentally prepared to not find out who the killer is. But what if we do . . .'

Pooja noticed the excitement in Shalini's voice. Finding the killer hadn't occurred to her. She hadn't thought that far ahead. Sanjay had pointed out her inability to think of the future several times, and she would always dismiss him for picking on her. But it seems he was right again.

'I didn't mean to stress you out,' Shalini said, backtracking.

'I don't think we will,' Pooja finally said, after thinking it through. 'We aren't interviewing suspects, just people who can vouch for Mira, who witnessed what happened between husband and wife.'

'Oh, but I thought . . .'

'I know I said this was a true crime podcast fighting for justice, but my goal is to fight injustice,' Pooja said, not wanting to appear dumb. 'We aren't finding the criminal. Where do we even have the resources for that?'

Shalini tried to hide her disappointment. 'But . . .' Pooja added, 'If we do come across something that we think is suspicious we will share it with the police.'

Shalini mumbled something about the police being incompetent, but she seemed less unhappy about the whole thing now. 'Remember the video of the news channel interviewing one of the apartment's residents?' she started, taking out her phone. 'The one who said that Rakesh had helped Mira kill Madhu? She seems like a blabbermouth. I was thinking . . . why don't we interview her?'

'We will,' Pooja said. 'But let's wait for Rakesh's reply first.'

84
Inspector Rakesh

'I DON'T KNOW . . . RAKESH SAID, STARING AT the message of a woman who claimed to be working on the podcast with Pooja.

Atif, who had come home to meet him, took the phone from his hands to look at it. 'I listened to the podcast yesterday,' he said, handing it back. 'It seems like they are on our side.'

Rakesh didn't show it but Atif saying 'our' side meant the world to him right now. 'Should I meet them?' he asked. 'Also, how did they get my number?'

'Most media houses have your number by now. Didn't you mention that you were getting call after call?'

'Yes,' he grumbled, finishing the rest of his coffee. 'Do you want to ask your father-in-law?'

'Death would be better,' Rakesh muttered. 'So, should I just do it? What do you think?'

'I don't think you should,' Atif said, after thinking about it for a couple of minutes. 'I know I'm not in your shoes, but unless they can guarantee that they will not make you look bad you shouldn't. Anyway, you should not do it unless you have approval from the department. You'll get into more trouble if you don't have their approval. Do you want me to look into the people behind the podcast?'

Rakesh was confused. Could he, by some chance, get a guarantee that they wouldn't air the episode until he secured permission? But who would grant him permission to give an interview?

Atif's phone rang and Rakesh came back to the present. 'Karthik sir,' he said, putting a finger to his lips. 'Yes,' he said, listening to Karthik. Then his eyes went wide. 'WHAT!?'

'Okay, I'm coming, sir,' he said, hanging up.

'What happened?'

'Mira ma'am is missing.'

'What do you mean she's missing?'

'She left a letter. She's gone.'

85
Pooja

POOJA HAD IGNORED ALL OF SANJAY'S CALLS and messages since 7.00 p.m. yesterday.

After editing the next episode she and Shalini had gone out to treat themselves at a local cafe. She had posted a picture of the two of them eating cake on her Instagram. The caption read: 'Who says you can't have a little fun while working? #NewEpisode #Cake4Life'

Sanjay had liked and commented on it, but she hadn't responded. He must be incensed; it had already been half a day.

She checked his comment again. 'A snack holding a snack. Damn' with the heart-eyes emoji. If she was a snack, who was the main course? Clearly, one of his multiple girlfriends. She knew it was meant to be a compliment and Shalini had said it was cute, but she found it rather offensive.

She wasn't planning on answering any of his calls right now. He was happy to behave as if everything was all right between them, but did he really think she was that spineless?

He called again. She didn't answer and turned the TV on to distract herself.

'Breaking news! Mira missing!' blared a local news channel.

'The infamous Mira has gone missing. Our sources tell us that when she didn't turn up for questioning like she should have, the police went to pick her up but found her apartment empty. There were no signs of a struggle so they're assuming that she has made a run for it. We wonder if her boyfriend, Inspector Rakesh, helped her escape. When contacted, the department had no comment to make.'

The channel cut to a live telecast of the front of Mira's apartment building. Two police vehicles were parked outside. A clip of Inspector Rakesh pushing past the crowd to run up the stairs kept playing on loop as the anchor cheerfully informed viewers about how urgently Rakesh had reached the location, how quickly he'd run up the stairs and what he was wearing. He seemed to be dressed in his pyjamas.

Mira was missing. Now even those who thought she was innocent would be convinced of her guilt. Fuck!

Pooja called Shalini and asked her to watch the news. They had to record a special episode instead of the one they had previously planned.

86
Inspector Rakesh

HE HAD INSISTED ON GOING WITH ATIF, running down the stairs in his T-shirt and track pants, past his protesting wife. When they reached the apartment, people had begun to gather outside.

'How the fuck do they know already? You just found out!' Rakesh said, craning his neck to see exactly how many cameras there were on them. Too many.

'I told you, there's a wonderful inside source.'

'Yeah, but this is going to make him look bad, not me,' Rakesh said. Atif found a parking spot a little further away. Rakesh jumped off his bike immediately and found the least crowded route to the front gate where the watchman was trying in vain to keep the crowd out.

As soon as he saw Rakesh, he pushed the gate open and let him in. Someone behind them yelled, 'Isn't that the inspector?'

'Wasn't he suspended?' another shouted. Atif, who was right behind him, raised his hands and said, 'He is just here to help. Nothing else. He's currently on leave, not suspended.'

'What's going on . . .' Rakesh heard Sunderesan ask as he ran towards Mira's house. He didn't wait for the elevator, taking the stairs two at a time, his bathroom chappals slapping against his heels as he ran.

Karthik was waiting outside Mira's house and stopped him. 'You know I can't let you in,' he said.

'I won't touch anything.'

'You have to come in for questioning.'

Rakesh stood there panting and staring at the man he thought was his friend.

'I am not the one who did this. You know exactly where I was all the time. Your little spy at the hospital would have confirmed that I didn't even visit Mira much . . .' He paused to catch his breath, '. . . I am not the one who dropped her home and I haven't seen her since that day.'

Karthik was about to protest when a constable came out of Mrs Krishnan's house. Karthik turned to him and Rakesh grabbed the opportunity to dart into Mira's house.

'Fuck!' Karthik yelled, coming in after him.

'I'll keep my hands in my pocket. I will leave when you are discussing the case. I will not interfere. Okay?' he said. Atif had reached the door by now and Karthik, glancing at the men in the living room, nodded. He always did maintain appearances in public, Rakesh thought, grateful for the audience.

The living room looked untouched except it wasn't. He could tell that all the drawers had been opened and shut.

There was a list on the table for them to make sure that nothing had gone missing, that Mira hadn't sold anything to get the money to escape.

'Are you convinced now?' Karthik said. 'She did it!'

'All I am convinced of is that she is missing,' Rakesh said, walking into the bedroom.

Karthik followed. Rakesh didn't ask and Karthik didn't volunteer information. Atif was the one speaking instead. 'What was in the note, sir? Any signs of a struggle?'

Karthik shook his head as Rakesh peered into the bathroom, at the shelves, looked into the clothes hamper and finally checked the washing machine before coming out of the room. He didn't touch anything.

'What did you learn from that little trip?' Karthik asked, sneering.

This was one area where Rakesh had an advantage over Karthik. He had a wife.

'Did you know that women hate leaving dirty laundry behind?' he asked, looking towards the bathroom. 'The washing machine doesn't smell of anything but dust. She hasn't done laundry since she came back from the hospital. The laundry hamper is full as well. Along with her clothes, you will find a man's trouser leg sticking out and a child's frock right on top. If you dig deeper, I am sure you will find more.'

'So?' Karthik asked.

'My wife does her laundry before going on a trip,' he said. Atif nodded. 'My girlfriend too, sir. She hates it if it isn't done.'

'Bindhu doesn't like leaving stinky clothes behind, especially mine. I sweat a lot, you see. Madhu was a drunken fuck. His clothes stank. Still, Mira didn't do the laundry.'

'She was too busy plotting her escape.'

'Sure. Or she was kidnapped. You and I both know there's a murky layer to this case. I take it you haven't bothered pursuing that angle.'

Rakesh thought about what he had seen next to the washing machine. The marks indicating that the washing machine had been moved were gone. He wondered if anyone else had noticed that.

87
Pooja

THEY HAD CONSIDERED CALLING INSPECTOR Rakesh, but it seemed like a bad idea. They had just spotted him live on a news channel, leaving Mira's apartment in a jeep.

'They're either questioning him or he's back to work.'

'If he's been asked to rejoin the team, he won't give us an interview,' Pooja sounded a little irritated. It was the first time she had personally spoken to someone for an interview.

'Anyway, let's start,' Pooja said, not wanting to think about losing their star interviewee.

Shalini had already begun writing the notes and Pooja settled in her chair with them. Shalini had tried calling the police station and the residents. She had even thought of driving to the building, but, in the end, they had decided to interview a psychologist. They needed do something the others hadn't thought about.

'Hello, hello,' Pooja started, adjusting the headphones as Shalini began recording. 'Welcome back to *The Accused*. If you are here for the first time, welcome. I'm Pooja, your host, and for our first case I'm talking about someone who despite not being accused by the police of murder has been subjected to a media trial. We are here to bring you the other side of the story.'

Pooja cleared her throat and continued, 'Today we have something important for you. As the news breaks right in front of us, let's go through everything that has happened so far. Mira, the woman at the centre of the storm, is missing, a few days after her husband was murdered. Police say that she has taken nothing from her apartment. This most likely means that she may not have actually run away.'

Shalini looked at Pooja as soon as she finished saying that and handed her a page. 'Doc says yes. In two hours.'

'We are pleased to welcome psychologist Dr Pushpa Michael to our show. She specialises in mob behaviour and the dynamics of large groups of people who aim to bring others to their side. Why do normal, thinking people become rabid when they are part of a mob? Is this how civilised people behave? Dr Michael will tell us more.'

Pooja asked Shalini to stop the recording and turned the TV on again.

'Do you think she did it?' Shalini asked as the channel showed a replay of everything that had happened that day.

'I don't know anymore,' Pooja said, staring at the photo showing on the TV screen, a photo of the woman who seemed to be trying her best to ensure everyone thought she was guilty.

88
Inspector Rakesh

HE'D BEEN ASKED TO WAIT IN THE ROOM reserved for suspects. As soon as Rakesh was done looking around Mira's apartment, Karthik had told him to come to the police station with them. He didn't think much of it then—after all he hadn't helped Mira escape—but now, sitting in this room, being made to wait till his colleagues decided to speak with him, was unnerving him.

This must be why no one wants to help the police, he thought, glancing around the dingy room for the hundredth time. He had forgotten how long he'd been here; in his hurry to reach Mira's house he hadn't picked up his watch. He was more aware of his outfit now, a tattered old T-shirt and checked blue pyjamas that he'd picked up in Luz Corner for two hundred and fifty rupees. The bargain shop clothes were making him feel small when compared with his uniformed colleagues and subordinates.

Finally, after what felt like ages, Karthik arrived.

'So,' he said, sitting across him. 'Atif says that you were with him this morning.'

Rakesh didn't respond. Karthik nodded and continued. 'We called your wife, she confirmed that you were with her the entire time. You went to an engagement party yesterday but apart from that, you were home all day. Your father-in-law confirms the same.'

Rakesh shrugged. 'I told you I don't have anything to do with this. You've known this the whole time, I don't know why you're claiming otherwise.'

Karthik smirked. 'In case you forgot I was at my sister's wedding when this happened. I only know what you've allowed me to know.'

Rakesh leaned forward and whispered, 'I could say the same. People know only what their source decides to tell them.'

Karthik jerked his head back and stared hard at him. Rakesh continued, 'I agree that I am a little slow, but I'm not as dumb as you think I am.' He leaned back with as much swagger as he could manage in the rickety wooden chair. 'You know my alibi. I have investigated the case with you right by my side. I may have goofed up a few times, but that speaks more about my abilities as a cop than my character. You know what we found on Madhu's phone. I notice that you haven't reported it or done anything about it. And this despite a child being involved? It makes you the more suspicious person here.' Rakesh watched Karthik's reaction while glancing up at the camera recording this conversation. Karthik didn't react the way Rakesh expected, so he tried again. 'I wonder why that is. Perhaps you really are helping someone else . . . doing what you accused me of.'

Rakesh was the type of person who would yell first and think later. But he needed to get out of here as soon as possible if he was to have any chance of getting timely answers to where Mira was. He stood up. 'My hands are clean, Karthik. I get that you're trying to find a scapegoat. But maybe it's time for you to use your detection skills and find the real criminal instead. I'd ask you to think like a villain but then. . . . ' he trailed off.

Karthik didn't say anything. He clearly hadn't expected Rakesh to figure out what had been happening behind the scenes. He just sat there with his mouth opening and closing before finally standing up himself.

'I haven't finished . . .' he started.

But Rakesh stopped him. 'I was at a wedding the day after I was asked to take time off. It was someone related to my father-in-law. You know how many policemen there are in that family. All of them were present at the wedding. You can check with them to confirm my alibi. I was at home for the rest of the day. After that, I was with Atif. If you check the CCTV cameras that Mira's building secretary installed after the murder, I am sure you won't see me on it. Anything else?' he asked, turning around and walking out of the room.

No one stopped him.

89
Pooja

SHE PACED THE FLOOR WAITING FOR RAKESH to reply. He probably couldn't. It looked like he was going to be charged for helping Mira escape. The case was getting more limelight and Pooja was starting to panic. She felt ashamed for wanting to maintain a distance from it. She didn't know what she had expected from the podcast because, as usual, she hadn't thought things through. She gritted her teeth as she realised Sanjay was right. She really should have stuck to a podcast about the film industry. Maybe *Pani Puri with Pooja* like *Koffee with Karan*.

She looked up at the TV and saw the vehicle carrying Rakesh leave the police station premises. The cameras now turned towards the other policeman who had started an impromptu press conference.

'Inspector Rakesh came by to help us and share everything he has found out about the case so far,' he said, looking around to catch all the cameras. 'We appreciate him taking time away from a family function to help us.'

'Did she really run away?' 'Is she dead?'

The policeman held a hand up, waiting for the reporters to pause with their questions. 'We are looking at the case from all angles. As you know, the victim, Madhu, had a lot of debt and we believe that his widow was worried about staying alone with collectors banging on her door. We request that you cooperate with us while we investigate this matter.'

He quickly turned around and went back inside, ignoring all the questions that were being lobbed at him.

'Is he Rakesh's boss?' Pooja asked.

'No, his badge said sub-inspector. He seems to be Rakesh's subordinate,' Shalini said.

'Maybe we should interview this guy instead.' He seemed to believe in Mira's innocence. But the case looked like a wild goose chase. Maybe it would be better to shut down the podcast and go back home. Her phone pinged. Sanjay. 'Respond and stop being a fucking bitch.'

Then again, maybe here was better.

90
Inspector Rakesh

AS ATIF DROVE HIM HOME, RAKESH LOOKED back to find Karthik speaking with the mediapersons. 'Fuck,' he muttered, wondering what he was going to say to them now.

When he checked his phone he found a message from Pooja. 'Don't hesitate to let us know if we can help in any way.' He couldn't think about that right now.

'Sir,' Atif said, turning towards the street that led to his home. 'About Mira's attached bathroom . . .'

'You noticed,' Rakesh said. He didn't have to ask; he knew Atif would notice. He just hoped that Karthik had not.

'Maybe we are mistaken,' Atif said quickly. 'I saw it that day when we went looking for Madhu's second phone.'

'So did I.'

'But today it's gone. I checked the crime scene photos from earlier as you had asked. Unfortunately, the floor wasn't captured in them. So maybe she wasn't the one who moved the washing machine. Could have been one of us. Maybe we're wrong.'

'We are not,' Rakesh said, in a resigned tone. 'You saw the pictures on Madhu's phone. He was hitting her. And he had a lot of debt. He was trying to sell his daughter, for Christ's sake!' Rakesh shrugged when Atif didn't reply. 'There is no way she would've spared him.'

'But didn't that lawyer say something about a divorce?'

'He said he was advising her . . . but what if she decided on a different way?' Rakesh said out loud what he had been thinking for a while.

'So . . .' Atif said, hesitantly.

'So . . . I'm not in charge of the case anymore,' Rakesh said, taking a deep breath to steady his nerves. The thought of Mira being a murderer was not easy to digest. 'If the officer in charge noticed what we did, then let him do something about it.'

'But, sir . . .' They had almost reached Rakesh's house now. 'Before we reach home,' he said, pulling his phone out of his pocket. 'Those podcast people contacted me. Asking if I needed help.'

'What did you say?'

'I didn't reply.' Atif was looking down the street to make sure people hadn't gathered outside Rakesh's house. 'But it seems like they don't mean harm, right?' Rakesh continued.

'I would still say it's a better idea to ask the higher-ups for permission.'

'Fuck,' Rakesh said as they turned into his street. Atif slowed down and quickly reversed. There was a crowd of people outside Rakesh's house.

'What do I do?' Rakesh said.

'Aren't madam and sir there?' Atif said, referring to Bindhu and her father.

They were. So was Anthony. 'Let's go face the mob,' Rakesh said, looking down once again at his horrible clothes. He certainly looked like he'd been unceremoniously suspended.

As they neared his house, Rakesh could make out a shrill voice over the others'. 'Dei, Pradeep! Hi, da! I'm on TV!'

His stupid son was hanging on to the grille in the veranda, waving at the cameras facing his house. Bindhu was trying hard to peel him off it while his father-in-law yelled at the journalists in his booming voice, asking them to get lost.

As soon as his vehicle came into view, the crowd turned towards him.

'See you later, sir. Be careful,' Atif said as Rakesh forced his way out, covering his face with one hand and using the other to elbow through.

'Did you help Mira escape?' 'Where have you hidden her?' 'Inspector Rakesh, are you suspended or fired?' 'How does your wife feel about you openly helping your mistress?'

'Fuck off!' he yelled at the one who'd asked the last question. But the short man grinned at him as he moved his phone closer. He wasn't even a real journalist! Rakesh finally reached the building gate where his father-in-law stood.

'I have no comment. Please get the fuck away from my house,' Rakesh snapped, shutting the gate behind him, all propriety forgotten.

His father-in-law silently glared at him as he entered the house. 'Sorry for the delay,' Rakesh said, smiling and ignoring the tense atmosphere. Outside, the reporters were making various statements about his involvement in the case, not one of which was true. 'Atif dropped me,' he continued, kicking off his chappals.

He could hear Bindhu shouting at Anthony in the kitchen for the stunt he had just pulled. 'But, Ma, I'm on TV!' he whined, the sound followed by a loud thump. The boy ran out crying.

Rakesh peered into the kitchen, hoping to see a lunch plate waiting for him. But there was nothing. Bindhu was roasting something on the stove. He could smell the aroma of warm spices and masala. It was a Saturday; she was most likely getting things ready for a biryani dinner. His stomach growled at the thought of it. 'I'm going to be staying with Amma and Appa for a while,' she said, not looking at him.

'Okay?' he asked, looking at his in-laws who were still staring at him.

'What else can I do but go with them?' she said finally, turning to look at him. 'I cannot be humiliated like this. The police keep asking me for your alibi and news anchors are blaring that you've made a fool of yourself and me. What kind of nonsensical things have you been up to? And now people are hounding us outside our home! This place has become unsafe now.'

Rakesh didn't reply, and after staring at him for a couple of minutes, Bindhu turned back to the smoking stove, cursing and adding ingredients to the blender jar. Rakesh went to his son's room. The boy was on his phone again, shooting and yelling for some idiot to move faster. He had recovered quickly from the thrashing he had received, so Rakesh went back to the kitchen.

As he waited for Bindhu to continue berating him, his phone pinged.

'Atif,' he said, without being asked. Bindhu kept muttering to herself while stirring onions in the ghee and he caught a few phrases. 'Entire family of cops.' 'Shameful.' 'Embarrassing.' 'What did I do?'

Rakesh finally spoke. 'This was just routine questioning. Karthik wanted to know if I had any clue about Mira running away.'

Behind him, he heard Karthik's voice coming through the TV. 'We appreciate him taking time away from a family function to help us with this.' Karthik was standing at the top of the stairs of their police station and talking to the press. He breathed a sigh of relief. Seemed like Karthik had a conscience after all.

But Rakesh still couldn't tell anyone what he knew about the case. What if the people Madhu owed money to had taken Mira because they couldn't get the kid? What if they hurt her? He trusted only Atif. He checked the message Atif sent.

'Heard the podcast on the way back. Sounds like they're being fair. Ask commissioner sir and take the risk?'

Rakesh had decided that he would take the risk of speaking with Pooja. But he was still unsure if seeking the commissioner's permission was right for him. He sent a quick message to Pooja and put his phone back into his pocket.

91
Pooja

THIS TIME WHEN THE PHONE BUZZED, IT HAD finally brought some good news. 'Rakesh,' Shalini said.

'And?'

'And . . . yes! He has agreed to do the podcast!' she said. 'Let's not wait for him to change his mind. Call him right now.'

Pooja muted the TV and moved from the sofa to sit next to Shalini. She called Rakesh and turned on the speaker. But he disconnected the call and messaged immediately. 'Can't talk, people.'

'Whoa! Shit must be bad,' Shalini said, quickly asking him if tomorrow was a better day to call him.'

A few seconds later, he replied. 'Will call.'

'I don't think he's got permission from his superiors,' Shalini said. 'If he had, wouldn't this communication be more formal?'

'You're right. Maybe he's going rogue,' Pooja laughed. 'I like it.'

On TV, the clip of Rakesh telling the journalists to fuck off while his son yelled 'hello' to a friend called Pradeep played repeatedly while the anchor kept expressing outrage at the inspector's apparent disrespect.

92
Inspector Rakesh

IT HAD ALL BEEN ARRANGED IN A SINGLE DAY. After Bindhu and Anthony left with her parents, Rakesh finally called Pooja Reddy back.

After a couple of hours of negotiations, she had agreed to his request—to show him in a fair light and to air it after he sought permission. Now, two days later, he was sitting in her small apartment and waiting for the recording to start. He had decided that if questioned by superiors, he would say, 'Isn't it better for me to get my story out there so Bindhu and the department aren't humiliated any further?'

He had expected a set-up much larger than this room. The launch video had showed a white, beautifully decorated room, but this one looked nothing like that. They were in an old bedroom with a dismantled bed propped against a wall that was covered in black foam. Thick curtains hung on the windows and a carpet that wouldn't look odd in a hotel room in Shimla covered the floor.

He had wanted Atif to be there, but Atif was busy. Instead, Rakesh had decided to record the entire interview on his phone. It was better to have proof of what he'd said in case the edited version didn't show the full picture. Plus, one clause of their agreement was about Pooja sending him a copy of the edited episode before it was posted. That was one more thing he was happy about.

He had Googled her after their discussion on call and realised with a start that he had been talking, quite curtly, to a bona fide celebrity. He couldn't believe he hadn't recognised the heroine of one of D's movies! Granted it had been years ago, but as a fan, it was no excuse. He watched as she gathered a few sheets of paper in the living room and arranged them. She wasn't behaving like some of the snooty celebrities he'd seen. She actually seemed nice. Maybe she would show him in a good light afterall. Moreover, she had just gone through a scandal herself. She would know, better than others, how he felt.

'Shall we start?' Pooja asked, walking in with a takeaway cup of coffee. 'Sure,' he replied, grabbing a glass of water to clear his throat.

'Don't worry. We will uphold our part of the agreement. You have my word,' Pooja said. Behind her, Shalini nodded in agreement.

'Sure,' Rakesh said, getting an odd feeling in his stomach. He had never done this before, and this seemed like a crappy situation to start.

'We don't want accusations of breaking promises. We want to build a long-lasting platform here. So we won't go back on our word.' Shalini's reassuring words helped him feel relaxed for the first time since coming to this house.

Shalini must have noticed the difference in his body language and she beamed as she set the microphone in front of him and connected it to a laptop. 'All phones on silent, please,' she said as she fiddled with some controls before Pooja hit the record button.

'Inspector Rakesh, it is wonderful to have you here with us today! I have been dying to ask you about the case.'

'Thanks,' he said in a clipped tone, suddenly conscious of how his voice sounded. 'I am happy to be here.'

'This case is your first homicide investigation, am I right?' Pooja said. Rakesh thought her voice too cheery for the subject. 'Your name has been dragged through mud simply because you and the victim's wife went to the same school. How does it feel to listen to these rumours?'

Rakesh suddenly felt hot and tried to loosen his top button before remembering he was wearing a T-shirt. 'I . . . it is horrible, Pooja ma'am.' She put her hand up and whispered, her voice normal again, 'Just call me Pooja, ma'am sounds terribly old.'

'Sorry,' he said and continued, 'It is horrible. As a member of law enforcement, there is nothing we hate more than fake news. These WhatsApp forwards and random "news" sites put real journalists to shame.'

Pooja waved her hand at him, encouraging him to go on.

'Do you remember that story about two men who got lynched for child abduction a couple of years ago?' he asked.

'Yes, I do.'

'Turns out that a business rival made up the story and then it went viral.'

'Are you serious!' Pooja gasped. Rakesh could tell she was acting, and she was good.

'Yes! With one forward, he destroyed the lives of two innocent men. And the idiots who believed this message did that man's dirty work for him!'

'Oh my God!'

'People who believe such forwards are playing God with another person's life, and they don't even know it.'

'So, you're saying that you're disappointed with people who are engaging in this kind of discourse?' Pooja said. Rakesh blinked at her, not understanding what she had just said. Thankfully, Shalini had better instincts and clarified.

'Yes!' he said, smiling gratefully at her. 'Yes, everyone in our profession hates it when people believe such things even though there is no evidence. You see, this habit of forwarding "news" and videos without verifying them has made life very difficult for us cops. We cannot police the internet; people have to do it themselves. When you receive any controversial forward, go to the nearest police station and show it to them. They will take action if it is true!' he protested, trying to temper his rising voice.

'Thank you, Inspector,' Pooja said. 'Now about the case . . . I know it is an ongoing investigation, but can you tell me how the process works at your end? Mira, the murder victim's wife, called you directly, right? She didn't call 100.'

Rakesh nodded, before remembering that this was an audio format. 'Yes. Actually, she didn't call me. Her neighbour called my police station. Mira had shared my visiting card with them since they wanted to install a police booth on their street.' Rakesh had lied, but if he mentioned the reunion they'd bring up that picture and he didn't want to remind people of that.

'I'm sorry?'

'That building's residents felt their street wasn't safe and wanted a police booth there for security. They wanted to talk to someone so, I believe, she had shared my office landline number since she knew me from school. They called me, not Mira.'

'Got it. Is that a request you can process?'

'No, ma'am,' he said. 'It is a long process that requires approvals from many government officials. I am not in any sort of position to approve such requests. Someone much higher up than me needs to be involved.'

'But that is how they got your number?'

'Yes . . .'

'Tell us what happened next . . .'

Rakesh addressed every rumour that was being peddled about him, including the one about why he was staring at Mira in the picture taken at the reunion. 'I wasn't looking at her. I was calling another classmate to join us. He was sitting at the table some distance away.' It wasn't true either. This is the same lie he had told Bindhu and his colleagues. It was best to stick to it. He didn't give Pooja the name of this classmate, so she wouldn't be able to cross-check this statement.

Finally, after a couple of hours, the interview was over. Pooja thanked him and promised to send him a copy of the episode before they posted it. Before he left, Rakesh messaged Atif to tell him he was done with the interview.

93
Pooja

A DEBATE WAS RAGING ON ONE OF THE national TV channels about the role of the public and the media in Mira's escape. Shalini and Pooja watched, pens poised over their open books, ready to make a note of anything they thought was a good idea for an episode.

The numbers of the podcast had fluctuated. They had dropped after listeners realised that D wasn't going to be a part of the episodes. But after Mira had escaped, the number of downloads had increased tenfold. Pooja, who had been having doubts about what she was doing with this podcast, was now ecstatic about the new subscribers who had been sharing her podcast and tagging her on social media. It felt like listeners had faith in her and she didn't want to let them down.

Of course, there was no running away from trolls who believed that she was using Mira to plan Sanjay's murder. But she was slowly becoming immune to such comments. Pooja watched as the news anchor, a legitimate one, factually recounted the information in the case.

As soon as the replay of sub-inspector Karthik's statement to the press ended, Pooja and Shalini looked at each other.

'We should call him,' they said in unison. Shalini grabbed her phone and Pooja went back online to see what people were saying about the latest bit of news.

'What if the person who killed her husband came back for her?' 'There were no signs of a struggle. That means she ran away, right?' 'I know someone who works at the hospital Mira was admitted to. Her husband wasn't the good guy everyone says he was. He used to beat her up, it seems.' 'Women always claim domestic abuse when they don't get their way. It's like rape cases, all a fucking lie.'

Pooja closed her eyes, inhaling deeply before scrolling past that last comment to read the rest. The theme was pretty much the same. Some women supported Mira, most women and men abused her.

Shalini managed to get through to Karthik and was convincing him to speak with them. This guy was going to be a no-go. Shalini hung up, looking disappointed.

'Let's just go with the building blabbermouth. What do you say?' Pooja asked, looking at the list of potential interviewees she'd made last night.

'The one who gave that sound byte about Inspector Rakesh? Sure. I can go to her apartment when it's a bit less crowded,' Shalini replied.

'We . . .' Pooja replied, getting up. 'And let's go now.'

94
Inspector Rakesh

ON THE WAY BACK HOME AFTER HIS INTERVIEW, Rakesh called Atif and asked if it was possible for him to get a copy of anything new that they had discovered in the investigation since his suspension. He knew he shouldn't have made that request, that Atif would get into trouble for helping him. But he wasn't going to be on the sidelines of this case.

Later that evening, Atif turned up to meet Rakesh.

'I don't think there is anything new,' Atif said as soon as Rakesh walked out to meet him. 'Karthik sir is thinking of sending a picture of Mira to state borders and toll booths to see if they can catch her.'

'Does he think what we think?'

'No, I don't think he's noticed. Oh, another thing came up today,' Atif said as he and Rakesh walked around the building compound. 'One of the neighbours, the lady living opposite . . .'

'Mrs Krishnan . . .'

'Yes. She saw a suspicious-looking man coming up the stairs and looking at Mira's house. Her husband called the watchman and told him to leave.'

'Picture? Description?'

'We have a copy of the CCTV footage,' Atif grinned, 'I've sent you a screen grab.'

A couple walked by, and the woman recognised Rakesh. Whispering to her husband, they crossed the street and walked down the other side. Rakesh glared at them and turned back to Atif. 'Has anyone mentioned me?'

'No one has brought up your name since you left after the interrogation. Karthik sir seems . . .' he trailed off, '. . . he seems a bit upset.'

'Let me guess, he expected to capture the murderer and solve the case in one day?'

'He also seems to be angry at the turn the case has taken. They were unable to track down the number to which Madhu had sent messages about paying back the loan with pics of his kid. The company it was registered to has shut down. He was using a prepaid SIM and recharging it with cash. We have no way of finding out if he topped up the card at a store or through the company's website. The company owner is taking time to respond.'

'If the information becomes public, Karthik will be in more trouble than me for not solving this.'

'It will quieten down as soon as something else comes up.'

'By the way, did you guys check and see if Mira's daughter is with her grandparents or if she left with Mira?'

'She's missing too. But obviously Karthik and the others are keeping that information under wraps for now.'

Rakesh remembered the little girl in Madhu's childhood home. He had assumed her to be Mira's kid but later realised she wasn't. Mira had probably run away with her actual daughter to someplace safe. Rakesh had no more questions to ask. He was about to bid Atif a good night but the head constable stood there with his hands in his pockets, as if he wanted to say something.

'What is it?' Rakesh asked, looking around to make sure his neighbours weren't out in their balconies watching them.

'About the podcast,' Atif said, scratching his chin. 'I believe they also asked Karthik sir for an interview.'

Rakesh stiffened. He had assumed that Pooja and Shalini were on his side; they had said they were. Why were they interviewing that asshole then?! 'When?' he asked.

'Before I came here, I heard Karthik speaking to them over the phone. Her name is Shalini, right? He said, "Not right now, Shalini ma'am, no comment." Then he said he'd get back to them, I'm guessing he realised there was a celebrity involved,' Atif replied, not looking at Rakesh.

Rakesh was already deep in thought, unsure of what to do next.

Atif said his goodbyes and promised to keep Rakesh posted if Karthik agreed to be a part of the podcast.

95
Pooja

POOJA AND SHALINI REACHED MIRA'S BUILDING and were surprised to see people still hanging out near the gate, even though it had been two days since Mira ran away and there had been no new information since. Didn't people have jobs to go to? Lives to live? Pooja thought.

Pooja covered her head with a cap and got out of the car.

'I don't think this is a good idea,' Shalini said. 'People in Chennai might not recognise you easily, but the journalists will certainly know who you are.'

Pooja looked around for a way to get into the building and realised Shalini was right. She got back into the car and pushed her seat back. This may not be the right time, but Pooja was determined to get what they had come here for. 'Looks like we will be here for a while,' she said.

Shalini whipped out her phone and called someone. 'Hello,' she said after a while, 'Sir, Sunderesan sir, this is Shalini, I spoke to you earlier . . . Yes. Sir, I wanted to ask if I can interview the lady who said that the inspector was having an . . . No, sir, I'm not trying to cause trouble. Yes, I am aware of your age, sir . . . No, sir . . . okay, sorry,' she said and hung up.

'No go? Why are you smiling then?' Pooja asked.

'He said that I could not speak to Joslin madam,' she said, her grin getting bigger.

'Ah, we have her name,' Pooja replied, tapping the Facebook app on her phone. Joslin was bound to have an account. They found her in less than ten minutes. 'I feel like a stalker,' Pooja said, sharing the profile link with Shalini.

'I feel like a detective,' Shalini replied gleefully.

After messaging Joslin, they went to a coffee shop nearby, waiting for her to reply. The same old news about the murder case was playing on the muted TV in the coffee shop.

'Should we go back and try again?' Pooja asked, looking away as the ticker on the channel mentioned a minister whose son had caused a car crash running his next rally.

'I can send her a link to the last episode so she knows we're legit.'

'No,' Pooja said, straightening up as an idea hit her. 'Send her the link of the launch. The one where D spoke.'

'Yes!' Shalini replied, furiously tapping away at her phone. 'For someone like her, this approach works best.'

A few minutes later, Shalini's phone pinged. It was Joslin. She agreed to meet them but didn't commit to anything else. Pooja and Shalini quickly paid the bill and drove to the building. The crowd had thinned, but they still waited for half an hour before going in.

'How did you find out my name? The channel didn't say anything,' Joslin asked as soon as she let them in. After they settled down, she kept glancing at Pooja from the corner of her eye, making her uncomfortable.

'It's my job to do that,' Shalini answered mysteriously. 'We wanted to ask you about the news clip that played a while back.'

'Oh God, I hate that. I looked horrible in it. Right?' Joslin asked. 'Look at me now. Don't you think they made me look bad on purpose?'

Joslin had dressed up to meet them. Her eyeliner and the too-light powder looked like they had been freshly applied and that glittery zari-covered outfit was not something people usually wore at home. Pooja took in the apartment. It was relatively clean. Behind her one of the bedroom doors was shut. It's probably where Joslin had dumped all her mess before letting them in.

'Yes, without proper lighting everyone looks bad,' Pooja replied, smiling at her.

'But you look nicer in real life,' Joslin said. Then she looked her up and down and asked, 'Have you gained some weight?'

Pooja grimaced.

'Anyway,' Shalini interrupted in a hurry, 'I was wondering how you came to that conclusion about the inspector having an affair with Mira.'

'What . . . oh yes. That other guy said it. Karthik. I overheard him when he was here to collect evidence,' Joslin said, waving dismissively. 'And now everyone believes that the crowd outside is my fault.'

It is, Pooja thought, but she nodded. Shalini continued, 'Okay, so the one in charge of the case now said that Rakesh and Mira were a couple and he helped her . . .'

'No, no,' Joslin shook her head. 'Wait, I will tell you exactly what he said.'

Scrunching up her eyes, she made a humming noise and then smiled. 'I think I heard him say, "Yes, they know each other but all this much romance is too much!" Or something like that,' Joslin said, grinning triumphantly.

'Wow, your memory is sharp,' Pooja remarked dryly.

'Thanks. I am known for remembering stuff like that,' she smiled, missing the sarcasm in Pooja's tone.

As they continued talking to her, it was obvious to both Pooja and Shalini that Joslin knew more about everything going on in the building than the other neighbours. She reminded Pooja of her mother-in-law. It made her dislike Joslin even more.

Joslin and Mira shared the same help, Divya, till she had been fired a few months ago. Their kids also went to the same school. Joslin shared that Madhu would beat up his wife every time he had a drink. 'Divya has so much to say about what goes on in that house. Madhu was useless! Mira must have been a rotten politician in her previous life to deserve this sorry excuse of a husband in this one.'

Pooja smiled and asked for Divya's number.

'Of course,' Joslin said. Pooja was glad they got something and got up to leave when Joslin asked, 'By the way, can you tell me what really happened between you and D? Does he really have abs like that? It's all Photoshop, right?'

96
Inspector Rakesh

RAKESH SAT ON THE FLOOR OF THE LIVING room of his empty house and went through the call list from Madhu's secret mobile phone. He was checking to see if any of the numbers overlapped with those on the phone he used more often. Rakesh smiled when he saw one common number. 'Got you!' he mumbled as he circled it, saving the number in a password-protected note on his phone.

The rest of the report had nothing new apart from what he had already added. The only change was the terminology used to describe Mira's current status. Absconding. He then flipped through the CCTV camera pictures taken around Mira's disappearance and noticed a grainy face staring up at the building. The man had been caught on two cameras that faced the front of the building.

Then he noticed another image, one of Mira walking out of the building with nothing in her hands. Since the cameras were facing the entrance, you couldn't see her face. But he could tell that it was her. He noted the time stamp. He was at the engagement party at that time. Karthik had had no option but to let him go.

97
Pooja

EVEN THE PROMISE OF ONE MONTH'S WAGES had not tempted Divya, the help who'd worked at Mira's house, to speak with them. So, they decided to follow up with Mrs Krishnan instead, as Joslin suggested. She even accompanied them to Mrs Krishnan's house.

Mrs Krishnan was a rotund, happy-looking person who was definitely unhappy to see them. She was about to shut the door on them, but Joslin stopped her and convinced her to let them in. She fidgeted a little with the sari, probably wondering if she could speak to them outside her house. But she glanced at the staircase and opened the door.

Pooja introduced herself and sat on the sofa she had been directed to. 'This is my colleague Shalini. Joslin told us that you helped Mira that horrible day.'

The woman's face fell. She got up to fetch them water but ran into the bedroom instead and shut the door behind her. A few moments later, a chubby face peeped out and vanished as soon as Pooja smiled at it. 'I can hear them whispering,' Shalini whispered.

Joslin smiled uncomfortably at them, embarrassed by Mrs Krishnan's behaviour, before going in to speak to her.

Finally, a man, presumably Mr Krishnan, came out the room followed by the two women. 'We just wanted . . .' Shalini started, but the man shook his head.

'We won't give interview and all,' he said sternly. 'Pictures of us have been plastered on various social media sites just for standing next to Mira at my son's birthday party. And now news channels have carried them too.'

'You don't know what it's like for people like us,' Mrs Krishnan added.

'This is not a regular interview . . .' Pooja interrupted. 'It is a podcast. We aren't going to question you. We just want to know about Mira. And maybe you can be a sort of character witness for her. For the public to know that she's not a crazy person.'

'You said that picture was taken at a party? The one that had been posted,' Shalini said hurriedly, not wanting to waste time. 'Some people had commented on the picture, saying an incident had happened at the party. We won't release any recordings without your permission. People won't even know your name.'

Mrs Krishnan looked at her husband for approval and he nodded. 'Mira was helping me in the kitchen. I made cheese and cucumber sandwiches for the party, like they showed in *Femina* magazine, and she was helping me remove the crust and cut the sandwiches into small triangles,' Mrs Krishnan was now speaking faster, stumbling over her words in a panic.

'It happened when we were eating. The party was in full swing in this living room. The door was open, and everyone from the building was coming and going, so I didn't see Madhu enter. But we could smell him. He was still in his office clothes; he didn't even bother changing even though his clothes were sweaty and smelly. I could smell alcohol all over him.'

'Oh God. At a children's party?' Pooja exclaimed.

'Yes! That too when his own child was present. Can you believe it!' Mrs Krishnan cried. 'My husband noticed and came over. He grabbed Madhu's hand and took him to one of the bedrooms. See, we are a middle-class family, we don't drink during children's parties. Only rich families do those kinds of things.' She looked at Pooja sharply when she said that.

'We don't do that either, madam!' Pooja replied, affronted. 'No one drinks at children's parties.' She was lying, of course. Sanjay did drink. But he wasn't violent. *You're lying* . . . a little voice in her head said. She pushed it away and concentrated on Mrs Krishnan.

'See! Even rich people don't do it. Mira was in the bathroom or the kitchen, I think. When she joined us in the living room, I told her that Madhu was here and that he had probably attended another party before coming here. She understood, and her face changed completely. She kept apologising. Then she pulled him out of the spare room and towards the door. But he didn't want to go. Madhu clapped and sang along with the song that was playing for the musical chairs game. Everyone was staring at him, but he didn't notice. My son later asked me if we sent Madhu uncle away for being a bad singer.'

Pooja laughed and Mrs Krishnan gave them a weak smile. 'He is an innocent boy. Anyway, she pulled him away, but he didn't move. He started shouting at her about how he wasn't troubling anyone. My husband and a few others, I think Mr Subramaniam and that Sharma boy from downstairs, finally dragged him outside. Joslin and I brought out the cake to distract the children.' She finished and took a deep breath.

'What happened next?' Pooja asked as soon as she was done.

Joslin jumped in. 'He slapped Mira. Right in front of us. She didn't even react, just continued trying to get him into their house. She told him to go inside and rest; not once did she say that he shouldn't embarrass her. She said, "Madhu, you look tired. Maybe you should eat and take a nap. Priyanka and I will come home in ten minutes." He looked at all of us and slapped her again.'

'Did she slap him back? What did he do next?' Shalini asked.

Mrs Krishnan shook her head while Joslin rolled her eyes. 'He struggled with the key and couldn't even open the door. That's how drunk he was. That Sharma boy took the keys from him and said, "It is dark, Uncle, I will help." Madhu didn't even thank him, just slammed the door behind him with the keys still in the lock.'

Joslin continued, 'Mira stared at all of us for a moment before saying it was late and it was time to go home. She took Priyanka's hand, wished my son a happy birthday again and left. Her face kept getting redder by the minute.'

When Pooja and Shalini left, they had two hours' worth of recordings. They promised, as usual, to send it over to the Krishnans before releasing it. Shalini was fuming the entire way home.

98
Inspector Rakesh

AFTER LEARNING ABOUT POOJA AND SHALINI'S intention to interview Karthik, Rakesh had to know what they were up to. He changed out of his lungi, grabbed his phone mid-charge and left home.

The two of them left Pooja's home early. He followed them to a café and waited on the corner of the street. If he went any closer, they would spot him. Shalini, the one who looked like she was a social worker, came out twice to buy cigarettes. Two of the twenty packs! He watched her in amazement. How much did she smoke in a day! That would certainly explain her raspy voice.

Half an hour of waiting and walking up and down the street later, they emerged, putting on their sunglasses and waving their hands in front of their faces as if the four seconds they'd spent out in the sun was too much. He looked down at his almost drenched shirt and grumbled.

They parked outside Mira's apartment and Rakesh, panicking, stopped one street away. He didn't need any new rumours. After waiting for two hours and drinking twelve cups of tea, he saw their car pass by to the main road and got on his bike.

Following them back, a safe distance away, he noticed another guy following him. He was a short, rotund guy whose stomach was large enough to rest on the basket of the scooter he was riding. Pooja and Shalini parked the car next to the gate of Pooja's building and went in. The guy stopped in front of the next building, typed something into his phone and rode away in a different direction.

He was becoming paranoid, Rakesh realised. Just because the man was on the same street as him didn't mean he was being followed. Sighing in relief, he made himself comfortable in front of a tyre puncture shop, which was diagonally opposite the window of Pooja's house.

Half an hour later, the puncture guy clicked his tongue. 'Sir?' the puncture shop guy said. 'SIR!'

'Yes?' he asked, focused on Shalini who had just come out to the balcony to smoke. 'Sir, can you please move so my customers can see my shop?'

He was about to yell at the guy for his audacity when Rakesh realised he wasn't wearing his uniform. He felt powerless without it. Rakesh apologised and walked to a tea shop, asking for a cup of piping hot tea and angling himself so he could see the building door on the mirrored sign behind the shop.

Nothing happened the rest of the day and he was about to throw in the towel when he spotted a man he thought he recognised. He struggled to remember the balding man, but couldn't quite place him. He stopped outside Pooja's building and spoke to the fat guy who magically reappeared. They looked up at the building and exchanged a few words. So he wasn't paranoid after all. They had been following him, or rather Pooja and Shalini. They hadn't noticed his presence.

He watched as one of the men pointed a finger at the building. Rakesh was sure he was counting windows, trying to figure out which one belonged to Pooja.

The balding man wiped his face with a handkerchief and put it back in his pocket. An old man stepped out of the house and asked him something. Rakesh was too far back to hear. So he moved closer, pulling out his phone and pretending he was reading something on it.

'Mr who?' the old man asked.

'Mr Pratik?' the man said, pointing at his phone.

'There is no Pratik staying here, sir. That house belongs to someone else.'

'Who?'

'How is that your business?' the old man asked, drawing himself up. 'Why do you want to know?'

'No, I thought maybe it belonged to Pratik's wife.'

'It does not,' the old man snapped and crossed his arms.

The man apologised, thanked him, and quickly walked away. Rakesh abandoned his post at the tea shop and followed the man around the corner where he took a left turn. Rakesh kept his head down and watched as the balding man got on to a bike parked in one of the side streets. Quickly typing down the bike's number on his phone, Rakesh sent it to Atif to check before making his way back to his spot.

When he came back, Pooja was peering out at the street from the kitchen balcony. The old man must have informed her about a suspicious man asking questions about her house. Rakesh crossed the street again and waited for her to go back in. Once he was sure she had shut the balcony door, he got on his bike and got the hell out of there.

99
Pooja

SHE HAD SPOTTED THE MAN AS THEY WERE driving back from the café. Her last encounter with the paparazzi had made her hyper aware and she knew the exact moment the short man started following them to the café and back home.

Pooja didn't mention anything to Shalini till they were inside her building. But as soon as she shut the gate behind her, she called the watchman.

'There's a man following us,' she told him, gesturing over her shoulder. 'He followed us to the restaurant too.'

Shalini was shocked and wanted to confront him but Pooja stopped her. She quickly described how the man looked to the watchman, who nodded and told them to wait inside.

The watchman was now an old man, but he had been there since she was a kid. She trusted him to keep an eye out for her as if she were his own daughter.

'How the fuck did you notice that? I was right next to you!' Shalini protested.

'I was driving; saw him too many times in the rearview mirror,' Pooja said, tossing her handbag on the sofa and double-locking the door behind her. She noticed him minutes after they left, but when he didn't park at the café, she had relaxed. But then she saw him on the way back and realised he was indeed following them.

It was probably Sanjay's little trick—get her followed to make sure she wasn't planning a divorce. This latest stunt was too much and she mumbled her herself, 'Why hire someone so incompetent to keep track of her!'

Shalini drew the curtains a crack and looked outside.

'Don't worry,' Pooja said, noticing her worried expression. 'It's my husband.'

'Your husband?' Shalini asked, shutting the curtain again.

'Yep,' Pooja said, turning on the laptop. 'I have been ignoring him for a while now. He has probably sent someone to make sure I'm not visiting divorce lawyers. Shall we finish editing Rakesh's episode?'

Shalini stood there for a bit as if she wanted to say something, then changed her mind and walked to the table with the laptop.

100
Inspector Rakesh

HE FOLLOWED THE MAN FROM A SAFE DISTANCE. He was now riding down Mira's street, looking up at the building. Suddenly Rakesh remembered.

He had seen the man just last night in the file that Atif had given him. In the screengrab of the CCTV footage.

He seemed to be patrolling areas that had something to do with Mira.

As they drove by, the man looked up at the building again and then across the street at the autorickshaw stand. 'Do they know?' Rakesh wondered as the helmet and Chennai heat made a line of sweat run off his nose. He turned left at the end of the road and stopped at an ATM. Rakesh rode past him and parked in front of a shop, getting off to buy a cigarette. The man got back on his bike just as Rakesh finished his transaction with the vendor. Sticking the change and the cigarette into his pocket, Rakesh jumped on his bike and started following the man again.

The man's final destination seemed to be a local bar. The same one where Madhu had had a fight. The owner had promised to send over the CCTV footage of the fight. Rakesh wondered if Karthik had followed up. He made a mental note to tell Atif to do so in case Karthik hadn't.

Rakesh walked by the bar, trying to catch a glimpse of the man, but the crowd outside didn't allow for much room. If Rakesh wanted to know what was happening, he would have to go in, but he couldn't do that right now.

He called Atif and was met with a busy tone. Instead of waiting for Atif to call back, he quickly opened the browser on his phone and checked if there had been any update with the case. There was nothing new except for a post from the podcast's social media page: 'An exclusive interview you wouldn't want to miss. Coming soon.'

He felt guilty about stalking Pooja and Shalini when he still wasn't sure he could trust them. They had, after all, called Karthik immediately after he had finished his interview with them. It was only natural for them to want more than one perspective. But everyone was currently believing Karthik's version of the events. Why couldn't people realise that Karthik's version was riddled with half-truths.

Sighing, Rakesh started his bike and rode home.

101
Pooja

IT WAS EVENING BY THE TIME THEY FINISHED editing, and Shalini sent a quick text to Rakesh, informing him that the episode was ready for him to listen to. Pooja had peeped out of the window regularly to spot the man again. But she could only see up to the big tree on the side of the building's entrance from her living room window. Now that it was dark, she could barely spot anyone. But she didn't want to step out into the balcony where she could be seen.

The busy day hadn't reduced her anger towards Sanjay. She waited for Shalini to leave before looking at her phone. She had ignored calls from Sanjay all day, but this time there were no angry messages.

She didn't want to give him the satisfaction of her calling him back. So she turned the laptop on and got back to work. The hastily designed Canva cover flashed before her as she checked their stats.

The podcast had gained even more traction now. In just one day, more people had Googled their podcast than all the other days combined. Shalini's SEO skills had really come to their rescue. That girl deserved more than Pooja could pay her right now, she sighed.

Her phone rang just as she started reading the comments on their Twitter page. She ignored it at first, recognising the ringtone. But when it rang for the third time, Pooja gave in.

'Yes?' she said as Sanjay's grinning face popped up on the video call.

'Oh shit, you're busy, aren't you?' Sanjay said, sounding artificially cheerful. It was the same tone he used in interviews.

'Very,' she replied, trying to sound less annoyed. She could hear the thump of electronic music in the background. Sanjay was at the club, but in a private room. 'We just finished editing a rather exciting interview. You're out?'

'I am. We are here to celebrate the successful launch of Ashish's new book. You know, I am trying to get the script rights for it.'

So, that's why he'd called her. He hadn't read a single one of Ashish's books. But she had read them all. 'My wife is a bigger fan than I am,' he said loudly, clearly for the benefit of others in the room with him.

Sanjay passed on the phone to Ashish, who reluctantly took it. She had met him a few times and knew that he hated the club scene. If Sanjay thought this was going to get Ashish to sell him the rights for his new book, he was going to be disappointed. Grinning at that thought, Pooja said, 'I'm surprised to see you agreed to a night out, Ashish. I thought you preferred staying at home.'

'I do. But your husband wouldn't take no for an answer,' Ashish said, laughing along. Behind him, Sanjay's face dropped. 'I heard about the podcast. Congratulations!'

'You'll have to give it a listen, I'll let you go back to your party,' she said smiling, then quickly hung up saying she was getting another call. Let Sanjay deal with this himself.

He called back an hour later at 2.00 a.m. and she gleefully answered.

'Why the fuck didn't you tell me he hated partying!' Sanjay hissed into the phone.

'First, I would have to know what you were up to, wouldn't I? Unlike you, I can't hire an investigator. And second, I have told you this multiple times.'

'No, you haven't!' he snapped back.

'Well, I had told you some time ago that I invited Ashish to join us for an evening out. But he declined, saying he didn't enjoy partying. And another time, when you had organised that launch party and asked me to invite my smart friends, especially Ashish, I had told you he didn't like going to loud and crowded places, especially at night. If you listened to anything I have to say, you'd know,' Pooja paused, happy that she'd stumped Sanjay. 'Anyway, now that you've woken me up, I think I'll get some work done.'

She hung up before he could protest. It was 2.15 a.m. She wouldn't be able to get to sleep now. She went through her notifications and noticed that more people had subscribed to the podcast from the US where it was daytime. Shalini had noticed this recent uptake in numbers and messaged her.

Pooja wasn't happy about this new development. She had only planned the podcast for an Indian audience because she wanted to be more than a one-film wonder, or Sanjay's wife, or rather Sanjay's ex-wife who got caught having an affair and lost both men.

Thankfully, the international position of their podcast wasn't high yet. 'This gives me time,' Pooja thought, putting her phone away.

Time for what? Pooja hadn't yet decided. It either gave her time to shut down the podcast prematurely or to make it the best thing she'd ever done. She would decide soon.

102
Inspector Rakesh

RAKESH WOKE UP THE NEXT DAY TO A MESSAGE from Shalini: 'Episode ready, come anytime. Call first.'

He told her he would meet them after breakfast. Then he checked Facebook, hoping that Mira had not deleted her account. But she had. Gone too was her profile on WhatsApp. When he typed in her number, it said the contact wasn't using the app and instead gave him the option to invite her. He got up and started pacing the room, wondering what to do next. Just then he got a text from Atif. 'Sir, I'm here.' Rakesh had sent Atif the grainy picture he had taken of the bar, the stalker's vehicle number and a side profile picture he had managed to capture at a traffic signal.

Rakesh let him in after making sure there were no journalists outside.

Atif pulled out a USB drive. 'It is the same bar. The vehicle is registered to a man called Kumar. Everything is in there.'

'Thanks. Do you have any idea why he was following them?' Rakesh asked.

'No, sir. I . . .'

'Why didn't you just send me all this via the phone?' he asked.

'Well, sir. I don't want any problems in case . . . No trail. Now if I am caught, I can just say I came to see you.'

Smart guy, Rakesh thought.

'Thanks, man. I will always appreciate this,' Rakesh said. Atif opened his mouth to say something, but seemed to change his mind. 'Th . . . Okay, sir,' he said instead and turned to leave.

'Want some coffee?' Rakesh asked, awkwardly, unsure if he was being ill-mannered.

'You made it?' Atif asked, raising an eyebrow. 'Well, yeah. I mean, Bindhu isn't here . . .'

'I'm good, sir. Next time I'll bring a flask from our tea shop,' Atif said, walking towards the door.

Rakesh ran to the bathroom to get ready to meet Shalini.

As he waited for the bucket to fill up, he looked at the files. Atif had included the CCTV footage of the fight Madhu had got into at the bar. One of the files was Kumar's picture. But he wasn't either of the men who had followed Pooja the previous day.

Rakesh scanned the remaining files. A name, Kumar, jumped out at him. It was the guy Madhu had regularly messaged. Was it the same Kumar who owned the bike that was used to follow Pooja?

Rakesh would have to check that. He stepped into the bathroom to turn off the tap. He should be getting ready to leave, but Atif had given him too much information. He clicked on the next folder and went through the CCTV footage of the fight.

The bar was a crowded place, but as the night wore on the patrons started leaving. Just past 1.00 a.m., Rakesh saw Madhu turning to the waiter and yelling at him while kicking his chair behind. The chair hit another customer who jumped up and grabbed Madhu. Soon, two guys, presumably his friends, tried pulling Madhu away. The other man's friends were doing the same thing with him. Only ten seconds were left and so far nothing had stood out. Suddenly, Rakesh realised something.

Going back a few seconds, he played the video again. The camera didn't cover one corner of the bar. It was focused completely on Madhu. Obviously, that's the footage they had asked for. But before Madhu's friends came to stop him, he saw a hand move into the frame from the corner of the bar and point at Madhu. He played it frame by frame, slowing it down as much as he could. One of Madhu's friends who had pulled him back from hitting the bar's cleaner was the bald man he had seen outside Pooja's apartment. The one who had driven down Mira's street the previous day and the one who was on the CCTV camera of Mira's building as he was loitering around.

Fuck!

103
Pooja

IT WAS MID-AFTERNOON BY THE TIME RAKESH finished listening to his episode. He requested a couple of corrections, which Pooja agreed to, and then asked if the episode could be emailed to, him before they uploaded it. 'Just to have a copy,' he said. Pooja smiled and agreed while Shalini looked disgruntled as she sat down to make the edits.

'Thank you for this,' Pooja said as he was leaving. 'It means a lot, and it will really help in getting the word out. Our listener count is increasing by a lot each day, and while we don't have the viewership of a prime-time news channel, we can definitely help in clearing your name.'

'Um . . .' Rakesh said, 'Are you planning on interviewing anyone else from the police station?'

So he had got word then, Pooja thought. 'We were planning to. But we aren't sure what to do now. We may have to stop the podcast.'

'Why?' he asked.

'Well, with Mira gone, we have no way of getting anything. The case has got too big for us to cover. We started with wanting to help her. But now . . .'

'It's probably for the best. You don't want problems,' Rakesh said instinctively, glancing at the street outside. Pooja noticed and stiffened. Did he know that someone was following them?

'We will keep you posted. We might do a few more interviews before we end this,' she smiled as she watched Rakesh leave.

As soon as she shut the door, Pooja went to window that faced the street and looked at him. Rakesh got onto the bike, but before he put on his helmet, he glanced up and down the street, as if he was looking for someone.

He looked wary.

'Um . . . I think we might be in trouble,' Pooja said, looking around at Shalini.

104
Inspector Rakesh

THE MAN WAS AROUND TODAY TOO. HE STOOD in the same spot from where Rakesh had observed Pooja's house the previous day. He rode off down the street, but took a turn and came back the other way. The man was still facing the direction in which he'd gone. When Rakesh was sure he wasn't being watched, he called Shalini's number.

'Hello,' Shalini answered, her voice cracking with a typical smoker's gruffness.

'Listen. I don't . . . I need to tell you something. Can you put Pooja ma'am on the phone?'

A few moments later, Pooja came on the call. 'Yes, Inspector. Is there a problem with the email?'

'No, I . . . haven't checked. I'm not calling about that,' he said, realising that the man hadn't noticed him thanks to his helmet. He was now looking bored, yawning and wiping the sweat off his face with a handkerchief while doing something on his phone. He still occasionally glanced up at Pooja's house.

'Come to the balcony, please. Make sure you aren't seen. There's a man . . .'

'A man who has come around asking about my house and other things?' she asked.

'Yes . . . he is here right now, wearing a grey, striped shirt, brown pants and black sandals. He is kind of balding and has a bit of a tummy,' Rakesh said. From where he was standing, Rakesh could see the man but not Pooja. It was obvious that she had come down though because the man spotted her and quickly ducked behind the tree next to him. He hadn't been obvious before, but now he clearly was.

'The one who . . .' she started, and Rakesh finished, '. . . hid behind the tree just now like a fucking idiot? Yes.'

Pooja laughed at his comment. 'Clearly, he isn't a professional. So what about him?' She must have gone back inside because the man came back out of his hiding place.

'He is connected to the case.'

'How?'

Rakesh hesitated. He couldn't say, could he? He was no longer in charge . . . but she made the decision for him.

'You can't say. Got it. Should I be worried?'

'Considering we know nothing about him, yes. It's better to be safe.'

'Thank you, Inspector,' she said, sounding like she meant it. It made him feel as if the effort and the stress of the last two days had been worth it. Rakesh started his bike again and drove home.

105
Pooja

SHE HADN'T EXPECTED THE INSPECTOR TO call. 'It's his hero complex,' Shalini said when she told her about it. 'He definitely suffers from a hero complex when it comes to Mira. And now he seems to have it with the two of us.'

'Maybe he's just a womaniser,' Pooja said, checking again to see if the stalker was still around.

'He looks like he couldn't get a woman to notice him if he tried,' Shalini replied, grabbing a slice of pizza that they had ordered some time ago.

The two of them were looking for another person to interview after they released the episodes featuring Joslin, Mrs Krishnan and Rakesh over the next two weeks. Pooja still hadn't decided if she wanted to keep the podcast going. If she did shut it down, where would she go? She couldn't stay here, not with that guy stalking her. Sanjay hadn't called since last night. It had only been a day, but he usually kept annoying her till she answered. Now that she knew it wasn't Sanjay who had hired someone to follow her, she wondered if he really was taking her silence seriously.

'Whoaaa,' Shalini said, putting her half-eaten slice back and sliding over.

'What?'

'Remember how you told me that we should stay the fuck away from Joslin because she's a gossip monger who tattles on everyone?'

'I'm guessing you didn't listen?'

'Obviously not. And she tattled,' Shalini said, triumphantly grinning and showing Pooja the phone.

Pooja adjusted her glasses and took it.

'I can get you his autograph for sure, tell me,' she read Shalini's message to Joslin.

'Whose autograph are you promising her?' Pooja asked her.

'D's,' Shalini said. Pooja rolled her eyes and continued reading Joslin's reply. 'No one knows, except our flat. But the watchman told us that she pawned some stuff and that she ran off with the money.'

'Any idea where?'

'It is a pawnshop nearby; I'll send you the address. You won't believe the kind of people who go there.'

'What kind of people?' Pooja asked. Joslin was still typing and Shalini took her phone back.

'That doesn't matter. I'll go. Also, I'm going to need D's autograph to give to this woman,' she said, going back to her pizza and refusing to look at Pooja.

'I'll come with you. Since I'm the one paying for this bloody information,' Pooja sighed as she got up to accompany Shalini to the pawnshop.

∽

'Hello. Yes.' The oily little man smiled, looking them both up and down. Neither Pooja nor Shalini was wearing any jewellery and as soon as he registered that, his eyes slid over to their handbags.

'We aren't here to pawn anything,' Shalini said dryly.

'Yes, sorry,' Pooja added, flashing him her brilliant red-carpet smile. 'I'm here for a bit of information. I am sure the police have already asked you, but have you heard of Mira?' She fished out her phone to show him Mira's picture, but she didn't need to. The grin slid off his face at the very mention of that name.

'I hate that woman!' he said. 'I have had lots of trouble, madam. I run a pawnshop. So many people come here with stolen things, but I have no problems once I report them to the police. But this woman, who only sold her own things to me, has brought more trouble than all these thieves combined.'

'What kind of trouble?' Pooja asked, pulling the worn-out metal stool towards her.

He shook his head, 'Sorry, madam, I don't want more problems than I already have,' he said.

Pooja smiled at him again. 'Sir, I'm not the police,' she said, putting on her fake smile again. 'I am just someone looking for information. See, we have this show, a podcast.'

'Yes, a radio show,' Shalini interjected. 'It's about true crime and it has been launched by some big people.'

'Yes,' Pooja continued. 'We are writing about this case for the show. And it will be very interesting if we know what happened here. It's a small but very important missing piece.'

'Big people?' the man asked, his expression eager.

'Yes, it was launched by D,' Shalini said, completely missing the glare Pooja gave her.

'D? Superstar D? *Aaja Nacho Nacho* D?' he asked, moving his hips around in a very poor imitation of D's exceptional dancing skills.

'Yes. D.'

Then his face cleared with recognition, 'Ah, madam, you are Pooja Reddy, correct?' She felt the smile slip away and she got up from the stool. 'Sorry for wasting your time,' she said.

'No, no, madam, I will tell you everything,' he said, the smile on his face lascivious. But Pooja shook her head, 'No, sir, it's okay. Thank you.'

Then she turned to Shalini and said, 'I have to get something else done, I'll see you tomorrow.'

She briskly walked towards her car. The way the man had looked was utterly disgusting. It was probably how other people looked at her as well these days—like she was a piece of meat. She kept her head down till she reached the safe confines of her vehicle.

106
Inspector Rakesh

INSTEAD OF FEELING DREAD, FOR THE FIRST time in weeks, Rakesh woke up with a strange sense of calm. He had listened to the podcast file with Atif last night, and it felt as if a load had been lifted off his shoulders. His version of events, the truth, was finally going to be out there.

He forced himself out of bed and checked the time. It was 7.40 a.m. He would get ready and check if that man was still stalking Pooja and Shalini. The picture on the bike registration Atif had sent over didn't match either man from the previous day. But Rakesh was sure he had seen this third guy somewhere too. He wasn't sure where, maybe in a recent past case. He would have to find out.

He checked his phone to see if Atif had a lead about the mystery man. Pooja and Shalini, however, had messaged, informing him that the episode would be up at seven that evening. That was it. There were no messages or calls from people asking him for bytes or sending him news about himself.

He heaved a sigh of relief and went to the living room.

As he ate a slice of bread that was both burnt and cold at the same time, he wondered if he ought to give Bindhu a heads-up about the podcast. People were bound to start hounding him when it released. But he changed his mind. She would only yell at him, and his father-in-law might try to stop the release. Instead, he drank a cup of the instant coffee Atif had dropped off and made his way to Pooja's street. He parked down the road this time, ensuring he wasn't parking in the same spot twice.

He was just about to get himself a cup of tea and settle down when a familiar raspy voice called him. 'Well, well. Looks like we have our own special bodyguard. Nice to see you, Inspector Rakesh.'

107
Pooja

SHALINI HAD CALLED AND MESSAGED HER multiple times after she left the pawnshop. She had ignored all of them. Shalini hadn't thought of her privacy when she kept dropping D's name. And why would she? She probably just thought the mention of a big actor might loosen the guy's tongue. After all, her one movie had released ages ago and only hardcore Bollywood fans would remember her. Also, they were in Chennai, a place that didn't care about Bollywood gossip. But it still annoyed her that one more person recognised her. Shalini had messaged this morning, telling her that she would come over and that 'No one but you cares about this.'

The disgusting messages Pooja received on Instagram almost every day would show otherwise. Nevertheless, she prepared herself for Shalini's arrival. They did have an episode to record.

Shalini came half an hour later and she had brought the inspector with her. 'Oh,' Pooja said, opening the door and looking him up and down.

'Yes, sorry,' Shalini said. 'I bumped into him at the tea shop outside. It seems he was spying on us.'

'Spying on us?'

'Sorry,' Rakesh said, not quite meeting her eyes, 'I didn't mean to . . .'

'Get caught?'

'I was just keeping an eye on you. Considering . . .'

'Considering your hero complex?' Pooja said. Even as the words left her mouth, she felt their venom. She shut her eyes tightly. 'Sorry,' she said after a beat, moving aside to let them in. 'I'm in a bad mood . . .'

Shalini poked Rakesh's back with her phone and he reluctantly slipped off his shoes. Once the door was firmly shut, Shalini looked at the two of them excitedly.

'Well?' Pooja said, her irritation with Shalini forgotten.

'Well . . . yesterday even after you left the man continued to be chatty,' she said, tossing her jute bag on the sofa. 'He seemed thrilled that he would be featured on a radio show hosted by the famous Pooja Reddy, D's girlfr—'

Pooja looked at Shalini sharply.

'. . . girlfriend in that one movie,' Shalini finished lamely. 'Anyway, he agreed to let me record him.' She pulled out her laptop and turned it on as they listened.

As they waited for Windows to finish installing its updates, Pooja offered the two of them chai. Shalini accepted and Rakesh refused, saying he just had coffee at the shop outside.

She brought out two cups and got ready to listen.

The beginning of the recording was a bit grainy. 'Sir, you said you've had more trouble than it's worth, right? Can you elaborate?' Shalini asked him in Hindi.

'Yes, see, first the police came. That inspector. He had so many questions for me and I obviously cooperated. Then two days after he left, another man came. He said he was from Mira's husband's office and was investigating the case for insurance reasons. He asked me the same questions the police had, except for one more question. He wanted to know whether Mira had tried to sell a phone to me.'

'A phone?' Shalini asked.

'A phone, yes.'

'What did you say?'

'I clearly told him that I did not run a cell phone shop. That she only came to sell her jewellery.'

'Did he leave after that?'

'He followed me for four days. Four days, madam! Even when I went to drop my children to school. He knows where I live, where my kids go to school. Now I don't let them come back in their usual autorickshaw. I pick them up every day. I won't let my wife take lunch for them. She is angry that she has to wake up early to make lunch for the children before they leave for school in the morning. Business has gone down so much since I saw him because I am scared. I keep asking people too many questions because I'm sure everyone is related to him.' His voice was getting hysterical.

'Okay. That is definitely bad,' Shalini said. 'What was your impression of the woman?'

'Nothing special, madam. I don't even remember her properly.'

'Anything else?'

'Everyone says that she killed her husband. But, madam, to me it seemed like she was preparing to run away. She must have wanted to leave him. That's why she was selling her stuff. But before that . . . see . . .'

'Thank you, sir . . .'

'So, that Pooja madam, is she really . . .' Shalini slapped the pause button and shut the laptop.

'He wanted to know if you quit acting to become a radio show host,' she said, laughing sheepishly.

'Someone is looking for Mira. Someone who has the resources to stalk the pawnshop guy, me and probably others in her life,' Pooja said.

'It makes sense,' Rakesh added.

'But why the cell phone?' Pooja wondered.

'Um . . .' Rakesh said. 'I might know, but . . .'

'You can't tell us!' Both Shalini and Pooja replied in unison.

108
Inspector Rakesh

RAKESH REALISED HE WAS HOLDING HIS HAND up like a school kid and put it back down.

'I might know. I can't give you the details, but I might know. Please don't mention it on the podcast.'

The two stared expectantly at him, so he continued. 'Madhu had a second phone. A cheap one,' Rakesh said, scratching his clean-shaven chin and wondering how to say it without saying it. 'We . . . we found some evidence on it that pointed to something else—something more serious. So, we have kept that under wraps.'

'An affair?' Shalini excitedly asked.

'Why would a random man be interested in both Madhu's affair and us? And how did the goons even know about the phone or the pawnshop?' Pooja said. 'There's something more to it.'

That was a good point, Rakesh realised. The men had contacted Madhu on his secondary phone, but how had they found out about the pawnshop?

'So, what did you people find?' Shalini asked, leaning forward.

'I can't . . .' he started and then turned to them. 'Wait a minute. How did you find out about the pawnshop?'

'It's not that hard when you have loose-lipped people all around,' Shalini snorted.

'Joslin?' Rakesh asked, raising an eyebrow. That woman would be the death of him.

'See!' Shalini laughed out loud.

'I wonder how many other people she's blabbered to,' Rakesh said. 'You did a good job. The pawnshop guy never gave me any of this information. I guess it makes sense considering it all happened after I questioned him. But I gave him my card and asked him to call back if there was anything else.'

'You should have bribed him with some money and the promise of an autograph. Speaking of which, I need to talk to you,' Shalini said, glancing at Pooja.

'Again?!' Pooja said, slapping her forehead. Rakesh looked confused.

'What did the pawnshop owner tell you?' Shalini asked Rakesh.

Rakesh repeated everything the pawn broker had told him, including the disappointment Mira felt at how little money she was getting for the jewellery. They listened to him and took notes. When he was done, they didn't speak for a couple of minutes.

Pooja was the first to break the silence. 'To be fair, the broker sounds correct. It does seem like Mira was planning to leave Madhu.'

Rakesh was still not sure if he trusted them enough to tell them that she had been speaking to a lawyer about divorcing Madhu. If it was included in the podcast, it might make Mira seem even more villainous. 'Which means she wouldn't kill him,' Shalini replied.

'Obviously,' he said, trying to add something meaningful to the conversation.

'But why do people think she did?'

'I don't . . .' Rakesh started, then decided to clarify his position before they suspected him. 'I got promoted instead of someone else. That someone else decided to ruin my reputation and, in the process, ruined hers too. I shouldn't have trusted him with some private information.'

'Karthik, right?' Pooja and Shalini asked in unison again and Rakesh was surprised. 'How did you—?'

'First, you're not very good at hiding things—someone I know, promotion, blah blah,' Shalini said. 'And second, there's something off about him.'

'Anyway,' Rakesh said. 'Now she's gone, and I have no idea about how to clear our names.' He stood up and started pacing, something he had been doing a lot of these past few days.

'What are you doing about it?' Pooja asked. 'I mean, apart from my podcast and stalking me.'

'I'm not stalking . . .' he started, raising his voice and stopped. He didn't want anyone else to hear. He had given them so much information already; he may as well give them a warning. 'I think the man following you is the man who went to the pawnshop. I know he was one of Madhu's friends. I know he wanted the cell phone to hide something because he is most definitely . . .'

'Drug smuggling,' Shalini said, snapping her fingers. Rakesh clicked his tongue, annoyed at being interrupted.

'It has to be drugs!' Shalini said, looking at him with an expectant air.

Rakesh nodded, not wanting to give her any insight into what he actually thought for risk of it ending up on the podcast. 'What if there are drug manifests in the phone!' Shalini exclaimed, waving her arms dramatically.

He nodded along as she continued detailing how she had seen something similar in a movie. His mind was completely elsewhere.

109
Pooja

INSPECTOR RAKESH LEFT AT LUNCHTIME, insisting that they call his colleague Atif in case they saw the stalker again.

'Do you think we need to hire a private investigator?' Pooja asked, peering out of the windows. The street below was crowded and there were way too many bikes next to the tea shop down the road. She wished the tea shop wasn't there. It gave men too much cover.

'I don't think we can hire someone who would do a better job than the cops.'

'True. But why not give it a try?' Pooja said. She didn't want to admit it, but she was a little scared. What if this man had killed Madhu? For the umpteenth time, she wished she had started a podcast on movies.

'Sure, if you think it'll help,' Shalini said, reaching for the balcony door with a cigarette in her hand.

'Use the one at the back,' Pooja stopped her. 'I don't want to give them one more opportunity to watch us.'

Shalini nodded and slid the bolt back in place.

Pooja already had the number of someone who could help her. Shyamal had sent it to her in the first couple of days after her podcast was launched, insisting that she use him to do all her research. He was used to do background checks on any new star Sanjay was launching. She looked at the number again, hesitating before jabbing the call button.

The man answered after a few rings and spoke in clipped tones, respectful but not really saying anything. He didn't seem too excited at the prospect of investigating a random housewife. But when she mentioned the housewife's name his tone changed. She had him hooked.

Pooja told him about the balding guy, why she suspected he was following her, and what she needed to know. All while leaving Inspector Rakesh out of it.

Shalini returned to the room while Pooja was talking to the investigator.

She didn't want Shalini to think she was scared, so she asked the investigator to find out whatever he could about Mira too.

'Soooo . . .' he began once she was finished. 'You want me to find out who this guy is, what their connection is, and also track Mira's movements from the day she disappeared. Correct?'

'That's right.'

'Then where she went and what she did there.'

'No, just where she went will be enough.'

'Okay. Obviously, I am not expecting trouble but, madam, this is a police case and if trouble comes knocking, I will vanish. I expect my name to not appear anywhere, in your podcart or anywhere else.'

'Podcast,' Pooja corrected. 'And, of course, I will not use your name anywhere. I don't know about the cops though.'

He laughed. 'I will handle them. Just give me a few days and I'll call you back.' He hung up without saying goodbye. He hadn't mentioned his price either. She assumed Shyamal had told him Sanjay would take care of it. Pooja let out a curse, wondering if she should give Sanjay a heads-up about the incoming bill.

'Is that it?' Shalini asked, looking disappointed. 'I was expecting us to go snooping down some shady gully and find a guy looking like Sherlock!'

Pooja laughed. 'I think we have enough excitement in our lives.'

110
Inspector Rakesh

RAKESH LEFT URGENTLY BECAUSE HIS WIFE had texted, asking why he was at Subham Colony, 2nd Street. How the fuck does she know where I am, Rakesh thought, before remembering the Finding Friends app she had installed on their phones. Did everyone have a stalker these days?

He would have to stay at home for the rest of the day if he wanted to avoid a fight with Bindhu.

So, he worked from home instead, checking if he had missed something important on Mira's second phone. He wanted to get the call and message details of her main phone, but Atif did not have access to them. Maybe Karthik suspected that Atif was on Rakesh's side and was keeping him out of the loop.

The number Mira had called the most was the lawyer's. She had dialled the other numbers just once or twice.

Rakesh hadn't bothered to check those, but now, with nothing better to do, he cross-checked them on the caller app. One belonged to a taxi company, the other wasn't listed.

He grabbed his mobile and dialled the second number, not sure what he would say if the person answered. He didn't expect the number to turn into a name as he clicked the call button. 'Contact card found, do you want to add Sudha Local?' his phone beeped with this message popping up on the screen.

'Sudha?' he said out loud, surprised.

Sudha was Mira's best friend from school. Even on the day of the reunion, it was Sudha who had dropped Mira home. Mira had also accompanied Sudha to an orphanage she was trying to adopt a child from. He hadn't spoken to Sudha after the reunion. If he recalled correctly, she had left with her husband and was back in the USA where they now lived. The number was no longer in use.

Rakesh went to the reunion WhatsApp group and checked if Sudha was a member. She wasn't. He typed the word 'reunion' in the chat conversation and started going through the messages right from the top. Thankfully, the old messages hadn't been deleted. As he scrolled though, something caught his eye. He whipped out his notes and checked them.

'Holy fuck,' he said out loud.

The first few digits of Sudha's phone number were the same as the number from which Mira had received a message in the hospital.

111
Pooja

POOJA THOUGHT SHE WAS BEING PARANOID, but then remembered the paparazzo jumping over her fence to get a picture of her inside her home. It made her shudder. 'Wish Lakshmi ma was here,' she said, checking the curtains again.

'Lakshmi ma?' Shalini asked from the sofa.

'Nothing.'

'We still need to find the guest for the next episode. We have just three episodes so far—one with Joslin and Mrs Krishnan, one with Rakesh that is releasing tonight. The recording of the pawnshop owner is really short.'

Shalini had been trying and failing to get either Mira's childhood friends or Karthik to appear on the podcast. The latter had informed them that he wouldn't say anything till the case was closed. And if they still wanted a byte from him, they were welcome to join the official press meet. Karthik's earlier friendliness had vanished after he heard that Rakesh had been interviewed.

As a bike roared passed her building, Pooja felt a prickling at the back of her neck. Once the detective did his work, I'll feel better, she thought.

'What about the other neighbours?' Pooja asked.

'Yeah, I can get their numbers from Joslin or from the inspector,' Shalini said. 'Should I take the car or a taxi?'

'Take the car. I'm not planning on going anywhere. It's cheaper anyway,' Pooja replied. As she said those words, something occurred to her. 'What's the date?' she asked, grabbing her phone.

It was the second of the month. She checked her account balance quickly on the bank's app. It had only eight thousand rupees left. She let out a low hiss. 'Eight thousand! The bastard,' she said, clicking the joint account to check the balance there. There were more digits here than necessary. Sanjay hadn't taken away her access to the joint account, but he was definitely issuing a threat. Leave him and she would suffer.

But Pooja wasn't going to beg him for money. She had her wits about her, she had her brain. She could earn money independently or use the account she had been secretly depositing money into for any emergency.

She called Sanjay. She wasn't going to touch his money, but she knew what to do to make him angry. He picked up on the second ring, something he hadn't done since their first year of marriage. 'Hello, darling,' he said loudly. He wasn't alone. 'How is the heat in Chennai? Is the AC fixed?'

What the fuck was he talking about?

'I was just telling Khanna sir how you were having trouble finding a good AC mechanic because of the weekend. Did he finally come? It's Tuesday, right?' he tittered clumsily.

'Sure,' she replied. 'I see that your standing instruction of automatic money transfer this month fell through. I assume this means you're ready to sign the divorce papers?' She was harsher than necessary, but it would get his attention.

'One second, darling, I can't hear you. Stupid network. Just hold on for a minute,' he said.

'No. It was a mistake . . .' he said after a while. 'I'll call the bank and find out what happened.'

'So many years and a mistake at this important juncture? One would think you're making up stories because some plan of yours fell through . . .' Pooja waited, hoping that Sanjay would react.

'Nothing like that, Pooja. Stop your bloody drama. It was a mistake, that's all,' he huffed. She could almost see him balancing his phone in the crook of his neck while lighting a cigarette.

'Just wanted to check, Sanjay. I thought this was an odd way to tell me that you wanted to leave.'

'I don't,' he spat. 'We don't have divorces in my family. We work through problems.'

'How am I supposed to work through what you did, Sanjay?' she asked. This was the first time she had mentioned what he had done to her that night. She didn't want to, but it had slipped out. Pooja waited, hoping he would say something, yell at her, deny it, but he didn't take the bait. She was surprised. Instead of snapping back, he asked, in a calm, even voice, 'How is the . . . show going?'

'The show? The recording is going well.'

'Good,' he replied, leaving behind an awkward silence.

'I have to go now,' she finally said. 'Shalini is coming with something.'

'Okay. Listen. . . . ' he said, '. . . before you go. I . . . sorry.'

'Sorry? For what?'

'Just . . . sorry.'

And he hung up. Pooja stared at the phone. Was Sanjay apologising for threatening to cut her off, or for what happened the night before she left for Chennai?

She didn't know, and right now she didn't care. Pooja vowed she wouldn't touch a paisa of the money he was giving her now. She logged out of the measly bank account and into one she had in Chennai. She had set it up while modelling in college. It had a grand sum of Rs 10,18,424.

Not everything was Sanjay's, in fact more than fifty per cent was hers.

She then checked her deposits and there was enough in there. She would be fine for at least a year.

112
Inspector Rakesh

ATIF CALLED BACK WHILE HE WAS CHANGING. 'Sir, the number you gave me is registered in the US. We can't check it. But the people you mentioned left for the US a couple of days before the murder took place.'

'Couple of days? That's no coincidence that Sudha and her husband . . . ,' Rakesh said.

'Three of them. Their child went back too. I asked my friend for the ticket details.'

Rakesh stopped trying to find a clean shirt to wear and stood up. 'What?'

'The three of them left.'

Sudha and her husband had come to India to adopt a child. At their reunion, she had casually mentioned that IVF wasn't working. Mira wanted to go with her to the orphanage, which is why they left early that evening. He remembered feeling bummed about it. That's when everyone had rushed to take the damn picture.

'Do me a favour, can you just find her address in India for me?' he asked, wondering if what he was thinking was even possible.

'Okay. Sure. Oh, and the guys from the bar? I asked the manager. Madhu's group goes there almost every night, but never miss Tuesdays.'

'Tuesdays?' he laughed. Most religious people didn't drink on Tuesdays. It's Tuesday today, he realised.

'Do you want me to . . .' Atif started.

'No, I'll go. You please find Sudha's address.'

'One second, sir. Someone's coming,' Atif said. He stayed on the line till Atif found a private corner.

Once he was in a safe area, Atif continued. 'Remember that fat guy? He has a few complaints against him, but nothing went through.'

'What do you mean?' Rakesh had asked him to check out everyone who was recognisable in the group at the bar. Everyone except the one who seemed to be the ringleader had cases against them. One for assault, another for stalking a woman, and everything else was related to smuggling.

'This is the guy who we saw in the video,' Atif whispered. Rakesh could hear him walking briskly. He must be looking for a better place to talk.

'Sure, babyma. I'll pick you up at seven, okay?' Atif said in a higher pitched voice and Rakesh did his best not to laugh and waited for Atif to be alone.

'Sorry, sir,' Atif said, finally. 'There were too many people around me.'

'No problem. Tell me, what are they doing about the case now? Are they looking into these characters?' He had put in too much hard work for it to end without an arrest.

'No, sir. Karthik sir said that he'd been asked to quickly close it since the media was finally looking away.'

'Must be leading back to someone big,' Rakesh muttered. To Atif, he said, 'But what have you discovered about the balding guy?'

Atif clicked his tongue. 'Sir, it's bad. Smuggling, one withdrawn assault case, I think that was an attempted rape, multiple bar fights, one ending in hospitalisation.'

'No murder?'

'Nothing we can prove.'

'Withdrawn, you said?' Rakesh asked, his mind trying to make a connection. 'Who withdrew it?'

'It seems the mother and daughter came to file the FIR and the father came back later and withdrew it. The girl was a minor.'

'Jesus!' he said, the seriousness of the situation dawning on him. 'How young was she?'

'Thirteen, I think. She was in the eighth standard.'

'Fuck . . .' Rakesh couldn't stop himself from cursing. But why had no one pursued the case any further? The answer was obvious, but he didn't want to admit to it. 'Can you—?'

'Send the files across? I can't, sir, I don't have access to it,' Atif finished and hung up. He said the last line in a hurry, so someone must have passed by. Rakesh hoped Atif was a better liar than he was; he needed to be if they were going to solve this case.

After the call with Atif, Rakesh left for the bar. Parking his bike in the adjacent street, he sneaked into the place. Both the balding guy and the fat man were already present with their friends. Rakesh ducked behind a waiter and pretended to look for someone in there.

The men were too immersed in their conversation to notice him. He put his phone on silent mode, ensured the flash was turned off and sneakily took a couple of pictures of the group from where he was standing.

They seemed to be discussing something serious. The balding guy looked around to make sure no one was listening before showing the fat man something on his phone.

The fat man was surrounded by people and had his head down, so Rakesh couldn't see him. He went to the counter, grabbed a beer and sat in a corner. As the people around Rakesh cleared out, he could overhear the gang talking even though his back was to them so they wouldn't recognise him. Rakesh took a sip of his suspiciously full beer. He wished he'd emptied half of it somewhere before taking his seat.

Turning on the camera on his phone, Rakesh turned it to selfie mode and started recording what was happening behind him. He slowly leaned forward and sneaked the phone over his shoulder, just high enough for him so it could record the conversation as clearly as possible, and catch their names so he could match them with faces.

113
Pooja

THE NEXT DAY, POOJA WAS WOKEN UP BY HER ringing phone. Cursing Sanjay for disturbing her so early, she was about to answer the call and yell at him when she noticed the name on the phone. She quickly sat up and cleared her throat before answering. 'Hello.'

'Ma'am, I have an initial report,' the private detective said, his voice too clear for this time of the morning. Her phone beeped. *Battery critically low.*

'Yes, please hold on; I'll get a pen and paper.'

'I will be sending you a report anyway, I can sum it up now.'

'That would be perfect,' she said, swinging her legs off the bed.

'Before running away, Mira spent most of her time at the hospital and at her house. She didn't leave her house any time prior to going missing. But we know that she had gone on a trip earlier; that was to Ooty. We will have the details on where she stayed in a day or so, if you wish,' he said. Her battery beeped again, this time sounding more urgent.

'And what about the balding guy who was following me?' she asked, while cursing herself for forgetting to charge her phone.

'He is a low-level goonda who works for one of the main political parties. I doubt they know about his extracurricular activities. He has some cases of violence against his name, so I would advise caution. I will send the report to you.'

'My address . . .' Pooja started.

'I already know,' the man said and hung up.

Of course, he knew.

Pooja rubbed her eyes and stared at the dead laptop in front of her. The all-important episode with Inspector Rakesh had dropped the previous day, and she and Shalini had spent all night dealing with angry comments and posts on social media. The vitriol that had spewed onto their comments section had been toxic. Pooja finally understood why Mira had vanished. Even though she had been a victim of online bullying herself, it had never been this bad. Some anonymous handles were threatening to find Mira or Rakesh and kill them.

Reporting them to the social media platform had made no difference.

She plugged in her phone to charge. She did the same with her laptop, which beeped to life, showing her the lock screen.

Shalini stirred in the living room. She had fallen asleep here after the late night, spending it on the lumpy old sofa. Pooja called her over. 'The detective called,' she said, as Shalini appeared in the doorway, her hair looking like a makeshift bird nest.

'So that was the annoying noise,' she said groggily. 'Please change your ringtone, it's horrifying.'

'And he's sending the report later,' Pooja continued, still too sleepy to bother giving her the rundown. Shalini rubbed her eyes and took the laptop, sitting cross-legged on the floor and squinting at the screen.

'So . . .' she said, pulling out a cigarette pack from the depths of her pants pocket. 'Listeners have increased!'

'Thanks to the internet mafia,' Pooja said.

'That's one way of describing them.'

Shalini shared the stats with her. Sorted by days, platform, number of listens and country. Their listeners were mostly from India, followed by the USA, Ireland and then South Africa. Pooja took the laptop from Shalini and clicked on the Indian flag icon to see how many were from Mumbai. She was sure her 'friends' were listening, more out of spite than any curiosity about the case. Mumbai and Delhi had a lot of hits, followed by Bangalore. She was surprised that Tamil Nadu had the least number of hits, considering the story was based here. Only 326 listens overall.

She clicked again and opened a smaller pool. With a start, Pooja realised someone was listening to their podcast on the website—not on an app, not on any platform, but on a browser. And it was coming from where Mira had gone before her husband's murder.

114
Inspector Rakesh

RAKESH WOKE UP FEELING IRRITATED. THE sun had crept into the room through the newly changed yellow curtains and kept bothering him till he reluctantly opened his eyes.

'Who the fuck puts on yellow curtains in summer,' he grumbled, sticking his face under the embroidered sofa cushions.

Thinking back, Rakesh couldn't remember how the fight had started last night. When Bindhu had called, asking him why he was at a Tasmac bar, he had snapped at her, drunkenly telling her something about clearing his name and Mira's too. Bindhu had lost it when he mentioned Mira and told him to go to hell.

He had a few more beers and didn't remember how he got home. He had one thing right though; he had managed to take a picture of the people at the bar and sent it to Atif, along with their first names, or at least whatever they had called each other. He picked up his phone and checked his messages.

Bindhu had texted four times, his father-in-law had called along with the police commissioner's assistant and a few others.

'What the fuck is happening?' Rakesh mumbled before remembering that his podcast interview had dropped the previous day. He had intended to inform the commissioner and Bindhu, give them both a heads-up, but he'd forgotten.

'I'm screwed,' Rakesh said, going into the kitchen to sober up before returning all the calls.

115
Pooja

'WHAT DO YOU MEAN WE SHOULD GO TO OOTY?' Shalini asked, raising her eyebrows.

Pooja handed her the USB drive and the sheaf of papers she'd just received from the detective. 'Look at that,' she said, pointing at the line she had highlighted.

'Last trip was to Ooty with her daughter . . . came back after a few days . . . Doesn't seem like her husband knew,' Shalini read and looked up at her. 'So?'

Pooja smiled, 'Now look at this.'

She turned the laptop towards her. Shalini stared at the page, not quite understanding initially. But as she scrolled her eyes grew wide. 'No fucking way!'

'Right?' Pooja said, slapping the table. 'I think we just cracked this fucking case wide open!'

'I . . . kind of feel like a stalker now,' Shalini replied.

'Come on!' Pooja said, worried her plan would fall through. 'Let's just go and see what happened. Aren't you curious to see if Mira is safe?'

Shalini pursed her lips and kept scrolling. But her eyes were on the wall above Pooja. She seemed to be thinking about it. Pooja waited.

'Okay,' Shalini said, setting the laptop back on the table and rubbing her hands together.

'Have you ever driven long-distance?' Shalini asked, sticking her suitcase into the car's boot.

'What does long-distance mean?' Pooja asked, tying her hair back and strapping on her seatbelt.

'Oh God, please tell me you've driven further than the grocery store,' Shalini gasped, eyes widening in horror.

'I have!' Pooja retorted. 'I've driven to the mall,' she said and started the car. Shalini looked like she wanted to say something but thought better of it.

Shalini read the file out, sometimes to herself and sometimes out loud as Pooja drove. 'Listen to this,' she said, reading from the police file that the detective had somehow got his hands on. 'Madhu is also suspected to have been doing business with known drug manufacturers and dealers in posh areas in Tamil Nadu.'

'Yeah, so?' Pooja asked, not sure why Shalini had pointed that out.

'What does "posh areas" mean?'

'Ah,' she said. 'Well, he means upmarket places, where rich people hang out, live, work.'

'I know that!' Shalini protested. I meant, was it the posh clubs or just general areas? Because I don't see parents being okay with druggies hanging around their neighbourhood.'

'The parents probably use drugs too. How do you know they don't have a stake in the business?' Pooja asked, turning on her indicator as soon as she spotted a coffee shop. She needed to pee.

Shalini didn't say anything till they got back into the car. But as soon as the doors were shut, she started again. 'What if Madhu was not just a dealer? What if . . .' she

paused, '. . . what if . . . he started doing drugs himself?'
Pooja sighed. Whenever Shalini latched onto an idea, Pooja felt like she was hanging out with an overexcited teenager.

'I think they would have found drugs in his system if he was a user. And Mira would have noticed it too. And probably mentioned it to someone.'

'She didn't tell anyone that they had money problems. Rakesh found out from the neighbours, and so did we,' Shalini replied and started recording notes into her phone. By the time they were halfway to their location, the file was lying shut on the car floor and Shalini had dozed off.

Pooja pulled over for minute, stuffed all the file papers into Shalini's backpack and tucked a small cushion between her shoulder and neck before driving away.

116
Inspector Rakesh

RAKESH WAS WAITING FOR ATIF AT THE BAR when he spotted the ringleader entering. Even though he had seen the ringleader the previous day, he was too drunk to remember it. He had saved the man's number from Madhu's second phone and checked his profile picture on WhatsApp; it was a shiny golden picture of some

God. In person, he was cherubic and looked like a happy middle-class citizen.

The second the man entered the bar the atmosphere seemed to change. With an ingratiating smile on his face, the manager Jayaseelan got up and led him to a table at the back. Rakesh would need to change seats to get a good view, but he didn't want to do it immediately; it would look suspicious.

Instead, he called over the skinny waiter, Gopal, who was taking orders and asked for a beer. Jayaseelan glanced over and recognised him but said nothing.

'What beer, sir?' the boy drawled in a bored voice. 'Kingfisher Ultra,' Rakesh said.

'Anything to eat?' he asked and walked away as Rakesh shook his head.

Rakesh pulled out his phone and checked his messages. The reply from Atif—'Coming, sir'—flashed on his screen for a second before he swiped it away.

He chanced another glance behind him. The fat man was seated comfortably in his corner with some minions around him. He looked like the kind of guy whose contacts could ruin your life. On his left sat the guy who had also been a part of the fight with Madhu. He was giving orders to the bar manager instead of the waiter.

Rakesh rested his chin in his hand and pretended to watch a video on his phone so the gang of men wouldn't notice they were being recorded. Rakesh leaned forward to hear them, but the three tables of drunken men between them meant they were too far away. All he could hear were the words 'sarakku', 'shipment' and 'load' a few times. Did they mean drugs? Were they drug traffickers? If so, why was Madhu sending pictures of his daughter in response to their repayment demands? He'd have to find a way to get closer.

Atif turned up a few minutes later. 'Sir,' he said, sitting down next to Rakesh and looking around the room. 'There he is,' Rakesh said, pointing with his eyes.

'Then why are you so far away?' Atif asked, looking genuinely puzzled.

'I didn't want to move immediately; it would be too obvious,' Rakesh replied, calling the waiter over. 'Same for my friend,' he said and the boy walked to the fridge and brought a beer back with him as Rakesh filled him on the meagre conversation he'd picked up.

Atif looked around the room and his eyes stopped at the TV. 'The cricket match is on?' he asked when Gopal came back with his beer. 'Yes, sir.'

'Let's sit there,' Atif said loudly, pointing at the table in the middle. 'I want to watch the match.'

Rakesh watched in surprise as Atif casually walked towards the seat, keeping his eyes trained on the TV. He got up and followed suit. Both men adjusted their chairs to face the screen and asked the waiter to increase the volume. 'Highlights, sir,' the boy said, making a face, but Atif dismissed him.

'For a true fan, highlights are even better,' Atif said, and then, after a pause, added, 'Bring us some chilli chicken.'

117
Pooja

IT WAS 6.00 P.M. BY THE TIME THEY REACHED the hotel in Ooty so they decided to rest for the day. Neither Pooja nor Shalini had a plan on how to approach Mira, but they were both sure that some food and rest would help them come up with something. Pooja hadn't driven much since marrying Sanjay and the long drive had exhausted her. After eating a heavy Indian thali, Pooja and Shalini hit the bed.

The next morning, Pooja and Shalini left in search of Mira with a photo of her in hand. According to the information the detective had given Pooja, Mira stayed at a hotel down the street from theirs.

The 'hotel' turned out to be a rundown lodge. The white paint on the pillars was smudged with handprints and paan stains, and the cracks in the walls hadn't been filled for so long that plants had started growing there. If Pooja wasn't here for work, she would have immediately left.

'Just go to the reception and ask if she stayed here a couple of months ago,' Pooja told Shalini. 'It doesn't look like they get a lot of guests anyway. They should remember her.'

'Be discreet,' Pooja called out as Shalini briskly walked away. The last thing they wanted was for someone to alert the media. God knows what Mira had been doing here. She could have just come here for a break from dealing with Madhu, but then again, she could have been running away.

A man walked slowly across the street, looking towards her car. Pooja sank further down in her seat and pushed her sunglasses up.

Shalini came out a couple of minutes later and got in. 'Nothing,' she said, looking annoyed.

'Nothing?' Pooja repeated. 'What do you mean nothing?'

'I mean she didn't stay here.'

'Okay. That I can imagine.' Pooja glanced back at the building and shook her head. 'Did they give you anything?'

Shalini shrugged. 'They don't have any digital records, just names written down in a notebook. A woman called and booked a room for two days—days that coincided with those of Mira's stay—but didn't show up.'

'A woman. Wow! That is helpful,' Pooja said, rolling her eyes, 'Did you find out her name?'

'No. I asked if it was Mira and they said no.'

Pooja glared at her, and Shalini got out of the car and ran towards to lodge again. When she came back, she looked excited.

'Well?'

'Mrs Krishnan.'

118
Inspector Rakesh

AFTER THE MATCH HIGHLIGHTS WAS OVER, the waiter switched channels to another sports channel, this one showing a football match. Atif began to enjoy himself even more, yelling at the screen every time the other team got possession of the ball.

A couple of other tables had also joined in. This was his first time watching a football match on TV, and Rakesh realised he needed to learn about other sports too. So when Bindhu's face flashed on his phone, he rejected the call and turned back to the match and tried to catch a waiter's eye to order another plate of chicken for the table. That's when he noticed a couple of people from the fat man's table looking at him. Keeping his eyes firmly on the waiter, he placed his order and went back to the match.

While he had wanted to stay incognito, now that those men had noticed him, he hoped they would befriend him in an attempt to keep a watch on him. So when the waiter came back, Rakesh loudly said, 'See what I have to do to get some food these days? She won't even cook for me anymore.'

He had expected Atif to be confused, but the man caught on instantly. 'Sir, leave it, sir. We can always eat outside. Or you come to my house. My mother makes the best biriyani,' he replied, equally loudly.

'Now that's an idea. Maybe I should go back to my village. I miss my mother's cooking. You know, no matter how angry she was, she never refused to make my favourite food.'

Behind him, the men who he hoped had overheard him laughed as Rakesh spilled some beer on himself. Atif put the bottle back upright and pushed the plate in front of him. 'Eat some more, sir. Tomorrow, lunch is at my place. No discussion.'

'Aren't you that famous inspector?' someone asked, tapping him on the shoulder. Rakesh turned around to see the balding man who had been following Pooja and Shalini.

'Aiyo,' he said, slapping his forehead.

'No, no, don't worry, sir, I'm not going to . . . just asked because I thought I had seen you before.'

'I promise I didn't do anything. Promise,' Rakesh said, doing a good job of whining.

'No, no . . .' the man started, but Rakesh didn't give him a chance. 'I can't believe this. I came to work thinking I would do some good, get an award. But look at what has happened. My life is ruined,' he cursed, turning back to the table and stuffing a spoonful of chicken into his mouth.

The man retreated and Atif apologised to him over his shoulder.

'Are they still looking?' Rakesh whispered and Atif nodded. 'Let's finish up and leave. Let them think I'm upset. You come back and pretend I'm drunk.'

They quickly finished up while trying to remain as casual as possible before leaving. Atif supported Rakesh till they were out of the bar and out of view. As soon as they were sure they couldn't be seen by the men inside, Rakesh straightened up and asked Atif to go back inside.

He would wait outside to follow them when they left.

119
Pooja

'WHAT THE HELL IS HAPPENING!' POOJA exclaimed.

They had just found out that a third hotel had received a call from someone called Joslin who had booked two rooms for the same dates as the other two they had visited that day. It had been an interesting morning. They parked overlooking a cliff and decided to stay in the car while thinking over what they had learnt. 'It was obviously Mira,' Pooja said.

'She has covered her tracks well. We don't know if she actually stayed in any of these places,' Shalini said, digging into a glazed chocolate donut that she had picked up from a coffee shop. 'I am not sure what to do now. The detective isn't really giving us anything helpful, is he?'

'I asked him to stop after he told me where she went in the days before the murder. What if he finds something he shouldn't and leaks it to the press?' Pooja replied, shielding her eyes from the sun with her scarf.

'Anyway,' Pooja said, trying not to let her exasperation show. 'What do we do now?'

'We've already gone to all the hotels in the area. I don't think we can do much here,' Shalini sounded apologetic even though she had no reason to be. 'I hate to say it, but this isn't Mumbai. Women can only get so much done here.'

'I agree,' Pooja said, pushing her seat back up and pulling the scarf off her face. An idea was forming in her head. 'What about a women's hostel?'

'A women's hostel?'

'Yes. If she was running away from her husband, the best place for her would be at a women's hostel where men aren't allowed.'

'But then . . .' Shalini said, her face falling. 'What if this whole trip is a hoax? What if she went somewhere else? What if she got another ticket?'

Pooja paused to think. 'We need to go to the bus stand.'

'Let me also call the inspector,' Shalini said, pulling out her phone.

'No,' Pooja grabbed the phone before Shalini could dial Rakesh's number. 'Let us exhaust all our options before we needlessly annoy anyone else.'

Shalini looked confused, but agreed. Pooja looked at Google Maps and turned towards the bus stop. There were too many tourists walking around. Families in colourful sweaters, the men and children in winter caps and the women hiding saris and kurtas behind woollen outerwear. Pooja kept her head down and her scarf up, her gigantic sunglasses covering most of her face. Shalini walked in front of her, trying to find a ticket collector and ask them about Mira.

120
Inspector Rakesh

HE BROUGHT THE CAMERA CLOSER AND PRESSED himself into the wall. No one could see him in the dark, but the streets were silent, and Rakesh was sure that the sound of the camera clicking would give him away. He had to record this meeting instead.

He'd brought an entire camera and mic kit with him and hidden it between his and Atif's bike. Atif was still inside the bar, probably watching the match and listening in to what they were saying about him.

The bar's door opened, and two more patrons stumbled out. One of them was in a state of disarray and yelling profanities, while the other was holding on to him so he wouldn't fall over.

It had been an hour already and Rakesh's knees were starting to lock. He stood up behind the bush and shook his legs out before trying to find a more comfortable position to wait in.

Bindhu would be pissed by now. She knew from her tracking app that he was at the bar. His phone had been vibrating at random intervals, with both calls and messages coming in, but he was sitting in a very dark spot and any light from his screen would alert people. He ignored his buzzing phone again and waited.

Ten more minutes passed before Atif called. 'Have you reached?' he asked. That was Rakesh's cue.

The door opened again and he was finally rewarded for his patience. Kumar, the one who looked like a God-fearing middle-class businessman and whose bike was being used to stalk Pooja, walked out with his hand on another man's shoulder. They were talking loudly, and Rakesh started to record their conversation, hoping he would catch them saying something useful.

'What can we do now! It's too late anyway,' the shorter man said, shrugging his free shoulder. 'Let's go home. Who cares! It's forgotten now. Only that inspector . . .' he started.

'Well, the idiot is done for anyway. It seems he gave an interview without permission,' said a man who had followed the two men out of the bar.

'Yes, he will be transferred to some nondescript place. His boss knows how the world works.'

'We need to worry about that Pooja woman.'

'Richard is following them. He will take care of it,' Kumar said.

So the bald man's name was Richard. Rakesh's ears perked up. He tried to listen harder, but the three men were already walking away. They bundled the largest one, Kumar, into an autorickshaw and walked to their vehicles. Once the brightness from their headlights completely faded away, Rakesh got on his bike and followed them.

121
Pooja

THEIR TRIP TO THE BUS STAND WAS AN absolute bust. No one could remember seeing Mira. They wondered if she had even come to this town. Even those who had immediately recognised the picture didn't recall seeing her. 'As if we wouldn't have informed the police, madam,' one shopkeeper said before dismissing them to attend to a customer.

'I didn't even know this was tourist season,' Pooja said as they looked around at the crowded bus stop to see if there was anyone left to talk to.

'This is so exasperating! How do we even know that she came back here again? Maybe someone else here is listening to our podcast,' Shalini said. Pooja was already getting tired, and the noise and honking at the bus depot was adding to her agony.

'Let's come some other time,' she said, tugging Shalini's sleeve.

As they made their way to the car, Pooja heard Shalini take in a sharp breath and hiss. 'Fuck, it's her, isn't it?'

Pooja turned to see who she was looking at. Shalini pointed at a small figure hurrying down the street, away from the bus stop. 'That's just a woman walking. How can you tell it's Mira by looking at her back?'

'Because she was standing there and looking at us.'

'She's too far away for you to know what she was looking at,' Pooja said, but Shalini had already crossed the road. Pooja sighed and followed, wishing she had worn her walking shoes.

The woman took a left down a smaller lane and sped up her pace. The road she was taking was getting narrower and narrower. Had this woman really spotted them and was now taking them on a wild goose chase or was she genuinely going back home, Pooja wondered.

She readjusted her scarf over her head and continued. After a couple of minutes of walking, the woman stopped. Pooja stumbled to a halt and tried to hide behind a bougainvillea bush. A few steps away, Shalini did the same. Pooja saw the woman turn back, take two steps and pause again. Pooja held her breath and looked down at her legs, hoping that her white pants had blended into the white wall behind her. If only she could get a look at the woman's face, but the bush was too dense. Suddenly, the woman turned and walked away. Both Shalini and Pooja peered out from behind their hiding places and, giving the woman a head start, continued behind her.

It was clear that she knew someone was following her. Shalini pulled out her phone, ready to click a picture or record a video if she turned around. Mira—or the woman they thought was Mira—stopped in front of a shop. It was one of those touristy dry fruits shops that sold overpriced nuts and seeds.

As she pretended to be checking the cashews kept in a tweed sack outside, the woman tilted her head ever so slightly in their direction. Pooja ducked again, behind a dustbin this time. All those days following Sanjay to see who he was sleeping with had paid off. Shalini, on the other hand, didn't seem to know what to do so she just marched past the shop, muttering to herself. The woman waited for Shalini to pass and left. Pooja, deciding not to risk discovery, gave her a longer head start.

By the time Pooja got up to follow her again, the woman had vanished. Pooja ran around the street, peering into every shop she'd passed, but the woman was nowhere to be found. She was wearing a dark brown sweater, the kind that could not be spotted easily in a crowd.

'Fuck!' she cursed, stomping her leg like a child. She'd lost her.

Pooja turned back, using her phone's parking location to find her way through the maze of streets she'd just walked through. She couldn't shake the feeling that she was being watched. When she reached the car, she called Shalini and waited for her to return.

122

Inspector Rakesh

RAKESH RODE BEHIND THE AUTORICKSHAW. The road was relatively empty, and he allowed a water tanker to get between them to make sure he was not spotted.

The autorickshaw turned into a residential street before coming to a halt in front of a gated community. Rakesh didn't want to go down the street since it was only for the residents of the area. He would be caught out in a second if any building's watchman stopped him.

He watched as Kumar paid his fare and stumbled inside. The auto did a quick U-turn and passed Rakesh. He waited for a couple of minutes before walking down the street to make a note of the building's name.

He could only make it a few feet into the street without being seen. The residents had installed CCTV cameras all around and the minute he caught the red LED light on one, Rakesh stopped and backed up. The board outside the street had the names of three buildings: Starlight Apartments, Los Angeles Bay View Apartments and London Tower Homes. Rakesh rolled his eyes at the names and took a quick picture of the board on his phone. He wondered how he would figure out which one Kumar stayed in when he realised that each building had the builder's logo installed right at the top.

'Ah, vanity plates,' he said, moving back so he could get a better look. London Tower Homes. That was the building Kumar had gone into. It was 3 a.m. and all the lights were off. But soon one got switched on in the middle block. Kumar had reached home.

Having got the information he needed, Rakesh got on his bike and went home.

123
Pooja

'WHY WOULD SHE ACT LIKE THAT IF SHE wasn't Mira?' Shalini asked, taking a bite of the naan they had ordered from room service.

'Maybe because two women she's never seen before followed her for a long time?' Pooja remarked, shaking her head. She couldn't believe how she had behaved today, that too with a stranger. She didn't consider Sanjay's girlfriends strangers since they practically shared him, but today's encounter felt weird.

'But we are women; we usually don't mean harm,' Shalini protested, sulking. 'Anyway, I know her sweater and handbag now. I'll be able to spot her next time.'

'People change clothes and handbags, you know,' Pooja replied.

'Yeah, people like you. People like her and me don't change handbags every day. We have one and we stick with it unless it's a special occasion or when it's finally in tatters,' Shalini said. Pooja immediately felt like a fool. Shalini was telling the truth. Pooja realised with a start that she had completely forgotten how she had been before Sanjay. She wondered if her old handbag from college was still in the cupboard.

'Anyway,' Shalini continued, 'she's cut her hair. It's short and only comes to her ears now. I've not seen her in person, but that woman seems to be of the same build and height as Mira, right? Should we ask Rakesh about her vital stats?'

'What?' Pooja asked, jerking back to the present.

'Should we ask Inspector Rakesh how tall Mira is? Will he think that's weird?'

'Not if we ask the right way,' Pooja said. 'Tell him we have an expert who wants Mira's height and weight to know if she could have overpowered Madhu. That might work. Ask him for Madhu's height and weight too.'

Shalini nodded and whipped out her phone. Pooja watched the girl enthusiastically talk to the inspector.

'He said he would send it later,' Shalini said, grinning from ear to ear. 'You know what? He sounded drunk. He said he was busy on a mission.' Shalini started laughing and Pooja smiled along with her.

124
Inspector Rakesh

AFTER THE LONG DRIVE BACK FROM KUMAR'S building, Rakesh now stood outside his front door, staring at it. He had forgotten his keys. He checked everywhere—his pockets, his bike's storage, even under the plant where Bindhu sometimes left her key. Pressing his hands to the window next to the door, he peered into the house. On the table, next to the box of eggs he'd bought that morning, were his keys.

'Fuck,' he hissed.

He walked around his house till he reached his back window and looked inside. The frosted glass that he'd installed was doing a good job of blocking the view. The backdoor wasn't unlocked either.

His phone buzzed and he saw that Atif had already called once. His battery had thirty per cent charge still left. He decided to answer the call before turning off his phone for the night. 'Sir,' Atif said as soon as he picked up.

'Tell me. What happened after I left?' Rakesh asked.

'After you left, I went back and watched the game for a while,' he said. Rakesh could hear his footsteps moving fast. He was probably walking up the stairs to reach his top floor flat. 'They waited for a while before asking about you. I told them you were trying to clear your name and that you had problems at home. They mentioned the podcast, only they called it a radio show.'

'And?' Rakesh asked, making his way back to the front of the house.

'I said you did that to tell your story. That you weren't a bad person. They were very curious about Mira madam. They wanted to know if we've found and arrested her, or if she is dead.'

Rakesh stopped in his tracks. 'How did they sound?'

'Curious. In fact, very interested. More interested than they were in you. I said that I was off the case since other people were handling it. They didn't say anything else after that.'

'I need to befriend them,' Rakesh said, sitting on the stairs that led to the terrace.

'Let's plan something. Did you find out where they went?' Atif asked.

'No, each one of them went in a different location. I followed Kumar to an apartment complex. He was the only one in an autorickshaw, so he probably didn't notice that I was trailing him. The other two left on their bikes. I still have a feeling I have seen Kumar before.'

Atif said he would try to find out who Kumar was, and Rakesh gave him the details of his building. Finding owner details wouldn't be that hard but finding if he was renting the house, it wasn't going to be that easy. Rakesh hung up and messaged Bindhu, 'Do you have your keys? I'm locked out.' He checked the charge on his phone battery again. It was down to twenty-five per cent now. Cursing himself, he turned his phone off and put it in his pocket.

125
Pooja

THE NEXT MORNING, POOJA WOKE UP TO TWO messages. One was from Shyamal, informing her that the detective had been paid. The other from Rakesh. It was meant for someone else, but it had come to her instead.

'That fellow who was following Pooja works for Kumar. Kumar lives in London Towers.'

'What?' she said, reading it again. He must have been drunk. She rolled her eyes and typed out 'Wrong number, Inspector-ji' and sent it before waking up Shalini.

An alert from Instagram popped up as she walked to the bathroom: Sanjay Reddy has uploaded a new story. She clicked on it and watched Sanjay showing off the dogs he was playing with at an animal rescue meet. He was holding an armful of puppies next to D and other actors from their upcoming movie. The cast was there to ask people to be kinder to other living beings. 'Adopt, don't buy,' Sanjay said before the story ended. She rolled her eyes, thinking of the three pedigreed dogs he had back in their farmhouse.

She didn't comment on his story. Instead, Pooja tweeted about the podcast episode that would drop later that day. Her phone beeped immediately. It was Sanjay: 'I know you saw my story. People are getting suspicious, it's almost been a month, for fuck's sake. Now that you have a detective doing the work for you just get your ass back.'

She had been away for three weeks and these weeks had gone by in a flash. Then it hit her. 'It's been three weeks since I came . . .' she said to herself, rushing through the dates in her head. 'Oh shit.'

126
Inspector Rakesh

RAKESH WOKE UP THE NEXT DAY TO THE sound of a squirrel screaming. 'Turn it off,' he mumbled, reaching for the sheets to cover his face, but there was nothing. 'And draw the curtains!'

When no one replied, he grumbled again and turned over. The mattress was really hard, and he ached all over. Just then a particularly loud caw followed by the sound of giggling woke him up. In an instant, the previous evening came flooding back to him and he jerked up right, banging his head on the water tank pipe.

'Appa,' Anthony laughed, 'what are you doing here?'

He looked at Anthony in the piercing morning light. He was on all fours, having crawled under the tank to see him.

'What are you doing here?' Rakesh asked, repeating the question to his son. 'Amma and I are home now; she said you forgot your keys.'

'And you saw a man sleeping under the water tank and decided to find out who it was? That's dangerous, isn't it?' Rakesh asked, his head starting to pound.

'You are not a stranger. I know how you snore,' the boy giggled again, crawling out. Rakesh followed him. 'Put my phone to charge,' Rakesh said, handing his phone to his son. 'Listen, is amma angry?' he called, but Anthony was already running down the stairs and didn't hear him.

Rakesh looked around at the terrace and realised one of his neighbours was looking at him. He waved and grinned sheepishly before hurriedly following his son.

Bindhu snorted as soon as she saw him in the living room and stalked off. She came back a second later with her hands on her hips. 'Have you seen this?' she said, showing him her phone.

It was a picture of a man sleeping on a roof which had been shared more than two hundred times on Twitter. 'What is this?' he asked, then grabbed the phone to see it for himself. 'Inspector Rakesh has been kicked out of his house, it seems. Here he's seen sleeping on a terrace in my neighbourhood,' the tweet read. He checked the account that had shared it. It was that fucking neighbour who'd just been staring at him.

'Only you are capable of undoing and then redoing damage in the same breath,' Bindhu said, a single eyebrow going up as she waited for his response.

'I mean . . .' he said, wondering when he could have a shower. Rakesh was starting to feel his back ache from sleeping on concrete. 'It's not like I did it on purpose.'

It was the wrong thing to say.

127
Pooja

THE MORNING HAD RUSHED BY IN A BLUR AND around lunchtime, Pooja drove to the spot they had seen the woman last. Shalini was yawning in the passenger seat and eating her second cream bun.

'I still can't believe it's been over ten years since you've eaten one,' Shalini said, putting the plastic bag into her pocket. 'It's my favourite!'

'Used to be mine too,' Pooja replied, her eyes straining to find a parking spot on the crowded street. They had taken a different, less frequented route today, hoping the traffic wasn't bad. But it was just as crowded.

As Pooja stood waiting for the car in front of her to move, her phone started buzzing. 'Is that Sanjay again?' she asked Shalini to check. She hadn't bothered to reply to his last message and now he'd started calling her. She knew it wasn't urgent because otherwise Shyamal would have called.

'It's not Sanjay,' Shalini said, turning the screen towards her. The caller ID read 'Mummy-ji'.

Pooja slammed the brakes and Shalini's coffee spilled onto her bag and shirt. 'Fuck!' Shalini swore, dropping the phone into the cup holder.

Pooja stared at the ringing phone as if it were a bomb. 'What is it? You look stressed,' Shalini asked, making a futile attempt to wipe the brown stain already spreading across her jute bag.

'My mother-in-law,' Pooja said. The wretched woman's face with the giant bindi flashing across her screen was enough to make her shudder.

'Dear God, she looks cheerful,' Shalini said.

'Does she ever,' Pooja replied wryly, still not sure if she wanted to answer the call. Her mother-in-law disconnected while she was making up her mind, and as she expected, a few seconds later, the phone started ringing again.

'I don't think she'll let up till you answer,' Shalini said. 'Better to rip off the band aid.'

'I don't want to,' Pooja whined, swiping on the green phone icon. 'Hi, mummy-ji!' she said cheerfully. 'Sorry I'm driving.'

'Oh, what happened to that driver you had? That Ram something. Where is he?' Her high-pitched voice came through the speaker.

'He's in Mumbai. I'm in Chennai now.'

'Accha, listen.' She had switched to Hindi and Pooja followed suit.

'Tell me?'

'When are you going back home? Sanjay misses you.'

'I don't know, mummy-ji, once my work is finished.'

'What's the need to work?' she said. 'You know we didn't want you to work after marriage.'

'You didn't want me to act after marriage. This isn't acting,' Pooja replied. 'I just want to do something to keep myself occupied. An idle mind is a devil's workshop after all.'

The silence at the other end meant she had won this round. Her conservative mother-in-law had fit in perfectly with her traditional husband. But Pooja hadn't, and that had always been a point of contention between them.

A car honked behind her, and she grabbed the opportunity to end the conversation. 'Achcha, mummy-ji, listen, the signal has turned green, I have to go now.'

'Wait, no, I still . . .'

'I don't want news articles saying Pooja Reddy was speaking on the phone and driving. Bye. I'll call you back!' She hung up as Shalini chuckled at her.

'Smart!' she smiled.

'I'll pay for it later,' Pooja said, changing gears and inching forward, eyes back on the road but her mind occupied elsewhere.

128
Inspector Rakesh

BY THE TIME HE HAD SHOWERED AND BOUGHT some vegetables that Bindhu wanted him to, Rakesh was exhausted. Bindhu still wasn't talking to him, and he was too preoccupied to fix it. Instead, he spent some time replying to all the messages that had arrived while his phone was off.

His classmates seemed to have made another group on WhatsApp and added him to it after his podcast episode released. 'Hi, guys. Sorry we needed to take a break, thanks to everyone for understanding. Welcome back @Rakesh. How have you been?'

Rakesh snorted at their audacity and left the group. But not before checking the members first. A lot of people hadn't been added, including Sudha, Mira's best friend. Behind him, Bindhu muttered something about lazy people before slamming the bathroom door behind her. She had to leave on a shopping trip, this time to finalise invitations for her cousin Lily's wedding.

He thought she had come back home for him. Turns out she wanted to get her things for Lily's wedding. As he was checking the image of him sleeping on the terrace again, this time with 2,734 retweets, his phone rang.

'Why did you leave, da?' the person at the other end said as soon as he answered.

'Who is this?'

'Fucker, you deleted my number as well? It's Uday!' It was his classmate, the one who had sat next to him in eleventh and twelfth grades.

'Why should I be part of that group?' Rakesh asked.

'It was just a misunderstanding, bro,' Uday said, his voice simperingly sweet. 'We know you didn't do anything. But the group admin said that the police may think everyone on the group is a suspect. He wanted to remove Mira first, but then decided everyone should leave.'

'Thereby making it look like just Mira and I were constantly talking?' Rakesh said angrily, not thinking.

'No . . . I mean history won't change and it'll show that we all left,' Uday faltered.

'I see that some people have still not been added,' Rakesh said. 'Do they not want to be involved with me? You can tell them that I've left the group. They can join again.' He knew he sounded like a sulky child, but he couldn't help himself.

Bindhu came out of the bathroom and raised an eyebrow at him. He mouthed 'Uday' at her, but she ignored him and walked past, taking out a bottle of water from the fridge and pouring herself a glass.

'That's not it,' Uday said. 'Joseph said he had enough problems of his own to deal with and Mona doesn't want to be part of any controversy. Sundari asked Sudha what happened, and she told Sundari that she didn't want to be part of a group that bitches about their friends. I wasn't surprised by Sudha's reaction since she and Mira have got really close of late.'

'Weren't they always close?'

'Not since Mira left school. But this time they even had lunch with their families.'

'What?' Rakesh said.

'Yeah, they even met a few times after the reunion. I saw them at a café,' Uday said.

Rakesh had been unaware about all of this. There was no mention of it in the group. He quickly asked Uday for the date and location before hanging up.

129
Pooja

'WHERE DO YOU THINK WE SHOULD START?' Shalini asked, looking warily at the bus stand in front of them.

'She came from that direction, right?' Pooja said, pointing at the streets leading away from the main junction. 'It's got two possible routes. I'll take the left one.' Shalini nodded and said, 'And I'll take the one she went down yesterday.'

As Pooja walked down the road, looking from building to building, she was sure this was a wild goose chase. No way was Mira dumb enough to come back to the last place she was spotted at, if that woman really was her. But Pooja thought she ought to give it a try anyway. As she walked past the church that was towering over the neighbourhood, Pooja noticed a man walk out with a bag that looked very similar to the one the woman was carrying the previous day.

It was a cloth bag that had the logo of a school. St. Agustus School for Children.

She turned around to look at the board on the church and it had the same name. 'So, there's a school attached to it,' she said to no one, her mind racing. She immediately called Shalini.

'I think I found out where that woman was coming from,' she said, quickly turning back the way she came. 'There's a church at the street I'm on. Let's take a look at it.'

Hanging up, she walked slowly around the church, taking pictures of the building and switching to taking a selfie whenever she thought someone was looking at her. The building must have been at least a hundred years old, but it was still standing magnificently. By the time she reached the end of the fence, Shalini joined her.

'That was fast,' she said.

'Yeah, I came as quickly . . .' Shalini panted, '. . . as I could. Did you find her?'

'No, but remember the bag she was carrying, along with that horrible handbag?'

'The tote bag?' Shalini asked.

'It has this school's logo on it.'

Shalini turned and looked at the board. 'Oh . . . So she works here.'

'That's possible. Or . . . she has a kid who goes here.'

The two of them looked up at the towering building.

130
Inspector Rakesh

HE HAD BEEN STANDING OUTSIDE THE CAFÉ that Uday had told him about for half an hour now, waiting for the manager to arrive. Finally, around 3 p.m., a shiny man in a white checked shirt parked his bike in the small lane by the side of the shop and walked to the café. Rakesh jogged over as soon as the shutters were up and showed the man his card.

'Which date, sir?' he asked, powering up the computer a couple of minutes later. Rakesh had told him to show him the CCTV footage from six weeks back when Uday had spotted Mira and Sudha there. Thankfully, they had back-ups of everything stored somewhere.

'The ninth,' he said. 'Sometime after 2 p.m.'

Rakesh watched as the man scrolled through the files. Finally, he opened one and vacated his seat. 'Is the audio available?' Rakesh asked.

'Sorry, sir. No audio. But our video quality is pretty good.' Rakesh thanked the manager and skipped ahead to the time mentioned in the text message. It took a while but soon he spotted Mira walking into the café with her little girl. The video was a bit washed out and didn't show faces too clearly, especially from this angle, but it was unmistakably her. 'Can you zoom in?' Rakesh asked.

'Yes, sir,' the man said.

Rakesh asked the man to zoom in on the child's face. He inhaled sharply when he realised it was the same girl whose images he had found on Madhu's phone. His mind was going a million miles a minute. He saw as Mira ordered for the two of them and waited. Five minutes . . . seven minutes . . . And then, just as he was about to skip forward, Mira waved. Sudha must've come.

Rakesh sped the video and watched as the order arrived. They ate, Sudha spent a lot of time playing with Priyanka and finally, almost two hours later, Mira got up to leave, leaving Priyanka behind with Sudha. Mira had probably gone to the restroom.

Rakesh watched as Sudha sat around a bit longer and then got a call. She spoke for a few seconds before asking for the bill.

Then, once she paid the bill, she got up to leave and reached for Priyanka's hand. He waited with his finger poised over the space bar. Mira would come any second now, he thought and waited. But she didn't.

'Can you fast forward?' he asked. The man nodded and sped through the footage. But Mira never showed up. He had reached the end of the video and was left with too many questions. Rakesh thanked the manager and asked for a copy of the footage before leaving. Maybe Mira waited outside. But why did Mira have a secret phone to call Sudha? And why was Priyanka leaving with Sudha instead of her own mother?

131

Pooja

POOJA WATCHED THE ROAD FROM BEHIND HER sunglasses, pretending she was a tourist taking pictures of the gardens. The white fence covered in bougainvillea flowers in bursts of violet, white and yellow provided the perfect cover for her to keep an eye on the street leading up to the church. Shalini was on the other side, keeping an eye out on the back entrance to make sure they didn't miss the woman they thought was Mira.

Her phone buzzed. It was Sanjay. Mother and son were ganging up on her, Pooja thought as she swiped a finger across the screen to reject the call before getting back to the job at hand.

She saw a woman walking towards her. She looked nervous, glancing around her from time to time. Pooja clicked a few pictures of her and sent them to Shalini. She definitely didn't look like Mira. Her hair was short and, unlike Mira who she had been told always wore a sari, this woman was wearing a salwar kameez. She wondered if she should send the picture to Inspector Rakesh as well but then changed her mind. What was she going to do after that, send him a picture of every woman she thought was Mira? No, she told herself, it would be better to wait and see.

The woman was almost at the church gate, but to Pooja's disappointment she passed it and turned right, walking away from both the church and Pooja. Her phone buzzed again. 'I don't think that's her,' Shalini had replied.

It wasn't.

Two hours into the exercise, around lunchtime, Pooja decided to give up. With her stomach growling more than usual, she walked over to the car and called Shalini. 'Are we done?' she asked, fishing around the glove compartment for the protein bar she usually kept there before remembering this was a rental car.

'Nothing here. Should we give up?' Shalini replied. Her voice was hoarse from smoking too many cigarettes due to stress. Sanjay sounded like this whenever a movie wasn't doing well.

'Yes, let's grab lunch,' Pooja said, instead of scolding Shalini about smoking too much. That never worked on smokers anyway.

'Okay, coming,' Shalini replied and hung up. Pooja reclined her seat and leaned back, angling her head towards the church, which was now completely out of view.

She saw another figure walking down the road, this time in a salwar kameez and sweater. Pooja chuckled at the thought of someone wearing a sweater during summer. That's when she was jolted out of her relaxed state.

Someone wearing a sweater at this hill station in the summer would not be used to the mild cold or maybe even air conditioning. She stayed where she was and took her phone out, recording a video of the woman walking.

'Come on . . . turn around,' she whispered, as if her saying this would make that woman turn.

The woman kept her head down, walking at a fast pace and looking nowhere. This had to be her. She kept recording, not wanting to risk taking a picture in case she missed the moment the woman looked up.

She was getting closer to the church gate. Pooja zoomed in and Shalini, who had come from behind, opened the door and slid in. The sound had caught the woman's eye because she turned her face towards them for just a moment. That was enough for Pooja. Thankfully, she didn't seem to realise someone was recording her because

Pooja was still lying in her reclined seat with her phone out of view.

She stopped at the entrance of the church, opened the creaky iron gate and made her way down the path.

'Was that her?' Shalini asked.

'I don't know,' Pooja replied. 'Her head was covered with her dupatta, but I think, if we go back to the room and watch the video on a bigger screen, we might just know for sure.'

Pooja dropped Shalini at the hotel and went to the market to pick up a spare memory card. As she drove around looking for an electronics goods store, she spotted a local medical shop. Pooja's mind went back to Sanjay's message, and she slammed the brakes. A bike behind narrowly avoided hitting her car and rode past, yelling about stupid female drivers. But Pooja barely paid attention as she pulled into a parking spot and, with the heavy heart, walked to the chemist shop.

Making sure her face was well covered, Pooja waited for another customer to finish. The fragrance of rasam was everywhere in the store, mixing with the smell of medicines and room freshener. Some of the store staff were eating. Her stomach growled and she hoped Shalini had ordered some lunch and that it would arrive by the time she reached the room. Once the old woman had left the shop, she approached the counter. 'Um . . .' she started, looking around. 'One bottle of Eno,' she said spotting the bottle on the shelf. 'One . . . pregnancy test and a strip of Crocin,' she rattled off the rest in one breath and looked around while the man went to fetch what she wanted.

'Cash or card?' he asked, placing the brown envelope on the counter.

She paid by cash and left. If she had paid by credit card, Sanjay would be notified and he would know she wasn't in Chennai anymore.

132
Inspector Rakesh

AS HE LEFT WITH A COPY OF THE VIDEO FILE, Rakesh didn't know what he was going to do next. Mira had met Sudha for coffee and left her child with her. No crime had been committed. He couldn't call Sudha and accuse her of being friends with a murder accused or of taking care of her daughter while Mira ran errands or whatever else she had intended to do, assuming she hadn't just abandoned her daughter. Then there was that message Mira had received in the hospital. He was pretty sure it was Sudha. So, what was he going to say to her? 'How dare you be friends with Mira and then cut off contact with her?' That was just ridiculous.

Rakesh had to make a stop outside Pooja's building and see if Richard was spying on them. It was the least he could do since her podcast was getting his so-called friends to talk to him again.

As he rode past the building half an hour later, Rakesh didn't see anyone watching them. Parking his bike at the end of the street, he searched for 'Rakesh + Mira + podcast' on Google and realised that the picture of him on the terrace was now on the news. There were at least three pages of search results about them in English and when he searched in Tamil there was much more to deal with.

He put his phone back in his pocket and was about to leave when he thought he saw some movement in Pooja's window. 'Maybe I'll just let them know the guy isn't watching them anymore,' he said to himself. He walked over and took the stairs two at a time and rang their doorbell.

Suddenly, the faint noise coming from inside stopped.

He rang the bell again and a door slammed from inside. But no one responded. He rang the bell again and heard something that definitely sounded like a 'shhhh'.

Why were Shalini and Pooja avoiding him? Had they stopped believing him? Had they interviewed Karthik? Had they seen the picture of him lying drunk on the terrace?

There was only one way to find out. He called Shalini.

She answered almost immediately. 'Yes, Ins—'

'I was telling you the truth!' he blurted out.

'Okay?' she said, sounding confused.

'Then why are you avoiding me? I am not lying, please don't believe what Karthik says.'

'Who? What? What do you mean we're avoiding you?'

'I'm standing outside your house. But you guys stopped talking as soon as I rang the doorbell. Never mind, I . . . sorry. I'm just a bit stressed.' He realised he was rambling.

'I just wanted to let you know the guy who was following you seems to have gone.'

'Stop! What do you mean you heard us talking? We aren't at home. We aren't even in Chennai. It's probably the housekeeper.'

'Oh, sorry,' Rakesh felt immense relief as Shalini started laughing.

'Pooja ma'am has a cleaner who comes once a week to maintain the house. Wait, let me ask her.'

He stayed on the line as Shalini asked if Pooja had given the house keys to the help. Pooja said something he couldn't hear. A few moments later, Shalini came back on the line.

'It's probably the housekeeper. He's old, might not have heard the doorbell. As I said, we're in another city, trying to track down someone for an interview.'

Rakesh apologised again and hung up.

Before he left, he pressed his ear to the door and listened for some movement. It was silent.

133
Pooja

WHEN POOJA REACHED THE HOTEL ROOM, Shalini had already started tucking into the mini meals the hotel had provided. Pooja's plate was sitting on the table covered with silver foil and a napkin.

She dropped the memory card on the table and went to the bathroom. 'I think it was her,' Shalini called out as she shut the door. Pooja opened the door and looked at her. 'Are you sure?'

'I am about sixty per cent sure,' she replied. 'Since we've never seen her in person. We've only seen a few images on the internet.'

'Let's try again tomorrow,' she said, shutting the door behind her.

Pooja had downed an entire litre of water on the way back, taking sips at every traffic signal. Dropping her handbag on the bathroom counter, she fished around for the pregnancy test kit. She knew how it worked; this was not her first time. Earlier, though, she had been filled with hope; now she was dreading it.

Taking a deep breath, she followed the instructions and waited. As she washed her hands, she heard Shalini's phone ring. She grabbed the stick again and stared at it, willing the result to be negative. She had been under a lot of stress of late, there were fights with Sanjay and irregular meals. The constant travel of the last few days wouldn't have helped. These could all result in a late period, right? That's what she'd read online.

Shalini banging on the door brought her back to the present. 'Did you give the key to someone?'

'What?' she asked, her mind still on the test.

'The house keys, does anyone else have a copy?' she shouted again.

Pooja opened the door a crack and peeped out. Shalini was still on the phone, looking stressed. 'What's wrong?'

'Inspector Rakesh stopped by. He said he could hear people in the apartment, but no one has opened the door. He thought we were avoiding him.'

'The housekeeper has a key. He's supposed to come tomorrow, but he comes and goes as he pleases.'

'Thank God,' Shalini said, walking back to the table. 'It's probably the housekeeper. He's old, might not have heard the doorbell. As I said, we're in another city are out of station, trying to track down someone for an interview.'

Pooja shut the door and went back to the stick. It was positive.

134
Inspector Rakesh

RAKESH LEFT THE BUILDING AFTER SPEAKING with Shalini, but he still couldn't shake off the feeling that something was off about the situation. Grabbing his phone, he texted Atif and rode back home. He needed to inform Bindhu where he was headed or she'd be furious. Thankfully, Atif was coming along to convince her to let him go out.

An hour later, after leaving a fuming Bidhu at home, Atif and Rakesh reached the bar. On the way, Atif had updated him on everything that had happened the previous night after Rakesh left. Atif had managed to initiate conversation with one man from the gang; it was the opening they needed. Tonight, the man sat with them and laughed about Rakesh's wife being a pain in the ass. 'Tell me, Rakesh sir,' he said between inebriated snorts of laughter. 'How did you manage two women?'

'Two women?' Rakesh asked, feigning ignorance even though he knew fully well what the guy was asking him about.

'You know, your wife and that Mira woman.'

'Even you don't believe me now, do you?' Rakesh slurred, keeping it together as best as he could. He wasn't as young as he used to be and drinking three nights in a row was giving him a throbbing headache. 'I didn't manage two women . . .' he said. 'I only met Mira after school that one time!'

The men laughed, shaking their heads. 'We've seen her, sir. She may be mad but she sure is hot.'

Kumar leaned forward. 'But crazy women are great in bed, aren't they?' he winked, and the table burst out in raucous laughter. Rakesh gritted his teeth and continued. 'How will I know that, sir? My wife gets crazy only when I am late reaching home.'

'In that case, she will be so angry with you tonight,' the short man sitting next to Kumar replied, glancing at the clock on the wall opposite him.

'She is at a party tonight. Didn't want to show her humiliating husband's face there,' Rakesh said.

The short man patted his shoulder in a show of comfort. 'It's okay, sir. She'll come around. Till then you are welcome to sleep on my terrace,' he said and everyone burst out laughing again.

'I can't even catch a fucking break?' Rakesh whined. He wasn't sure anymore if he was acting or serious. Everything was starting to blur. 'I deserve some points for not cheating, but I keep getting into trouble.'

'Of course you do!' Kumar slapped the tabletop. 'Men are like animals. We have a strong urge to spread our genes everywhere. The fact that we are married and forced to be monogamous is punishment enough. These women should be grateful we don't leave them!'

There was some murmurs of agreement as Kumar added, 'See, I can easily get a younger, prettier wife. But I remain loyal to my wife. I deserve a reward for that.'

Rakesh nodded. But he knew that Kumar had no choice but to remain loyal to his wife. Atif had briefed him about Kumar on the way here. A no-good rowdy who'd befriended the businessman father and married the not-so-pretty daughter. Like Rakesh, Kumar owed his career, his money and his entire life to his wife's family. If he ever stepped out of line his father-in-law would skin him alive.

Rakesh poured another glass for everyone, topping off their alcohol with sodas and Coke. He had managed to get them more drunk than usual. 'To our crazy wives!' he said, raising his glass.

135
Pooja

A NIGHT OF LYING ON THE LUMPY HOTEL mattress wasn't helping things but Pooja had forced herself to wake up early to go to the church the next day. She had called the orphanage associated with the church earlier that morning to book an appointment and the woman who answered the phone seemed taken aback. 'Someone told me you're doing good work with children. I just wanted to know how I could help,' she explained as sweetly as she could. With a 9 a.m. appointment with the head of the orphanage, Pooja parked their rented car on the steep driveway and got out.

She walked along the building towards the entrance with Shalini following her. Suddenly, she felt Shalini grabbing her by her elbow and pulling her to a corner. 'I think someone inside is watching us.'

'What!? How do you know?'

'Someone was watching us and as soon as I looked up, they moved away. I saw the curtain move,' she said.

But Pooja dismissed it with a wave of her hand. 'It's probably a kid.' But as Shalini passed her to knock on the door, she glanced up at the first floor to see if there really was someone watching them.

'I think I'll stay out here,' Shalini said, taking a step back and pulling out her camera. Pooja nodded and watched her go.

The heavy wooden door opened after a couple of knocks, and a smiling nun stood on the other side, 'You must be Mrs Reddy,' she said, moving back to let her in.

Pooja turned around to check if she could spot Shalini. She was already a dot disappearing around the end of the main building.

'So, you wanted to have a look at our facilities and maybe make a donation for the children?' the sister said, pointing at a chair in her small office.

'I'm sorry I didn't quite catch your name,' Pooja said, smiling as she sat down. She'd dressed up well today. Thankfully, she'd had the foresight to pack some nice clothes for the trip. Pooja pushed her sunglasses on her head and waited for a response.

'Yes, I'm Sister Rose.' She pronounced it as Rosy instead of Rose and Pooja wondered where she was from.

'Sister Rose, I have to tell you I'm here for completely selfish reasons.' Pooja had decided to play the sympathy card. 'My husband and I, you know film producer Sanjay Reddy, have been trying to get pregnant for a while,' Pooja said, dropping Sanjay's name shamelessly. Her stomach lurched when she said the word 'pregnant' but she pushed the thought aside. The sister's expression didn't change. 'I just thought that if I did something for kids, maybe karma will do its job and help us?'

The sister raised her eyebrows and smiled vaguely. Pooja realised she had made a mistake and hurried to clarify. 'If I don't end up having kids, at least being able to help others kids in some way. So, in a way, this is a selfish endeavour.'

'Understood,' the sister said, standing up. 'You mentioned on the call that you wanted a small tour of the facilities? Would you like to start now?'

'Sure,' Pooja said, looking behind her again to try and spot Shalini through the windows. But she was nowhere to be seen.

136
Inspector Rakesh

HE HAD NO IDEA WHAT HAD GOT INTO HIM. But when he saw a set of keys sticking out of the bags of one of the men, Rakesh grabbed it. It was burning against his leg now as he sat in the autorickshaw that was taking him home. The same rickshaw had taken Kumar home the previous night. Rakesh didn't indulge in his usual banal conversation with drivers in case this one was under their employ. Instead, he thanked the man, stumbling a bit as he got out, and paid in cash.

The house was empty when he went in. Bindhu was clearly spending the night at her parents' home again, and Rakesh was okay with that. It gave him more time to follow through with his plans. Hungry and alone, Rakesh went to the fridge and removed a plate of leftover rice mixed with pickle for dinner. On the way to the sofa, he picked up a packet of chips.

When he woke up the next morning, Rakesh had no idea how he had ended up in bed. The last thing he remembered was eating a second dinner and throwing up. He looked down the front of his shirt and thankfully, there was neither vomit nor food stains on it. Quickly putting his phone to charge, he rushed to the bathroom to wash up and leave for Kumar's house. It was time to follow his movements.

Rakesh made it in the nick of time. It was quite a feat, he thought, considering he had to go to the bar first to pick up his bike. But once he was on it, he raced through the streets, unconcerned about breaking speeding laws, and reached just in time to see Kumar leave on a scooter. It was a little odd considering the posh area he lived in and the kind of house he owned, Rakesh thought, as he hid his face with his visor and rode a safe distance away.

After a few minutes, Kumar stopped to get fuel and continued till he reached a nondescript building with a commercial sign on it. He had driven eight kilometres from home. It was in a residential area, which was surprising considering the risky nature of his business. Rakesh rode past the house next to which Kumar had parked his scooter. Rakesh memorised the door number. Then, hiding his bike behind a tree, he waited.

137
Pooja

BY THE TIME SHE FINISHED THE TOUR OF THE orphanage, Pooja was exhausted. Her feet were aching and she'd had to dislodge her stilettos from the cobblestone pathways quite a few times. The children seemed amused by the predicament her sky-high heels were putting her in.

None of the staff or caretakers in the church resembled Mira, though. Pooja was disappointed they hadn't found her there. She promised Sister Rose that she'd call back later and left. On the way out, she noticed a pregnant woman waiting and a sister ushering her in.

As she got into her car, Pooja's phone pinged again. It had pinged the entire time she was with Sister Rose who had glared at her several times for it. She finally checked it.

Shalini had sent close to twenty WhatsApp messages, including a few pictures and a location.

'That woman, I saw her.' 'She came out and went to some building.' 'Here's where I am. Too far to walk back. Pick me up please.' 'Wish I had brought the camera. It's in the car. Can you come here?' 'She's gone out. I know which street she's in. It could be either the yellow building or the slightly less yellow building.' And on it went.

Pooja clicked on the link to the location and started her car. As she pulled into the small street, wondering how she would back up if another vehicle came from the opposite direction, Shalini darted out to the street from a florist's shop.

'Why were you inside the orphanage for such a long time! My God!'

'You could've walked back, you know.'

'And missed the location?'

'You mean this place you sent me?' Pooja asked, manoeuvring between two badly parked bikes.

'The street next to this one is wider. Park there,' Shalini said, guiding her till Pooja parked the car rather uncomfortably between a small truck and a covered pushcart. They waited in the car next to a quiet building for half an hour before Pooja spotted the woman. Next to her, Shalini had gone to sleep and was now snoring loudly.

'Wake up!' she hissed and nudged Shalini with her elbow.

'Wha . . . who. . . . whatdidido?' Shalini said, waking up with a start.

'Look! Isn't that her? The one who looked like Mira?' Pooja said, pointing at a woman who was walking towards the building with cloth bags containing groceries in both hands. They ducked back down as she approached the gate and their car. Thankfully, she didn't notice them as she walked inside and shut the gate. A couple of minutes later, a light in the back room on the ground floor turned on.

'Should we?' Shalini asked.

'Go! Go!' Pooja whispered and Shalini slipped out of the car with the camera. Shalini's dark kurta vanished behind the rose bushes and Pooja lay back in her seat, keeping watch. Nothing happened for at least half an hour but then the gate opened again, and two women stepped out. Pooja was parked two houses down, and neither one of them gave her dark, dusty vehicle a second glance as they hurried down the street towards the main road.

A few moments later, Shalini emerged from the bush.

'They were talking about some woman or girl,' she said, getting into the car.

'Something about how she was safe now and nothing could harm her anymore—that she was in a better place.'

'Sounds like whoever they're talking about died.'

'Yeah. But they didn't call that person Mira, they called her Priyanka.'

'But did the woman look like Mira?' Pooja asked, feeling hope slip a little bit. They had been tracking her so long that she wanted her—actually any woman—to be Mira.

'Honestly, I couldn't tell. The windows were half shut, and the frosted glass didn't help matters. I only saw her profile.'

'I guess it can't be helped,' Pooja shrugged.

'There's a "to let" board up front,' Shalini said suddenly. 'I could . . .'

'No . . .' Pooja replied. 'What if she gets scared?'

'I won't be meeting her. I can just ask the owner the name of the person living there!' Shalini said, jumping out of the car and walking away before Pooja could protest.

138
Inspector Rakesh

HE HAD DOUBLE CHECKED BY DRIVING PAST A few times. It was definitely empty. Kumar's little scooter was nowhere to be seen and as far as he knew, everyone else came by cycle or by public transportation.

Later that evening, Rakesh parked his bike a street away from Kumar's office and walked to the building. He scaled the wall easily, his cap hiding his face from any cameras the owner might have installed.

The door had just one lock and it opened without a creak. Rakesh was suddenly glad he regularly forgot to oil the hinges in his house. He quickly looked around the office to make sure no office boy had slept over. Once he was sure the coast was clear, he locked the door and pocketed the key.

The office comprised four rooms. The main one had chairs everywhere and also a plaque on the wall that said 'Lalli Import Export'. He clicked a picture and continued to the second room which seemed to be the actual office, complete with plush chairs and a brand-new split AC. The walls were covered with various pictures of gods adorned with floral garlands. The smell of incense—artificial rose—still clung to the air

Rakesh donned the gloves he'd brought with him. He wasn't sure what he was going to find here, but he knew it would be something interesting. He remembered Kumar telling a short guy at the bar the night before about carefully locking this place. 'I'll be going to the factory,' Kumar had said. 'Make sure you go to the office every day, we shouldn't leave the place alone.'

One of the keys he'd had stolen looked like it would fit the cupboard on his left. It protested loudly as Rakesh opened it and he stopped for a bit, straining his ears to make sure no one was nearby.

It seemed Kumar really did run an import–export business. There were invoices and bills in most of the files inside the cupboard, and by the time he finished going through the last shelf Rakesh was sure he had risked breaking into this office for nothing. The one place he hadn't checked was the locker that was placed on top of the cupboard. None of the keys from the bunch could open it. It had to be with Kumar himself.

Rakesh went back to the files he found. It had order numbers, invoices, addresses for delivery—all with dates and times mentioned on them. They were all for construction material but some of it made no sense to him. One truck of bricks was selling for way more than the market price.

When Bindhu and he had built their house a few years ago, bricks hadn't cost so much. Another invoice, this one for cement and bricks, was once again too high. All the trucks carrying the construction material started their journey from a godown in Red Hills, somewhere in Chennai's industrial area. He clicked a picture of the address.

Back when he was working under Parameshwaran he'd been part of a drug bust. They had raided a restaurant that was the front for the operation. It sold drugs in tiny quantities to college students and the like. But to get the right drug, they had to order something that wasn't on the menu, a code word known only to those who were aware of how the whole operation worked. Since Rakesh was much thinner and fitter, he had posed, along with Karthik, as a college student and asked for a magic blue falooda.

He had got a regular falooda in a takeaway drink mug. But in the takeaway bag was a pouch with a party drug that had been doing the rounds at that time. Rakesh remembered that he had been charged two thousand and eight hundred rupees while a regular falooda would have cost only two hundred.

Rakesh concluded that the company was either smuggling something under the guise of building materials, or their customers were using their services to cheat the income tax department.

Rakesh carefully took pictures of each invoice till he was satisfied that there was nothing more to see in that cupboard. He shut it and went back to the safe. His phone pinged and Rakesh's heart skipped a beat. The sound of the notification was jarring in the quiet office. 'Someone is coming,' it said. Tucking everything back into place, Rakesh rushed out of the office and locked the door behind him.

He had made it out just in time. As he tucked himself behind the staircase leading to the top floor, he saw

Richard, the one he'd spotted outside Pooja's apartment, open the door and go in.

Rakesh quickly jumped over the fence into the next building. Then, bending low to keep himself out of view, he duck-walked along the wall and walked out of the gate that was thankfully open.

When he reached his bike he checked his phone again, zooming in to see the pictures he had just clicked. Among the invoices was a picture of the safe. Next to it was a framed photo of Kumar shaking hands with a man. Rakesh zoomed to see who the man was. He could recognise that outfit and that dual-coloured hairdo anywhere. It was a regular picture of Kumar. But it was the man he was shaking hands with, the one who had opened his factory, that interested him.

It was the minister who was in the news recently, whose son had mowed down a few people some weeks ago.

139
Pooja

POOJA QUICKLY GOT OUT OF THE CAR AND ran after Shalini. The young woman was much too fast for her, and Pooja's heels weren't helping. She slowed down to a walk as an old man stared at them, readjusting her dupatta and her hair. Shalini was already knocking on the gate.

The door opened and Pooja could see an older woman's head pop out. Shalini smiled, pointed at the white board on the building, and a few moments later, Shalini went into the building. Pooja walked back to the car and her phone rang just as she reached it. She got in, reclined her seat and answered.

'Madam, you need to come back,' her housekeeper Bhasker said as soon as she answered.

'What happened?' she asked. He sounded aggrieved.

'I think a thief came to the house, madam,' he said, almost wailing this time.

'What!' What do you mean by thief?'

'Madam, there is mess everywhere.'

Pooja immediately switched to a video call. But Bhaskar wasn't tech savvy and Pooja kept her anxiety at bay as she tried to teach him how to flip his camera. When he finally succeeded, she was aghast at what she saw.

It looked like a tornado had passed through the house. Clothes and papers were strewn everywhere. Every room was in the same condition. She instructed Bhasker to not touch anything and called Rakesh immediately. When he didn't answer, she messaged him to call her back immediately and then dialled Shalini's number.

140
Inspector Rakesh

ATIF WAS WAITING NEAR HIS BIKE FOR HIM. They hid behind a parked truck and watched Richard leave a few minutes later. 'Let's go back in,' Rakesh said and went to the gate. He stepped in the compound and a short, young man stepped out, zipping his backpack.

The two of them stared at each other, both unsure of what to do. Rakesh saw a look of panic cross the younger man's face. He looked like a cornered rat. 'Listen,' Rakesh said, putting his hand out to calm the man.

Just then the man spotted Atif and taking one look at his police uniform, turned around and bolted.

'STOP!' Rakesh screamed, following him. From the corner of his eye, he saw Atif giving chase as well.

The man was quite fast for his size and Rakesh was having trouble keeping up. He turned into the small gully between two stores and leapt over a fallen garbage bin. 'Stop!' Rakesh yelled again, but this time it came out as a gasp. Atif was next to him now and Rakesh stopped to let him pass; he was faster anyway.

Rakesh caught his breath for a moment and continued running. By the time he reached the two men, the man was sitting on an upturned flowerpot with Atif twisting his arm behind his back. 'Sir,' he said, nodding at the bag the man had dropped. 'He has some weed with him, seems like he's a ganja dealer.'

The man looked at the backpack nervously, not saying a word.

'So that's why you ran,' Rakesh said, picking up the bag and checking it. Atif was right, there was a small bag of ganja in there, but it wasn't enough to make him a dealer. Then, he saw it. A hard drive hidden behind some books and a pair of jeans. He looked at Atif who was trying to communicate with him through his wriggling eyebrows.

He looked back into the backpack and took out the small bag. 'Out of stock, huh? You're lucky. Else you'd have definite jail time,' he told the young man. Atif looked worried and continued raising both eyebrows, looking at the bag and making an angry face.

Rakesh tried his best not to laugh while rummaging through the bag. 'Nothing else in here.' He pulled out the book, bent down to meet his eyes and asked, 'College student?' The man nodded.

'Which college?'

'Sir, online, sir. PG, sir,' he panted.

'MBA?' he asked, looking at the book cover.

'Yes, sir. Sir, sorry, sir. I won't do it again, sir. Please, sir,' he begged, his eyes looking more scared than he needed to be. Rakesh put the books back in the bag and closed it.

'No need to worry. We will let you off with a warning this time,' Rakesh said and watched Atif's eyes go wide. 'Come to the police station tomorrow evening, pay the fine and collect your bag.'

'Sir, sir . . . Please, sir,' the man begged.

'What's your name?'

'Sir, Ranga.'

'Ranga, just come to the police station tomorrow and take it, all right. Why are you so scared? I'm not arresting you, right?'

'Sir exams, sir. I have to study.' His voice was almost timid now.

Rakesh had had enough. 'If you had to study, then why the fuck are you outside selling drugs? Let's take him to the police station now,' he snapped, getting up and dusting off his pants.

'Sir, please, sir.'

'Either go home and collect your bag tomorrow. Or come with us now and we'll keep you while we write up charges for selling drugs. Don't worry, you can study in your jail cell. Some of your clients will be under eighteen, right, since you're a college student? That's selling drugs to minors.'

The man remained silent, glancing between the bag and the two of them. 'Do you have more drugs in here?'

'Sir, no.'

'Then what are you staring at?'

'Sir, house key . . .' he said meekly. Rakesh rolled his eyes and asked him where it was. He pointed at the bag's front pocket where Rakesh found a bike key, a house key and a wallet.

'Don't you keep your wallet on you?' he asked, handing it over to the man after checking the driving licence inside. 'Rangan Gopal, born in 1996, resident of Vellore.' He had around four hundred rupees in there; he was clearly not a drug dealer.

Ranga didn't answer. Instead, he mutely took the keys and the wallet, tucking them awkwardly into his pants pocket. Atif was still holding him down.

'Tomorrow,' Rakesh said, nodding to Atif who told the young man which police station to come to.

The two of them followed Ranga as he walked back the way they came. He got on a small red scooter that was parked in front of an internet café and zoomed away after another fearful look at them.

'You could be a kathakali dancer, Atif,' Rakesh laughed as the young man rode away from them.

'Sir?' Atif asked, looking confused. Rakesh imitated his eyebrow movements from earlier, bursting into laughter at Atif's horrified expression. 'I was just trying to . . .'

'. . . to tell me a story through your eyes. A perfect kathakali dancer,' Rakesh said, laughing again as Atif's face went red.

141
Pooja

POOJA AND SHALINI RUSHED BACK TO THE hotel and quickly packed their things. They were on the road in an hour, racing to get back to Chennai before dark.

'Who the fuck would do this!' Shalini said, calling Rakesh again.

'He must be busy,' Pooja said. Her mind was racing. Her entire childhood was in that house. Thankfully, all the valuables had left with her parents to the US. Except for some old clothes and furniture, there was nothing in the house of much value. But every precious thing she owned was there. Her school pictures, certificates, memories. She shifted gears as soon as the truck in front of her gave way and pushed ahead.

Next to her, Shalini sat clutching onto the seat, her knuckles white.

'Do you want to tell Sanjay?' Shalini asked, after a while.

'No,' Pooja replied. 'Not before I tell my parents. It's their house. I need to inform them first.' She wondered how they would react. She would probably get an earful. They were disappointed by her recent behaviour; in fact, she doubted they were ever even proud of her. Would they kick her out? She didn't have another place to go without Sanjay's help.

'Can you call Rakesh again?' she asked, shaking her head to clear her mind. 'First things first. We need to talk to the police.'

142
Inspector Rakesh

HARRY, THE HACKER, WAS STILL IN HIS PYJAMAS when he opened the door. 'Hi, sir,' he said, scratching his stomach and moving aside to let him in. He had moved back with his parents since the last time Rakesh had seen him. The house was starkly different from where he'd lived before; it was clean, didn't smell like weed and sweat and, most of all, Harry looked actually groomed. Rakesh chuckled at the difference.

'You're looking like an actual human now,' he said, taking a seat on the long L-shaped couch.

'And dating two women doesn't suit you,' Harry shot back, pointing at Rakesh's tummy.

'I'm not . . .' he started and realised Harry was chuckling. 'What happened?' Rakesh asked, pointing at Harry's clean-shaven baby face.

'Amma made me remove the beard,' Harry replied, rubbing his chin. Rakesh could see why his mother had done that; Harry had gone from looking like a middle-aged hooligan to looking like a teenager. No one would guess that a year ago he had been brought to the police station for hacking into his professor's computer and leaking every single question paper to his classmates. His boss back then, Parameshwaran, had been brought in quietly so the college wouldn't lose face, but, of course, everyone knew. It was an open secret that a mere teenager had leaked Winston

University's engineering papers. Harikrishnan, Harry for short, was a legend there.

'Tell me, sir,' Harry asked now, sitting on the sofa with a bottle of water. 'I didn't do anything, you know.'

'I know. This time, I need you to do something,' Rakesh replied, taking out the hard drive from his bag. 'This is important. Is there anyone else here?'

'No, mum and dad have gone on a pilgrimage to pray that I stop drinking,' he said, rolling his eyes.

'You're just twenty, right?' Rakesh asked.

'Yes. I don't drink though,' he smiled. 'Only weed.'

'I will pretend I didn't hear that,' Rakesh said, handing the drive over to him.

'What is it?'

'A hard drive.'

'Duh! That's obvious. What should I do with it?'

'I don't know if anything was deleted. I need to retrieve everything that was ever in there.'

'Whose is it?' he asked.

Rakesh decided to answer honestly. 'It belongs to a suspect in a human trafficking ring. This could be the evidence we need.'

'Whoa! Wait a minute, why can't you ask your cybercrime team to do this?'

'I am suspended. And anyway . . . this case is related to some bigshot,' Rakesh started, remembering Harry's conspiracy theories. 'I need to make a copy of the evidence and then return it before anyone finds out. I have a day.'

'Let's get started then,' Harry said, leaving the drive on the sofa and vanishing behind a beaded curtain. When he came back, he had a heavy-looking laptop with him. 'It will take some time,' he said. 'In case you want to come back.'

'Can't leave it and go . . .'

'I'll have you know I am going to do some illegal stuff here,' Harry said, pulling out a slightly squished joint from his pocket. 'You can't say anything.'

'I'm asking you to do illegal stuff, boy. I won't say anything. Go on.' Rakesh said, pulling up a chair.

143
Pooja

THEY REACHED HOME AROUND 10.00 P.M. AND ran up the stairs, leaving their luggage behind in the car. As promised, Atif was waiting for them. Rakesh had finally answered his call and when he heard what had happened, he said something that surprised Pooja. 'Well, that was fast.' She would ask him to clarify later.

Atif waited for Pooja to open the door. Bhasker, who had returned, stood next to the watchman who was beside himself. Atif stepped into the room, took out his phone and snapped pictures of everything.

'The police station didn't send anyone else?' Pooja asked, following behind. She could hear Shalini cursing softly behind her as she looked at the mess.

'This isn't my station's jurisdiction. I need to have someone from your area come in,' he replied, moving on to the recording room and taking pictures. The kitchen seemed untouched. So did the other bedroom which Pooja hadn't opened since coming back. The only rooms they had gone through were the two Shalini and she had used these past few weeks.

Pooja waited for Atif to finish as she called her brother in the US. As she finished telling him what happened, she could hear the disappointment in his voice. 'I knew this would happen. The watchman is old, and the house has been empty for so long. Bhasker also has a loose tongue. I bet he's gone around boasting about his sweet gig, cleaning an empty house once a week. If that.'

Pooja didn't say anything. She didn't want her brother to know this was probably all her fault. This was better. She would replace any damaged items and it would end at that. Provided nothing was stolen.

'I will tell mum and dad,' her brother sighed. 'Are you guys safe?'

'Yes, we are.' In the background she could hear his kids screaming for their mother.

'I have to go. Let me know what's stolen and if you're filing a case,' he said and hung up.

'Tell—' Pooja started but her brother had hung up already. She shouldn't have expected much from him. He was a busy man. She watched as Atif gingerly lifted a pair of pants with his pen.

He finished five minutes later and came back to the living room.

'Do you want to file a complaint?' he asked, putting his hands in his pocket. 'Of course we want to . . .' Shalini started, but Pooja put her hand up.

'What happens if we do?'

'Nothing,' Atif said, shrugging his shoulders. 'If you'd had CCTV cameras, we could have done something. We can check for fingerprints, eliminate yours and the cleaner's. But we have to have something in our records to match it to. Basically, nothing will happen.'

'But other CCTV cameras . . .' Pooja said.

'There is no forced entry. Whoever it was seems to have a copy of the house key,' Atif said. 'We can call the local police station, but apart from an hour of inconvenience don't expect anything. Now if something is missing, especially electronics or jewellery and you can give me an image of it or the serial number, we can actually do something.'

'How did they get a copy of the key?' Shalini said, looking at the housekeeper. Bhasker looked as surprised as them.

'I will file a complaint,' Pooja finally said and Atif nodded, taking out his phone. 'I know someone at the local police station. I will see if they can come over now.'

144
Inspector Rakesh

AS HARRY WORKED, RAKESH WALKED AROUND his living room, looking at the photo frames on the walls. There were a lot of pictures of him receiving prizes. And those trophies were all displayed in the show case. 'Second in Chess', 'Best Debate Team', 'First in Chess'—the list went on. The boy had won awards in everything except sports and cultural events.

'Why the guitar in the corner? From what I can see, you haven't participated in any musical competitions?' he asked, walking around the dining table and approaching the haze of marijuana smoke.

'The guitar is to get girls. They won't pay attention to me otherwise,' Harry replied, squinting at the screen.

'Doesn't work that easily, you know.'

'It does when their ego has been crushed by an idiotic ex-boyfriend.'

'How much longer?'

'It's not as easy as they show in the movies, you know,' Harry replied dryly.

'Sorry. Just asked.'

Harry looked up. 'There's some pizza in the fridge if you're hungry. I suggest you get comfortable. This will take a while.'

Rakesh didn't want the day-old vegetarian pizza, so he ordered something fresh and went through the photos he had taken in Kumar's office. One of them said there was a shipment due on Friday. This Friday. This must've been the one they were discussing in the bar.

If he could be there, maybe take some pictures, maybe some evidence. Just as he was thinking this, his phone rang. It was Shalini again. He didn't want to discuss anything with the boy around, so he typed out a message saying he'll call back and waited for his food as quietly as possible. A while later, Harry let out a gasp.

'Holy fuck!' he said, leaping off his seat in a panic.

'What? What!' Rakesh asked, jumping up. The boy looked utterly terrified.

'I am NOT involving myself in this disgusting shit. No fucking way. No, I won't.' He was backing away from the laptop. Rakesh climbed over the sofa between them and looked at the screen.

Rakesh looked at the open folder and a chill ran through him. 'I knew they were up to something. I thought drugs but this? Bastards!' he growled.

'I am not—'

'You have to,' Rakesh whirled around at Harry. 'You absolutely have to. This is important evidence! I need a backup.'

'Sir, I don't want even a slight hint of this on my system. I refuse to be involved,' Harry said. His false bravado was now gone and he was close to tears. 'I cannot. *Chee*. It is so disgusting!'

'Harry,' Rakesh said, walking towards the boy. 'These are bad people. Do you understand that?'

'Obviously I do!'

'Okay, so these bad people need to go to jail. Right? I need evidence to ensure that happens. You see what they did to me the second I found out what happened? I got suspended the day we found proof on one phone,' Rakesh asked. Harry nodded, defeated.

'They did that to me when I had barely scratched the surface,' Rakesh continued. Harry looked like he was calming down. 'If I don't preserve this evidence, I will not be able to punish these guys. If I could copy it myself, I would do it. But I needed you to figure out a way to do it so that no one knows this file was accessed. You know I would never put you in a position like this if I had a choice.'

Harry was looking at him nervously. The joint he had been smoking earlier lay forgotten on the floor. 'Listen, brother,' he said, affectionately calling him younger brother, 'there was a little girl whose fath—, eh, whose parents found out about this. Her mother's life has been ruined because she wanted to save her child. She's gone now. But these other children . . .' he pointed at the screen behind him. 'They are still here. If we don't save them, can you imagine what they will go through?'

Harry looked distressed and didn't speak for a few minutes. But Rakesh could see that he was getting his determination back. Rakesh stepped back and let Harry go back to work. He copied all the images and slowly transferred them to the other USB drive. As he did so, Rakesh noticed that he was trying not to look at the horrible pictures in front of him. He couldn't bear to look at them too. In all the pictures, young boys and girls were holding up a small blackboard with various numbers written on it. Some of them in various stages of undress.

145
Pooja

BY THE TIME THE POLICE LEFT, IT WAS CLOSE to midnight.

Pooja had gone through all the shelves after they were checked for prints and found that nothing was missing. Except for one packet of chips. She wasn't sure if she had eaten it herself or if the intruders had munched on some snacks while ransacking her apartment.

She had promised to visit the police station the next morning to file an official complaint. After she escorted them out, Shalini went to the car and brought back their suitcases along with the laptop and camera. The housekeeper handed over his key to Pooja and left as well.

'What do you want to do?' Shalini asked, 'Are you going back to Mumbai?'

'No . . . I don't know,' Pooja said.

The police had promised to go through the CCTV footage from a nearby building, but Pooja doubted they would find anything useful there. If the intruders had managed to get a copy of her keys, they would have been careful to avoid the cameras too. 'Where are the hard drives which have the recordings?' she suddenly remembered.

'I brought them with me,' Shalini replied, pointing to her backpack. 'Moreover, everything is backed up as well.'

'They took nothing . . .'

'They did damage the microphones,' Pooja replied.

Neither of them spoke for a while. Finally, Pooja sat up straight. 'I'm buying a CCTV camera,' she said, whipping out her phone and placing the order online. It would be here the day after.

'You wanna sleep?' Shalini asked. She had already brought sheets from the bedroom cupboard and was curled up on the sofa.

'I can't,' Pooja replied. 'What if . . .' She knew this latest upheaval in her life had something to do with the podcast. With Mira. But she couldn't help thinking that Sanjay and his mother wanted her back home in Mumbai. A copy of the keys to this house was in Sanjay's cupboard since they got married. She wouldn't put it past him to do something like this to make her go back to him.

It wasn't going to work.

She checked her phone. There was no communication from Sanjay.

She got up and took photos of the damaged room from multiple angles. Then, she began composing a tweet.

146
Inspector Rakesh

THE BACKUP WAS SAFELY STORED AWAY AND Atif had given the keys he had stolen to a locksmith to make a second copy. Rakesh had picked it up and was on his way to the bar to return the original. He had to do it before someone realised it was gone.

Once there, he took his usual seat. He was early today and the others hadn't arrived yet. He placed his order and, when no one was looking, slipped the key behind the dustbin. It was close enough to their regular table for them to believe they had dropped it. Once he was satisfied that he had done a good job, Rakesh joined the other patrons in front of the TV, ready to scream at the cricket match being telecast.

When Rakesh woke up the next morning, Bindhu was gone again. There was no text from her informing him of her whereabouts either. He called her and got a busy tone. Then he called Atif.

The boy they'd caught the previous day had collected his bag. Rakesh had made sure to put everything back the way it was. Except the weed. He'd handed that over to Harry who was quite disappointed at its average quality. That didn't stop him from taking it though. 'He seemed really worried,' Atif said. 'I asked if he had hidden any other drugs in the bag and he almost ran away from the police station.'

'Good,' Rakesh replied. They needed him to believe they hadn't checked the backpack. It was crucial that no one knew that they knew.

'Pooja Reddy madam has filed a case,' Atif informed him. Rakesh had completely forgotten about that.

'What happened? Was anything stolen?' he asked.

'Nothing. But they broke their microphones and cut the wires. Clearly, it's related to Mira's case. She tweeted about it last night, didn't you see?'

He hadn't. He immediately checked and found the tweet. Pooja was smart. She hadn't mentioned the podcast. Instead, she had said that the city wasn't as safe as it claimed to be, but thankfully her secret CCTV had captured the perpetrators and that the police would nab them soon.

'Do we have the footage?'

'She doesn't have a CCTV installed. The building nearby caught something though.'

'Can you send me images?' Rakesh asked.

'The other police station has them. You'll have to ask Pooja directly.'

'Dammit! Okay I'll do that,' Rakesh said and hung up.

147
Pooja

HER TWEET HAD RECEIVED THOUSANDS OF likes and retweets by the time she woke up. She had also received calls and messages from journalists who had her phone number. She added a second tweet, saying that she and her staff were safe. And finally, she returned Sanjay's many calls.

'Yes,' she said as soon as he answered.

'Come back,' he said. Pooja sat on the sofa just as Shalini yawned and woke up.

'Why?'

'WHY?' he sputtered. 'Someone BROKE into your house. And you want me to give you reasons?'

'That just means I'm on to something,' she replied as coolly as she could.

'Poo, that means you're not safe. Come back.' Pooja stood up and walked into her room before finally saying what she had kept buried inside her. 'And am I safe around you, Sanjay?'

'I . . . stop being a fucking bitch! I apologised, didn't I?'

'Moreover, who is to say you aren't trying to scare me into coming back! You have a copy of the keys,' she said angrily and hung up. He called again but she ignored his call. Her friend Dhakshi called next, but she rejected her call as well.

'All good?' Shalini asked, when she went back to the living room.

'Yes,' Pooja said. 'Let's have breakfast before going to the police station. What do you want?'

The visit to the police station was fruitful. She wasn't sure if her tweet had done the trick or if Inspector Rakesh knew someone there. But the cops had procured the CCTV footage from the next building. Pooja and Shalini went through it and realised that it had happened the night Inspector Rakesh had called Shalini in anger, asking why they weren't letting him in.

The inspector in charge, Praveen, sat with them as they went through the footage.

'Look here,' he said, pointing at the time stamp in the corner of the frame. 'That's when this guy broke into your house.' Pooja gasped. She recognised him. It was the same man that Inspector Rakesh had warned her about, the one who had been watching their apartment. Even on the grainy footage, Pooja could recognise his balding, shiny head.

'Do you know him?' Praveen asked, pausing the video. Pooja nodded. 'I've seen him before. Quite a few times actually. Outside my building.'

'Looks like he was doing a recce,' Praveen said and pressed play. The man looked around, covering his face with one hand, and went into the building.

They sped through the rest of the video. They saw Inspector Rakesh enter and exit the building in a span of two minutes. Pooja had to explain to a curious cop why he was visiting her. 'I told him to collect the recorded interview,' she said. 'We interviewed him for the podcast, and I had promised to give him a copy.' None of them asked why she didn't just email it to him.

The video showed that the man left shortly after Inspector Rakesh. He must have been spooked. It didn't look like he had taken anything with him, but Pooja insisted on proceeding with the case. She wasn't taking any chances, not with two women living alone.

By the time Pooja and Shalini left, it was late. But as soon as they were in the car, she told Shalini to call both Atif and Rakesh. 'We are going to meet them and get to the fucking bottom of this,' she said, slamming down harder than needed on the clutch.

148
Breaking News

'POOJA REDDY IS TRENDING ON TWITTER AGAIN and as usual the supporters and trolls have been active. One group has concluded that she was trying to stay relevant because she was no longer popular. The other group is sure that men broke into her house because of the podcast. Reddit and Twitter are both abuzz with people trying to solve the Mira mystery. They have also come up with multiple theories on why someone would want the case shut down. The popular opinion right now seems to be that the people who killed Madhu had done the same to Mira as well and are now coming for Pooja Reddy.' The news anchor was her usual animated self.

'It remains to be seen if the reason for the break-in at Pooja Reddy's studio was because of the podcast or, as Mrs Reddy herself said, because it had remained empty for too long.

'This is News Views, you heard it here first.'

149
Pooja

WHEN THEY CAME BACK FROM THE POLICE station, Rakesh was waiting for them outside the building. They walked up to Pooja's apartment and Shalini started speaking as soon as they shut the door. 'Guess who it was?' she asked. 'That guy who was spying on us.'

Rakesh stopped mid-step and looked at the two of them weirdly. 'Richard,' he said.

'Who?'

'His name is Richard, I just found out. He works for a guy called Kumar,' Rakesh explained.

'Okay, I've filed a case . . .'

Rakesh laughed.

'What is it?' Shalini asked, narrowing her eyes at him.

'He has friends in high places,' he replied, taking out his phone and showing them the picture he had found in Kumar's office.

'Oh,' Pooja said, 'high places.'

As they all thought about what it meant, Rakesh's phone rang and he excused himself. 'Sorry, I need to attend this,' he said and rushed out of the house. A USB drive lay where he was sitting.

'He dropped that,' Pooja said, picking it up and placing it on the table. 'Do you think it has evidence?' Shalini said, looking eagerly at it.

'Don't . . .' Pooja said when her phone vibrated as well. 'Just leave it be,' she said, going into her room.

Sanjay had messaged her: 'Granted my behaviour hasn't been the best and I have made some mistakes, one horrible one. I apologise for that. I am not sure what came over me. We fight a lot, Poo, but I would never knowingly and willingly harm you. The fact that you think I'm a goonda, a thug, like the guys I hate and avoid . . . I don't know anything anymore.'

Shyamal messaged at the same time: 'Sanjay sir said he will talk to you when you come back.'

Sanjay was clearly manipulating her. She wasn't going to dignify his message with a response. She didn't want to. Not till she figured out whose baby she was carrying.

Shalini came barging into the room. 'You need to see this,' she said, shutting the door behind her. She had her laptop in her hands. Rakesh's USB was sticking out of one of the ports.

'I told you not to do that! We are going to get into trouble,' Pooja said urgently.

'He's outside fighting with his wife,' Shalini replied. 'Forget about him and look at this!'

Pooja took the laptop from her and froze. 'What the fuck is that . . .'

The folder was full of pictures of people tied up together and sitting on a dingy floor. The next folder contained mug shots of hundreds of people, each one holding a slate with a number written on it. She scrolled through them feeling completely disgusted and stopped at the photo of a little girl. She was dressed in a slip. Her hair was frizzy and unkempt but had been pushed back to show her face. Someone—a vile creature—had attempted to add some make-up to her face. A garish pink lipstick smeared across her unsmiling lips made her look like a character from a tragicomedy. Only this was real life.

'What . . .' Pooja started, but Shalini had already moved on to the next image of a little boy who looked freshly showered.

'Is this a human trafficking ring?' Pooja asked. She watched as Shalini sped through the images. Most of them were women and children. There were some men too, but they all looked younger than thirty-five.

Pooja closed the folder and hovered over the next folder, unsure if she wanted to see more of these repulsive images.

'Open it,' Shalini whispered, putting her hand on Pooja's and clicking on the folder.

The doorbell rang and the two of them looked at each other. The inspector had finished his phone call.

'Open the door,' Pooja whispered.

150
Inspector Rakesh

'SORRY, I HAD A CA—' RAKESH FROZE WHEN HE saw what the two women were looking at.

'How did you . . .' he said angrily, trying to grab the laptop.

'Don't,' Shalini said, pulling it away.

'Are you in on this, Inspector?' Pooja asked, grabbing a pen from the table and holding it between them like a weapon. 'Is that why you keep coming around? To make sure we don't find out?'

'No!' he gasped. These two had lost their minds, he thought. The apartment door was open behind him and he turned around.

'Don't you dare try to lock it,' Pooja snapped. 'You're in on it, aren't you? That's how they had a copy of the key.' Pooja looked at the door and calmly continued, 'I keep my key by the door. When you came back that evening, you were returning a stolen key, right?'

'What! No! Have you lost your mind?' he said. 'This is evidence in a case.'

'You're suspended.'

'This is evidence in Mira's case,' he said, the words struggling to come out. He couldn't believe they had gone through the USB drive. 'I swear! Look at the folder that says CCTV. There's footage of Madhu having a fight in a bar with the guy who has been following you.'

'Why wasn't your house broken into then?' Shalini asked. It stopped him in his tracks. They were right! Why wasn't his house broken into?

'I don't know. Maybe because the minister had Karthik on his side,' he said. 'She's missing and I'm just trying to find her.'

They watched him for a few seconds and seemed to give him the benefit of the doubt. 'Is this where you think she's gone?' Pooja asked as Shalini placed the laptop on the bed.

'I don't know.' He looked away. 'Maybe.'

Shalini opened the folder he'd mentioned and played a video.

'Can you put the pen down?' he told Pooja. But she clearly hadn't believed him because she backed up a few steps and watched the video, her hands still holding the pen in front of her.

They watched the video for a couple of minutes and Pooja admitted, 'It is them.' She finally put the pen back on the table.

'Her kid . . . ?'

'I DON'T KNOW!' he yelled and the two of them shut up.

They stood there like that for a while, the atmosphere thick with tension, before Rakesh took a deep breath and sat down in a chair.

'Sorry,' Pooja said.

Rakesh shook his head at them and shrugged. 'Let me guess, the USB drive fell out of my pocket?'

'Yep,' Shalini replied, shrugging like she had no choice but to check it out.

'Trafficking?' Pooja asked.

'Based on whatever we've learnt from the case, Madhu owed them a lot of money. He. . . . ' Rakesh couldn't bring himself to say it.

'He was planning on paying them back another way,' Shalini said for him.

'I can't prove it yet. I only have this evidence. I need to . . .' Rakesh didn't know what he needed to do. If he sent the evidence to his colleagues, this would get buried as soon as they realised the minister was a part of it. They were surely paying off some cops to pull off an operation this big. If he sent it to the media, the same reporters who'd had a field day with him . . . No, he didn't trust them.

'I'm lost,' he finally admitted.

He looked at Pooja but she was sitting on the other side of the bed, her mind clearly elsewhere. Finally, after a couple of minutes, she looked at him and said, 'Well, if it's any consolation, we think Mira is safe.'

151
Pooja

ONCE THEY SHOWED RAKESH THE photographs Shalini had taken of the woman they believed was Mira, he was surprised. 'How did you find out where she is?' he asked.

'We have our ways. We're telling you because you don't need to worry about Mira's whereabouts,' Pooja replied. 'Now, why don't you just leak the trafficking information to the press?'

'The same press that destroyed my career? No way! I don't trust them.'

'Inspector,' Shalini said calmly, 'they would jump on this. There is no way they would pass up the opportunity to share this with the rest of the country.'

Rakesh shook his head vehemently and sat back looking sullen. Suddenly, his face brightened. 'Can you keep a copy of it?'

Pooja was taken aback. She didn't want that filth anywhere near her.

'You can release it to the media if something happens to me tomorrow.'

'What do you mean by that? And why tomorrow?'

Rakesh pulled his phone out and showed them the pictures he had taken of the invoices. 'See this, a "brick" shipment booked out for tomorrow.'

'Bricks?' Pooja asked, confused.

'It isn't bricks. That's the word they're using for . . .' he jerked his head towards their laptop and the women understood. 'I have to be there to see if it's really what I think it is.'

'Mira? But we told you . . .' she started.

'I know. But there are others!' he snapped. 'Anyway, can you keep a copy of this and give it to Atif? In case something happens? I've informed him about it.'

'And you're going to do this whole thing alone?' Pooja asked, rolling her eyes. He really did have a hero complex.

'I don't have a choice,' he said, standing up. 'Can you please keep a copy?'

Pooja agreed and Shalini saved a copy of it on the laptop, promising to encrypt it so it didn't fall in the wrong hands. 'I'd recommend you also do the same,' she told him, as he left the house, pocketing the USB and mumbling about taking his wife shopping.

Once he left, Pooja and Shalini spent the day sorting through the evidence that Rakesh had left behind. It was now compiled into a neat folder. The images were sorted by name, place and date. Shalini is really good at this, Pooja thought, as she went through the files.

They had found addresses in the invoice pictures that Rakesh had sent and narrowed it down to three potential places. 'The office,' Shalini said, ticking that off.

'There is a godown and a factory.'

'How do you know?' Pooja asked.

'It says factory in the title and it's in an industrial area.' Shalini moved aside so Pooja could read her notes.

'Do you really think they would have written down their addresses? Like actual addresses?'

'Only one way to find out,' Pooja said grimly.

As they were winding up, Pooja realised that in all the excitement of the day she had forgotten to take the second pregnancy test. 'I'll be right back,' she said to Shalini before grabbing her purse and leaving for the medical shop right down the street.

She kept an eye out for the men she had seen in the CCTV footage. There was no one around, so she was safe for now. Ten minutes later, she was back with her test and a pack of sanitary napkins just in case she was wrong.

This test took ten minutes longer than usual but gave the same results. 'Fuck,' she shouted, staring angrily at the test kit in her hands.

Her phone pinged.

It was a message from Sanjay. 'Why did you go to a medical shop? All okay?' She'd forgotten to use cash.

Fuck.

152
Inspector Rakesh

RAKESH WAS FEELING RESTLESS AS HE WATCHED Bindhu fawning over the mehendi being applied to her hands at the salon. His mind was on other things.

He texted Atif while he wandered around the salon. 'Tomorrow is the shipment. I'll be checking it out to see if it's real.'

When Atif didn't reply even ten minutes later, he called his old boss, Parameshwaran.

'Hello, Rakesh.' It had been a few months since he'd heard this familiar, serious voice. Parameshwaran had been a good boss to him. He was a man of principles and had disapproved of Rakesh using family connections to secure the police job and then a promotion. Despite his misgivings, Parameshwaran had treated him fairly, and Rakesh would always be grateful for that.

'Sir, how are you?'

'I'm doing well, Pa. It's been a while. I was surprised you didn't call earlier, especially with all that I was hearing on the news.'

'I . . .' Rakesh started.

But Parameshwaran finished the sentence for him. '. . . have a problem asking for help. I know.'

'I'm . . . asking now,' Rakesh said. He hated the fact that he was in this position.

'Go on.'

Rakesh told him everything that had happened since Madhu's murder, while looking over his shoulders constantly to make sure no one was listening. When he finished, Parameshwaran sighed. 'You've certainly been carrying the weight of the world on your shoulders, haven't you?'

Rakesh wanted to cry when he heard that. Finally, someone understood. Rakesh informed him about the plan he'd made with Atif and Pooja. Parameshwaran agreed to help him if it went awry.

'I hope my pension isn't affected because of this,' Parameshwaran laughed and Rakesh immediately felt guilty.

'Don't worry, Pa, I'm only kidding. If it does, I'll come live with you, okay?' he said and hung up.

When Rakesh went back, Bindhu's other palm was stretched out for the mehendi application. He smiled and told her it was a lovely design. Then he messaged Atif, summarising what Parameshwaran sir had said. He couldn't believe he had teamed up with a retired cop, a constable, a hacker, a movie producer's wife and a podcast editor to solve a case. What a strange bunch of people they were.

153
Pooja

SHE QUICKLY INFORMED SANJAY THAT SHE just needed some supplies.

Pooja felt guilty about lying to him. But what would she tell him when she wasn't sure whose child it was? While Sanjay and she had been trying to get pregnant for a long time, they'd stopped when she discovered his latest affair. She had always used protection with D. 'But condoms aren't a hundred per cent safe, you idiot,' she mumbled to herself while checking her period tracking app to see whose it could be.

The thought of the press finding out about this made her head hurt. 'Pooja and D have a baby'. 'Sanjay Reddy cuckolded by his main actor.'

Pooja shut her eyes tightly for a few moments and checked the test result again, hoping against hope that it would change.

'Fuck!' she swore before tossing the stick in the bin.

When she came out, Shalini was holding the medical shop's bag and staring at her. 'Um . . .' Pooja started.

'Are congratulations in order? Or . . .' She asked holding up the bill.

'I haven't decided,' Pooja said, her shoulders slumping.

'Oh,' Shalini said awkwardly. Pooja had been feeling nauseated of late. She was sure it had more to do with the stress she felt about the pregnancy than the physical changes. Shalini cleared her throat and sat down. 'We need to record the next episode.'

'Let it be the last,' Pooja said.

'What?'

Pooja looked at her. The girl seemed upset so she had to be the practical one. 'If this is as big a situation as the inspector claims it is, we can't be interfering with this investigation. In the next episode we will tell the audience that something big is happening in the case and that we will get back once the case is resolved.'

'What if it isn't resolved?' Shalini countered. 'Aren't we giving things away?'

'We . . .' Pooja sat down exhausted. Going out in the afternoon sun had been a mistake. Her head was starting to throb. 'Let's just do it tomorrow,' she said. 'I'm tired.'

Shalini got up as if to help her up, but then stood back and scratched her head. Pooja shuffled off to the bedroom and took out her phone to call D. Her finger hovered over the call button before she decided against it and climbed into bed. It was going to be a long night.

154
Inspector Rakesh

'I'VE KEPT FRESHLY IRONED CLOTHES ON THE sofa,' Bindhu said in the car on their way back. She was waving her hands in front of her, waiting for the mehendi to dry. He'd had to open the car door for her, put her seatbelt for her and move strands of hair off her face whenever they irritated her. It felt like they were a newly married couple, only now she didn't blush. She just got annoyed if he didn't follow instructions fast enough.

'Do I have to come to the reception?' he said, once he'd opened the main door for her and served food for Anthony. 'I mean, after that picture went viral . . .' he trailed off.

'Which picture exactly, Rakesh?' Bindhu asked, not looking at him. 'Quite a few have gone viral.'

He kept silent and called out to Anthony to come and have his food. The boy was always in his room playing games with his online 'friends'. He wondered who the fuck these new online friends were who were happy to play video games with a kid. He should check them out. Maybe Harry could help.

'You know what I mean,' he told Bindhu instead.

'You went back to Shubham Street today. Are you giving those women another interview?' she asked. 'You better not be doing that.'

'No. No, I'm not,' he replied, releasing the cooker's pressure as she'd instructed, and waited for the hissing to stop. 'They had a break-in. I was trying to help them. Policemen from their area were also present.'

'I'm going to wash up,' she said, gingerly touching a mehendi line to see if it had dried. It broke off and fell to the floor.

'I'll clean that up,' he said immediately. Bindhu gave a non-committal sound and went to their bedroom. When he came out of the kitchen, Rakesh noticed that his pillow and bedsheet were back on the sofa. He turned around to find the bedroom door firmly shut. Of the plates he had set on the dining table with food, only his was still there.

'Fine, I'll come,' Rakesh yelled out loud and sat to eat his dinner. He would have to get away from the house early if he was going to make it to the factory. He would tell Bindhu something urgent had come up and he couldn't make it to the reception. That is, if she ever spoke to him again.

155
Pooja

SHE SLIPPED THE TORCH, THE EXTRA BATTERY pack and two protein bars into her old school backpack that smelled of mothballs and looked around the bedroom. They had secured their hard drives, scheduled an email that would go out two days later in case they were in trouble and, finally, they used up all the milk in the fridge.

'Do you really have to go?' Shalini asked.

'Why shouldn't I?' Pooja said, sipping her third cup of chai that day. She had decided that they were going to the addresses they had discovered on the invoices. The one that mentioned a brick shipment. Rakesh had said he would be there but she really didn't trust him a hundred per cent. Shalini had been less than enthused about the idea.

'Do you have pepper spray?' Shalini asked.

'No.' Pooja realised she'd never had one.

'I have a spare one. Take that,' Shalini said, reaching into her bag and tossing it to her. Pooja caught it and looked at the instructions. 'Scary,' she said, slipping it into the side pouch for easy access.

It was quite late, and Rakesh still hadn't answered Shalini's calls. 'Maybe it's a sign we shouldn't go, he wouldn't want us there anyway.' Shalini told her.

'Aren't you the one who's usually excited about stuff like this?' Pooja asked, raising her eyebrows.

'Yeah, but now you're pregnant. That changes everything.'

'No. Let's go,' Pooja said, putting on her backpack and opening the door.

Shalini sighed and followed.

156
Inspector Rakesh

THIS TIME, RAKESH TOOK A TAXI, TOLD THE driver to drop him off in front of a tile factory and waited for the driver to leave before walking the rest of the way to the address he'd noted down.

Rakesh had made a copy of all the keys he had stolen from Kumar. Maybe one of them would work at the building looming in front of him. He felt the clump of keys in his pocket and waited. There was no guard at the gate and this building looked a lot more decrepit than Rakesh had expected.

He sent his location to Atif, Shalini and Pooja, then deleted the evidence of those messages from his phone.

Rakesh walked carefully behind the parked trucks, making sure before moving between each one that there were no sleeping drivers or cleaners around. The last thing he wanted was an angry, drunk trucker chasing after him. He heard light snoring from somewhere around him and slowed down. 'Where are you . . .' he whispered to himself as he knelt to check under a truck.

Nothing.

He covered the length of the vehicle and checked under the next one. He was getting closer to the sound. He looked behind him and spotted a boy sleeping on top of one of the trucks. He looked harmless, so Rakesh quickly backed away and continued on his way, checking above and under each truck to make sure no one else was around.

He had reached the building now. Rakesh tried pushing back the small gate but it was latched. He slipped his hand through the grille. It took a bit of manoeuvring, but Rakesh managed to bring the bolt to the middle. Slowly, trying to be as gentle as possible, he wiggled it back and forth till it slipped open. There were a bunch of quick squeaks as he opened it, but it didn't seem like he had disturbed anyone. Behind him the boy was still sleeping soundly and no one stirred from inside the building in front of him.

He ran to the building, which looked like a warehouse, and tried to open door after door. It took a while to try each of the keys in his pocket and four doors down he was ready to give up. 'Just a few more,' he told himself. He looked back to make sure the boy was still sleeping. He was.

Rakesh cracked his knuckles and went to the fifth door. Seven keys later he heard a click. He opened the door, sure that someone in the room would jump out at him but no one did. It felt empty. Slipping inside, he locked the door behind him and turned on his phone's flashlight.

He looked around the plain room which had inbuilt shelves on the walls. It couldn't store much. There were makeshift beds rolled away against the walls and small piles of clothes in the corners. The smell of sweat and grime had hit him the minute he opened the door. It looked like a room where labourers slept. What if he had got this all wrong? Maybe Kumar and his friends were keeping illegal immigrants here. But that didn't explain the pictures of children, especially little girls with faces full of make-up.

Using one end of a broomstick he found behind the door, Rakesh picked up one of the shirts. It clearly belonged to a small child. 'Child labour?' he wondered. Then he spotted a pink dress peeping out from the pile. 'Fuck,' he whispered. He moved the pile with the broom till he found the dress and picked it up. No girl older than five would fit into it.

The knot in his stomach tightened some more and Rakesh quickly dropped the dress.

He turned around and continued nudging the pile. On closer inspection, he realised that everything there belonged to young children; some of the clothes were small enough for babies. This isn't looking good, he thought. Suddenly, his phone vibrated. It was Bindhu. He hit ignore and sent the standard rejection message, 'Driving, call you back.'

Hoping that the message would keep her satisfied for half an hour, Rakesh continued checking the room. It looked more and more like a makeshift home for children to sleep in. Well, to call it home was stretching it.

He took pictures and uploaded them to his cloud. He had already shared the folder with Atif and Harry who had promised to make a copy of everything as and when it was updated.

Once he was done with the room, he locked the door behind him and made his way to the next building in the compound. He had just rounded the corner when he heard footsteps.

157
Pooja

'STRAIGHT, THEN LEFT.' POOJA FOLLOWED Shalini's directions, cursing the traffic that seemed to be endless on the road.

'The one we just passed?' she asked, frantically looking back at the lane she had missed. She couldn't have gone into it anyway; there were huge lorries parked on either side.

'No, the next one,' Shalini said. 'You better move into the left lane now. Else we'll get to our destination only tomorrow.'

Pooja turned on the indicator and honked angrily. She was a patient driver, but this was her first time encountering such horrible traffic. She was sure whatever they wanted to witness would be over by the time they reached.

'Son of a . . .' Shalini said, showing her phone to Pooja. But she couldn't exactly take a look at the screen. The signal had turned green and bikers around her were swarming into all the gaps.

'Read it.'

'Rakesh has sent us his location.'

'Well, at least he's including us.'

'No, he isn't,' Shalini replied. 'It says, "Save my location, just in case."'

'He really believes he's James Bond.'

'That's Rakesh, Inspector Rakesh,' Shalini said, chuckling. 'We are going to the same place. Let's keep going.'

They found themselves in front of the row of warehouses in about twenty minutes. Once Pooja left the main road, there was hardly any traffic.

Pooja parked in one of the side lanes. They cursed as the car went over something and landed, with a metallic grind, into a pit. 'Well, that's just brilliant,' Pooja said, peering into the side mirror. She had already turned off the headlights and couldn't see exactly what she had parked on; it was probably some garbage dump on the road.

'What do you want to do?' Shalini asked. It was quite clear to her that neither one of them wanted to get out. The street was as quiet with the only sound coming from the horns and rumbling vehicles on the highway.

'Are you okay?' Shalini asked.

Ever since she had found the pregnancy test, Shalini had been extra careful with her—generously making her extra cups of chai and even offering to give her a hot water bottle for her back.

'Yeah,' Pooja replied.

'No nausea? Stomach ache?'

'Shalini,' Pooja snapped. 'I take it you've not been around a pregnant woman? I'm not in pain, I'm not dying and you don't have to keep looking at my stomach. This isn't alien vs predator!'

A rap on the window shocked Pooja who screamed as she turned around. It was Atif, the constable who had come to their house when it was ransacked.

'What the fuck are you two doing here?' he growled when she opened the window.

158
Inspector Rakesh

RAKESH STOOD CONFUSED FOR A SPLIT SECOND before giving chase.

'SIRRRR!' the boy yelled, already running away. The boy had a head start; Rakesh could hear his chappals slapping the soles of his feet as he ran towards the line of trucks. As Rakesh gained in on him, he turned back and, with a look of panic, dove under the wheel of one of the trucks and vanished.

'Fuck!' Rakesh said, skidding to a stop. He squatted behind the wheel and peeped around it. The boy wasn't there. 'I'm not gonna hurt you,' he whispered, hoping the boy could hear him. Nothing. All he could hear was the distant rumbling of heavy trucks on the highway.

A small distance away he heard a twig snap.

He crept around the truck. He wished this area was better lit, but the trucks were blocking the light coming over from the streetlights. He could barely see the outline of the trees, let alone a person.

But something told him that there was someone behind him.

A soft scoff came from behind him. He turned around a second too late.

Something hit him on the side of the head, and he felt a searing pain before blacking out.

159
Pooja

'DON'T YOU HAVE ANY COMMON SENSE?' ATIF snapped, 'This is real life, not the make-believe world you live in. This is serious stuff. Not like what happens in your films.'

'I haven't . . .' Pooja started but stopped when Shalini tapped her shoulder. She was pointing at something. The three of them peered through the fence. There was a commotion happening near one of the buildings. 'Come fast,' someone yelled, and two figures ran towards them from the distance. They seemed to be carrying something. 'I can't see . . .' Atif said. Pooja squinted, wishing she'd brought her glasses with her. But as the two men walked away from the building the moonlight did the trick.

'Is that . . . !' Shalini swore. Rakesh was being carried past trucks by a skinny man and Richard, the man who, according to the CCTV footage, had broken into Pooja's house.

'That's the group's right-hand man,' Atif whispered behind them.

'What do we do now?' Pooja asked.

'I cannot leave the two of you alone to chase them. Not to mention the guy has a gun.'

Shalini showed her phone. 'I'm recording this. Just in case. I wonder where they're going with Rakesh.'

'Maybe they're keeping him in another building,' Atif said.

'There is no other building,' Pooja said. 'I got a satellite view of the place before coming here. They don't have another building. I think . . . they're taking him somewhere.'

Pooja was right. A few moments later, a truck rushed out of the compound, right past them. They hid down deeper behind the trees and waited.

'You two, go home,' Atif said sternly and ran in the direction opposite to where the truck had carried Rakesh. Shalini and Pooja looked at each other and started chasing him. 'Jesus fucking Christ!' Shalini cursed.

Atif's car was parked on the side road, and he ran to unlock it. Pooja was close on his heels and climbed into the passenger seat. 'What the fuck . . .' Atif said, starting the jeep. 'Get out.'

'No.'

Shalini had reached as well by now and climbed into the back seat. 'What the fuck is wrong with you two?' he hissed. He didn't have time to wait for them to get out. So he drove, cursing them till he caught sight of the truck.

'I have more than a million followers on Instagram,' Pooja said. 'And the podcast has at least ten thousand.'

'Now is not the time to boast about your influencer status,' Atif replied incredulously. Pooja was sure he thought she was stupid, but she kept calm and continued, 'If they try something, if they hurt Rakesh, would they be able to get away with it if someone with one million followers goes live and shows people what's happening as it happens?'

Atif turned to look at her, his mouth wide open.

He had nothing to say. 'Shalini, keep your phone ready. Go to the podcast handle in case we have to go live. Email that video you just recorded to your journalist friend. Tell her to wait for an hour before posting,' Pooja said, taking her phone out of her pocket and keeping it ready as well.

'Aren't trucks slower than cars anyway?' Shalini asked. 'Loaded trucks, yes. Not empty ones.'

Pooja could feel her heart pounding. They were chasing someone. A car chase! Well, a truck chase but that didn't make a difference.

Just then, the truck turned off its headlights and vanished off the road.

160
Inspector Rakesh

WHEN RAKESH WOKE UP, HE WAS INSIDE A moving truck. His head was throbbing. He cursed, but no words came out of his mouth. He had been gagged.

Kumar's lackey, the one he'd stolen the keys from, was sitting in front of him. 'So, you *are* a piece of shit,' he said as soon as Rakesh opened his eyes.

The boy whom he'd followed peered in through the small window between the front and the rear of the truck. He looked like a dog expecting a treat after successfully performing a trick. He also looked much younger in the light than he had when Rakesh was chasing after him. Another idiot child who'd been brainwashed by these creeps.

'Did you really think we wouldn't find out what you were up to?' the man asked, yanking out the cloth out of Rakesh's mouth. He stretched his jaw, moving it around till it felt more settled.

'You didn't come to the bar because you were upset about being suspended,' he continued. 'You came to spy on us!'

Rakesh didn't know what was worse, being kidnapped or being kidnapped by someone stupider than him. Rakesh shrugged, eliciting a snort from the man squatting in front of him. The truck bounced over a speed breaker and turned left, rolling into a kutcha road. The boy's head appeared again and he said, 'Sir.'

It seemed to be some sort of code.

The lackey nodded and took out his phone. Rakesh remembered his own phone and realised instantly that it was missing. He looked around him but he couldn't spot it. 'Hello, sir. Yes, sir, we are here. We have something, someone. I caught someone . . .' he said gleefully. 'Yes. Him. Yes. Okay, sir,' he replied before hanging up.

Rakesh caught a glimpse of the time on his phone. It was 11 p.m.

It had been a few hours since he'd been knocked out. He estimated that they were outside Chennai now. Where he wouldn't have jurisdiction. Where Atif couldn't follow him. He also realised he'd missed Lily's reception and Bindhu would be furious.

161
Pooja

'FUCK! THE TRUCK'S GONE!' POOJA YELLED.

'Yeah, thanks, I hadn't noticed,' Atif said dryly, speeding up.

After a few silent minutes, Atif finally said, 'I think we've lost it.'

'Stop,' Shalini said. 'Maybe it went down a side road?'

'We might have heard it in that case. All the side roads are kutcha,' Atif replied.

'His wife!' Pooja said. 'Do you have her number?'

By now Atif was nearing a fork in the road, not sure which way to go and not wanting to take a wrong turn.

'Yeah, but how will that help us? I'll figure something out. You ladies please keep quiet while I think.' Atif looked annoyed.

'Sir, do you know me?' Pooja asked. She was getting tired of him thinking she was useless.

'Yes, madam, I know you, you have a million followers, blah blah blah,' he said, looking through the contacts on his phone. He wasn't even looking at her. Pooja glared at him and said, 'I also have a cheating husband. Which means I know of at least five to six ways of tracking him. Doesn't the world think Mira and Rakesh were having an affair, including his wife?'

Atif's jaw dropped. Again.

Soon, they had Rakesh's location and were back on track, following the red dot on Atif's phone.

162

Inspector Rakesh

'WHO ELSE KNOWS ABOUT US?' A BEARDED GUY who Rakesh had never seen before asked, pulling a chair out. They had reached their destination a few minutes ago and he had already been roughed up. He had been welcomed with a left hook to the face and a kick to the stomach before being tied to a chair. His already sore stomach groaned and he felt his rear clench.

Rakesh raised an eyebrow at the man instead of replying. How could he reply with a gag on his mouth?

'Remove that thing,' the man instructed and waited as Richard came over to yank it off. 'Now tell me.'

'I have to save my reputation. I was just snooping. I thought . . .'

'So no one else knows?'

'I never said that,' Rakesh replied, hoping it would give Atif time to track him. He had no way of knowing if Atif had managed to get the truck's number and alert the traffic cops. But he had to hope.

'So someone knows.'

'Who are you exactly in this company?' Rakesh asked. He was deliberately stalling, hoping his attitude would piss off the man long enough for him to try and get away.

'No one important.'

'Clearly you are,' Rakesh said, glancing around. 'They brought me to you. So you're the head of operations here. More important than that Kumar anyway.'

'So you know Kumar.'

'Yes, he's a friend.'

The man looked at Richard in surprise.

'You don't know, do you?' Rakesh grinned.

'I . . . don't know what?'

'We are drinking buddies,' Rakesh said.

The bearded guy looked irritated, then suddenly got up and left the room, followed by Richard. He heard a loud slap first, followed by muffled yelling. Taking advantage of having been left alone, Rakesh frantically looked around the room, trying to find something—anything—that would help him escape.

163
Pooja

POOJA'S PHONE BUZZED. IT WAS SANJAY. BUT she couldn't answer right now. She looked at road ahead and rejected the call.

'If it's an unknown number, answer it. It might be Rakesh,' Atif said, eyes still on the road. She shook her head. 'It is a work thing,' she said. Her phone buzzed again. This time, it was a text.

'Why can't you answer. I've been . . .' The preview ended there.

She turned her phone face down and went back to staring at the blinking red dot on Atif's screen. 'Your phone's battery is low,' Shalini said.

Pooja looked at Atif's phone and noticed it was at twenty-seven per cent. 'It will last till we get there,' Atif said, but he didn't sound confident.

'I have a battery pack,' Shalini said.

But it was back in their car. As she watched it drop by another per cent, Atif pressed down on the accelerator, and they continued down what seemed to be a never-ending road.

'Just half an hour more.'

Suddenly, a beep went off.

'Shit!' Atif exclaimed. 'No, dammit, I was hoping this wouldn't happen!'

'What happened?' Shalini asked.

'Fuck,' Pooja said, grabbing the phone off its stand on the dashboard. She had tracked Sanjay's location enough times to know what had happened.

'Rakesh's phone has been turned off,' she told Shalini.

'What are we supposed to do now?' she asked, looking at them for answers. Neither said anything.

164
Inspector Rakesh

HE WAS IN A WAREHOUSE OF SORTS. TO HIS left, Rakesh could see a large door that was locked from the outside. He couldn't turn but when he was brought in, he had taken in a quick glance and remembered that there were tyres behind him, some truck repair equipment and a large work table. There was also a metal cupboard, like the ones found in old stores.

Behind that were rows and rows of shelves. It looked like something had been stored there. The smell of chemicals still lingered in the air. There was a small wrench on the floor. It had no sharp edges, but he had to get it. Something was better than nothing.

The shouting outside had got louder. He could hear some bits of the exchange. 'Do I look like a fucking idiot to you?' The sound of another slap followed it.

Rakesh shuffled his chair as quietly as possible to the wrench that lay three feet away from him.

It took considerable effort, but he managed to put one foot on it and dragged it back with him and his chair. It was quiet outside. He was still a whole foot away from where he had started. Taking a deep breath, he decided to jump with his chair to the original position and hope for the best.

He saw the line on the floor that showed he had moved his chair. It was visible even in the dark. 'Fuck,' Rakesh muttered, his mind racing. Before he could come up with something to explain the line, the shouting stopped and he heard hurried footsteps walking towards him. Maybe they wouldn't notice what he'd done.

Maybe.

165
Pooja

THEY WERE ON THEIR WAY AGAIN. THIS TIME they had got the address from the files Rakesh had collected. Some kid called Harry had been kind enough to send it to Atif.

Unfortunately, Bindhu had also noticed that Rakesh's phone was off and kept texting constantly to see what was happening. Atif finally got tired and muted her.

'Just send me the location and turn off your phone,' Pooja said, annoyed. Bindhu realised that Atif wasn't replying to her messages so she called instead. Pooja rejected the call. 'She'll thank us later,' she grumbled and took out her phone.

'She isn't going to like that,' Atif said, handing his phone to them to turn it off. 'How far away is it?'

'Not too far, but... I don't know what's happening there.'

They drove down the muddy path for a bit before their headlights lit up the smooth surface of the highway tar road. Shalini's face appeared once again between her and Atif. She had stopped paying attention to their instructions to lean back and wear her seatbelt.

'What will they do if we don't get there on time?' she asked, saying out loud what both she and Atif were keeping to themselves.

The car was silent. Atif finally spoke up, 'They are human smugglers.'

'They traffic women and children,' Pooja replied.

'The intent is clear.'

'The people are mostly uneducated and incapable of escaping,' Shalini said. 'Which means Rakesh is of no use to them, so he should be safe.'

'Or they might not keep him alive since he knows what they're up to,' Pooja said.

'I'd rather not think about that,' Atif said tersely. The vehicle was gaining speed now that they were on the highway, and he was completely focused on the road.

A Scorpio crossed them, followed by another, political flags proudly marking them. 'Isn't that . . . ?' Pooja said, sitting up to get a better look.

'Fuck,' Atif replied.

'Do you think they recognised your car?' Shalini said.

'I don't think so.'

'They were going to fast I couldn't see any of the vehicle numbers,' added Pooja.

The car was quiet again. She was sure they were all trying to convince themselves that they were safe. No one spoke till the map mentioned they take the next turn. The politician's car turned the same way. They better get to Rakesh soon.

166
Inspector Rakesh

THE BEARDED MAN CAME BACK, FLEXING HIS wrist. Rakesh was sweating from the effort it had taken him to get the wrench. It was still under his shoe and would remain there till someone untied him. He still had no idea how he would use it. 'It's a little hot in here. I thought the human trafficking business would have made you rich. Where's the air conditioning?'

'Don't be a fucking smartass.'

'You sound like my wife.'

'She seems like a smart woman with bad taste. I'd listen to her if I were you,' the man said, returning to his seat. 'Now what am I to do with you?'

'I think I'm good-looking enough for you to traffic,' Rakesh replied, laughing.

'You wouldn't fetch one paisa,' he sneered. Then his expression changed.

Rakesh pressed down on the wrench. He could just about feel it through his shoe. He heard a truck start outside and the headlights flooded the room. His ride was leaving.

Rakesh wished he knew the time, but his phone was with Richard and he couldn't see his watch since his hands were tied behind him. 'They have work to do,' the man replied, cracking his knuckles. He looked like a TV villain, straight out of Bindhu's soaps.

The man's phone buzzed. 'Sir,' he said. 'Yes, sir. The second place, sir. Yes.'

He nodded for a bit and then said, 'Okay, sir. He told me a bit. It seems Suresh fucked up.' He nodded again, 'I am taking care of it, sir. Don't worry.' Then he hung up and turned back to Rakesh.

'So here we are. Would you like to discuss life? Or perhaps give me some tips on how to make money?' Rakesh said. He was blabbering now, but it didn't matter. He hoped it would buy him time till someone would hear or see him.

'Sure,' the man said, standing up and stretching his arms up with a fake yawn. As his shirt rode up, Rakesh saw the hilt of a gun. The man cracked his neck and sat down with a smile. 'Should we discuss life?'

167
Pooja

THEY TURNED OFF THE HEADLIGHTS, followed the vehicles from a safe distance and parked discreetly behind one of the gigantic trees in the area. Atif put his hand out to stop them from getting out. Instead, they watched while the group of men exited the SUVs and marched into the factory.

They looked determined.

'Looks like he's in there,' Atif whispered.

'You're a cop, right? Can't you just go in and bust them?' Shalini asked.

'I'm a cop? Do you even live in the real world? I'm a constable, I've got no backup and if I do go in there, they'll probably shoot me and bury my body,' he hissed angrily.

'Let's get out,' Pooja said, her stomach clenching; she wasn't sure if it was excitement or anxiety.

Atif nodded and they opened the doors as quietly as possible. The drivers of the SUVs were still near their vehicles and if they heard any noise, it was game over. Celeb or not, Pooja would be in some serious trouble.

'I don't have any of the things I got for this evening,' she mumbled as Shalini slipped into place behind her. They had, in an absolutely idiotic move, left everything behind in their car. If Atif hadn't been so insistent on making them stay back, they would have everything they needed.

'I only have my phone and my lighter,' Shalini said.

'I have my phone and your bottle of pepper spray.'

'Stop talking,' Atif whispered and pointed at the drivers idling some distance away.

The three of them crept along the wall next to the road, careful not to step on anything that would give them away. The grass growing by the side of the road provided ample cushioning but also meant they couldn't see any twigs.

They made it to the gate just as one of the two drivers went off into the darkness. The other stayed behind, lighting a bidi and leaning on the hood.

Pooja and Shalini crouched next to the dilapidated entrance and watched as the driver blew smoke rings in the air. 'Show-off,' Shalini mumbled and Atif waved his hand to shush her. They could hear the second man peeing somewhere to their right. Pooja cringed, the nausea getting worse.

The other driver came back and the two of them started talking. Atif indicated that they move again and Pooja obliged, almost tripping as something sharp scratched at her leg.

'Fuck,' she hissed, rubbing the back of her leg.

Atif turned back sharply. 'Careful,' he whispered after making sure she wasn't bleeding.

It was the factory's sign board that must have fallen down what seemed like ages ago. The rusty peeling yellow letters read, 'Fireworks'. Pooja and Atif looked at each other and gulped.

168
Inspector Rakesh

WHEN HEADLIGHTS HAD ILLUMINATED THE room a few minutes ago, Rakesh thought it was Atif coming to rescue him with backup. But it wasn't.

The bearded guy glared at Rakesh and walked towards the man who had entered the room. They whispered to each other, occasionally throwing glances at Rakesh. He heard his father-in-law's name and tried to hear the rest of the conversation. But he couldn't hear anything else.

He looked outside the window and saw tiny headlights driving past. Would they hear if he screamed? He doubted it, and he'd get murdered before that. The man in white raised his hand and came closer. It took Rakesh a couple of seconds to realise it was the minister he had met the day his son had run over a few people.

'Hello, sir,' the minister greeted him in English.

'Is this why you were so worried about your son? Because the boy might ruin this operation?' Rakesh asked.

'My son?' the minister laughed. 'That idiot boy knows nothing.'

Rakesh watched the man and the minister leave and slipped off his shoe to try and pick up the wrench when he was alone. His socked toes weren't helping. But he still managed to get the wrench in his grip. A second later though it fell to the floor with a loud clang.

He stared at the door, hoping the noise couldn't be heard outside. When no one came running into the room after a few seconds, he quickly tried to lift the wrench again. He wasn't as flexible as he used to be, and the angle was so tight that Rakesh was sure that either his hamstring or his pants would tear. Finally, after a few minutes, he managed to slide the wrench up the leg of the chair and under his right thigh. The car outside started and the bearded man came back in, this time with one of the politician's goons in tow.

Rakesh didn't have time to put his shoe back on, so he made a show of trying to scratch his other leg with his sock-covered foot. 'Maybe you can untie my hands so I can at least slap that bloody mosquito away?' he said, looking at the goon up and down.

The man ignored him and spoke to the bearded guy. 'Did you find anything else on him or just the phone?' he asked.

The man shook his head and handed over Rakesh's phone.

'Sir, don't delete any data, okay?' Rakesh called out in what he hoped was an arrogant drawl. 'My son's game progress is saved there. If it vanishes, he will kill me.'

Neither responded. The politician's man walked out, leaving Rakesh alone with the thugs again. And one of them grabbed his throat.

169
Pooja

'ARE WE LIVE?' ATIF ASKED. THEY MANAGED TO duck out of sight when the politician was walking out. Pooja had whipped out her phone faster than he could imagine and within seconds she was streaming while Shalini was recording on her own device.

'Guys, please record your screen in case we are unable to save the livestream,' she whispered for the second time, nodding at Atif.

'Vehicle number 0007,' Shalini said. 'Really? Maybe they didn't have the budget for 007.'

Pooja's phone started vibrating. It was Sanjay calling her again. 'Fuck!' she hissed and rejected the call.

'Who was it . . . madam?' Atif asked, realising that at least three thousand people had joined the live stream and he had to maintain formality.

'My husband. He's going to be pissed at me for this,' she replied.

Someone commented, 'Is she showing us a live stream of her affair with someone else?'

Pooja didn't say anything, but Shalini noticed her pained reaction and took over the narration.

'Our investigation has led us to this place,' she said, whispering. 'We believe there is a human trafficking group here and that the victim of this case, Madhu, knew about it.' Pooja panned the camera back to the warehouse entrance where a dim light was on. 'Inspector Rakesh has been taken hostage. He is currently being held here . . .'

A yell came from inside and Pooja almost dropped her phone in surprise.

'What are we going to do?' she hissed. 'Do we know how many people there are in there?'

'Holy shit, are they serious?' 'I'm recording.' 'Me too. Recording.' 'Stay safe, madam.' 'Fuck, she has balls.'

Pooja ignored all the comments except one—Sanjay's. 'I TOLD YOU NOT TO GO THERE IN YOUR STATE,' he had commented in all caps.

She turned around to Shalini who looked away. She would have to deal with this later. 'Something just occurred to me,' Atif said. 'If you're streaming live to . . .' he stopped to check, '14,000 people now, and they broke into your studio to get you to stop the podcast, doesn't that mean they're following you? They probably know we are here . . .'

170
Inspector Rakesh

THE MAN'S HAND CLOSED AROUND HIS THROAT as he tried to wriggle out of his grip. All Rakesh could do was thrash around like a pinned animal. He was paying the price for not working out for months. His body was letting him down. He tried to take a deep breath, but it was getting impossible. His heart was starting to pound in his head. He tried to find something around him that would throw the thug off him.

There was nothing.

He was struggling to breathe. The dots in the corner of his eyes became little white lights. He continued feeling around for something that would help. His other arm was straining to be set free. But nothing was helping. His hands were still tied behind his back. The wrench was still under his leg, but it was going to be of no use if he couldn't get his hands free. He couldn't hold it with his legs.

His legs!

Rakesh pushed himself and his chair behind. The bearded man lost balance and cursed. Lifting his legs up to his chest, Rakesh pushed the stumbling man off him. The chair swung wildly on its two back legs and came crashing onto the floor behind him, on top of his arms.

'AAARGHHHHHH!' he screamed as bits of splintered wood stung his hands. But he was free.

The man got up again and rushed towards him. Rakesh finally heard voices from outside. The truck driver who had driven him here stared at him from the entrance of the room before making a dash for him along with the young boy who had first spotted him. Rakesh pushed himself up on his legs and ran.

171
Pooja

THE SCUFFLE INSIDE WAS GETTING LOUDER. Atif had started walking towards the entrance, half crouched to keep himself hidden. The loud crash and the scream had propelled them into action. Pooja sneaked off to the other side to see if she could find another entrance. Shalini followed her.

Pooja's phone was still receiving multiple pings, but she ignored them all and continued streaming. Sanjay was calling her again. She ignored him once again.

As they passed one of the smaller buildings, the strong smell of sulphur from firecrackers flooded Pooja's nostrils. She reached a door that was swinging open and looked inside. The room was filled with all types of crackers, from rockets to sparklers. How had that idiotic driver smoked near all this, she thought, as they moved on to the next building. Shalini pinched her nose as they continued.

Behind the warehouse was a dilapidated building. Pooja went around it and came face to face with Rakesh. He was standing by the window screaming for help. They couldn't hear him though. The trucks on the highway were drowning out his voice.

He paused when he saw them, taking a moment to realise they were there in the flesh, and then, looking behind him, he started screaming again. Pooja gestured at her phone and Rakesh looked at it. Behind him, Pooja could see a bearded man gaining in on Rakesh. She yelled, 'Move, move, live . . . let's capture the man's face.'

Rakesh didn't seem to understand. Pooja turned the phone around and showed him the screen. Finally, he got it. Rakesh moved out of the way and the man crashed into the window.

That's when Pooja yelled, 'Everyone, take a screenshot now, please. He is one of the thugs in the operation.'

The man froze as he noticed their phones.

172
Inspector Rakesh

AS HE DARTED AROUND THE MAZE OF STACKED boxes and equipment, hoping the man wouldn't catch him, Rakesh finally found a back door. But this led him away from Pooja and Shalini. He ran out into the open ground. There was no one outside. Everyone had gone into the warehouse to hunt for him.

Ducking between some trees, Rakesh tried to get his hands in front of him. It was a struggle because his ass was much bigger than he remembered. Using his legs one by one to rest on the tree trunk, he managed to slip his hands under his thighs. Now he was stuck in an awkward position.

'Need some help?' a voice asked and he turned around, relieved at the familiarity of it. Atif removed an army knife from his pocket and soon Rakesh was free.

'Those two . . .' he said.

'Are hiding,' Atif said, pulling him into the trees.

'No shipment is being despatched from here. I don't think this is the place,' Rakesh said. He had realised that a while ago. Atif gave him his keys. 'Go to the Jeep.'

'No, you go.'

'And what about you?' Atif said, his eyes constantly darting around to make sure they were safe.

'I'm getting those two,' Rakesh said and walked in the direction he came from, this time with his hands free.

173
Pooja

POOJA SAW TWO MEN WHO WERE IN THE SUV with the politician come running towards Shalini and her. Pooja wasn't a runner. She only excelled in yoga, but slow movements weren't going to do her any good today.

As soon as one of the guys yelled, 'Come back, you whores,' she made a run for it, with Shalini following her. The men were quicker and were gaining ground.

They ducked behind one of the buildings and Pooja stuck her phone in her back pocket, with the camera part sticking out, hoping that it would continue recording and not lock itself. Shalini and she slowly made their way to the back of the building where the smell of piss was overwhelming. It was stronger than the smell of sulphur from the room with all the firecrackers.

Pooja suddenly had an idea.

'Gimme your lighter,' she whispered to Shalini, looking around to make sure no one had found out their hiding place. Shalini pulled it out and handed it to her. 'When I signal, run,' Pooja whispered. Without wasting any more time, Pooja got up and started running towards the buildings they'd passed earlier.

The men saw her and immediately charged towards her. 'SHE'S THERE!'

Pooja pushed her useless legs to move faster as they gained ground.

'GRAB THAT BITCH!' someone else yelled and Pooja glanced behind, only to trip and fall, the lighter slipping from her hands.

They were going to grab her. She could hear them coming closer as she scrambled back to her feet. Pooja's heart was in her mouth and her mind went blank.

Suddenly she heard Shalini's voice. 'I'M RECORDING EVERYTHING, YOU BASTARDS, SAY HI TO INSTAGRAM LIVE!' The footsteps stopped and Pooja managed to get back on her feet and lunge for the lighter. The building was just a few feet away. She didn't have time to check if Shalini was okay. She looked wildly around her for an escape route, seeing a small gap in the fence behind her.

Then, before the men changed their mind and came after her again, she slipped into the room with the firecrackers.

The first box she found was of sparklers. She hoped the contents hadn't gone bad from being out in the open for God knows how long. She lit the lighter and pressed it against the top of one sparkler. It didn't take.

She could hear shouts coming from outside and wondered if they'd caught Shalini. What the fuck were Atif and Rakesh doing if they weren't saving them? Pooja wondered if they had escaped like cowards, and then she heard a gunshot. Who had fired?

'Come on . . . ,' she pleaded. Her phone vibrated in her back pocket and she ignored it, tossing the sparkler and grabbing the next one.

It didn't take either.

She grabbed a third box of crackers, the ones obnoxious cricket fans burst when their team wins a match. It was dry to the touch, so she yanked it out and held the lighter to the tip.

It sparked immediately and she threw it on the other boxes in the room. She ran to the gap in the fence, crawled to the other side and waited.

A second passed.

Then another.

'Fuck,' she said. 'It didn't work.'

Then, the first BAM came from the room with a flash of light that almost blinded her.

She turned and ran.

174
Inspector Rakesh

'WHERE ARE THEY?' HE MUTTERED TO HIMSELF. He was waiting behind the trees searching for Pooja and Shalini. He hoped they didn't go to the Jeep. It was the first place the goons would look.

But Atif was already near the Jeep, signalling him to come as well. Suddenly, he saw Shalini bursting out from the gates and running towards their vehicle. On seeing her, Atif immediately jumped out from behind the car, gun in hand. Rakesh ducked down, ready to jump at them if they tried to grab her. But then, Atif took a shot.

It rang loud in the otherwise silent night. Everyone seemed to freeze for a moment, and then a louder bang came from behind them all.

Someone on their team had a gun, thought Rakesh. He's a politician; of course his men would have guns.

But the sound was quickly followed by more bangs.

'Fuck, someone's set off the firecrackers!' one of the guys screamed.

'SIR!' another one shouted and they split, half of them running back into the factory while the other half ran past Atif who quickly jumped out of the way.

Shalini stood confused for a second before turning and running towards Atif and Rakesh.

'Pooja is still there,' she whispered. 'We need to get her, she's pregnant.'

Atif jumped into the Jeep and turned it on.

175
Pooja

SHE MANAGED TO COME OUT OF THE BUSHES only slightly hurt. Her palms were scratched up and bleeding but she was fine otherwise. She removed her phone from her back pocket and realised the live stream had ended when it had locked. She unlocked her phone and sent her location to Shalini.

Moments later, Atif's Jeep had reached her, and she jumped in.

'Are you okay?' Shalini shouted over the din of the bursting firecrackers.

'Yes, let's go now,' Pooja shouted, climbing in with their help.

They rode away as fast as they could from what would soon become a blazing fire. Pooja was glad there were no homes nearby.

'Were we wrong about the date?' Atif asked, as they drove back. 'I was sure that it was today,' Rakesh said, a little dejected.

'It is,' Pooja said, leaning forward from the back seat and showing him a message she had just seen. 'Someone messaged me: "Four trucks urgently left that warehouse. Here are the numbers."'

A follower had sent her a few photographs of the trucks. The pictures were unclear, but the numbers were visible. Sanjay called once more and she ignored the call again. Her phone was full of notifications from the posts she'd been tagged in. Shalini's journalist friend was following up on the evidence she had sent across, but the gossip pages were busy posting about how Pooja had lost her mind and was trying to make the previous news go away by causing a sensation without proof.

Calls had also started pouring in. She wished she had changed her number after the previous scandal.

Sanjay called again. 'Just answer it,' Shalini said. 'If you don't, he'll keep calling.'

'He wouldn't be calling if you hadn't told him about my pregnancy,' Pooja snapped and tapped the green icon.

'Are you okay?' he yelled into the line. She had to move the phone away from her ears. 'Where are you now? Come back home.'

'I can't come back to Mumbai now . . .' she replied, keeping her voice low. It was bad enough that Shalini now knew what was happening between husband and wife, but she didn't want two strangers to know about it too. Sanjay wasn't helping by shouting. She may as well have put her phone on speaker mode.

'I'm in Chennai. You've changed your locks.'

'You're in Chennai?' she asked incredulously, turning around to Shalini. She shook her head and put her hands up, mouthing something.

'I'm outside your house.'

'Sanjay, it's midnight, go to a fucking hotel!'

'No, where are you? I'm coming to help,' he said. He was sounding quite determined. An image of Sanjay in his shorts and a T-shirt stretched over his paunch trying to crawl in that warehouse flashed across her mind and a chuckle escaped her mouth.

'I'm not kidding, Poo. Come back, or I'm coming there.'

'How do you know where I am?'

'Are you stupid? Shalini had posted the location of the godown. She also livestreamed that stunt you pulled! Are you trying to get yourself killed? Come . . .'

'My battery is low. I have to go. I'll see you soon,' she said.

'I love yo—' he said as she hung up. No one said anything. Atif and Rakesh were focused on the road and Shalini was emailing the video to a friend of hers. Pooja went to her direct messages and sent the reply she had been typing out.

'Thank you. Any idea where they are headed?'

'Yes, madam. They went left, which means they are heading to the harbour.'

'He says they're going to the port,' Pooja said out loud, handing the phone to Rakesh.

176
Inspector Rakesh

HIS HANDS WERE STILL SHAKING FROM THE splinters in them and the aftershock of the whole experience, but Rakesh tried to hide it when he took Pooja's phone and looked at the messages. 'Can you send these images to a number I tell you? Those men took my phone,' he asked. The phone was smudged in his blood, but Pooja didn't flinch when she took it back.

She just said, 'Sure,' and typed out the number.

'Can I borrow your phone?' he asked Atif, who nodded and pointing to the glovebox. Rakesh retrieved it and turned it on. There was just nineteen per cent battery left.

'Calling Parameshwaran sir?' Atif asked.

'Yeah. He knows enough traffic cops,' Rakesh said and waited as the phone rang. His former boss answered on the fourth ring. 'Tell me, Atif,' he said, sounding as authoritative as ever. 'You need help, right? I hope Rakesh is not too burnt,' he said.

'Sir, Rakesh, sir,' Rakesh said, his voice shaking a bit. 'I need some trustworthy traffic cops stationed on the way to the harbour. It's urgent, these smuggler's trucks cannot get in.'

'Do you have . . .'

'I've sent you the truck numbers, but it might be best if we stop all of them in case . . .'

'. . . in case they switch vehicles or plates. Got it. I'll send you the numbers of some traffic policemen,' he said and hung up.

'I can see why you like him,' Atif smiled as he pressed harder on the accelerator.

Pooja tapped him on the shoulder and showed him her phone. On Twitter there were photos of him and Pooja next to what seemed like satellite images of the factory with the firecrackers alight. #SaveInspectorRakesh #SavePoojaReddy were trending along with people sharing videos of the livestream they'd captured.

'What the fuck?'

'Welcome to the power of the internet,' she said, rolling her eyes as she got yet another call.

177
Pooja

WHEN RAKESH'S CALL WITH PARAMESHWARAN ended, Pooja had an idea. 'Let's do one better,' she said to Shalini and pressed speed dial 4. Shyamal answered on the first ring. 'Madam, why, madam . . .' he wailed into the phone. She controlled her laughter and jumped to the point.

'Shyamal-ji, I need contacts in Chennai. Journalists. Proper investigative journalists. I'll explain later.'

'I'll send you a list,' he said.

She hung up and waited. The contact cards came almost instantly.

'Send them a message about what's happening,' she told Shalini. 'Share some basic information. Suspected human trafficking, related to Mira case, Inspector Rakesh chasing them and Pooja Reddy from *The Accused* podcast doing a livestream at a warehouse from where people were trafficked. Tell them we will send them the location as soon as we know. Mention the port.'

'This won't be an issue, right?' Pooja asked Rakesh, leaning forward.

'In fact, this is better. This way, it will at least be on camera. No one can deny anything.'

Her phone started pinging immediately and the constant sounds were starting to stress her out. 'Also, send them the recorded video,' she instructed, taking deep breaths to calm herself down.

178
Inspector Rakesh

AS THEY DROVE PAST THE BARRICADES WITH their car's siren blaring, Rakesh answered his phone. 'Inspector Rakesh?'

'Yes.'

'Parameshwaran sir gave your number. This is Stephen.'

'Hi, Stephen sir, were you able to—'

'We are stopping all trucks headed to the port,' Stephen continued, ignoring the interruption. 'Please tell us what we need to look for.'

'People,' Rakesh said. 'Children and women possibly being smuggled out of the country.' He couldn't hear clearly over the loud sound of the siren, but Rakesh definitely made out a sharp intake of breath.

'Okay, sir. Please make sure you reach soon. There are just eight of us here.'

They were just two minutes away and saw the flashing lights of the police cars the moment they entered that stretch of the road. A line of trucks stood one after another. Rakesh jumped out of the vehicle as soon as Atif slowed down.

Shalini started recording and walked past them, making sure to tape every truck. Rakesh continued walking and saw another police SUV at the front of the line. He recognised that one; it was from his police station. Atif stopped too.

A familiar figure walked towards them with two others and stopped. 'I'm Stephen,' the other man said, reaching out to shake his hand and stopping when he saw the state Rakesh was in. 'Karthik sir said you had asked him to come here too.'

'Yes,' Karthik said, looking at Atif and him. 'We seem to have reached at the same time.'

'Parameshwaran sir?' Rakesh asked as they walked down the line of trucks.

'Who else?' Karthik said. He wasn't unfriendly, but Rakesh didn't trust him as yet.

'I didn't know that minister . . .' Karthik started when they spotted a truck reversing out of the line-up.

Stephen and Atif noticed it too. 'That one,' they yelled and started chasing it. Pooja, who had been observing the scene, took out her phone and chased after them. Shalini was already there. 'STOP!' she yelled, pausing to throw her chappal at them.

'Anna, stop that truck,' Shalini yelled to the driver behind the reversing truck, who jerked into action and moved his truck slowly to block the route.

'They're here,' Pooja yelled, waving her phone.

Confused, Rakesh looked around and saw bikes stopping and young people, holding cameras and handheld mics, run towards them.

Rakesh stood back and waited as Stephen and his team yanked open the truck's door. The driver jumped out of the vehicle and made a run for it. Atif chased after him. The cleaner, unfortunately, wasn't as fast and was caught immediately by Karthik.

Shalini opened the back doors and the cameras crowded around. Lights were shone in and from behind large wooden pallets, a group of kids stood up, peering at the bright lights in front of them.

Rakesh breathed a sigh of relief and felt his legs give out under him.

179
One Week Later

THE CAMERAS CLICKED WILDLY, BLINDING them with their flashes.

'The operation was successful,' the police commissioner said, sitting next to Rakesh and smiling at the journalists around him. 'Four people from a human trafficking ring who were kidnapping and smuggling women and children have been nabbed. We will consider the extent of their cooperation in helping us catch the bigger names. But as of now we consider this a win.'

'Sir, who were these people?' 'Any big names involved?' 'Any other suspects?' 'How many children have been affected by this?' 'Where were they taking them?' 'Have you managed to identify any victims?'

The commissioner put his hand up to slow down the onslaught of questions and took a deep breath before reading the paper in front of him.

'We have managed to identify about fifty-seven children in the first truck we found. Since they are minors, we will not share their names. Those who have families have been returned to their homes, and the others are being taken care of by the government. We cannot reveal the names of any other suspects right now as it is still an ongoing investigation. But we would like to commend the people involved in nabbing these criminals. Inspector Rakesh and his team, who went undercover and discovered the location of the godown where the children were being held captive, the traffic police department, especially Inspector Stephen and his team, who stopped the trucks on time. SP Lakshmiprasad and DSP Joseph who took timely action to stop those who were trying to make a getaway at the border and of course . . .' He stopped reading and looked at the press assembled there, 'You, the press, for coming on time and covering the news, which helped in nabbing those who were involved.'

Rakesh chuckled under his breath. He did not seem happy about what he was saying; nevertheless this was a win for the police force. Now, not only was he the hero who stopped a human trafficking gang but he could also go back to his wife without getting into trouble. The commissioner continued, 'We would also like to extend a special thanks to *The Accused* podcast run by Pooja Reddy and Shalini Madhan. They came forward with the information they had discovered, which also helped us immensely.'

Rakesh glanced at his wife sitting in the front row and looking proudly at him. His son looked starstruck.

Rakesh smiled as the cameras flashed to get the picture that would be printed in every newspaper the next day.

180
Pooja

POOJA FOLDED THE NEWSPAPER SHE HAD BEEN reading and stared out at the perfectly manicured lawn in front of her. Sanjay was still asleep, hungover from the previous night's party. With more alcohol served than snacks, it hadn't seemed like a baby shower.

Rakesh had thanked her for all the help she and Shalini had given him. One of the bigger names involved in the scandal had worked in Sanjay's films, and both he and D had begged her to keep it out of the papers. She had told off Sanjay then. How could she trust him to be a good father if he was involved with people who smuggled kids? He had backed off quietly.

As if on cue, her phone buzzed. It was Shalini. 'Done', she had messaged.

Pooja had sent Shalini some money to send to the orphanage to make sure Mira had support to get back on her feet. Mira didn't have a lot but at least she had a friend she could trust her child with. She wondered what little Priyanka was doing in the US. One of Pooja's friends worked in the same company as Sudha. She could check on Priyanka if she wanted to. But she wouldn't. Some things were better left alone. Moreover, she needed to focus on building her own friendships in case she ever needed to leave. Pooja sent Shalini a thumbs up emoji and put her phone away.

Sanjay and she had decided to keep news of the pregnancy quiet for another month. In case D's name cropped up again. Her paternity test had cleared all doubts though. Her stupid husband was the father.

The gate creaked and her mother-in-law's signature booming voice called across the gardens. 'Where is my darling daughter-in-law!'

Pooja took a deep breath to steady herself and got up to greet her suddenly friendly foe.

Epilogue: One Year Later

Newspaper article

AN ARREST WAS MADE YESTERDAY IN WHAT has become the longest running investigation into a child sex trafficking ring. Two men, Suresh and Manivannan, were arrested while transporting two drugged children. The two minors have been handed over to a children's centre run by the government to be physically and mentally examined and then reunited with their families.

Inspector Rakesh, who is in charge of this case, made the arrest after receiving an anonymous tip about a little boy they were looking for. 'Yes, we have been searching for a little boy who had gone missing about three months ago. He was taken from outside his house while he was playing. We got a tip that someone who looked like the little boy had been found and we followed up. It wasn't him but we won't lose hope. I am sure he will be found when we question the suspects.'

Madhukumar who was murdered a few months earlier was known to the traffickers. His wife, Mira, who is still missing, was originally blamed for the murder but the investigation cleared her of all charges. The police suspect that Madhukumar found out what he was involved in and tried to keep himself and his family safe. But it was too late.

Earlier this year, Inspector Rakesh nabbed a notorious ring of human traffickers who had been smuggling people to work in the Middle East and other countries. An international investigation is currently ongoing to identify them and bring them back home.

Children have been going missing for a while now in certain suburbs of Chennai and this arrest has come in the nick of time. The public, and the higher-ups, are commending Inspector Rakesh for a job well done, again.

Acknowledgements

I HAVE TO THANK MY MOTHER FOR HELPING keep me on track to actually finish this book. My uncles, Balu and Babu, for reading short snippets and confirming that I do indeed have it in me to write and my sister, Appy, for being critical of everything I create and keeping me grounded.

Many thanks to Ravi Subramanian for encouraging me and being a mentor.

The entire team at Westland Books, especially Gautam Padmanabhan, Sanghamitra Biswas, my editor Sonia Madan and the designer Saurabh Garge, for caring about this book as much as I do.

Lastly, to Rithika for checking my cop portions and keeping facts on track.